FORSAKING ALL OTHER

FORSAKING ALL OTHER

Catherine Meyrick

Courante Publishing

Published by Courante Publishing, Melbourne, Australia: courantepublishing@gmail.com

Author website and blog: catherinemeyrick.com

Cover Design by Jennifer Quinlan, Historical Fiction Book Covers

A catalogue record for this book is available from the National Library of Australia

ISBN: 0648250814
ISBN-13: 978-0648250814

For B.A.K

Characters

The Allingbournes—Essex and London
Bess Stoughton, a widow, a waiting woman to Lady Allingbourne
Florence, Lady Allingbourne, wife of Sir Hugh Allingbourne
Lucy Torrington, a well-born young woman
George Raynsford, Lady Allingbourne's nephew
Philippa Beckingham, a well-born young woman
Avisa Gerville, a well-born young woman
Anthony Compton, serves Sir Hugh Allingbourne
Thomas Rawson, serves Sir Hugh Allingbourne
William Goodwin, a lawyer
Alan Fossett, Lady Allingbourne's steward
Clemence Higden, a waiting woman to Lady Allingbourne
Mall, a maidservant

The Wyards—Northamptonshire
Edmund Wyard, a soldier recently returned from Ireland
Margaret, Lady Wyard, Edmund Wyard's mother
Robert Hayes, Edmund Wyard's serving man
John Wyard, Edmund Wyard's elder brother
Eloise Wyard, John Wyard's wife
Kit and Jack Wyard, the children of John and Eloise Wyard
Hester Shawe, a waiting woman to Lady Wyard
Cicely Ramage, a waiting woman to Lady Wyard

The Askews—Suffolk
Nicholas Askew, Bess Stoughton's father
Emma Askew, Bess Stoughton's stepmother
Joyce and Sybell Askew, two of Bess Stoughton's sisters
Richard Litchfield, Nicholas Askew's neighbour
Elinor Hervey, Emma Askew's sister
Jane Hervey, Elinor Hervey's daughter
Maggie Drayton, a friend of the Askews
Lady Gleybrook, wife of the local Member of Parliament
Mary Perris, Emma Askew's servant
Perris, Nicholas Askew's groom of the stable
Tom Hornebolt, Nicholas Askew's servant

Part 1

1

July 1585

Bess Stoughton shivered as the icy wind snatched, yet again, at the hood of her mantle. Her dark hair was plastered to her head, her ruff flattened and, after a downpour an hour earlier, her clothing damp beneath the mantle.

In the gloom she glared at Hornebolt's back as he rode ahead of her. From the moment they had set out at daybreak, her father's man had set such a punishing pace that, at times, Bess had difficulty keeping up. He had assured Lady Allingbourne before they left that he had arranged for them to travel with a group of merchants once they reached Chelmsford—there was greater safety in numbers. Yet here Bess was, one of Lady Allingbourne's waiting women, travelling alone. Hornebolt was so far ahead that had she been attacked by brigands, she doubted he would have noticed.

Hornebolt had barely spoken to her except to give gruff directions. They had not stopped often enough to rest the horses well and would have eaten in the saddle had Bess not insisted otherwise. Her pleas to give thought to the horses had been met at first with mutterings and later by silent contempt. The journey, which usually took at least a day and a half at a moderate pace from Allingbourne Hall to Bess's father's manor near Ipswich, would be completed in one long day.

Bess sank back into a miserable reverie. She had no wish to return to her father's house. She had never before been required to attend the christening of his children by the young wife who had replaced her mother ten years ago. Besides, Philippa was to be betrothed in a week. Philippa Beckingham was the eldest of the young women in Lady Allingbourne's care, learning the skills and duties required of a woman in the running of a large household. Nearest in age to Bess, she had become her closest friend. Bess doubted she would be back at Allingbourne Hall in time for the betrothal.

The road wound past a small copse and there, nestled in the folds of the grey hills, was her father's manor house. Not a single light flickered in any window.

As soon as they clattered across the bridge and into the courtyard, Hornebolt dismounted and led his horse towards the stables without a backward look. Perris, the groom of the stable, a familiar face from Bess's childhood, came out buttoning his doublet. He greeted Hornebolt as he passed but Hornebolt merely grunted in reply.

Exhausted, Bess remained in her saddle.

'Let me help you down, Mistress,' Perris said as he walked towards Bess's horse.

Bess fought back tears. 'Thank you, Perris.' Her feet finally on firm earth, she stumbled against him. 'My legs are like jelly,' she forced a laugh, holding his arm for support.

'A long journey?'

'Too long to be done in a single day unless it is a matter of life and death.' Doubt swept through her. 'It is not...? My father...?'

'No Mistress, all are well here. Mistress Askew and her babe, a little lass, are both thriving.'

Perris ran his hand along the quivering palfrey's flank and grumbled, more to himself, 'I'm surprised this horse is still standing. That man should never be allowed near horses.' He called to a lad who had just come out into the courtyard, rubbing sleep from his eyes, 'Ralph, bring Hornebolt's gelding out here.' He led Bess's palfrey around the yard.

'Is there something wrong with Rosie?'

'Not if I do my job properly. But no horse should be ridden as hard or as far as this one has been. Did you stop to rest the horses at all?'

Bess nodded weakly. 'Yes, but not as often or for as long as we should have. Hornebolt was in a hurry. I tried to explain but he would not listen to *an empty-headed woman prattling about matters beyond her ken.*' Bess made a fair imitation of Hornebolt's gruff voice.

'That's the pot calling the pan burnt-arse,' Perris muttered under his breath.

Bess stood staring up at the dark windows of the house. 'Perris,' she said, 'do you think anyone else is awake?'

His attention drawn away from the horses, Perris took in her bedraggled state. 'You get yourself inside, Mistress. Mary is up. She'll help you out of those wet things and find something to warm you.'

Before Bess reached the great door, it was flung open by a stout woman, grey hair escaping from beneath her coif. She bobbed a curtsy then threw her arms around Bess. 'Sweeting, you've come home.'

'Goody Perris,' Bess blinked, forcing back sudden tears. 'I am so glad to see you.'

Mary Perris stepped back, her hands resting on Bess's shoulders. 'But look at the state you are in! Up to the parlour with you. I've stoked the fire and I'll get something for you to eat.'

She chattered as she led Bess through the darkened hall into a small parlour at the end. 'Everyone's abed. We did not think to see you until tomorrow.'

'Hornebolt made sure we made the journey in a single day.'

'A single day?' Mary glanced over her shoulder. 'But he left five days ago.'

'He arrived at Allingbourne Hall late yesterday.' She did not trust herself to explain more.

Mary clicked her tongue in disapproval. 'I would be letting your father know that, if I was you.' She held the door to the parlour open for Bess. Inside a fire crackled and the candles had been lit. 'Now get that cloak off and sit by the fire.' She settled Bess into a chair, plumping a cushion behind her, and hurried from the room, Bess's cloak on her arm.

Bess dragged the chair closer to the fire and held out her hands. She sniffed, again fighting the urge to cry. Mary Perris and her husband had been part of Woolham Manor for as long as she could remember. In her way, Mary had been mother to Bess when her own mother had died. She was part of Bess's idea of home.

In the flickering candlelight, the parlour appeared unchanged despite the presence of her father's second wife these past ten years. The legs of a doll poked out from beneath a cushion lying on the floor beside the chair at the other side of the hearth. Bess

3

eased herself out of her chair, bent stiffly and picked up the doll. She stood in front of the fire staring at the doll's carefully embroidered face and wondered what growing up in this house was like now. Her own childhood, until the day her mother died, seemed to have been sun-filled even in mid-winter.

Within a year, a stepmother had arrived, a young woman five years older than Bess. Her father had been besotted to Bess's mind, fawning over his new wife, barely able to keep his hands in check. Bess's sullen incivility had ensured a place was quickly found for her in service with her mother's distant cousin, Lady Allingbourne. The years had not altered Bess's attitude to her stepmother—she was her father's wife, her children her father's children, no real kindred to Bess.

~

Mary bustled in with a goblet of mulled wine and a plate with slices of bread and cold mutton. 'Here we are—this will take the edge off your hunger until I can heat up something else.'

Bess placed the doll in the chair opposite her and took the plate and cup. 'I am not that hungry Goody, this will do.' She nibbled at the bread. 'I would like to go to bed soon.'

'You'll be in with Joyce and Sybell.'

Bess frowned, she did not want to share a bed with children.

Mary rushed on, 'They are the eldest, eight and nine, both good girls. The others are in the nursery. Joyce has been so excited at the thought of you coming.'

Bess sipped her drink and said nothing.

'I'll go and put your things in your room.' Mary closed the door quietly behind her. Despite the appearance of always being in a rush, Bess remembered Mary could, when she wanted, move silently, appearing from nowhere—especially when you were indulging in the most entertaining of mischief.

Bess placed the plate on a small table beside the chair and pushed off her shoes, wriggling her damp stockinged toes in front of the fire. Her skirt steamed with the warmth.

'Bess.'

Bess's father stood at the door. Perhaps it was the dim light of the parlour, but Nicholas Askew seemed to have aged since she had last seen him two years ago, his hair and beard now heavily peppered with grey. Bess rose wearily from her seat; tomorrow every muscle would ache.

'No lass, stay where you are.' He squeezed her shoulder gently as he passed by and took the seat opposite her. Frowning, he pulled the doll out from beneath him and tossed it across the room onto a pile of cushions in the corner. 'We were hoping you would arrive today.'

'Hornebolt made sure we did. He set such a pace that he near killed the horses.'

'He's a driven man when he sets his mind to something.' Askew tugged his fur-trimmed night gown tighter around himself. 'Still, you seem to have survived the ordeal.'

Bess bit back a sharp reply and sipped her drink, staring into the fire.

'Mary is seeing to your needs?' her father asked.

'Ay, she has gone to prepare a bed for me with two of your children.'

Askew's eyes darkened. 'We have little space at present. Emma's elder sister, Elinor, and her daughter came for the lying-in and will be staying until the churching.' He forced a smile. 'Joyce and Sybell will no doubt plague you with questions when they wake. To hear them talk, their sister is waiting woman to the Queen.'

Bess gave a slight smile, acknowledging the thought, we are sisters even if we have different mothers. I should not blame them for it.

Askew rose and bent over her. 'Well daughter, I will leave you.' He brushed his dry lips against her forehead. 'The christening will follow the church service tomorrow morning.'

Bess's face betrayed nothing of her feelings. 'I will be ready. No doubt Joyce and Sybell will make certain I am up early.'

Askew's face relaxed. 'That I do not doubt.'

~

Mary Perris led Bess to the bedchamber by the light of a single candle. She whispered as they climbed the stairs, 'All your belongings are damp but I'll make sure they are dry for the morning. You will have to wear a bed smock of the Mistress's.'

Much as she wanted to, Bess could not refuse.

Mary opened the door. 'You'll find the bed well warmed by those two little angels in there.'

Bess's eyes brimmed as a surge of jealousy swept through her. This was *her* Goody Perris loving other children. Bess held herself taut, as much against her unreasonable emotion as the cold, while Mary helped her undress and combed out her hair. She told herself sternly that it was not rational that she, a grown woman, should be jealous of children near a third her age.

Bess climbed into the large bed and stretched out alongside the two girls with their flushed cheeks and angelic curls, careful not to disturb their sleep. She watched the wavering light of the candle as Mary moved towards the door and fell soundly asleep as soon as darkness claimed the room.

2

Bess sensed she was being watched. She opened her eyes to find two small faces not inches from hers.

'Who are you?' asked the older of the girls.

'Elizabeth Stoughton.'

The girl stared hard at Bess, calculation in her washed blue eyes. 'You are my sister. Most people call you Bess.'

'That is right,' Bess answered. 'And who are you?'

'I am Joyce Askew,' she said seriously, 'and this is my sister Sybell Askew. What are you doing in our bed?'

'This was my bed once. I shared it with my sister Ann.'

'That would be Ann Lovell. She is my sister too.' Joyce tossed her head, her golden curls catching the morning light, her pride in her older sisters obvious. 'She has a baby called Elizabeth.'

Bess was overcome with a startling rush of affection for this earnest child. She saw the aged family historian the child would become with memory for all the intricate connections life forced on men and women.

Joyce's small face broke into a sudden grin. 'Elizabeth Lovell is older than her aunt, my new sister.'

'That she is,' Bess answered. And, no doubt, a number of others too, she thought.

'Do you have a baby?'

'No.' Bess closed her eyes against the intense scrutiny and wondered if a child would have made a difference.

'Oh,' Joyce gasped, 'I forgot. He died.'

'Two years ago,' Bess added, matter of fact. It was strange but she now had a fondness for her husband Myles that, for the most part, had been lacking while he was alive.

Joyce was thoughtful. 'Agnes White, in the village, is not married but she has a baby.'

'I dare say someone will marry Agnes. They'll be happy to see that she can have babies. It does not always work that way for girls like us.'

Joyce nodded. 'I heard Aunt Elinor whispering to Mother about a cousin who had a baby. She was not married and she could not get a husband because everyone thought she was light. The baby's father must be light too. Would he have trouble finding a wife?'

'Nay, wanton behaviour by a man is rarely held against him. Life can be very unfair, Joyce.'

Sybell, who had been rolling on the end of the bed while Joyce and Bess were talking, crashed into Joyce. Joyce turned to her sister, her mouth a flat line of disapproval. 'Fie, Sybell! Stop it! You are such a baby.'

Bess smiled at Sybell who took it as an invitation to crawl up the bed and nestle against her. Bess wrapped an arm around Sybell. 'How old are you, Sybell?'

'Eight. And Joyce is only nine.'

'When I was eight and Ann was six we used to do somersaults on this bed together. I even did it when I was nine.' She gave Joyce a sly grin.

Joyce looked down at her, her mouth open. 'Were you not a good girl?'

'Not always.'

'I'm not always good either.' She lay down and curled in beside Bess.

'And what is the new baby's name?'

'Dorothy,' Sybell answered.

'We can call her Doll,' Joyce said. 'Babies are just like dolls,'.

'Except they are noisy and hungry and wet all the time,' Bess added.

'And cack-ey,' Sybell giggled.

'And that too,' Bess agreed.

The door creaked open and a maid came in and bobbed a curtsey inside the door. 'Excuse me, Mistress, but it's time for Joyce and Sybell to get up. They need to break their fast and dress for church.'

The girls kissed Bess loudly, one on each cheek, scrambled off the bed and followed the maid from the room. Outside Bess heard their squeals as they greeted someone.

They had barely gone when Mary Perris came in carrying a tray with bread, cheese and small beer. She glanced out at the sky as she put the tray on a chest beneath the window. 'It will be a fine day for certain—yesterday's showers have blown away.' Her face shone with happiness as she said, 'It is good to have you home, Mistress. Now, while you are eating, I'll bring up your clothing and help you dress.'

Once Mary left, Bess slid out of bed and padded, barefoot, to the window. She sipped the small beer as she gazed out at the landscape of her childhood—the garden that had been her mother's delight sloping gently to the moat that wound around the house; the orchards and the fishponds; and beyond, the fields, some under crop, some grazing sheep. The eyes of experience she now possessed told her it was not the grand manor she had imagined it to be as a child, but it was prosperous and could provide a more than satisfactory living to someone not blessed with an unending supply of daughters.

~

After the Sunday service Bess, with Joyce and Sybell beside her, watched as their youngest sister was baptized. The godparents stood at the font, the most senior of the women, Lady Gleybrook, wife of the local Member of Parliament, holding the child. The baby roared as she was dipped in the water and her forehead signed with oil. The second godmother, Mistress Byfield, the rector's wife, then took the baby and wrapped her quickly, saying, 'There sweeting, that's the Devil gone out of you.' She handed Dorothy back to her nurse, a placid woman from the village.

The party made its way on foot from the church on the rise at one end of the village towards the manor house. It was a beautiful summer's day like the remembered days of Bess's childhood—the sky a clear blue, the breeze gentle, carrying the bleating of sheep. Nicholas Askew was busy with Lady Gleybrook and had not bothered to present Bess. No one spoke to her; but for the company of Joyce and Sybell she would have felt an intruder. Sybell ran back and forth picking cornflowers and daisies from the verge. Joyce, chattering incessantly, held Bess's hand as they walked.

'Do you really think the Devil lives inside unbaptized people? He would not fit.'

'Not in a little baby,' Bess grinned, 'but do not say that too loudly, especially near Mistress Byfield.'

'I do know,' Joyce lowered her voice, 'or Aunt Elinor. She is a pray-er too.' She furrowed her brow, 'Why are pray-ers such busybodies? Aunt Elinor likes to know everybody's business and tuts all the time. Goody Walters in the village prays a lot, but she is kind.' She looked up at Bess. 'She's the midwife. She can do baptisms too.'

'Only if the baby's life is in danger.'

'She baptized our two little brothers.' Joyce clapped a hand over her mouth. 'I'm not meant to speak of them. Father gets angry and Mother weeps.'

Bess said nothing. She did not want to think about her father and his wife. Eight children in ten years was excessive and, at this rate, there would be at least another eight.

Two thin, pale-haired women were walking on the opposite side of the road, staring openly at her. Bess nodded at them and smiled insincerely. They quickly turned away. She bent her head towards Joyce and whispered, 'Who are the two women?'

'That's Aunt Elinor and cousin Jane. They are talking about you.'

Bess's eyes widened at Joyce's bluntness.

'They said earlier that you should have visited Mother this morning.'

'I did not have time,' Bess snapped.

'I wanted to tell them we all woke late. I did not visit Mother either but Aunt Elinor is always telling me I talk too much.'

'I do not think you talk too much.' She squeezed the child's hand. 'We will both go and see your mother as soon as we get back to the house.'

~

Bess followed Joyce into Emma Askew's bedchamber. It was a large room dominated by a great carved bed with heavily embroidered hangings. She paused inside the door, gripped by an overwhelming anguish. She was sixteen again, standing at this door gazing at the alabaster face of her mother lying in the great bed, and beside her the still, swaddled form of the son she had died giving birth to.

Now it was the scene of festivity, a musician playing a lute in one corner. Around the room women sat on stools and cushions gossiping, drinking ale and eating comfits and wafers, others drifted in and out through the open door.

Bess pushed the image of her mother away and forced herself to move towards the group of women surrounding her stepmother. Three days having passed since giving birth, Emma Askew was now seated out of bed on a high-backed upholstered chair.

Before Bess could reach her, a rosy-cheeked woman touched her on the arm.

'It's Bess, is it not?'

Bess nodded, not trusting herself to speak.

'My eyes are not what they were.' She beamed at Bess and swept her into a tight embrace. 'You are the image of your mother.'

When she released Bess, she stepped back and said, 'Your mother would have been proud to see what a fine woman you have become.'

Bess fought back prickling tears as she rummaged in her memory. 'Mistress Drayton?'

'You do remember. Your mother was never one to forget a friend, dear soul that she was.' Maggie Drayton barely drew breath, 'I was heartsore when I heard of your husband's death.'

'It is over two years now.'

'That long? Still, I imagine you will soon wed again. Someone is sure to snap you up.'

Bess opened her mouth to protest but stopped, realising it sounded ungracious.

Maggie glanced across at Emma Askew. 'Emma is starting to get some colour back in her cheeks. I was here for the lying-in and we feared we would lose her. I do worry about poor Emma—she is not strong enough to have so many children so quickly.'

'Mistress Drayton, *please!*' Bess held up her hand. 'This is not a matter...'

'Sorry dear,' she said quickly, 'but she is so like my Mabel. I think of her as a daughter.'

Bess felt weak with betrayal. This woman had been her mother's closest friend yet here she was, fawning over the girl who had replaced her. 'Mabel has children now?' Bess asked.

'Oh yes,' Maggie said proudly. 'Mabel was made to be a mother—a child every two years for the last ten with not the slightest trouble.' As Maggie launched into the long story of Mabel's numerous confinements, Bess watched the women who came and spoke to her stepmother, women who had been her mother's friends. They were all older, all changed but still familiar. There was a gentleness and care in their approach to Emma that spoke of both love and a deeply felt concern. Emma sat in the middle of a group between Lady Gleybrook and Mistress Byfield, her hands pressed against her stomach as she laughed at the tale Mistress Byfield was telling.

Bess put her hand on Maggie's arm. 'I should go and pay my respects to...' She was unsure how to finish. She had always said *my father's wife* but that would not do here. *Emma* was too familiar but for certain she would never call her *Mother*. Bess mumbled and moved away.

Emma smiled as Bess approached her. 'Welcome Bess, I am so glad you arrived in time. I was worried when you were not here by nightfall yesterday.'

'Thank you, madam,' Bess curtseyed. 'Hornebolt was determined we make it.'

'Sit here, Bess,' Mistress Byfield rose. 'I'll see what delicacies they are keeping for themselves below. The servants are a bit tardy today, no doubt enjoying themselves as much as we are.' She patted Emma's hand and moved away.

Emma turned to Lady Gleybrook and introduced Bess. Bess curtsied and took a seat. Before anyone else could speak, Emma's sister Elinor said, 'We are indeed pleased you deigned to come home.'

Bess blinked, taken aback by the naked criticism.

Lady Gleybrook looked from Elinor to Bess and said, 'Bess, Emma tells me you serve Lady Allingbourne. Sir Hugh Allingbourne is my husband's cousin.'

'Yes, I have been with my lady for eight years in all,' Bess was relieved not to have to deal with Elinor. 'We usually spend summer at Allingbourne Hall but a good part of the year is spent in London when Sir Hugh is at court.'

'My, you do move in exalted circles.' Malice glittered in Elinor's pale eyes. 'You would be more useful here. Emma has her hands full with so many little ones. You should not need to be told where your duty lies.'

Emma leant across and placed her hand on top of Elinor's. 'Bess's life is elsewhere.'

Bess saw that Emma meant what she said. Emma had changed; she was quite different from the girl who had come to take Bess's mother's place. There was still that gentleness about her, which Bess had seen as weakness then, but she could now see the inner strength that lay beneath. She was pale and tired, thin rather than slender and she appeared more than the five years she was older than Bess, passing for nearer forty than thirty.

Bess met Elinor's judgmental gaze. 'I am well content with my life with Lady Allingbourne and have no wish to leave.'

Emma looked directly at Bess. 'Nor do I wish you to leave there.'

Elinor jerked her head, her lips pressed tight together.

Joyce skipped up to the group and knelt beside Bess, resting her head against her thigh. Bess gently stroked Joyce's hair. Emma smiled at them and Bess found herself smiling back.

'Mother, may I take Bess down and show her Dorothy's gifts?' Joyce asked.

'Of course, my sweeting.'

Bess rose and curtsied to Lady Gleybrook, extending it to Emma as well. Towards Elinor she merely nodded.

Joyce ran to her mother and hugged her, smacking a kiss on her cheek.

As Bess and Joyce left the room, hand in hand, Lady Gleybrook said, 'Joyce is a delightful child.'

'I believe Emma is too lenient with her, my lady,' Elinor sniffed. 'Throwing her arms around her mother like that is disrespectful, and she has an opinion on everything.'

'She is not alone in that,' Lady Gleybrook said evenly. 'There is nothing more charming than a child showing affection for her mother.'

'Joyce is the joy of my heart,' Emma said vehemently. 'I would be lost without her.'

~

The hall of the manor house was as crowded as the bedchamber, but here were male guests as well as female. A pair of viols and a shawm struggled valiantly against the rising conversation. Bess glanced around the room, unchanged since her childhood. Beneath the high beamed roof, an armorial banner hung behind the high table. Painted cloths depicting hunting scenes hung on the wainscotted walls around the room.

A light breeze carried the scent of roses from the garden through the open windows. Bess swallowed a lump in her throat as she again thought of her mother.

Joyce tugged at her sleeve. 'What is the matter, Bess? You look as if you want to cry.'

She thought she had left that sadness behind. 'Nay,' Bess smiled sadly, 'I am remembering what this was like when I was your age.'

Joyce pulled her by the hand to the cabinet where most of the family plate was on display. There were a number of new additions—apostle spoons, covered cups, a coral teething ring with a silver handle.

Bess's gaze strayed to a silver goblet decorated with vine leaves—her christening gift from her godfather, now dead. She had danced with him at her own wedding—a kind ruddy-faced man with sparkling blue eyes and a great booming laugh. Death had been cruel, taking one by one those who meant most to her, those who would have made a difference to her life—her mother, her godfather, even her husband. She took a deep breath. She was being ridiculous, like an old crone in her cups.

Joyce had lost interest in the gifts and slipped through the crowd to join a group of children beyond the hall screen. From the sound of the squeals as they ran out into the garden followed by a sudden silence, they were beginning a game of hide and seek.

'Bess,' Nicholas Askew said, beaming. 'I did not say it last night—Welcome home, daughter.' He kissed her cheek.

Bess noted the glint in his eyes and perfume of his breath and concluded that he had already partaken well of his own hospitality. 'Thank you, Father.'

'You have no drink?' He beckoned to a servant who brought over a goblet of wine. Askew pressed it into Bess's hands. 'Have you eaten anything?'

'Nay, Father, but I am not hungry. I am still tired—we rode from sunrise to well after sunset.'

'I will speak to Hornebolt. He left near a week ago with time enough for a leisurely journey. I fear he took the time to look to his own interests rather than mine.'

'Not the most mannerly of men.'

'Never was. Still, he is useful. Manages to extract rents that are not forthcoming.'

By what means, Bess wondered. She felt a prickling along her spine and turned to find an elderly man standing close.

Askew beckoned to him. 'Bess, you will remember Master Litchfield.'

The old man simpered as he bowed and took her hand. Bess did remember him. He had been one of those too friendly men who always had an apple or a sweetmeat ready for any child. Her father, like so many others, had seen him as a kindly man yet she and Ann had not warmed to him. Bess supposed he was approaching the allotted span of three score and ten. Time had not been gentle. He stepped forward and kissed her. His breath was rank and his lips moist. Bess resisted the urge to wipe her hand across her mouth.

His smile was unnerving. 'Mistress... Ahhh...'

'Stoughton,' Bess finished for him.

'No need for formality, Dick,' Askew beamed. 'You have known Bess since she was a baby.'

'Bess,' he said, still holding her hand, 'you have grown indeed.' When his eyes finally settled on her face, he said, 'I was sorry to hear of your loss.'

'Thank you, Master Litchfield.' She wriggled her fingers free.

'And you still serve Lady Allingbourne?'

'Yes.' Bess was surprised he knew so much of her life.

'A lively household, no doubt.' His eyes once more travelled over her body. 'No doubt you have many young men dancing after you. You'll be married again in no time.'

Bess opened her mouth to speak but, in face of his unwavering lascivious gaze, could think of nothing to say. All her training had deserted her—the ability to make light conversation, to lead it away from uncomfortable or unpleasant subjects without making the other party feel reproof.

'Your..., your family, Master Litchfield,' she stuttered, 'how..., how are they?'

'Ah Bess, I am quite deserted.' His eyes moistened. 'Both my daughters know nothing of their duty. Once married, they have never visited me. It has been nigh on fifteen years since I have seen either. I know only of their fortunes through others.' His pale face was narrow, his sparse hair combed across his balding pate. He had made Bess uneasy as a child and nothing had changed. Her mother had no liking for him, declining all invitations for Bess and Ann to stay when his wife had been alive.

'I visited my Joan once,' he said. 'Her husband was away. She barred the door against me, would not let me enter under her roof.' He smiled his oily smile again. 'But you are a dutiful daughter, Bess, you come at your father's bidding. You follow his direction, do you not?'

'I suppose I do,' Bess said. She looked for a way of escape. Her father had disappeared, but she caught the eye of Maggie Drayton.

'And you have no children, do you?' Litchfield asked.

'No.'

'So sad. A young woman in her prime, so ripe...'

'Dick,' Maggie broke in, 'you will have to excuse me, there is someone Bess must meet.'

'Till tomorrow,' he smirked.

Bess gratefully allowed Maggie to steer her across the room.

'I know Dick Litchfield is a good neighbour but he seems to forget he's not twenty-five anymore and a delight to a girl's eye,' Maggie laughed.

Bess gazed at the crowd. 'Who am I to meet, Mistress Drayton?'

'No one at all. I thought you needed saving from Dick Litchfield.'

Bess laughed, 'That I did.'

'I'll keep you under my wing tomorrow too.'

'Tomorrow?'

'Dick's grand dinner. It appears he is looking to marry again, so he has invited all the eligible women in the neighbourhood, and a few of us old matrons for decency's sake.'

'Fortunately, I've not been invited.'

'Oh, yes you have,' Maggie said. 'I heard your father saying young Joyce and Emma's niece Jane have been too. I made sure he invited me, although all my girls are married. I've not seen the inside of that house since Ellen Litchfield died and I want to have a good look,' Maggie laughed. 'Do not worry Bess, we will have a merry time at Dick's expense and you will come away safe with no thought of marriage to a man old enough to be your grandfather.'

3

A stocky man of around thirty stood alone in the chancel of the village church staring at the stone slab set into the floor. The lettering on the stone was newly carved.

Christopher Wyard
Knight
1585

Nothing more, nothing that said anything of the man whose remains lay beneath.

Edmund Wyard, his hand resting on his sword-hilt, closed his eyes and threw his head back and groaned. He took one final look at the slab, his face now rigid with self-control, and strode down the centre aisle to the door.

~

Margaret, the dowager Lady Wyard, sat embroidering the neck of a child's smock. Beside her, her good-daughter, Eloise had laid her own sewing aside. Dame Margaret was well aware that Eloise had no liking for sewing, be it plain or embroidery. Eloise's mother may have been willing to complete what Eloise left unfinished, but Dame Margaret would have none of that. Eloise had complained it was an endless task, but it was one of the many duties expected of a wife, and Dame Margaret would make sure Eloise fulfilled her duties. She had lost count of the times she had reminded Eloise of her responsibility to set an example for the other women in the household.

The room was unusually quiet. Even Eloise's cousin, Cicely Ramage, had ceased her endless chatter. All that could be heard was the slither of thread through cloth and, outside, the sleepy cooing of doves. Eloise rose from her seat and wandered to the window. She stood, both hands in the small of her back, arching backwards, the swelling of her belly obvious through the folds of her gown. She leant forward, resting her hands on the windowsill, a frown on her usually cheerful face.

'What is it, Eloise?' Dame Margaret asked, her voice sharp with concern. 'It is far too soon.'

Eloise turned back to the room and brushed her hand impatiently through the air. 'No, nothing like that. We have visitors. One is the image of Sir Christopher.' She smiled at her good-mother. 'Perhaps I should go down and greet them.'

Dame Margaret concentrated on her sewing. 'Wait here—let whoever it is seek you out.'

Eloise returned to her seat and took up her sewing. After a few stitches she put it aside once more and sat back, her fingers spread on her belly, smiling to herself.

Dame Margaret held her needle still in her fingers and waited as the door to the solar swung open and her youngest son, Edmund, was led in by the footman. So like his father! He had Sir Christopher's build and light brown hair. He would have been as handsome too but for the discoloured pockmarks spread across his forehead and his cheeks above his neatly trimmed beard.

Dame Margaret did not rise to greet him.

Edmund stopped six feet from her chair and bowed formally. He was still in his dusty travelling clothes, the faint smell of sweat and horse a sharp reminder of his father too.

Dame Margaret wrinkled her nose. 'You have arrived, finally.'

'I came as quickly as I could, Mother.'

'But a month?' she asked, incredulous.

'I could not walk away from my responsibilities at a moment's notice. Travel from Ireland is nothing like an unhurried ride from London.' Edmund scowled at his mother, 'I supposed Father had been buried long before I even received the news.'

The other women watched him from beneath their lashes while pretending to sew. Only Hester Shawe, Dame Margaret's woman, stared openly at him.

'I have been to the church. Is that all that will be done for Father—a flat stone in the floor?'

'Oh, no,' Eloise said as she rose from her chair. 'John will explain when he returns home.' She laid a hand on his arm and smiled, 'I am John's wife, Eloise, and I am delighted to meet you, Edmund.' She stood on tiptoes and kissed his cheek. 'John has organised a mason to come from London and is planning a monument with both your parents and all the children on it. He is certain your father would have approved.'

Dame Margaret watched as Edmund turned his attention to Eloise, saw him take in the glowing skin, the reddish-blond hair, dark eyebrows and smiling eyes. She pressed her lips together in a tight line. All men were the same—it was the nature of the beast.

'Father would indeed be pleased,' Edmund said.

'Now Edmund, you must come and meet your nephews.' Eloise linked her arm in his and guided him through the door.

Dame Margaret glared after them. Eloise should not have pushed herself forward and drawn attention to herself. She would need to remind her, yet again, of the standard of behaviour expected of her as John's wife.

~

Dame Margaret had hoped for a private word with Edmund but as soon as the evening meal was finished both he and Eloise had disappeared.

The meal had been surprisingly agreeable. Eloise, in her element with a guest to entertain, had drawn Edmund out and had him talking of the more pleasant aspects of his life in Ireland these past ten years. She had done her job so well that Dame Margaret had little need to ask any questions. But he had given no intimation of his plans for the future. Edmund had changed, she used to be able to read him so well. He was guarded now but, all the same, he had been at ease with Eloise, laughing as she talked of her children. The girl had been as good as flirting with him. Indeed, Dame Margaret would speak severely to her.

Dame Margaret could not fault Edmund's manner, yet she wondered if it was innate—he had been awkward in the company of decent women as a younger man. She wondered what manner of women he had mixed with in Ireland, other than whores. And there would have been whores—he was his father's son. No doubt, he would also have his father's view that a mistress of many years was not a strumpet.

Dame Margaret decided to wait until tomorrow to speak with him. He had said he would stay a few days, at least until John returned.

As she made her way towards her own chamber she heard squeals and laughter coming from the nursery. What was that nurse thinking? At this hour the children should be asleep. She swung the nursery door open, her mouth set in a disapproving line, and halted, stunned by the sight of her younger son on his knees with his four-year-old nephew, Kit, on his back. Jack, Kit's little brother, was bouncing on his toes yelling, 'Me! Me! Me too!'

Eloise and the nurse were red-faced with laughter. Kit was wearing his uncle's hat as he bounced along.

Edmund swung Kit down from his back and said to Jack, 'And where do you want your trusty steed to take you today young sir.'

'London,' the boy lisped, his eyes alight. Edmund galloped around the nursery, Jack squealing with delight.

'I wish to speak with you, Edmund,' Dame Margaret said as a sudden silence descended on the room.

Edmund halted in front of her. He did not rise, remaining on all fours with his now quiet nephew jouncing on his back. He looked up at his mother. 'I will be with you as soon as Jack has had his turn.' His good humour had vanished.

Margaret Wyard swept from the room. Edmund took Jack on three more circuits then galloped to the nurse and tipped him into her arms.

Eloise raised her eyebrows at him.

'I had better be going.' He retrieved his hat from Kit and dusted his knees.

'Will Grandmother beat Uncle Edmund for being naughty?' Kit asked as Edmund left the room.

'Nay,' Eloise answered, 'he's much too big for that.'

Edmund turned at the door, 'When you get to my age, Kit, they beat you with their tongues.'

The boy screwed up his nose, disgusted. 'You'd better have a bath.'

Edmund grimaced at Kit, amused.

Jack, who was kneeling in the window staring out into the courtyard, gave a squeal of happiness and scrambled down. He caught his mother's hand. 'Mammy, Mammy, Daddy's come,' he said, tugging her towards the door.

~

Dame Margaret had a good view of her sons from her chair beside the parlour fire. They were seated at the table, sharing a jug of wine, Eloise with them, sitting so close to John, she may as well have been in his lap.

Her sons were unalike physically. John favoured the height and blondness of her family and Edmund the darker colouring and build of his father. And John had always seen the wisdom of his mother's counsel whereas Edmund, even as a young child, had been stubbornly set on his own way. Yet you could tell they were brothers, especially when you saw them in profile. The odd mannerism was the same, even the way they threw their heads back as they drank—so like their father. She pressed her lips together. She would not think on that. Despite the five years between them, there had been an easy camaraderie through their childhood that they had not lost.

John's approach was blunt. 'Well Edmund, you are quite a man of property—your Irish estate and, now, what Father has bequeathed to you. Have you given thought to marriage?'

'No.' Edmund busied himself refilling his cup and missed the look of sympathy that passed between John and Eloise.

'Do you intend returning to Ireland?'

'I have done more than my duty,' Edmund shrugged, his mouth twisting, 'but I have not decided either way.'

'With property you will want children to pass it on to.' John put his arm around Eloise's shoulder and pulled her closer.

'In time, perhaps.' His eyes rested on Eloise. 'The suggestion does have merit.'

John glanced towards his mother. 'Mother chose Eloise for me.'

Edmund said nothing.

'I am sure she could do as well for you.'

Dame Margaret rose from her chair and came to the table. She took the seat opposite Edmund and sat erect, her hands neatly clasped on the table. 'I did take an active role in your brother and your sisters' marriages. If you are willing, I will do the same for you.'

Edmund gave a mirthless laugh. 'I suspect I am the victim of an ambush.' He looked from his mother to his brother. 'It appears you two have discussed this matter already.'

'Only in the most general terms,' John said evenly.

'Who do you have in mind for me?' His hazel eyes were cold.

'No doubt Mother could suggest a number of suitable young women.'

'I get a choice?'

Dame Margaret ignored the sarcasm. 'The daughter of Sir Peter Torrington may interest you. She is one of Lady Allingbourne's young women. You could pass Allingbourne Hall on your way to...' she paused then said the name as if it were something distasteful, '...Bucklings Hall.'

Edmund frowned, 'It is only on my way if I am attempting a roundabout route.'

'They will be celebrating the betrothal of Anthony Compton to another of Lady Allingbourne's young women.' Eloise's eyes sparkled, 'You could go and represent the family and see what you think of Mistress Torrington without anyone knowing.'

'If you have no liking for the girl, nothing will have been lost,' John added. 'And if none of Mother's suggestions suit, we can look to Eloise's endless tribe of cousins.' He squeezed his wife's shoulder.

Edmund turned his head and stared out into the dusk.

When he did not reply, Dame Margaret said quietly, 'Edmund, we do have your welfare at heart.'

Edmund drained his cup and placed it on the table. 'I suppose I should be thankful I am not a girl to be kept locked in my room until I agree to whomever you decide upon.' He rose from his seat and said as he walked from the room, 'I will give it some thought.'

4

From her seat on the chest beneath the window of the bedchamber, Joyce watched Bess as she tied her riding mantle. 'Master Litchfield invited me too, and Father said I could come,' she said as she softly banged her slippered feet against the chest. 'But when he told Mother she shouted at him and said she would never let me go there. She has only ever shouted at father once before—when Master Litchfield wanted Sybell and me to visit after Christmas. Father says she is being silly, that Master Litchfield has known us so long he is like an uncle.' She pouted, 'And Master Litchfield told me yesterday that his cat had a new litter. He said I could visit him any time I wanted.' She gazed at Bess, appeal in her eyes. 'I love kittens.'

Bess sat on the chest beside Joyce and took both her hands. 'Your mother is right. No matter what Master Litchfield says, he is no kinsman of ours and it would not be right—there are no women in his household.'

'But there are today.'

'Joyce,' Bess held tighter to the child's hands, 'promise me you will do as your mother says.'

Joyce scowled.

'Promise me,' Bess pleaded. 'You are never to visit him by yourself even if he promises you two kittens to bring home.'

Joyce wriggled off the chest. 'Very well,' she mumbled. After a few moments sullen silence, she said, 'But what if you marry Master Litchfield, can I visit then?'

'I am not going to marry Master Litchfield.'

'Everyone says he is looking for a wife.'

'That well may be, but I would not marry him even if he were the last man on earth,' Bess grimaced. 'He is far older than Father.'

Joyce giggled, her mood put away, 'Mother says it is not a good thing to comment on the way a person looks because they cannot help it. But when we visited Grandmother at Bury St Edmunds, I saw a grave with a stone skeleton on it that looked just like Master Litchfield.'

Bess screwed up her nose in mock disgust. 'Now I will think of that whenever I see him.'

Joyce grinned, 'You will tell me everything that happens?'

'That I will, sweeting.' She bent and kissed Joyce on the cheek.

~

As Bess rode beside her father, he pointed out the improvements he had made over the last few years. 'The boundary to our land was once the river, but my father sold a parcel this side to Dick Litchfield to finance repairs to the manor and the barns. I have tried to buy it back but Dick wants more for it than I can afford. In truth, more than it is worth.'

As they rode across the bridge, ahead of Elinor and Jane, Bess gazed around at Litchfield's estate.

'I see he has not started reaping yet. With the recent rain, the hay could spoil.'

'You surprise me, Bess,' Askew chuckled. 'Most women have no understanding of these things.'

'Many most certainly do,' Bess said, a flare of anger colouring her cheeks, irritated by his amusement. 'From the highest to the lowest, men are often away from home and their wives have to manage in their place.'

'Sensible men employ a bailiff or steward to manage in their absence.'

'A steward is, in the end, a hired man. Surely a wife, who has a man's best interests at her heart, would be far more reliable?'

Askew grinned, 'You have the makings of a farmer's wife.'

'Unless I married a merchant, my life would be on an estate of some sort. Only a fool would not try to learn something of it.'

'Do you have a farmer in particular in mind?'

'It is too soon.'

'Many marry within two years.'

'Many marry with indecent haste.' Bess noticed the hardening of her father's expression and did not care. He had not waited much more than a year, and must have been plotting marriage within months of her mother's death.

As the gatehouse of Litchfield's manor came into view, Jane drew alongside Bess. 'Rather dismal, is it not?' Jane stared at the squat building with its small windows. 'What is it like inside?'

'I have no idea. I have never visited here. My mother had no liking for Master Litchfield.'

'Aunt Emma is the same and will not explain why. I thought him a personable old gentleman.'

Bess blinked. 'Master Litchfield?'

'He complimented me on my gown,' Jane said smugly. 'Word is he will choose a bride from today's guests.'

'He may choose all he likes, but there is no guarantee anyone will accept him.'

'But there is much to recommend him.'

Bess gaped at Jane, lost for words.

'He is old and may not live long,' Jane said with a sly smile. 'His bride would then be free to choose as she pleases.'

'Even were she so fortunate, I fear a day with Dick Litchfield would be a day too long.'

'Why did you come if you have no interest?'

'Father wished it and I did not realise I was to be part of a parade of cattle.'

'That is a coarse way of putting it,' Jane sniffed.

Bess turned on her saddle to face Jane. 'You would accept if he asked you?'

'I can see advantages.'

'Jane, have a care. Marriage can be Hell on earth for a woman married to the wrong man.'

'Most can be controlled,' she smirked.

Bess's first impression had been that Jane was dull and unintelligent, but seeing that knowing look on Jane's face, Bess wondered if she were cunning. Perhaps cunning was the answer to life with the likes of old Dick Litchfield.

~

Litchfield greeted his guests in the hall of his house. The room was gloomy, little of the bright sunshine outside made its way through the small windows. He was dressed in new velvet and spotless linen but a liberal dousing with scent had done little to hide the sour odour of his unwashed body. He greeted his guests effusively, bending over the women's hands, drawing them slowly to his lips with all the ostentation of a Spanish grandee.

Bess waited until he moved on to wipe her hand against her skirt. Several other neighbours and their daughters arrived a few minutes after Nicholas Askew's party, the Byfields among them. Bess bit back a smile when she saw their daughter, Grace, quickly do the same.

The guests soon separated into two parties, the men eager to sample the ale and wine and the women to feast their curiosity on the inside of Litchfield's house.

As Bess stood talking to Maggie Drayton, she forced herself not to stare around the hall. Mistress Byfield had no such scruples. She ran her finger along the carving on an oaken cabinet as she eyed the tarnished plate, absentmindedly brushing the dust from her fingers. She quickly dropped her hand to her side when she realised what she was doing. She glanced at Maggie who winked back at her, the flicker of a smile on her lips.

Maggie turned to Bess and said, 'There's an uncontrolled housewife in all of us that must be kept in check when we visit houses that lack a lady.'

'I am certain I can control her here.'

'I can too,' Maggie said in a loud whisper.

~

Despite Bess's misgivings, it was a merry meal, all the guests intent on making the most of Litchfield's largesse. The meal itself would have brought no shame at Allingbourne Hall, although the linen was yellowed and the salt and finger bowls tarnished. Courses of beef and lamb and carp, vegetables and custards were served while a trio of musicians played. When the meal was finished and the tables cleared, a group of tumblers began to caper in the space set aside in front of the hall screen.

'This is grand,' Jane whispered to Bess.

'Indeed.'

'Do you know if Master Litchfield has anyone in mind?'

'I have no idea, but I doubt his affection would be returned.' Bess wondered which lucky lass was the object of Master Litchfield's affections, other than one who had been forbidden by her mother to come.

Jane gazed along the table towards Litchfield. 'I think he is rather agreeable.'

'I suggest you go and chat to him. Look at him closely and consider whether it would be so agreeable to permit him to have free use of your body, for years on end, to do with as he pleases.' Anger simmered beneath Bess's words. 'And keep in mind he is not the sort to die conveniently within a month or two of marriage—he has already buried one wife.'

Jane gaped at Bess, speechless, and quickly gave her attention to the tumblers.

The leg of a chair scraped behind Bess as Litchfield sat himself near to her.

'I thought I might see better from here,' he simpered.

Bess gritted her teeth and concentrated on the antics of the tumblers. The audience laughed, Litchfield with them. With each burst, his breath, with more than a hint of rotten teeth, blew past Bess's face.

When the tumblers finished, Bess slipped away to find the privy. As she returned to the hall, Litchfield stepped from behind the screen separating the hall from the entrance to the house. Bess sensed he had been waiting for her.

'Bess,' he said, 'I would have a private word with you.'

Bess paused, at a loss how to refuse his request. He indicated a seat beside the front door where those entering the house sat to pull off their muddy boots in winter. Litchfield grasped Bess's hand and drew her onto the seat beside him. Bess pulled her hand away and, under the cover of rearranging her skirts, moved as far as she could from him without falling off the seat. Beneath her feet, dried mud crumbled.

Litchfield leant close and tried to grab Bess's hand again but she kept her hands firmly clasped in her lap. He contented himself by resting one hand on top of hers.

Although Bess held herself taut, no warmth in her face, Litchfield was not deterred. 'Bess, my dear, I wonder if you are aware of the depth of feeling I have developed for you in the short time we have been reacquainted.'

'Sir,' Bess said carefully, 'it has been no more than a few

minutes of conversation. It is too short a time to know anything.'

He waved his unoccupied hand, dismissive. 'I have known you since you were a babe in arms. I know you are dutiful—you come to your family when called, you married the husband chosen by your father, all without demur. To my mind, you have all the excellent virtues wanted by any man in a wife.'

Bess stared at Litchfield, not wanting to comprehend what he was saying.

'No doubt this comes as a surprise to you but I would be greatly honoured if you would agree to become my wife.'

Bess remembered not that her mother had disliked this man but that she had detested him. Her mother's voice had been low, indecipherable, but full of anger and disgust and her father's voice, louder, dismissive. 'It's women's imaginings—false malicious tales.' Bess had no idea what that had meant then but now she could guess more accurately.

She called on her training. This was her father's neighbour; she could not destroy his goodwill by acting on her instincts and rejecting him outright. 'This is indeed a surprise, sir.'

Litchfield leant close to her. 'No need for formality, my dearest.' His hand slithered over hers. 'Call me Dickon,' he rasped, 'my first love did.'

Bess could not imagine Dick Litchfield was ever an eager unspoiled boy named Dickon. 'Master Litchfield,' she continued, appalled at the prospect of the slightest familiarity, 'I cannot answer you yea or nay yet. If you will grant me a few days' grace, I will discuss it with my family.'

'Of course, but you will find your father is well disposed to this. Nicholas and I have already touched on this matter and,' he added smugly, 'we have begun negotiations regarding the financial arrangements. I will ensure you receive all that is owed you by your late husband's family. It is a scandal they would deny you, a delightful widow, access to the income due to you. I hold your family in such esteem that I will give management of my jointure into your father's hands during my lifetime.'

Bess swallowed, understanding dawning. 'Your jointure?'

'The land I will settle on you, the land I hold on your father's side of the river.' He tried to insinuate his fingers between hers.

'And, when we are married, you may invite anyone you choose to stay here—your friends, your family,' his voice was hoarse, 'your young sisters.'

Bess fixed her eyes on her lap where her clasped hands rested, covered by Litchfield's bony hand with its flaking skin and liver spots, its ragged nails rimmed with dirt. 'You are most generous.' Her voice betrayed a tremor of anger as she rose from her seat.

Litchfield stood too and, before Bess could move away, his arms were tight around her, his mouth grappling hers, his tongue battering against her clenched teeth. She struggled but he was far stronger than he appeared and forced her against the wall. Despite the layers of clothing, she could feel his excitement as he increased the pressure of his body against hers. Bess strained her head away from him. 'Sir! I am not a strumpet to be tumbled against a wall.'

Litchfield, chastened, sprang back. 'Forgive me! Sweet Bess, I was quite swept away by your beauty. I could not help myself.'

Bess moved away towards the screen, holding herself erect. 'It is time we returned to the hall.' She was as imperious as Lady Allingbourne at her best.

'Ay, the others will wonder what has become of us.' His eyes travelled slowly up her body. 'Bess,' he said, 'if you were to wear your hair loose, you could pass for at least ten years younger.'

Bess fled back into the hall, past her father, Master Byfield and Harry Drayton with their tankards of ale and talk of sheep and wool, trade and war; past Elinor deep in conversation with Mistress Byfield. She made her way straight to Maggie Drayton who stood talking with two other guests.

Bess touched her arm and drew her away from the others. 'Stay with me Mistress Drayton. Please do not leave my side until it is time to go.'

Maggie followed Bess, her brow furrowed. 'You look as if you have seen a ghost.'

'Worse than that.' She grabbed a goblet of wine from the sideboard and drained it, shuddering, hoping to wash away the taste of Litchfield's rotten mouth. 'The gaping pit of Hell. Master Litchfield has asked me to marry him.'

Maggie laughed, 'We all knew he would be proposing to someone today. There is no question of you accepting.'

'He believes the conclusion is foregone.' Her eyes glistened. 'He says he has Father's agreement. Oh,' she groaned 'here he comes.'

Grace Byfield had pulled her father to the centre of the hall where they had begun to dance. Bess caught Maggie's hand. 'Come, let us join them.'

They made a set together and danced their way through the almain and Salinger's round, the rest of the company joining with them. Wherever Bess was, whomever she was with, Dick Litchfield's eyes were on her, a smile plastered to his face.

When the musicians stopped for a rest, Bess waited with resignation as he wove purposefully through his guests towards her. Before he could reach her, Jane and Elinor stopped him. Elinor gave a smug little smile as Jane linked her arm through Litchfield's and drew him towards a settle on the other side of the room.

'Well, well,' said Maggie, 'You have some competition there.'

'She is welcome to him. As we rode in, she commented that there was much to recommend him—his age being his greatest asset.'

'I would not count on that. That one will make dry old bones.' Maggie stared hard at Jane, now sitting beside Litchfield, appearing to hang on his every word. 'She does not appear to possess great wit but, sometimes, such women do better than the rest of us. They possess a certain type of cunning that ensures they get what they want.'

'She is a fool,' Bess said.

'Excuse me, honoured guests.' Litchfield stood at the edge of the dais at the other end of the hall. 'Friends.' He cleared his throat. 'The day is drawing to a close and any of you who wish are most welcome to stay the night.' He beamed at Bess.

'That is a delight I must force myself to forgo,' Maggie whispered.

'And I am not staying a moment longer than I have to.'

'That's the spirit, lass.' She hugged Bess. 'Now let us get these men to bestir themselves.'

Nicholas Askew had settled in. He was sitting, comfortable, in a grubby padded chair beside the great hearth, talking companionably with Harry Drayton, a jug of ale on the floor between them. Maggie spoke over them, 'Time to go, Harry, if we are to be home before dark.'

Harry rose slowly and rolled his shoulders. He grasped Askew's hand, then gave Bess the quickest of kisses. 'Good to see you again, Bess.'

'We should go as well,' Bess said.

Askew poured himself another drink. 'No, we will accept Dick's offer of hospitality.'

'Father, I do not feel well.'

'All the more reason to stay.'

She lowered her eyes and swallowed as she lied, 'It is a woman's problem.' She would do anything to get away.

'Lord save us,' Askew said irritably. He drained his mug and got up from the chair. 'Go and find your aunt and cousin, I will meet you in the yard.'

He wandered off in the direction of the privy as Bess muttered between gritted teeth, 'They are not my aunt and cousin.'

~

Dick Litchfield was disappointed they had not accepted his invitation to stay. He rode beside Bess as far as the boundary between the two manors. He sat on his horse and watched until they disappeared over the rise.

The whole time, Bess was aware of Jane's eyes boring into her back. When Askew's manor house came into view, Bess galloped off, leaving the others to make whatever they wanted of her behaviour.

5

B ess started as the bedroom door slammed open.
Nicholas Askew stood in the doorway glowering, 'Your behaviour today was a scandal.'

'I thought I behaved most civilly in the circumstances.'

'You did little to disguise the contempt you apparently felt for our host.'

'I doubt he noticed it, so taken up is he with his own fantasies.' She grimaced, 'He kissed me.'

'What man is not entitled to kiss the girl he is courting?' There was puzzlement in his scowl. 'That is no reason to show lack of respect to him.'

'I did not show lack of respect. I merely attempted to avoid his company, once I knew what he wanted.'

'There are others interested and, if you are not careful, he may withdraw his offer.'

'Jane is welcome to him! I am certain with her flat chest she would be more to his liking.'

'You women talk such nonsense! I do not know what ails you, girl. It is a good offer.'

'The man is ancient, his breath is foul, he is unclean and he makes my flesh crawl.'

'Rubbish! You cannot afford to be particular.'

Bess bridled, 'What do you mean by that?'

'A widow of two years and not a single offer in that time.'

'And why is that?' Bess took a sharp breath, her nostrils narrowed. 'An unmarried woman brings a dowry to her marriage, a widow her jointure. The Stoughtons have cheated us. They took the dowry you offered but refuse to pay the jointure that is my right now Myles is dead. I have nothing to live on yet you have not lifted a finger to help me. If I had my jointure, I would have more hope of a decent offer.'

'Bah! I do not have the money to throw at useless legal cases. I have six other daughters to provide dowries for.'

'As my only male relative it is your duty to ensure I receive the income that is rightfully mine.'

Askew's face was mottled red. 'You lecture me on duty?' A nerve flickered at the corner of his eye.

'Why not? I know enough about duty—I did my duty when I married according to your wishes. I am a grown woman now, a widow, should I not have some say in the running of my life?' She rushed on, 'Yet you have begun negotiations with Master Litchfield without attempting to discover what my wishes are.'

'You know now,' he snarled.

'And you know now that I despise the man and will not marry him.' Bess lifted her chin. 'I see no point in staying here any longer, I will be returning to Lady Allingbourne on the morrow.'

'Hornebolt has work to do here. I'll not have him wandering the countryside on ladies' fancies. Life with Lady Allingbourne has given you airs—you consider yourself better than the rest of us. No,' he crossed his arms, his pointed beard jutting out, 'you will remain here and be ruled by your father like a dutiful daughter. You can help your mother with the children until you are married to Dick Litchfield.'

'I swear I will never marry that vile man,' Bess spat back. 'I will stand in church and say that I do not take him, tell the whole congregation that I have been forced.'

Askew glared at her, his fists clenched. Bess braced herself but he turned on his heel, slamming the door behind him.

As Bess heard the key scrape in the lock, she shouted after him, 'She is not my mother.'

~

Askew entered his wife's bedchamber to see Elinor and Jane gabbling excitedly, each trying to fill in the details of the day's events the other had missed. The wet-nurse sat in the corner feeding the baby.

'I wish to speak to my wife,' he spoke over them.

No one moved.

'Alone,' Askew added roughly.

Elinor rolled her eyes at Jane but both women rose and left the room. The nurse remained where she was, aware only of the baby suckling contentedly at her breast. Askew glanced across at her then sat, his back to her.

'You heard all that happened this afternoon?'

'Almost minute by minute,' Emma said. 'Jane seems to have a liking for Master Litchfield.'

'He proposed to Bess.'

'And she did not agree.'

'How do you know?'

'She is not an empty-headed girl captivated by the idea of marriage. She knows the pains and blessings marriage brings and would not enter it lightly.'

'It is a fine opportunity. Dick has a good landholding although it could be better managed. Bess has been widowed two years without a single offer of marriage.' His colour rose as he spoke. 'She has an inflated idea of herself. It is time she was taught her place,' he finished angrily.

Emma's eyes widened at the force of his words. She leant forward and placed her hand on his arm. 'Nicholas, please.'

'She *will* learn her place.'

'But you cannot force her to marry.'

'If we are not careful, Litchfield will look elsewhere. Jane is willing enough and what benefit will that bring to us? In the end all cats are the same in the dark.'

Emma shut her eyes and rubbed the spot between her eyebrows.

'Emma,' Askew said softly. 'I was speaking from Dick's point of view.'

She opened her clear blue eyes. 'I am afraid Master Litchfield prefers kittens.'

Askew frowned, not understanding. 'Bess is to stay in her room until she comes to her senses, on bread and water if need be. She is not going back to Lady Allingbourne either. She can help you until she marries. Dick was thinking after Christmas but if we can agree on the details, it will be sooner.'

'Oh, this is not right if she is set against it.' Emma shifted uncomfortably in her seat. 'I would not want to marry Dick Litchfield.'

'You are not being asked to.' He saw her quail at his sharp words and took her thin hand in his. 'You are a good woman Emma, you have always done what was asked of you.' He shook his head. 'I do not understand it, Bess was always a dutiful child.'

'She is no longer a child, she is a grown woman.'

'She still owes me obedience.'

Emma winced. 'If you wish, I will speak with her.'

'Do you think it will help?'

'It may.' She stifled a groan.

'What is wrong?' he asked, anxious.

'Nothing for you to worry about.' Her face was pale, dark smudges beneath her eyes. 'Will you send Mary Perris to me?'

Askew jumped up. 'Straight away.' He brushed his lips against her forehead and hurried from the room.

~

Bess sat staring out the window at the darkening landscape. She turned, immediately alert, as the key creaked in the lock. Mary Perris entered and hurried about lighting the candles.

'Is there anything I can get you, sweeting?'

'Nothing at all,' Bess sighed.

Mary came and patted Bess's shoulder. 'Do not be so glum. The sun will rise, no matter how dark the night.'

Bess smiled—Mary had a saw for every occasion. 'Perhaps you are right.'

Mary left without locking the door but Bess had no desire to leave the room and face another argument with her father, or the prying eyes of Elinor and Jane.

She stared out the window into the darkness, ignoring the light tapping at the door a few minutes later. There was another burst, sharper now. Bess rose reluctantly and opened the door. Emma leant against the door frame, supporting herself with one hand, the other resting on her still swollen belly.

'May I come in?'

Bess held the door open and Emma walked slowly to Bess's empty chair. She sat and laid her head against the back of the chair and sighed.

'Bess,' she began.

Bess stood in front of her. 'Madam, the answer is no. I will not marry Master Litchfield. Never. Ever.'

'I have not come to press you, I merely wish to know what you truly want.'

'What I want?' Bess said resentfully. 'Could my father not ask me that?'

'He is too angry to hear anything you say.'

'I can tell you what I do not want. I do not want to marry Dick Litchfield, nor do I want to be your unpaid waiting woman, or nurse to your children.'

'I do not wish that either, and I know of no one who would want to marry Master Litchfield—for love or money.'

'Your niece Jane would consider him.'

'Jane is eager to marry and has given no thought to the life that follows the wedding.'

As Emma spoke, Bess became aware of the effort this was costing her.

'I see no merit in Master Litchfield but your father does, so I will give you his arguments. He is known to the family. Married to him you would not be in the company of strangers but close to home so we will be at hand should you need us. He has a more than adequate income.'

'There are as many arguments against,' Bess answered. 'For one, he is very old.'

'That could be an argument in his favour,' Emma smiled weakly. 'You would not have as many years to put up with him as with a younger man.'

'With my present luck, he will live to be a hundred. Besides, he makes me feel ill. I could not bear the thought…' She would not finish.

'Who could?' Emma gave a tired shrug. 'First he asked for Joyce, said he would wait until she was fourteen to marry her.' She shook her head to clear it of the unpleasant thought. 'I told your father I would not stand for it so he suggested you. Master Litchfield was happy enough at that, but he came to me afterwards and suggested that once you were married I could place Joyce with you, and later the younger girls. He said it would be better than sending them further away to learn their place.'

Bess shivered. 'If I were forced to marry him, I would never take any young girl into my service. Master Litchfield has an unnatural interest in young girls. My mother could not abide him and, until now, I was not sure why.'

'I suspect you are right. Your father wants that piece of land this side of the river and this is the price Master Litchfield asks, although it is tied up and hidden as part of the jointure.'

'Surely Father would not sell us for a piece of land.' Bess sat heavily on the chest and sighed, 'What can I do?'

'Your father intends to keep you locked in this room until you agree. If you are to find your way out of this, you will need your freedom. Promise the earth if you must, be demure, even tolerate visits from Master Litchfield. I will have Mary Perris stay with you so you never need be alone with him.'

'But would Father believe my change of heart?'

Emma shrugged. 'He has little idea of the way another's mind works. All he would see is that you are doing as he has told you to, that should be enough. You will need to think of a ruse to get yourself back to Allingbourne Hall. Say you must finish your term with Lady Allingbourne, or you must stay until she can replace you.'

'She would never insist—she would be happy to hear I was to be married.'

'Your father need not know that.'

'Why are you doing this for me?'

'Oh Bess, why would I not help you?' Emma leant forward in the chair. 'I know you hated me because I married your father. I was not much older than you and did not know how to treat you. What you did not know was that I did not want to marry. I did my duty and married the man my father chose for me. I was too young to do otherwise. Nicholas is a good man and I have come to love him as a wife should, but it makes my heart bleed when I hear of others forced to marry when they do not want to. I am certain you could never come to love Dick Litchfield, even given all the time in the world.'

'I am deeply sorry.'

'For what?'

'For all my ill thoughts—I was young too and I did not understand.' She bent and kissed her stepmother. 'But what will you tell Father?'

Emma rose carefully. 'That you agreed reluctantly but you now see some merit in the match. Leave it for a few days, at least, before you mention finishing your time with Lady Allingbourne.' She slumped back into the chair.

Bess knelt in front of her and grasped her hand. 'What is wrong?'

'I am still weak and the pains that follow birth still trouble me. I need to rest a while longer. Will you get Mary to help me to bed?'

'When you are ready, I will help you myself,' Bess said.

~

Bess lay through the long night, kept awake by a swelling anger. There was no justice in life. She had always been dutiful and sensible, yet what had she gained? One marriage that despite her misguided dreams had been based on duty alone and, now, another that would be a hell on earth. Her first marriage had not brought her joy but, apart from one humiliating argument, Myles had treated her with courtesy and, at surprising moments, with kindness. But this... She tried to force away the memory of Litchfield's foul mouth, the pressure of his lecherous body. She tossed in the bed and rubbed her hand back and forth across her mouth until it hurt. This marriage... She would never, never, never agree to it. All her obedience had earned her was her father's expectation that she would agree without demur, that she would accept that her own wishes were of no importance.

Emma's support was a slender thread. But would her father trust her change of heart enough to allow her to return to Lady Allingbourne? Her worst fear was that he would write to Lady Allingbourne to tell her she was marrying. If he did that she had no hope of going back.

Bess remembered her father as a happy man before her mother died. The house had always been full of guests but many, she supposed, were her mother's kin. His love for her must not have been deep though, for he married in little over a year. Bess heard it said so often—a man with children needs a wife, but she and Ann were nearly grown. If he had married a woman closer to his own age, it would have been easier to accept. She had seen the way he had looked at Emma. No, he did not marry for his children. This proposed marriage was not for her benefit—it was for his own, again. Angry tears pricked at her eyes.

Bess was drifting towards sleep when the door creaked open. She lay still in the bed, alert. A small voice whispered 'Shhhh' as if willing the door to be quiet.

Joyce tiptoed across the room in the grey dawn light and climbed onto the bed.

'Bess, are you awake?' she whispered.

'Ay, Joyce. Should you be here?'

'No one will know, they are all still asleep,' Joyce answered as she burrowed under the blankets beside Bess. 'It's better here,' she wriggled, comfortable. 'Are you really going to marry Master Litchfield?' Joyce's forehead crinkled into puzzled lines. 'I thought you did not like him.'

'I despise him but, at the moment, I can think of no way out of it,' Bess groaned. 'At least, if I say I agree, I will not have to stay in this room.'

'You could run away.'

'I doubt I would get far. Father would come after me and, besides, it's not safe for a woman travelling alone.'

Joyce sat up, cross-legged, pulling the blankets away from Bess. 'If I wanted to run away, I would dress as a boy then no one would bother me. I would go to London and make my fortune. I would be so rich I could do exactly as I wanted.'

Bess drew the blankets up a little. It was a child's fantasy but Joyce was so earnest. Bess played along. 'Where would I find the clothing?'

'You know Father never throws anything out—*Might have use for it one day*,' she forced a gruff voice. 'He even has clothing from when he was a young man in the chest in his chamber. I am sure some will fit you.'

'How do you know this, Joyce?'

'I notice things.' Joyce's face was a picture of innocence.

Bess tried not to smile.

'I heard Father say he is going back to see Master Litchfield on Wednesday morning. You could go as soon as he leaves.'

'But even if I did leave, he could come after me.'

'He would be looking for a girl not a boy.'

'But…' Bess paused, hope sparking in her. 'It might work. If I were to leave a letter… If he would give me a year… If I tell him I will come home willingly next year if I am not at least betrothed to someone better than Master Litchfield.' She sat up and hugged Joyce. 'If I put my mind to it, surely I can find someone else within a year.'

'And Master Litchfield will have to marry someone else as well.'

They both lay down again.

Bess turned on her side and beamed at Joyce. 'You are a most wonderful girl. When I am married to a nice husband with my own home, you can come and stay with me. And, when you are older, I will help you find an excellent husband who will take good care of you, not an aged man with foul breath.'

Joyce giggled, 'Sybell says he smells like he eats cack.'

Bess wrinkled her nose. 'I doubt even Master Litchfield would do that.'

6

Rain dripped through the branches of a massive oak, splattering in large drops off the brim of Bess's hat. She huddled closer to her palfrey as a rough gust of wind blasted rain against them. Rosie shook her head and gave a complaining snicker.

~

Bess had spent the previous day in her room, alone except for surreptitious visits by Joyce bringing her articles of her father's clothing, and by Mary Perris with food.

Nicholas Askew had come to see her mid-afternoon, unmoved despite her apparent acquiescence, insisting she would remain in her room until the betrothal. He had dismissed her complaints as he left the room with an airy wave of his hand. If he could finalise the details tomorrow, she would have her freedom when she was betrothed the day after.

Bess's only hope was Joyce's plan, hare-brained as it seemed by the cold light of day. She spent the rest of the afternoon composing a careful letter to her father. She was certain Emma would plead her cause and Elinor, although she had no liking for Bess, would not encourage Askew to pursue her, seeing the way clear to encourage Litchfield's interest in Jane.

The day had dragged and the night seemed endless. As soon as the room was washed in grey light Bess had dressed. With her father's heavy jerkin over her own doublet, her shape was well hidden. She wore his old breeches beneath her skirt, intending to remove the skirt when she was out of sight of the manor. Bess then positioned herself at the window to wait for the sight of her father on his way to see Litchfield. She put on her cloak as soon as she saw him ride out mid-morning. Bess placed the items Joyce had brought her earlier in her capcase—bread and cheese, a stoppered flask of small beer, as well as an apple and a small bag of oats for her palfrey. Joyce had thought of everything. When she had hugged Bess, she had advised her, her small face serious, that she would spend the rest of the day in the nursery so no one would suspect she had helped Bess. Joyce had the makings of a consummate schemer.

Bess left a letter for her father on the chest beneath the window.

> *To my honoured Father,*
>
> *I realise I am less than dutiful in this, but I need time to reconcile myself to your wishes. At this time, I have no desire for marriage to Master Litchfield, remembering well my mother's dislike of him. I am certain, were she here, she would stand firmly against this match.*
>
> *I did my duty when I married Myles Stoughton and I still want to obey you but find I cannot. I cannot promise before God to love and honour and obey a man I despise. I cannot say I give myself willingly, for the Lord would know that it is a lie.*
>
> *I am mindful that any marriage I make must bring benefit not only to myself but also to my family. Allow me a year or so, until Michaelmas next year at the latest. In that time, I will find for myself a husband who will please you far better than Master Litchfield, a husband who will bring with him the hope of happiness for me and the prospect of advancement for you. If I fail in this, I will come home to you and submit myself to your will, whatever that may be.*
>
> *I acknowledge this may cause you difficulties with your neighbour. Tell him I have been summoned by Lady Allingbourne, that I cannot gain my release from her until next year. Tell him I am as willful and thankless a daughter as his own if you wish, but grant me this space of time, Father, for the love you bore my mother if not for me.*
>
> > *Your loving daughter,*
> > *Elizabeth Stoughton.*

~

Bess's heart had raced as she moved quietly through the house; she was not sure whether it was from fear or excitement. She did not know what she would say if she met Elinor or Jane, even how she would explain herself to Perris.

Perris was nowhere in sight but Ralph, the stable-boy, was standing at the entrance to the stables, staring up at the sky.

Bess swallowed, afraid her voice would creak with nervousness. 'Ralph, saddle Rosie for me.'

She too stared at the sky as she waited for Ralph to bring the horse out; a storm was sure to break in the next half hour. Perris called to Ralph from inside the stables so he darted back in as soon as he had handed the reins to Bess. He had not helped Bess mount, nor questioned her as Perris was sure to have done.

~

It was the first time Bess had ever travelled alone. Fear that her father was pursuing her had kept her going at first, but as the distance grew from Woolham Manor, other fears had crept up on her. It was unsafe for a man to travel alone, worse for a woman. Bess watched the road from beneath the dripping branches of the oak. Surely even cutthroats and highway robbers would stay indoors in this weather. She shivered and thought grimly that if she did not get herself killed, she was like to die of fever at her journey's end. Still, a swift death was better than a living death married to old Dick Litchfield.

Bess suspected she had been travelling for over four hours and had not seen a living soul since the rain started. It had taken near eighteen hours to ride to her father's house and the journey back would take her much longer; she would be lucky to make Allingbourne Hall by tomorrow night. Bess wrapped her scarf around the lower portion of her face. Nothing was to be gained by lingering under wet trees.

'Come, Rosie.' Bess led the horse out from beneath the tree and mounted in the easing rain.

~

It was hard to tell in such nasty weather but Bess thought the sun must be near setting as she rode up to the small farmhouse. The house was in darkness but the smell of wood smoke lingered in the air. A dog yapped frantically, out of sight.

Bess dismounted and pulled her hat down and her scarf up. She walked to the door and banged loudly. The mutter of voices inside fell silent.

She banged again. 'Halloo! Anyone home?' She deepened her

voice, sounding more a youth than a man but, she supposed, she looked like a youth. 'I'm a traveller seeking shelter.'

'How many of yer?' a gruff voice called through the door.

'I am alone.'

The door remained firmly shut.

'Use the barn.'

Bess led Rosie into the barn. It was dry at least. She put her in a stall at one side and unsaddled her. The horse blanket was damp so she hung it over the partition hoping it would dry by the morning. Bess filled a bucket with water from a trough beside the house. As soon as she placed the bucket in front of Rosie, the horse dropped her head and began to drink. Bess inspected the barn in the gloom and found a tattered old blanket behind the door among a pile of what appeared to be rags. After using one of the rags to scrape the sweat and rain from Rosie's back as best she could, Bess spread the blanket across the palfrey. She then climbed the ladder to the loft which was newly packed with hay. She dropped a bundle to the ground and climbed down again to feed Rosie.

Back in the loft, Bess took off her boots and cloak and lay them out to dry. She settled into the straw. Although it prickled, it was warm and dry—and better than life with old Dick Litchfield. Bess smiled to herself. It was becoming a measure of the pains of life, anything that was better than life with Dick Litchfield could be borne. She munched on the apple that was meant for Rosie and ate the last of the cheese. She tossed the apple core towards the door of the barn, shut her eyes, and fell immediately into a sound sleep.

~

Bess woke with a start to find luminous green eyes staring into hers. They slowly closed and a low rumbling purr started up beside her. She went straight back to sleep comforted by the thought that there were unlikely to be rats in the barn.

~

A rooster crowed.

Bess woke and stretched, stiff from yesterday's ride and her night on the floor of the hayloft. She pulled on her still damp boots and tried to pick the straw from her hair. Twisting her thick plait tighter, she pushed it into the back of her jerkin, and wound the scarf loosely around her neck. She climbed down and led Rosie from the barn to the water trough near the house. As the horse drank, Bess bent and splashed water over her face.

She straightened up to see the farmer watching her from the doorway—a short wiry man of indeterminate age, his face riven with lines above a grizzled beard.

'Maken off without payen was yer?' He looked her up and down, his dark eyes calculating. 'Who yer runnen away from?'

'No one.' Bess met his gaze. 'I am a messenger. Got lost in the rain last night.' She could see his disbelief. 'You made no mention of payment.'

'Said yer could have shelter, not food.' He scratched his beard. 'Horse that size eats more than her share.'

Bess took a coin from her pouch and tossed it to him, careless. He caught it one-handed and bit it. 'It'll do,' he grunted.

The aroma of cooking drifted from the house. She would not ask directly, nor be polite but behave as a young man would—demand and expect. 'Where's the nearest town? I need to break my fast and find feed for the horse.' She tightened the girth strap and made to mount the horse.

'Cobbenham's an hour's ride.' He bobbed his head. 'Sir.'

The sudden servility told Bess she had the upper hand.

'Could help yer out—pottage, bread, cheese, apples, oats fer the horse, more t' take with yer.' The surly knave was falling over himself to be helpful.

~

Bess lounged on a bench beside the door to the house, her legs stretched out in front of her, and stared out at the sullen landscape. The weather was better than yesterday but still striving to forget it was summer. The unspiced pottage of meal and vegetables had been warm and filling. She sipped at a surprisingly strong small beer. A sense of well-being thrilled through her. She had ridden near twenty miles, alone, and come to no harm and was answerable to no one for the space of a day. This was life as men had it. Bess stood, her legs apart, and drained the mug. She was no longer Bess but Geoffrey Stoughton, free to ride where he pleased. Geoffrey swaggered as he walked, the way young men often did.

The farmer strolled over once Geoffrey had swung into the saddle. He laid a hand against Rosie's rump. 'Fine horse this.'

'Ay.'

'How'd a lad like yerself come by such a beast?'

'Belongs to my lady.'

'Who'd yer say m'lady was?'

'I did not say.'

'Where yer off to?'

'Allingbourne Hall.'

The farmer raised a bushy eyebrow. 'Y've a fair day's ride ahead.'

The sun was fighting to break through the clouds but the wind was still biting. Geoffrey wrapped the scarf across his mouth and chin, pulled his hat down, and muttered a reply. He saluted the farmer and cantered away, the farmer's intent gaze on his back.

Certain in the disguise, Bess could have whooped aloud in pure joy.

7

The silence of the evening was broken by the chatter of nesting birds and the thud of hooves as Edmund Wyard and his man, Robert Hayes, breasted the hill. Ahead, against a sky reddened by the setting sun, was Allingbourne Hall.

A solitary rider rode almost at a walk along the road towards the dark puddle of a sizable coppice of chestnuts. The rider appeared more interested in the pattern of the clouds than his surroundings. As he came level with the coppice, two shadowy figures darted from the cover of the trees, one tugging at the horse's head, the other pulling at the rider, trying to dismount him. The horse reared but the rider clung on, lashing out with his foot.

Wyard yelled to Hayes and they charged down the hill, swords drawn, bellowing an incoherent war cry. The attackers loosened their grip on both horse and rider and, with a jolt, the horse broke loose, galloping off towards the Hall. The attackers fled for the cover of the trees.

As Hayes turned towards the coppice, Wyard yelled, 'I'll see to the rider.' He dug his heels into his mount and sped in pursuit, gaining quickly on the tired palfrey.

'Hold up,' he called, his horse now level. He saw the glint of a blade in the rider's hand. 'Stay! We are friends.'

The rider glanced at him, his eyes shadowed by the brim of his hat. He slowed his horse, his chest heaving as he gasped for breath.

Wyard saw the smooth cheeks above the rider's scarf and guessed his age at not much more than fourteen or so.

The lad swung sharply in the saddle as Hayes joined them.

'It's my man,' Wyard said.

'Got away into the trees, but not without a pinprick to the arm,' Hayes laughed, his white teeth flashing in the dusk.

Wyard gave a satisfied grimace. 'So lad, where are you riding to?'

'Allingbourne Hall.' His voice was light and still breathless. He was too young to be out alone.

'We are bound there too. Ride with us—it will be safer.' The boy held a knife in one hand. 'What have you there?' Wyard leant towards the lad and took it. 'Blunt and rusty,' he said, running his finger along the blade. 'You'd need a hammer to drive this in if you wanted to do damage.' He handed the knife back to the boy. 'What brings you out alone?'

The boy was reluctant to answer. 'A message,' he said finally.

'For Lady Allingbourne?'

'Nay, Mistress…' He seemed to be racking his brain. 'Mistress Stoughton.'

'Have you come far?'

'Beyond Stowmarket.'

Wyard raised his eyebrows. 'Alone?'

'Yes.' The answer was almost a challenge.

'What's your name, lad?'

'Geoffrey.'

'Well Geoffrey, my name is Edmund Wyard. Find me tomorrow. I'll see that blade is sharpened for you and, if you wish, I'll give you some advice on taking care of yourself on the road.'

Geoffrey muttered a thanks but said little else. He clearly had no desire for talk so Wyard left him to his silence.

~

They rode together into the almost deserted yard at the rear of the Hall. The household appeared to have settled in for the night but light still flickered from the stables. Wyard watched as Geoffrey dismounted clumsily and led his horse towards the stables. He appeared to know his way around.

'You're not stabling that horse straight away, are you?'

Geoffrey shrugged.

'You cannot ride a horse to a standstill then leave her in a stall. Walk her around the yard for a few minutes to cool her down.' Wyard dismounted and started to lead his own horse. 'You have a lot to learn if you are to survive as a messenger.'

Geoffrey scowled at Wyard but said nothing as they continued their circuit of the yard. A stable-boy ran out to take the reins from Wyard but he brushed him away. 'No, lad, bring out a couple of blankets.'

The lad rushed back with the blankets. Wyard tossed one to Geoffrey who caught it clumsily. 'Now spread it over the loins, you do not want your mount to take a chill.'

They paced the yard for a few minutes more, Wyard watching Geoffrey.

'That's long enough. Notice, she is no longer sweating and quivering. Take her into the stables.'

As Geoffrey entered the stables another boy looked over from the horse he was brushing and frowned, puzzled. Geoffrey said something about a masquerade that Wyard, who was following him in, did not quite hear or understand. The boy asked, deference in his manner, 'Do you want me to see to Rosie?'

'I'll see to her, Wat.' He gazed at the full stalls. 'You're very busy—guests for Mistress Beckingham's betrothal?'

'They started arriving yesterday. The house is so full some are sure to be sleeping on the floor of the hall.' He nodded towards the rear of the stables. 'There's a free stall half-way along.'

Geoffrey picked up a lamp and led his palfrey into the gloom.

Wyard followed as another stable-boy took his horse to the back. He waited, judging the quality of the care his horse was getting, reprimanding the lad sharply for anything that was not to his liking. Finally satisfied, he walked toward the entrance but halted half-way watching Geoffrey as he brushed his horse. There was something sinuous about the way he moved—feminine almost. Clearly he was still little more than a boy, with no sight yet of the changes that sometimes so quickly turned a boy into a man.

Geoffrey glanced over his shoulder at Wyard.

'You make sure you come and see me tomorrow.'

'Thank you, sir.' Geoffrey turned back to his horse.

Wyard walked out into the courtyard and stopped, waiting for Hayes to join him. He leant against the wall of the stables and stared up at the glittering pinpricks in the inky sky.

Geoffrey came out with his bag held against him. He carried it close, the way a woman would. Half-way across the courtyard a swagger crept into his step. It was almost as if the lad, aware of

Wyard's scrutiny, was trying to prove he was a man.

~

Bess moved quickly through the house to the chamber she shared with the other women of Lady Allingbourne's household. With so many strangers in the house, a boy hurrying up the stairs was barely noticed.

Lucy Torrington, dressed in her smock and bodice, screamed as Bess pushed the door open. Avisa Gerville, sixteen and sure of herself, was unconcerned. Seated on a stool, she stretched out a long stockinged leg and began, slowly and carefully, to roll her stocking down, her vivid blue eyes on the boy at the door the whole time. Only Philippa recognised Bess instantly.

'La! Girls, it's Bess.'

Avisa looked at Bess, disgusted. 'What games are you playing?'

Bess dropped her bag beside the bed. 'I did not reach my father's home,' she gave a mock sigh. 'We were set upon by brigands not far from here. I was taken captive and sent to a stew in Southwark. Before they could set me to work, I overpowered the guard, stripped him and stole his clothing. Disguised as a boy, I made my way here.'

Philippa stood at the other side of the bed, struggling not to laugh.

Lucy blinked, open mouthed.

Avisa muttered, 'A likely story,' as if hoping it were true.

'You'll not have eaten then?' Philippa said.

'Not for hours.'

'I'll get something brought up. And you'll want water to wash.' She opened the door and called to one of the maids arranging pallets on the floor in the room beyond.

'It will not be long, Bess. Let me help you with your clothing.' She helped Bess out of her jerkin and shirt and unlaced her bodice beneath.

The other women continued with their preparations for bed.

'So, what is the real story?' Avisa asked.

'I told you the real story.' Bess pulled her bed smock over her head and dropped her breeches to the floor.

'Lady Allingbourne will have something to say about you riding about dressed that way.'

'And how will she find out?' She picked up the breeches and folded them. 'No one here will tell her.'

'If she does, we will know where to look,' Philippa stared at Avisa.

'Find out what?' Clemence Higden, the most senior of Lady Allingbourne's women, asked as she bustled in, pulling the pins from her headdress. 'I hope you girls are not planning mischief of some sort.' She carefully secured a night kerchief over her unnaturally red frizzed hair and began undressing.

'Now is that likely with sensible Bess here to keep us in order?' Avisa smirked at Bess as she climbed into bed.

Lucy sat on the side of the bed slowly plaiting her hair, humming to herself, oblivious to everything around her.

Bess looked from Lucy to Philippa, questioning.

Philippa rolled her eyes and shrugged.

~

The bedchamber was dark but stifled giggles came from behind the curtains of one of the two large beds.

'And then do you know what he did?' Avisa's voice descended into a whisper that could be heard only by her bedmate.

'No!' Lucy gasped.

Bess could imagine the horror and incomprehension on Lucy's face, the glitter of mischief in Avisa's eyes. She sat up and called across the room. 'Avisa! Enough! Go to sleep.'

There was silence for several minutes, punctuated only by Clemence's dainty snores. The whispers started again but Bess could no longer hear what was said. She was drifting toward sleep when Lucy snapped, 'You are a liar! I will not hear another word, I am going to sleep.'

'That girl knows more than she should,' Bess muttered to Philippa who had woken with a start.

'I think most of it is talk,' Philippa said sleepily.

'Talk she is too young for.'

Avisa's whispers continued, stopping only when they were met by a loud snore. Bess lay silent, staring into the dark, savouring the warmth and softness of the bed. The sensation of the cloth of her bed smock against her skin was luxury after her damp and uncomfortable ride. This was exactly where she should be. She had escaped Dick Litchfield and she would do whatever was needed to make sure she did not have to go back.

Philippa turned on her pillow and yawned. 'So, what happened?' she whispered.

Bess moved closer. 'He brought me home to marry me off to a vile old man.'

'Oh Bess, how dreadful.'

With the warmth of Philippa beside her, her familiar scent, and the genuine concern in her voice, tears sprang into Bess's eyes. She shook with silent sobs. 'I would rather be dead than married to him.'

'Surely your father…'

Bess cut her short. 'He was arranging for me to be betrothed today.' She started to sob again.

Philippa rubbed her hand against Bess's shoulder. 'And you escaped.'

'Yes,' Bess sniffed, fighting the tears. 'It was safer to travel dressed as a man. Still, I was set upon by brigands a mile from here. I do not know what would have happened but for the arrival of one of your guests and his man.'

Philippa groaned, pulling Bess closer. 'Will your father come after you?'

'I hope not. I left him a letter. I promised to find a more advantageous match by Michaelmas next year.'

'Do you have anyone in mind?'

'Nay, but he must be rich and,' Bess added bitterly, 'this time my jointure will not be an annuity but gold or land of my own. I'll make him grant it to me as soon as we are married.'

'You are planning to outlive him?'

'Indeed! A wealthy widow has more hope of being her own mistress, and that I want more than anything.'

~

Bess woke from a dreamless sleep. She sensed movement in the room. Someone was moving slowly, surreptitiously—a pause after each action in the hope it had not been heard. Bare feet padded on the floor. Bess waited for the sound of the chamber pot, but instead there were more furtive sounds, the rustle of clothing as whoever it was dressed quietly. Slippered feet tiptoed to the door.

With the whisper of a creak, the door opened and closed.

Whoever it was would be well out of sight by the time Bess could get out of bed, even if she were willing to follow in her night gown in a house filled with guests. She should check who it was, but as she tried to struggle upright every muscle protested. Bess groaned and lowered herself back onto the mattress.

Fool girl! She would find herself in trouble. Bess supposed it was some sort of lovers' tryst. It could not possibly be Clemence, she was nearing forty and her sense of what was proper was deeply ingrained. Lucy was more likely to be led astray by flowery words and empty promises but she constantly worried about doing the right thing. Avisa, with the certainty of youth, would not even consider there could be consequences. Bess would work it out tomorrow. Perhaps the girl's behaviour would give her away. Bess would have to tell Lady Allingbourne. Lady Allingbourne did not tolerate light behaviour in her ladies as it reflected upon her own reputation.

8

Florence, Lady Allingbourne, turned at the sound of a light rapping on the door of her chamber. She peered over the pair of unbecoming spectacles she wore only in the company of her private household, watching as Bess closed the door quietly and curtsied.

Lady Allingbourne held out her hands, beckoning Bess closer. 'I did not expect you back so soon.' She drew Bess into a brief, scented embrace.

'I arrived on dusk last night, my lady.'

'Bess dear, do sit down,' she nodded towards the stool beside her paper strewn table. 'I will be a moment.' With a slight frown, Lady Allingbourne continued to add to the list in front of her.

Bess gazed out the window at the early morning beauty of the estate with its neat orchards, its rolling hills and meandering river.

Lady Allingbourne wiped her pen and placed it on the table and gave her full attention to Bess. 'Now tell me of your visit.'

'It was pleasant. The baby is well, my stepmother tired but contented.'

'And the baby's name?'

'Dorothy. Joyce, my sister, has decided to call her Doll. In her opinion babies are very like dolls.'

'Joyce is nearing nine or ten years of age?'

Bess was well aware that in the past she had always referred to Emma and her daughters as my father's wife, my father's children. Lady Allingbourne would not have missed the change.

'She is nine and a delightful child. They all are.' Bess felt shame that she had clung for so long to the angry judgment she had made as an unhappy sixteen-year-old.

The distant baying of hounds carried across the fields.

'Has Philippa gone coursing?'

'Nay, my lady, she has just risen.' Bess grinned, 'I imagine she will take all morning to dress.'

Lady Allingbourne smiled, 'These are such happy occasions, and Philippa and Anthony well matched.' She glanced away from Bess as Alan Fossett, one of her stewards, entered the room. 'If you will excuse me, we had best get back to business. She took up a long list from the table and handed it to Fossett. 'Bess, tell Clemence to come to me mid-morning.'

Bess rose and curtsied. 'My lady.'

She had hoped to ask Lady Allingbourne for help with finding a suitor but the opportunity had passed. She would wait until all the guests had left.

~

It had taken more than two hours for Philippa to dress. Over her smock and bodice and layers of petticoats, she wore an ornate gown with heavily embroidered sleeves and forepart, held firmly in place by dozens of small pins. She sat patiently as Mall, the maid the young women shared, combed her hair and pinned it in place with decorated combs. Philippa appeared nervous, barely pausing for breath as she asked Bess question after question about her own betrothal. Bess, seated by the window, looked out at the few high clouds and tried to answer without thinking too deeply of hopes long faded.

Mall pushed the last comb in place and took up a pot of crimson.

'One moment, Mall.' Philippa turned towards Bess. 'Would you mind getting me something to drink? My mouth is dry and I do not want to sound as if I am reluctant because I cannot get the words out.'

~

Bess took her time on the way to the kitchens. The hunt had not yet returned so there was no need to rush. She glanced out a window into the rear courtyard as she passed by. Tom, the brew-wife's five-year-old son drove a flock of geese through the yard— a small task for a small boy but the first step on the way to service within the household.

With the sudden rumble of hooves, yapping of dogs, the shouts and laughter of riders, the hunt thundered through, scattering the geese in all directions. Bess opened the window, leaning out, searching the crowd for sight of Tom. She saw him finally, crouched at the far end of the yard against the stable wall, terrified by the noise and the stamping hooves of the towering horses.

Lifting her skirts, Bess ran from the room, speeding down the stairs and out onto the steps to the yard. The riders were in high spirits, some had already dismounted, others were still coming through the gateway. Bess paused, wondering how she could make it safely through the crush of hunters and horses to the stables.

Geoffrey's saviour of the night before stood below her with Tom, tear stained and grubby, in his arms. Bess reached out and took Tom from him.

'Thank you, sir.'

In the daylight his hazel eyes were gentler than she had expected of a man who could see off brigands at sword point and harshly rebuke a stable lad for the way he unsaddled his horse. There was a deep sadness in them too. Bess wondered if the scars marking his face made him appear sterner than he was.

Wyard met her gaze. Puzzlement flickered in his eyes but he said nothing. With an awkward bow, he disappeared into the crowd.

Tom clung to Bess. She carried him into the house and gently lowered him. 'Can you walk, Tom?'

Still hiccuping, Tom nodded.

'You are not hurt?'

'No, Mistress.' He wiped his nose across the back of his hand.

'Let us go to the kitchen and see if they have a wafer or two to spare.'

Tom sniffed, smiling through his tears.

The kitchen was more of a madhouse than the stable yard had been with servants rushing about, the clatter of pots and pans, cooks shouting orders. Bess would have turned back but she had promised Tom. She stopped at the doorway and stared around. On a table inside the door among the platters of tarts and pies, custards and breads, stood a subtlety in the shape of a horn surrounded by comfits moulded into small fruits. Bess darted in and grabbed a small apple and a pear, quickly rearranging the other comfits to hide her theft. A pot boy glowered at her. Bess grinned at him and slipped out the door.

She caught one of Tom's hands and placed the sweetmeats on the palm. 'There were no wafers, but here is some marchpane.'

Tom bit warily into the small apple, delight lighting his face as the sweetness melted onto his tongue.

Bess took his other hand and said, 'Now, we should find your mother.'

Tom nodded and skipped along beside her.

~

The betrothal took place in the small parlour next to the hall. In front of family and the more select of the guests, Philippa Beckingham and Anthony Compton were betrothed. Philippa was almost as tall as Anthony, willowy and graceful, her long dark hair hanging loose. Anthony was a well-proportioned muscular man, a couple of years older than Philippa. He was dressed in the height of fashion—snowy ruffs and green doublet embroidered in gold, hose of peacock blue.

Bess thought this a marriage on which the stars shone. It pleased and benefited both families and, better yet, the couple had a genuine liking for each other that with time could grow into something deeper.

Philippa and Anthony held hands and vowed to marry at a time meet and convenient, sealing their vows with a kiss. As a token of the promise, Anthony placed on the third finger of Philippa's right hand a ring worked into a love knot and set with a diamond. She gave him a brooch set with pearls.

As Bess glanced around the room at the assembled guests, her eyes met Edmund Wyard's. He was watching her. Bess quickly looked away.

The guests trooped from the parlour to the great chamber above the hall to begin the feasting. The chamber was decorated with garlands of boxwood and ivy interspersed with rosebuds and jasmine. The tables were dressed with pristine linen, an ornate salt, finger bowls of polished silver. The greatest of the guests were seated with Sir Hugh and Lady Allingbourne at the high table, Philippa among them beside her intended husband.

Bess was seated further from the high table than either Lucy or Avisa. Avisa was enjoying herself thoroughly, flirting openly with an older man seated beside her, while casting eyelash-veiled glances at a young man opposite. Lucy sat beside Edmund Wyard. Her face glowed with a greater joy than could be seen on Philippa's. It had nothing to do with her dinner companion, for whenever Bess glanced along the table neither seemed to be interested in talking to each other at all. Wyard appeared as though he would rather be elsewhere.

So, Bess thought, Lucy was the foolish girl who had crept from the bedchamber last night. One look and anyone could tell she was besotted. She wore a secret smile and every so often her hand would drift to her breast as if she had a love token hidden there. Bess thought it should not be too hard to discover the object of Lucy's passion. She need only follow Lucy's gaze but each time she looked towards Lucy, she caught Edmund Wyard's eye. She would have to find another way—she did not want him thinking she was trying to attract his attention.

The feast was lavish with course upon course: beef and lamb and kid; salmon and duck; dishes of eels, of peas, of artichokes, crabs and pigeons; custards and sallets; pies of chicken; tarts of gooseberry and cherry and suckets. It finished with the subtlety that Bess had raided earlier.

While the guests ate, musicians played at the far end of the chamber, tumblers capered and, at the end, a small troupe of players, with music and verse, declaimed the joys of love.

9

The hall was a sea of swirling colours as guests in their silks, brocades and satins danced the first measure led by the bridal couple, Lucy among them with one of Sir Hugh's men. Bess watched her closely. Each time the dancers moved down the hall, Lucy's gaze strayed to the corner where a group of the guests' attendants sat, to a man of about forty with faded blonde hair and a neat pointed beard. Their eyes met once and both looked away instantly. Someone's serving man with neither wealth nor position. The girl was a bigger fool than Bess thought. She would try to talk some sense to her. But it could wait until later, Bess would enjoy Philippa's celebration.

Too tired for dancing, Bess made her way back to the small parlour. Here tables were now arranged for games of cards and dice.

Clemence was playing Primero with Edmund Wyard and two of Sir Hugh Allingbourne's men, Henry Smythe and Thomas Rawson. Clemence smiled as Bess entered the room and said something to her companions.

'Come, take my place,' she called to Bess. 'I've already lost more than I can afford. Besides, I need to attend Lady Allingbourne.'

Wyard nodded to Bess by way of greeting.

Thomas Rawson rose and gave a courtly bow. 'You are welcome, Bess, provided you do not do as Clemence has warned and win back all she has lost and more besides.'

Bess half-smiled, inclining her head towards him. 'That will depend on whom Dame Luck is smiling today.'

'You think skill plays no part?' There was a challenge in Thomas's handsome, smiling face.

Bess took Clemence's seat between Henry Smythe and Edmund Wyard. 'For certain it does, but luck is needed in equal measure.'

'She has been a kind mistress to me so far,' Thomas said smugly.

Bess placed her ante. Wyard dealt two cards to each player and the wagers were made. He dealt two more then spread eight cards face down on the table.

Bess held two sevens, a six and a five; she doubted she could do better. She sat at Wyard's left and was the last to play. The other players had all passed, discarding one card and drawing another. When the play reached Bess, she knocked on the table.

Thomas sighed theatrically, 'It appears Dame Luck has changed her allegiance.'

The wagers were increased and the next round played. Wyard knocked this time. The cards were shown, Bess winning the hand.

They all played on. Bess's face betrayed nothing of her hands and, by increments, she began to build a pile of coins.

'Bess has always been lucky at cards,' Henry said as he discarded two cards.

'Would you not rather be lucky at love, Bess?' Thomas asked.

Bess kept her eyes on the game. 'Nay, I am well content with my present luck. Gold is far more likely to keep me warm in my old age than a man.'

'But with the right man…,' Thomas said, one eyebrow raised.

Bess studied Thomas over her cards. He had a well-earned reputation as a master of the game of love but, unlike the poets of old, he saw each passing object of his desire as attainable.

'I have not met him yet,' Bess said, both exasperated and amused at his persistence.

At the next round, Thomas failed to bid.

'Perhaps, Master Rawson, we should finish now,' Bess said, 'while you still have something left.'

'You would deny me the chance of making good my losses? Besides, my friend Wyard here is still in the game.'

Wyard had played in silence, concentrating on his cards.

With the next round Thomas and Henry failed to bid, but Bess met Wyard's. The games around them slowly ceased, attention drawn to what had become an intense game between Bess and Wyard. Wagers were made on the outcome.

'You take the game seriously, Master Wyard,' Bess said, trying to break his concentration.

Wyard frowned, 'There is more to life than cards and dice and wagers.'

'But is life not one long game of chance? We seize what Dame Luck offers us—sometimes we win, sometimes we lose.'

He said nothing, intent on his hand.

'In love for certain,' Thomas agreed.

Bess ignored him, her attention on the cards and her opponent.

Wyard, silent, continued to stare at his cards.

'If you are short of money, Smythe here has plenty to spare,' Thomas said.

Smythe opened his mouth to protest but before he could speak, Wyard snapped, 'I'll not borrow to meet a wager.'

Thomas pulled a face. Bess sensed that Wyard was not a man that fitted easily with the carefree young men here.

'I could put up a manor in Ireland,' he said gruffly.

'That would be worth far more than this pile of coins,' Bess said, surprised.

'It is worth what I am willing to wager it at,' he said testily.

'What would I do with a manor in Ireland?'

Thomas gazed at her as if she were the only woman in the room. 'Bring it as your dowry when you marry me.'

'I heard, Master Rawson, that you are about to become betrothed to a well-dowered young woman of your father's choosing.'

'But Cupid's darts have pierced me through. I am willing to throw aside family and fortune for the game of love.'

Bess glared at him. She had no time for games or dalliance. She was intent on the serious business of finding a husband, something that could not be done with a head full of romantic fancies.

'You are too serious, Bess,' he laughed. 'You need someone to teach you to play.'

'Love is no game for women,' Bess snapped, 'the price is far too high. Only a simpleton would be won by hollow words.'

Thomas, stung, sat back and said nothing more.

Wyard watched the exchange, showing nothing of his thoughts. 'I pass.'

Henry and Thomas said in unison, 'Pass.'

Bess made a token bid and laid out her cards, three sevens and a six. 'Primero 79. I suspect I win.'

Wyard put down his hand, three sixes and an Ace—Primero 72.

Thomas considered the hand and smirked, 'Perhaps, Wyard, you will be luckier at love?' He gave a slight jerk of his head in Bess's direction.

Unsmiling, Wyard ignored Thomas and pushed Bess's winnings across the table to her.

Bess pressed her lips tight as she collected them up.

Alan Fossett, the steward, had been standing behind Bess among the crowd watching the game. He stepped forward and briefly rested a comforting hand on Bess's arm. Bess placed her own hand on his and rose from her seat. She forced a bright smile. 'We should find Philippa and offer her our best wishes.'

'And your duty done there, Bess, you can oblige me with a dance,' Thomas said with a bow.

'We shall see, Master Rawson,' Bess said with a smile that did not reach her eyes.

Thomas stood aside, clearly puzzled at the failure of his charm.

As Bess neared the door of the parlour, Wyard who had been waiting there said, 'May I have a word, Mistress?'

Alan moved off and Wyard walked with Bess into the hall.

'You play a reckless game, sir. I never wager more than I can afford to lose.'

'Nor do I.'

Bess wondered what manner of man could afford to lose a manor at a game of cards. Perhaps she should have taken his offer; she would not have to worry about her unpaid jointure if she had a manor of her own. 'You wished to speak with me?'

'I wondered how your son is?'

'My son?' Bess's brow wrinkled. 'Oh, you mean Tom,' she laughed. 'He is not my son but one of the brew-wives'. I saw his predicament from the window.' She smiled at Wyard. 'It was kind of you to look to him, many would not.'

Wyard did not acknowledge her compliment. 'And what of your brother?'

'My brother?' Bess frowned.

'You are Mistress Stoughton?'

'Yes, but I have no brother.'

'A lad, Geoffrey—he brought a message for you last night.'

Bess's heart thumped. She was a fool to have mentioned her own name but it was the first that had sprung to mind.

'I received no message.' Bess kept her eyes on the dancers.

Wyard studied her profile. 'For certain he bore a resemblance to you.'

She turned to him, clear-eyed. 'As I said, I have no brother—my father was not blessed with sons.'

'A cousin?' Wyard persisted. 'He said his name was Geoffrey and he had a message for Mistress Stoughton.'

'I know nothing of it. Now, if you will excuse me.' Bess gave a shallow curtsey and walked away from him. She caught up with Alan Fossett and linked her arm in his. 'Keep me company a while, Alan.'

Alan glanced over her shoulder. 'Avoiding Edmund Wyard?' he laughed. 'Word is that he's a prickly one. Unhappy at his losses?'

Bess changed the subject. 'Let us find Philippa.'

~

Wyard made his way around the edge of the hall towards Anthony Compton who sat drinking with a group of men.

'Anthony, I have not yet congratulated you.' He grasped Anthony's arm.

'Thank you, Edmund. Philippa is a prize indeed.' He smiled towards the dancers where Philippa skipped beside a showily dressed redhead. 'Well-dowered and delightful, she is all that a man could want in a wife.'

'A fortunate combination,' Wyard said as a courtesy.

'Here, have a drink.' Anthony poured a goblet of wine. 'Are you glad to taste civilization once more?'

'Civilization has more than a toehold in Ireland, and among the Irish there are men I would call honourable enemies.'

'Surely not,' Thomas Rawson scoffed. 'You have not changed

allegiance, have you?'

Wyard glared at him.

'Look, I spent six months on that vile island. For certain it is the worst place upon this earth, the entire people unreliable, worthless and barbaric.'

'You belittle those in Ireland who, like you, took the Oath of Association to protect our Queen,' Wyard snarled. 'While they may not be as many in number as here, daily they fight against the Irish rebels and their Spanish allies to protect both England and our Protestant faith. That oath means more to them than those who play at soldiers in the comfort of London and think a round or two with a fencing master is preparation enough to face the enemies that surround us.'

Dislike plain in his face, Rawson did not back down. 'I'll grant you a few may be civilised but the weather is foul and the food worse,' he sneered.

'And the Scots are as bad,' said the redhead who had now joined the group, 'cousins to the Irish in barbarity and duplicity. The border reivers are natural thieves and brigands.'

Thomas and the young man, drawn to each other in their enmities, set about topping each other's stories of atrocity.

'You have an estate in Ireland, Edmund?' Anthony asked.

'In Kildare. The spoils of war I suppose, granted to me by Lord Grey. It is well managed, I have a good steward there.'

'And land here too,' Anthony added, slapping Wyard on the shoulder. 'Time to consider marriage?'

Wyard shrugged. 'My mother thinks as much.' He gave a half-hearted grin. 'She has compiled a list of eligible ladies but I do not know that I want the inconvenience of a wife.'

'I can see nothing but benefit.'

'Provided she does not change once you are married.'

'I doubt that. We have known each other for years. There is no duplicity in Philippa.'

'A pity all women were not the same.'

Anthony Compton glanced sharply at him, fleeting pity in his eyes but Wyard did not see, he was concentrating on Bess Stoughton, seated on the other side of the room.

'Do you know anything of Mistress Stoughton?'

'You are interested in her?'

'No,' Wyard frowned. 'I met a lad on my way here with a message for her. He was young and ill-prepared. I hoped to give him advice for his homeward journey but he seems to have disappeared.' His scowl deepened. 'She denies all knowledge of him. Some unfortunate by-blow of her father's, or a lovers' go-between, I suppose.'

'A go-between for Bess?' Anthony laughed. 'I doubt it. Bess puts a man in mind of his sister.'

'Not Rawson.'

'I will concede that, but Thomas will flirt with anyone. He would even make a play for your mother if he thought there was the slenderest hope.'

Wyard saw nothing amusing in the comment.

'I have never heard a word of scandal about Bess,' Anthony said, serious now.

'You think she is a faithful wife?' Wyard scoffed. 'She is not married to that blond serving man, yet they act like long established lovers.'

'Alan Fossett?' Anthony's deep blue eyes twinkled. 'They are old, old friends. Fossett plays court to all the ladies but seems to have no real interest in any. As for Bess, she is a widow and, I would say, it is time her father gave thought to finding her another husband. So far she has not shown the slightest interest in arranging anything for herself.'

Wyard continued to stare across the room.

'If I were you, I would look elsewhere if I was hoping for a dalliance.' Anthony grinned at the affront on Wyard's face.

~

Philippa slumped into a chair beside Bess.

'My feet are about to fall off,' she said. 'So many men all wanting to dance with me, but I would rather spend the whole day dancing with Anthony.'

'And you say you are not in love.'

Philippa gave a sheepish smile. 'I am, a little,' she tried to appear serious, 'but not intemperately so. They say too much love makes for an unsteady marriage.'

'Some love is necessary,' Bess murmured, 'without it...' She forced a bright smile. 'So, Philippa, you do not love Anthony *too* much?'

'Not *too* much. Temperately,' Philippa sighed, 'and eternally.'

Bess leant across and kissed her cheek. 'You deserve to be the happiest of women.'

'But what shall we do with you? We cannot have you married off to a crabbed old man.'

'I would be happy enough to marry one if I could be sure he would be dead within three months of the wedding.'

'I know you are not so hardhearted. We need someone younger. Look, that one talking to Sir Hugh, would he do?'

'I do not mind as long as he is rich and does not have too many nasty habits.' Bess turned. 'Oh him! No.'

Philippa was not deterred. 'He is old Lady Wyard's younger son. He has spent years in Ireland and is quite wealthy. His father died not so long ago and, Anthony said, bought property for all his children beyond that entitled to the eldest son. And he has never married.' Philippa giggled, 'Perhaps he does have some nasty habits.'

'He does not seem the most pleasant of men.' Bess pushed aside the memory of his concern for 'Geoffrey' and for Tom, concentrating instead on his sharp rebuke of the stable-boy, his intensity at the card table, and his gruff interrogation earlier. Wyard was now deep in conversation with Sir Hugh Allingbourne. From the forceful way Sir Hugh was speaking, Bess had no doubt he was reliving past military glories. Wyard seemed more relaxed in Sir Hugh's company than she had seen him all day. Avisa approached the pair, eyelashes fluttering no doubt. Sir Hugh grinned at her, indulgent—he regarded Avisa as little more than a child. Wyard shook his head, impervious to her charms. Avisa moved away with a toss of her hair in search of easier prey.

'It would be best if Avisa were married soon,' Bess said.

'I'm not so sure—she would have to limit her flirting to one man,' Philippa laughed. 'I doubt she would like that.'

Bess stared across the room. 'And as for Lucy, the silly girl is in love.'

Philippa knitted her brows. 'Lucy has been more lost in daydreams than usual.' She glanced around the room. 'Is the object of her affections here?'

'Yes. He is a serving man of some sort. I have not yet been able to find out more. He looks to be forty, at very least, and has a certain disreputable charm. He studiously avoids watching Lucy but she cannot help herself and looks longingly at him now and then.'

'It sounds as if he has experience of underhand liaisons.'

'Married, no doubt.'

'We should let Lady Allingbourne know.'

'I will speak to Lucy first. If it has not gone too far and Lucy is sensible, there may be no need to trouble Lady Allingbourne. The fewer people who know the better. But,' Bess groaned, 'love and sense rarely seem to walk hand in hand.'

~

Determined to catch Lucy as she slipped away to meet her lover, Bess made sure she was in the bedchamber before the others. She removed her skirt and sleeves, laid them on the chest at the end of the bed and pulled her bed smock over the rest of her clothing. She climbed into bed, feigning sleep when the others came in chattering.

Bess fought to stay awake but the exhaustion of the past few days overtook her. She woke to a pitch-dark room. Philippa muttered in her sleep as Bess eased herself out of the bed. She tiptoed to the other bed and slowly parted the curtain. Avisa slept stretched out in the centre of the bed. Clemence lay on her side at the far edge. There was no sign of Lucy.

Bess pulled off her bed smock and dressed quickly. She crept into the adjoining room where the maids lay sleeping on pallets but was struck by the hopelessness of her task. She would discover far more than she wished to if she prowled through the house prying into darkened rooms. So, she sat on a stool beside the door and waited for Lucy to return.

Despite her best efforts, Bess nodded off. She shuddered awake after what felt like no more than a minute or two, sensing a change in the room. She went to the bed and pulled back the curtain.

'Lucy,' she whispered.

Lucy lay still, her eyes squeezed tight shut.

Bess bent and whispered in Lucy's ear, 'Lucy, I know you are awake. Be warned, this must stop.'

Lucy snored loudly in answer.

10

When Bess woke, Lucy and Avisa were already gone from the room. Philippa was still dressing, Mall putting the finishing touches to her hair.

'I'm surprised you slept so late with the clatter the others were making.'

Bess stretched and yawned. 'I was tired out.' She climbed out of bed and walked to the window. Rain pattered against the small panes.

Philippa stood and adjusted her bodice. 'We were to go hunting but it has been raining all night. We'll have to find other ways to entertain the guests.'

'I am sure all Anthony needs is a window seat and your eyes to stare into, but we will have to find something else for the rest.'

'Oh,' Philippa said brightly, 'Anthony says Edmund Wyard is looking for a bride. It seems his mother has made him a list of eligible ladies. Anthony says he is not much interested though. Probably would rather be off somewhere fighting.'

'If he does not care whom he marries, why does he not let his mother choose the bride?' Bess said irritably.

'Indeed! At his age, a man should not always be doing what his mother tells him.' Her eyes glittered with mischief as she added, 'So Bess, if you could catch his attention...'

Bess remembered Lady Wyard well, an elegant imperious woman with a firmly held belief that the world should run according to her wishes. 'Lady Wyard would never consider a penniless widow, and me least of all.'

~

Bess moved swiftly up the stairs towards the long gallery where Sir Hugh and Lady Allingbourne's guests were entertaining themselves with a rowdy game of bowls. She heard a door creak open ahead of her. On impulse she followed the sound, catching a glimpse of skirt as the door at the other end of the room swung shut. Whoever it was, and Bess had a fair idea, was heading for the armoury. Another door banged shut farther on.

She pushed the heavy door to the armoury open.

Lucy stood by the window, staring out at the rain-sodden landscape. She turned, expectant. Disappointment instantly changed to wariness as Bess picked her way through the disorder of the room. Ancient shields and helmets and discarded breastplates lay in untidy piles against more carefully packed chests.

'Lucy, what are you doing in here?'

Lucy opened and shut her mouth, her eyelashes fluttering.

Bess stopped in front of her. 'I know what you are up to. He will not marry you—men who make secret assignations with silly girls never do.'

Lucy stammered, 'I... I... have no idea what you are talking about.'

'Your secret meetings with that man—knavish, middle-aged, blond.'

'He is no knave!' Lucy said, indignant.

'So, you do know whom I mean. And he is most certainly married.'

'He is not!'

'You have discussed marriage?'

'No, but I know he is not married.'

'Do not trust a word he says,' Bess's voice was harsh. 'This is a game men play—they will say anything to get what they want from you. This man will have forgotten you as soon as he sees his next quarry. In a week he will not even be able to remember your name.'

'No! No! You do not understand.'

'I understand too well. Even if he believes what he says when he is with you, he will say the same words with as much passion to the next girl.'

'He would die rather than deny the words he has said,' Lucy said quietly, her eyes shining.

'If you will not take notice of me, you will heed Lady Allingbourne.'

The colour drained from Lucy's face. 'Oh Bess, you've not told her?'

Bess scowled at her.

'I swear I have done nothing to be ashamed of. I never would. He is leaving tomorrow and, although we have never spoken of it, I am sure he would regard a woman's chastity as her greatest gift.'

'Her greatest gift to *him*.'

'It is not like that at all.'

'Well,' Bess said, sceptical, 'tell me what it is like.'

'I cannot.' Lucy's eyes were wide open, pleading honesty. 'I promise you I would never do anything to damage my virtue.'

'The only promise I want from you is that you will not see him again. Promise me that and I will take it no further.'

'I cannot promise, but you have my word that with F...,' she stopped herself from saying his name, '...with him I am as safe as I am with you or Philippa.'

'You are a fool.'

'Please, Bess,' Lucy wailed.

'One look at you and anyone can see you are smitten. It would not take much for him to use that to his own advantage.'

'I swear to you there is nothing improper between us.'

Bess stared hard at Lucy—her pale face, the tears glistening on her lashes. If she were truly duplicitous, if this were Avisa not Lucy, she would have promised not to see the man again but would have done exactly as she pleased.

Lucy took a deep breath. 'He would never behave with me in any way that was not honest, and I am not so foolish that I would allow a man to take liberties. I am not in love with him. I promise you, one day I will explain it all to you.'

She seemed so honest. 'I will hold you to that,' Bess said. 'Now go to the long gallery and help keep the guests amused.'

Lucy sped from the room before Bess could change her mind.

Bess crossed her arms and frowned, wondering if she had done the right thing. Lucy was innocent but not simple. Bess had assumed, until now, that Lucy was one who would regard an overlong kiss as unchaste. She would take Lucy at her word and pray no ill would come of it.

~

Bess hurried after Lucy, wanting to make sure she went to the gallery, not off to another assignation with the man.

'Bess,' Thomas Rawson called to her as he strolled across the parlour. 'Stay a moment.'

Bess stopped, her hand on the handle of the door to the gallery.

He smiled, 'Dearest Bess.'

Bess, knowing what he was about to say, glared at him, her mouth pressed into a tight line.

His long-lashed brown eyes were intent on hers. 'You know I truly care for you. Of all the women...'

'For Heaven's sake, I have heard you use these very words with other women.'

'But this time I mean them,' he said earnestly. He caught her hand with both of his.

'I am certain you do, and will until you get what you want and move on to the next woman.'

One hand dropped to his side. 'You think me faithless?'

'Oh Thomas, do you know yourself so little?' Bess considered him seriously for the first time—handsome, wealthy, well-connected. She understood why women wanted to believe him. 'Your attentions seem to last as long as a spring flower and I cannot afford dalliance. I need to marry. Are your pretty words a prelude to an offer of marriage?'

He blinked, surprised. 'It is a game, a pleasant game.'

'It is not to me.' Bess withdrew her hand and marched ahead of him into the gallery.

~

Edmund Wyard walked out into the long gallery from the small chamber where those less interested in playing bowls were intent on games of cards and dice. His luck was no better today. After three quick losses, he had given up. It was a pity the weather prevented further hunting; he hated being shut in with nothing to do but play these frivolous games. If the rain cleared a little, he might go out riding anyway.

He watched as a young woman dressed in willow green bowled. She was, for certain, the most appalling player he had ever seen. Each time she missed, which was often, managing not to strike a single pin, she collapsed into giggles. She had been seated beside him at dinner yesterday, lost in her own daydreams.

Mistress Stoughton came in, the shadow of a frown on her face. She was followed by Thomas Rawson who attached himself to Anthony Compton's team. He did not seem his usual assured self. Wyard wondered if the two were connected.

Perhaps Anthony was right to see her as above reproach. She was no beauty but a pleasant-faced woman with clear grey eyes. He had noticed that when her smile lit her whole face, a dimple appeared in her left cheek. Although she was clearly of gentle birth, she was older than the other young women and dressed more soberly. She seemed to be one of Lady Allingbourne's waiting women rather than a young woman placed with Lady Allingbourne to be educated in the running of an estate.

Mistress Stoughton was watching the woman in green intently. With a surprising twinge of disappointment, Wyard realised that her glances along the table had been directed at the young woman, not himself.

Anthony's betrothed called to her, 'Bess join us, we are one player short and I am certain Lucy is playing for the benefit of the other team.'

The woman in willow green, Lucy, handed Bess Stoughton a ball.

Her eyes narrowed with concentration, Bess bowled slowly and carefully. The ball rolled along the floor demolishing the whole arrangement.

Bess took a step backward, satisfied, and collided with Wyard. He caught her in his arms but did not enclose her as many of the other men would have. He wondered where they learnt that ease with women.

Bess stepped away from him, her face flushed. 'I am sorry, sir, I did not see you.'

'It is no matter, Mistress.' Now would be the time to make a playful comment but nothing occurred to him and, if it had, he doubted he could deliver it confidently. He supposed he appeared humourless.

He stood to one side and watched the game. He wondered which of the women was Sir Peter Torrington's daughter. He would ask Bess Stoughton, she seemed more approachable than the rest.

The game finished, the players drifted apart, some to the gaming room, others to join a group singing at the virginal at the other end of the gallery. Anthony and his betrothed sat close together on a seat beneath a window, fingers entwined.

Mistress Stoughton glanced towards them with a fleeting wistfulness. She was a widow, was she not? Wyard wanted to say that pain does fade but, still, there were times when it caught you unawares. He doubted she would welcome such a comment.

She moved down the gallery towards the singers but turned back. 'Would you care for another game of cards, Master Wyard?'

Her duty to entertain her lady's guests, no doubt.

'Thank you, Mistress, but I have lost more than enough for one day, not counting my losses last night.'

'Think though,' she smiled, 'it would have been worse had I taken you at your word and accepted your manor in Ireland.'

'Ay,' he nodded. He wondered why he had offered it; he was not a reckless man. It surprised him she had not accepted the offer, most would have—Rawson, certainly, if he had her hand.

He was sure she wanted to be in more congenial company but she said politely, 'Would you care to join in the singing?'

He might as well ask her. 'Which is Mistress Torrington?'

'Lucy Torrington is the woman in the green dress.'

The appalling bowls player. She stood at the edge of the group singing a madrigal. When she sang alone, her voice was clear and pure.

'You sat beside her at dinner yesterday.'

Wyard studied Lucy Torrington. Was this the manner of woman his mother thought would suit him best? She was well-dowered and, no doubt, malleable. But she was not to his taste; insipid was probably the best way to describe her. It had been a mistake to allow Eloise to talk him into coming here; he should have gone straight to Bucklings Hall.

He glanced at Bess Stoughton. Of all the women present she was the most appealing. Despite his initial misgivings, she seemed honest and sensible. She was not predatory or flirtatious, nothing like that bold piece who had tried to get him to dance last night.

Perhaps Bess Stoughton's relationship with that serving man was some sort of protection—life could be difficult for a widow. And she looked at him with neither pity nor revulsion.

'You know Mistress Torrington well?'

'As well as any. Lucy is a good and gentle girl who deserves to be treated with kindness and respect.'

'Who does not?'

Her eyelashes fluttered as if surprised at his comment. 'Lucy would bloom best married to someone who loved her.'

'Few have that blessing. Kindness and respect are the best that most of us can hope for.'

She bit her lip, frowning. 'Are you considering marrying Lucy?'

Wyard shrugged, 'She is one of a number of young women my mother thinks would make a suitable bride.' He gave a wry smile. 'It may be more accurate to say would make a suitable good-daughter.'

'Do you have a list of requirements—number of hands high, girth, teeth, temperament? A list such as you would take to a horse market.'

It sounded ridiculous the way she described it. He gave a sudden bark of laughter. 'In truth, I have no list.'

'Do you always do as your mother wishes?'

'Rarely, but it is probably time I married and she fears that, left to my own devices, I will either never marry or choose someone highly unsuitable.'

'Who would be unsuitable?'

'From my mother's position, someone without money or connections.'

'And from your own?'

'I have not thought so far.' If you could not marry the most loving woman you had ever met, it really did not matter.

'Well you should. Can you imagine what it is like for a woman married to a man who is forcing himself to his duty, who does not like her company or her person, who married her simply because his mother or his father told him to?'

He had never thought of it from a woman's point of view. 'Was your own marriage like that?'

'You lack courtesy, Master Wyard.'

'But you sound as if you speak from experience.'

'That is none of your business,' she snapped, colour flooding her cheeks. 'If I were a man, if I had your freedom, I would do exactly as I pleased. I would never accept a bride who had been bundled up for me by my mother.' She glared at him, 'Now, if you will excuse me.' She swept away towards the group of singers, her back straight and her head held high.

Wyard wanted to stop her, to explain it was never so easy. He watched her go, wondering why he had never imagined he could truly do as he wished.

11

Lady Allingbourne and her women sat sewing in the parlour overlooking the knot garden. The guests had all left and the household had returned to its usual patterns.

Lady Allingbourne had seated herself at some distance from the other women, out of earshot. Bess sat on a stool beside her, staring at the letter that lay in Lady Allingbourne's lap.

'Your father's letter is most disturbing. Not only that you would be so undutiful, but that you would risk your safety by riding unaccompanied over such a distance. Anything could have happened to you.'

'Forgive me, my lady. I did not think. I was too upset and fearful.'

'Bess.' She shook her head slowly, two lines between her brows. 'You are usually so sensible. I accept what you say about your father's neighbour. A marriage with such an age difference can be quite difficult. I do find it hard to credit that your father would force you to marry a man you clearly despise.' Lady Allingbourne looked intently at Bess. 'You do want to marry again?'

'I do, but I also want a say in whom I marry. Love is no guide but there must be a degree of liking.'

Lady Allingbourne nodded. 'I need to give thought to this but, perhaps, I can help you.' She smiled at Bess, 'I quite enjoy the role of matchmaker—I suggested Anthony Compton to Philippa's father. And while we are speaking of marriage,' her brow wrinkled again, 'I saw you chatting with Edmund Wyard. Do you know if he has an interest in Lucy?'

'No, my lady. Whilst he wished to know who she was and asked me what I knew of her, I doubt he passed a single word with her.'

'That means little with Edmund. When he remembers, he can

be quite charming, but he does not remember often. His mother's opinion is that he needs a woman's influence in his life. Perhaps the next time he visits he will speak with Lucy. She is the young woman Margaret favours most as a bride for him. I am certain Lucy's father would be well pleased with such a match.'

'I suppose this visit, to use a military metaphor, was merely reconnaissance.'

'Indeed, I will tell his mother as much when I write to her.'

~

'So?' Philippa said as soon as Bess came over.

'It was not so bad,' Bess shrugged, picking up her sewing from the basket on the floor beside Philippa. She sat and arranged her skirts. 'She scolded me for my lack of duty to my father and for my rashness in returning alone. Thankfully, she does not know how I was dressed. Then she asked how much interest Edmund Wyard showed in Lucy. It seems she is the one his mother wants him to marry.'

'Did he speak to her at all?'

'Not that I saw.' She threaded her needle and began to sew. 'I suggested to Lady Allingbourne that it was a reconnaissance sortie.'

Philippa frowned.

Bess lay her sewing in her lap. 'It's a term I heard Sir Hugh use. Soldiers sneak into enemy territory to see how the land lies there.'

Philippa rolled her eyes. 'Allingbourne Hall is hardly enemy territory. Do you think he will come back?'

'If his mother tells him to.'

'He seemed far more interested in you than Lucy. The night before last he could not keep his eyes off you.' Philippa gave a sly smile. 'And he even danced with you, which was more than he did with Lucy.'

'I asked him to dance. I could not walk off and leave him seeing he had made the effort to apologise.'

'What had he done?'

'He asked some tactless questions earlier in the day.'

Wyard had approached Bess following the evening meal and made an awkward and bald apology. He had given no shallow explanation, as many would have. In so taciturn a man, perhaps his question and his apology should be considered something of an honour.

'He found me easier to talk to—I made the effort Lucy did not.' She frowned. 'He is a puzzling man.'

'I doubt he likes women much.'

'It may be that he is wary of them.'

'You could be right. Anthony said that when he was about eighteen he was smitten by the daughter of a London vintner. He even claimed they were betrothed, nothing formal, nothing accepted by their parents. He went to Italy for a year with his father and by the time he returned, she had married someone else. She denied there was ever anything between them, said nasty things about his pockmarked face. He lost all reason for a while. Anthony says he made a fool of himself, started sending her the most appalling love poetry. His father then packed him off to Ireland with Sir Henry Sidney.'

'I could forgive much of a man who wrote me poetry,' Bess murmured.

'There is worse.' Philippa lowered her voice. 'He came back from Ireland about seven years ago with Sir Henry and became involved with a harlot.'

Bess stifled a gasp.

'He was raising a band for service in Ireland. How would he have time for that sort of thing?' Philippa said primly. 'This woman had a child and Edmund supported her and the child. Not in a grand fashion, but enough for her to give up harlotry. He even had the child sent to school, said he would find a place for him when he was old enough. And the child was not even his.'

'And he is still supporting them?' Bess asked.

'Nay, they both took the plague two summers ago.'

'I suppose,' Bess said slowly, 'it shows honour of a sort.'

'But look at it from a wife's point of view. How could you trust a man who was likely to go off and set up house with a whore? The shame would be so hard to bear. You know,' Philippa whispered, 'his father did the same, but the woman was no common harlot.' She stopped and said earnestly, 'I'm glad he's not interested in Lucy.'

Bess felt she should defend Wyard although she barely knew

him. She was certain there was some injustice in the way Philippa had described him. Philippa was right about Lucy though. Bess was certain that a marriage between Wyard and Lucy would be a disaster. Marriage for a man capable of that sort of passion would only work if he were married to someone who returned his love with equal fervour.

~

As soon as Wyard was past the gatehouse of Allingbourne Hall, he urged his horse to a gallop. The journey took two days; for much of the time Wyard was lost in memories of his father. At the final rise, he reined his horse in and paused to survey the rich and well-run farmland—his inheritance.

The timber and brick manor house was built around a large central hall with wings at each end and a small courtyard to the rear. Wyard and Hayes rode through the gatehouse into the large courtyard at the front of the house and dismounted. A chapel, stables and barn surrounded the yard. Wyard strode through the imposing entrance, past the servants running from all directions to greet their new master. He stepped from behind the carved screens into a spacious hall bathed in dappled light from tall stained-glass windows. He gazed around at the panelling, the carved ceiling beams, the ornate fireplace. This beautiful house was his.

Despite the ache he felt at the loss of his father, he smiled. He welcomed this gift in the spirit he knew it was given. His mother hated this place, was only able to speak of it with distaste, but he knew his father had been happy here. The world may have considered it wrong, but it was here that his father had lived with his mistress of many years. Wyard suspected that her death, a little over twelve months ago, had sapped his aging father's will to live.

He wondered if it were possible to find a wife he could love as deeply.

Part 2

12

January 1586

Lady Allingbourne and her women made their way through Cheapside, the sights and sounds of the London streets around them: the rumble and squeak of carriages pulled by horses and of carts trundled by hand; the hammering and clatter from workshops; the cries of pedlars and of apprentices standing beside stalls and in doorways: 'What do ye lack, do ye buy?'.

The streets were crowded—porters sweated under heavy loads despite the cold; merchants and aldermen strutted in long robes and furs; men and women well clad against the wind, shopkeepers and shoppers, gossiping, laughing, haggling; pickpockets and cut-purses moving silent and unseen. Ahead of the women, Lady Allingbourne's footmen pushed through the crowd, shoving away those who did not step aside for them.

No sooner had Lady Allingbourne stepped into the mercer's shop than Master Stephen Goodwin was at her side. He escorted her to an upper chamber and sent apprentices scurrying for more seats for her ladies. Bolts of costly cloth, brocades and velvets and fine silks, were paraded before the women although they had all bought lengths of cloth when they had first arrived in London little more than a month earlier.

Bess alone showed little interest. She stood by the window staring down into the street. Below, a group of young men dressed in the height of fashion in showy hats, bright coloured hose and long rapiers, pushed through the crowd. Their vivid silks and satins flashing out beneath their furs and capes as they swaggered, careless of those around them, laughing at anyone who dared admonish them.

Behind Bess, Avisa and Lucy held a bolt of marigold silk between them, looking as if, at any moment, they would begin a tug-of-war. 'Bess,' they called in unison, 'does this suit me?'

Bess turned back to the room. 'That would suit Lucy better

than you, Avisa.' Avisa's eyes narrowed but Bess added, 'The gingerline brocade young Master Goodwin is holding would be beautiful on you.'

William Goodwin, accompanied by a frowning apprentice, had entered carrying several bolts of cloth. A young man in his late-twenties, William's features were cast from the same mould as his father's although his lips were not so hard, nor his grey-green eyes as calculating. At least, not yet. His face was pleasant rather than handsome and his manner matched.

He handed the brocade to the apprentice who brought it to Avisa.

'This is beautiful.' She brushed her fingers against the reddish-violet cloth. 'And it truly suits me?' She almost pleaded for a compliment.

'In a gown made of this cloth, with your dark hair and clear complexion, you will draw all eyes.'

'And Mistress Stoughton,' William asked, 'is there anything here that I can tempt you with?'

'It is all so beautiful.' Bess gazed at the rich array of colours and textures laid out on tables. 'But, at present, I have no needs.'

William draped a length of sea-green shot silk across his arm and moved it in the light. 'Surely, there is never a time a woman does not need a new gown?'

Bess traced her fingers against the fabric, for a moment entertaining the thought of a gown made of this beautiful expensive cloth.

'I am sorry, sir,' she said, 'today I am not buying.'

'Not even at sixpence a yard?'

'Surely, it cannot cost so little?' It was far below its true value. 'Perhaps you should point to the flaws in the cloth,' she said, her eyes alight with amusement. 'It will not fall apart at the first wearing or leach dye into everything it touches?'

'You are a shrewd customer, Mistress.' A smile twitched at his lips. 'In truth, it is a bargain designed especially for you.'

'Many thanks Master Goodwin, but I could not take advantage of your kindness. Besides,' she added, 'I doubt your father would be pleased to find you throwing his profits away.'

'William!' Stephen Goodwin called his son from the other side of the room.

Smiling, William bowed to Bess. 'Forgive me Mistress, my father calls so I must obey.' He carried the cloth to his father who was serving Philippa and Lady Allingbourne.

Avisa and Lucy were arguing now over a length of sarcanet, Bess tried to give her attention to them but would rather have been in Clemence's place, attending Lady Allingbourne. When she glanced over, William Goodwin winked at her. Bess turned away and forced herself not to look back.

~

On the opposite side of the street from the Goodwin's shop, not far from the Great Conduit, was Goldsmith's Row with its fine houses and shops, all four storeys high, decorated with coats of arms. Her purchases of cloth made, Lady Allingbourne walked towards the Row, Clemence beside her, the footmen clearing the way ahead, her women chattering behind.

'What will you do with that beautiful silk?' Bess asked Philippa.

'A bodice and sleeves.'

'Do you not have enough already?' Bess laughed. 'We have spent the last six months preparing your clothing for this wedding.'

'This is a gift from Lady Allingbourne. She is arranging a tailor to make it for me, otherwise it will not be ready in time.' She grasped Bess's wrist. 'Oh Bess, I have so enjoyed my time with Lady Allingbourne. I will miss you all.' Her eyes glistened in the winter sunlight.

Bess squeezed her gloved hand. 'But Philippa, you will have your own household soon and then you may invite whomever you wish to stay.'

'And I can invite all of you.'

'Even Avisa?' Bess laughed.

'At the moment I believe I will miss her too.'

Lucy, walking a few steps behind them, said, 'And will you miss me, Philippa?'

Philippa glanced over her shoulder at Lucy's eager face. 'Of course, I will.'

Lucy skipped across a puddle, her pattens clattering on the road as she caught up with Bess. 'He was nice, was he not?'

'Who?' Bess frowned slightly.

'Master Goodwin's son.'

Bess opened her mouth to answer but Avisa spoke over the top, 'Taking an interest at last, Lucy?'

'No, no,' Lucy stammered.

Bess glared at Avisa. 'You should mind your own business.'

'I thought men interested us all,' Avisa said. 'He would be a reasonable catch for someone,' she added, disdain in her voice.

They followed Lady Allingbourne into a shop at the middle of Goldsmith's Row. Natural light fell from large windows onto the display cabinets with their array of plate and covered cups and candlesticks.

Once again Lady Allingbourne was immediately recognised and waited on by the Master Goldsmith who listened, attentive, as she described a necklace of amethysts and pearls she wanted made for the following month. She planned to wear it when she attended court with Sir Hugh.

Avisa caught the attention of a journeyman and was soon poring over the contents of a velvet-lined tray: rings, finely wrought, enamelled, set with stones. Bess stood a few steps away from Avisa and stared at the rings—all desirable, all costing far more than she could ever dream of spending.

'I think young Master Goodwin was interested in Bess,' Lucy said to Philippa in a loud whisper.

Philippa's eyes lit up. 'What makes you say that?'

'He offered Bess the cloth you bought for next to nothing. And he was flirting with her.'

Bess turned away from the tray of rings. 'Lucy, you will learn soon enough never to take a merchant's word, or indeed his smile, at face value.'

'But Bess,' Philippa laughed, 'he is not a merchant but a lawyer. He was visiting the shop, not working there.'

'He was there the last time we visited and was watching you the whole time too,' Lucy added.

'Perhaps he was there for a reason today,' Philippa said. 'William Goodwin is worth considering. His family have been mercers for generations and are wealthy. There has even been a Lord Mayor in the family.'

'For Heaven's sake, Philippa!' Bess tried to sound cross but smiled all the same.

~

As Lady Allingbourne and her retinue pushed through the tight pressed crowd near the Royal Exchange, a gentleman stood aside to let Bess pass. As she went to thank him, she gasped—it was Lucy's *friend*. He acknowledged her with a nod of his head, gentle amusement in his clear blue eyes. In that moment Bess understood how Lucy was drawn to him. He was surrounded by an air of peace, a light shining from within. Bess glanced at Lucy whose face was suffused with joy, and Bess knew that Lucy was lost. When she looked back, the man had melted into the crowd.

13

Philippa and Bess sat together in the parlour, free of the company of the younger women. Bess was embroidering the sleeves she planned to wear to Philippa's wedding, Philippa putting the finishing touches to a scarf for her betrothed.

'Did Lucy try to avoid going with Lady Allingbourne to visit Lady Wyard?' Bess asked.

'Yes, she suspects Edmund will be at home.'

'So Master Wyard has decided Lucy will make a satisfactory wife.' Bess stabbed her needle into the cloth.

'His mother is determined on the match but Anthony says Edmund is anxious to join the Earl of Leicester's army in the Low Countries. He is keen to leave as soon as he can, though Heaven knows why he imagines he's needed. Think of all the men who volunteered to go when the Queen announced we would give aid to the Dutch against the Spanish.'

'Many of them are still here.' Bess carefully unpicked her last few stitches. 'It is a relief that Lucy need not worry until he returns.'

'Oh, Lady Wyard is determined they marry before he leaves.'

Bess looked up from her sewing, 'That could be any day.'

'I doubt it. Anthony says Edmund has arranged to go with Sir William Pelham. He served with him in Ireland when Sir William was Lord Justice. Sir William cannot leave until he has the Queen's permission and she will not give it until a debt he owes is paid.' She waved her hand as if it were all beyond understanding. 'Whatever the reason, it will be some time yet.'

'Does that mean whenever the Wyards are invited, Lucy will be forced to attend Lady Allingbourne?'

'Well, it is not likely to be you.'

Bess rolled her eyes and groaned. 'That child was about to be sick. If I had not hurried him out, he would have vomited all over the floor. With the way her Ladyship walks about with her nose in the air, she would have skidded in it and landed on her backside.'

'You practically bowled the woman over,' Philippa grinned, 'after ordering her to get out of the way.'

'She was standing in the doorway, making a grand entrance. A sensible person would have seen what was happening and stepped aside.'

'I doubt anyone has ever shown her such lack of respect.'

'So Lady Allingbourne said,' Bess sniffed, still stung eighteen months on. 'And the whole time Lady Allingbourne was reprimanding me, the old creature was peering along her nose as if I were muck on her slipper.'

'You can see where her son gets his fine manners.'

'He is nowhere near as bad.' She thought of Tom. 'I'm certain he would have had the sense to move out of my way. Still, he will not do for Lucy.'

'Perhaps William Goodwin would make a better husband.'

'For Lucy?' Bess asked, surprised, and noticed Philippa's smile. 'I do not know him well enough to guess.'

'He will be at our wedding.' Philippa glanced at Bess who continued stitching. 'You can get to know him better then.'

'Get to know who?' Anthony Compton asked as he strolled into the room, followed by Thomas Rawson.

They both bowed to the women. Anthony stepped forward and kissed Philippa. Bess looked away. There was passion there for certain, a passion kept in check. She hoped it would last, so often it died soon after marriage.

Thomas raised an eyebrow at Bess. 'Who are you hoping to get to know better?'

'William Goodwin,' Philippa said, tidying away her sewing. She moved along the settle, making space for Anthony and took hold of his hand.

'You are interested in him?' Anthony's eyes twinkled.

Bess shrugged. 'He seems personable but I barely know him.'

'Personable!' Thomas laughed as he threw himself onto a cushion beside her. 'And how would you describe me?' He sprawled his long legs just inches from her skirt. 'Handsome, courtly, brave?'

Bess gazed into the handsome face, her needle, still, in her hand. 'I would describe you as betrothed.'

'Ah,' he sighed with mock disappointment, 'the stumbling block.'

'William will be at the playhouse, Bess,' Anthony put in. 'I'll make sure he sits next to you.'

Bess saw the look Philippa gave him and the little smile they exchanged.

She packed her sewing away and stood. 'Are you two playing Cupid?'

'It is a pleasant game.' Philippa's face was alight with happiness.

'Poor Master Goodwin may have none of it.' Bess moved towards the door.

'Nay,' said Thomas as he took her seat. 'Since you arrived last month, he has been unable to speak of anything but your charms.'

Bess frowned, wondering if this was his usual exaggeration or there was some truth in it.

'Do not be so sceptical, Bess,' Anthony said, 'William has deputed me to make the first approach.'

'Ay,' Thomas laughed, ''Tis always amusing to watch when such a sensible fellow is love-struck.'

Bess paused. There was something in his tone—she was not sure whether it was malice or irony. 'If you will excuse me, I will tell Mistress Higden that you are here.'

'Good Queen Clemence is coming?' Thomas groaned. 'No chance of secret kisses then.'

Bess rolled her eyes. 'There was no chance without her either.'

'And what of the delightful Mistress Gerville?'

Bess nodded, 'Avisa is coming too.'

'That is something to be grateful for—a woman who appreciates my charms.'

Bess shook her head at him as she would with a naughty child.

~

The group moved briskly along the street, accompanied by their footmen, cloaks pulled tight against a biting wind. Thomas took Bess's gloved hand and linked it through his arm.

'Bess, it is good to see you interested in someone at last.' For a moment, he put aside his façade. 'Even if it is Goodwin and not me.'

Bess smiled weakly. 'Do you know him well?'

'Anthony and I were at Lincoln's Inn with him.'

'I believe Edmund Wyard was there too.'

He glanced at Bess, speculation in his eyes. Bess was afraid he was about to accuse her of interest in Wyard as well. Instead he said, 'He was at the Middle Temple for a while, before his father packed him off to Ireland with Sir Henry Sidney. He is five or six years older than us.' He gave a nasty laugh. 'Wyard. Now there is one who knows how to lose his heart.'

Although Bess was not sure she liked Wyard, she did not want to hear him ridiculed. She changed the subject. 'When are you to be married?'

'Not for some time yet.' Thomas placed his free hand on hers. 'Bess, say the word and the betrothal can be broken.'

'Thomas, do you never give up?' Bess said, amusement and disapproval fighting within her. 'Who would break an advantageous betrothal for a penniless widow?'

'Rich not in money but in beauty and wit.'

Avisa, who had been walking ahead at Clemence's side, skipped back and slid her hand through Thomas's free arm. 'Who is rich in beauty and wit?'

'You, sweet Avisa,' he turned the full force of his charm on her, 'rich in all the ways a woman can be rich.'

It would be so easy for a woman to slip under his spell, Bess thought. It was hard not to smile when someone so handsome smiled at you as if you were the only woman present. She knew that, to Thomas, it was a game of chase he hoped would end in bed. He seemed to enjoy the chase as much as she supposed he did the goal. He was rarely unpleasant if rebuffed, particularly if it was done with grace and humour.

~

The playhouse at St Paul's was a small establishment, its higher entrance price ensuring the nobility and gentry who frequented it could enjoy the theatre without the press and reek and rude behaviour of the common populace.

Lady Allingbourne's women and their escorts arranged

themselves around the room among the rest of the audience. Clemence sat down beside Anthony and Philippa and frowned at the sight of Avisa pressed close to Thomas Rawson. Bess fought a smile at Avisa's sullen pout when Clemence rose and asked Thomas to move so she could sit between them. Avisa was another to watch. Now almost certain that Avisa's claim to knowledge and experience was mere affectation, Bess feared such a girl could easily be led into trouble. She did not want to bother Lady Allingbourne but this was one situation that could easily get out of hand. She would talk to Clemence.

William Goodwin slipped into the seat beside Bess. 'Are you regretting now, Mistress, that you did not accept my offer?'

'Your offer?' she asked warily, her mind full of Thomas's double meanings.

'The cloth last week.'

Understanding lit Bess's eyes. 'I am sure your father does not regret it.'

William pulled a rueful face. 'Alas, you are correct. My father has ears everywhere, even when serving an illustrious customer, and roundly disabused me of the idea that I could sell his cloth cheap to put myself into a lady's good graces.'

'I could have told you that, Master Goodwin. It is a sure way to penury.'

'Perhaps that is why my father encouraged me to the law, knowing I did not have a merchant's sense. In fact, he has banned me from the shop.'

'Oh dear. Does that upset you?'

'Not at all,' he grinned. 'I have achieved what I wanted.'

'And what was that?' she asked, expecting the sort of answer Thomas Rawson would give.

'All I wanted was the opportunity to know you better.' His answer was empty of any other meaning.

The boy players took their places, clad in sumptuous costumes, and began to work their magic. With music, song and elegant words, they told a classical tale of love's entanglements. As she watched, captivated, Bess wondered why these tales charmed the audience when in reality such love was an illusion.

~

The following Sunday was a bright but chill winter's day. Lady Allingbourne, wearing a thick cloak lined with marten fur, accompanied by her women, listened as the sermon was preached from the stone pulpit at St. Paul's Cross.

Bess's interest in the preaching waned after the first five minutes. While Lady Allingbourne and Clemence listened intently, Avisa used the opportunity to exchange sidelong glances with a showily-dressed gallant sitting across from their group, and Philippa lost herself in dreams of love. Lucy was at home in bed with a blinding headache. She was a robust girl but often, by Saturday, she was laid low by myriad aches and pains, needing a day in bed before she was fit to fulfil her duties on Monday.

At the other side of the Cross, William Goodwin appeared to be enthralled by the preacher, but occasionally his gaze would stray to Bess. She tried to avoid looking at him, instead staring steadily at the preacher and fighting off her own daydreams.

By the time the sermon finished, leaden clouds had hidden the sun and were threatening icy rain, if not snow. Lady Allingbourne's footmen pushed a way for the women through the crowd. Despite the press of worshippers eager for their dinner, William managed to catch up with them. He smiled at Bess but bowed courteously to Lady Allingbourne.

'Master Goodwin,' Lady Allingbourne's eyes twinkled as she spoke, 'a fine sermon was it not?'

Bess could tell by her playful tone that she thought he, like so many others, had come to be seen or to make a show of piety rather than out of interest in the preaching.

'Indeed, my lady,' William fell in step with her, 'a sermon that should be preached in every church, large and small, throughout the land. I have never heard a better refutation of the errors of the Papists.'

'If all would take heed, we could live without fear.'

'Most Papists are too far gone in error to be won by argument. They need to be rooted out from our midst,' he said vehemently. 'Did you hear, another priest was taken and lies imprisoned at the Wood Street Compter?'

Lady Allingbourne shivered.

William continued, 'The weak and gullible are prey to such as these because they do not know their faith well enough.'

Lady Allingbourne regarded him with interest. 'You think the knowledge given at Confirmation is not enough?'

'Many know those answers by rote alone and have no understanding. To defend the faith well, we must not only have it written in our hearts but understand it deeply too.'

'You are right,' she said. 'In these fearful times it is most necessary. Your family takes faith seriously?'

'We do. We are not zealots but I am convinced that anyone with a claim to faith should know enough to defend it in argument.'

Bess walked behind them half-listening. She was as fearful as anyone of the constant rumours and plots of the Papists and their foreign allies. She knew God existed and, without hesitation, fulfilled all her religious duties but, beyond that, she had little interest in theological argument.

As they neared the Goodwin's shop in Cheapside, William took his leave of Lady Allingbourne with a warm glance towards Bess.

Lady Allingbourne called Bess to her side. 'I believe young Goodwin has an interest in you, Bess.'

'I am not sure, my lady.'

'I am.' A smile hinted at her lips. 'I have reports of your visit to the playhouse. And just now, while his manners and his intelligence are most admirable, I sensed he would rather have been talking to you, and not about religion.'

'I am sorry if he was less than courteous.'

'His manners are faultless but I can tell when a young man would rather be in other company. You have my permission to encourage him. I am certain that would be a match to please your father well.'

'My lady,' Bess said quickly, 'I had not thought so far.' But that was not true, she knew he was interested and had fought not to imagine where it could lead.

'You would bring benefits to his family too—your lineage will enhance their standing. There are many who believe a gentleman is one who has the means to live as one. Better a wealthy merchant or lawyer than a poor gentleman.' Bess nodded in agreement. 'I have invited him to dine with us tomorrow.'

As Bess thanked Lady Allingbourne, she warned herself not to think too far ahead. But William was exactly what she had hoped for as she rode away from her father's manor—wealthy, of an age with Bess, pleasant, charming. And he was not following anyone else's instructions.

14

As guests began arriving for Philippa's wedding and Lady Allingbourne's household swelled to nearly twice its size, meals took on a festive atmosphere.

Following dinner, the guests and other members of the household drifted into small groups. Some moved to one end of the hall and began to dance, some took to games of cards and dice, others sat about talking.

William Goodwin was at ease with the men of Sir Hugh's household. Bess supposed his family's long history as citizens of London, and their wealth, gave him the standing that others had through lineage alone. Blood was what allowed Bess to hold her head high in distinguished company—her mother could trace her line to one of the knights of the Conqueror. There were moments when Bess wondered at the use of such ancestry if a family lacked wealth and influence.

William's eyes lit up as Bess came and sat next to him at the end of the hall, away from the music. He was in a heated discussion with Anthony on the merits of the native breeds over the Barbary horse. Anthony was still extolling the virtues of a Barb his father had recently acquired as Philippa drew him away to dance.

'How do you know so much about horses?' Bess asked. 'I would have thought that here in London...'

'...and me the son of a poor shopkeeper,' he aped the accent of a London pedlar, tugging an invisible forelock.

Bess flushed, 'I did not mean that.'

'Be truthful, Bess,' he laughed then added, suddenly serious. 'I may call you Bess?'

'Of course, William,' she said without hesitating. 'I did not mean to be discourteous.'

'I know you did not,' he said gently. 'You are right to wonder.

While many Londoners do ride, few know much of the breeding of horses. I spent my earliest years on my grandfather's estate in Surrey. My mother was a true London girl though and could not stand the endless grass and trees, nor the deathly quiet. As soon as my youngest sister was walking, we all returned to London.'

'Do you still visit your grandfather's estate?'

'On occasions, but my life is here. I like the bustle and the thrill of London. It is the greatest city in the world,' he said, emphatic.

'I hardly dare ask, but do you know many others?'

'Venice and Florence, Strasbourg and Paris. Three years ago, I went with Lord Willoughby's embassy to Denmark to invest their king with the order of the Garter.'

William spoke honestly of what he had seen and done. He did not boast but neither was he falsely modest. He was no mere lawyer but a courtier of sorts, with influential connections.

'You are a close family?'

'My father believes in keeping ties strong. He says it makes for greater loyalty. It also means he can keep an eye on what we do and bring us to heel when we make missteps like offering cloth cheap to pretty women,' he said with pretended sheepishness.

'Does it often work?' Bess asked.

'I have tried it once and I would say it does—here am I speaking to you, and I know you well enough to call you Bess. That will do for now.' His words were reassuring but his eyes asked for more.

Perhaps she had misjudged him and he was like the rest. Lawyer and courtier, he was one who used words to convince others to act, in the end, to his advantage. His face seemed honest, but Bess could put on an honest face on the rare occasion a lie was necessary. Perhaps he was no different from Thomas Rawson, his aim the same although his words were more subtle and his chase more leisurely. Bess needed a husband, not a lover. She had nothing but herself to offer in the marriage market and she doubted that was enough. A man might want her, but without a solid dowry, his family would not. She did not know what arts a woman needed to make a man desire her so much he would be willing to marry her in the face of opposition.

'What are you thinking?' His fingers brushed her hand.

Bess pushed her thoughts away. 'Nothing and no one.'

'You look so sad.' He took a deep breath and caught her hand in his. 'Grief does not run to a calendar. If it is too soon for you...' his voice trailed off.

She felt no thrill at his touch, but there was comfort. Bess placed her other hand over his and looked away to the dancers at the centre of the hall. 'Not at all.' She stood up, still holding his hand. 'Come William, let us dance.'

~

The night before the wedding, the women's chamber was crowded. Bess and Philippa shared their bed with Philippa's younger sister, Kate. Avisa, Lucy and Clemence were in the second bed, other young women and their maids slept on trundle beds and pallets on the floor.

Philippa snuggled close to Bess and whispered, 'This is the last time we will be together like this. I want so much to marry Anthony but I will miss you.'

'I'll miss you too,' Bess whispered. The younger women were more like charges but Philippa was her friend. There would be no one to share her secrets.

Philippa laid her head against Bess's shoulder. 'Bess,' she breathed, 'it will not be too bad? I have heard...'

'Hush,' Bess whispered, 'Anthony cares for you and he is no green youth.' She rolled on to her side to face Philippa in the dark warmth of the bed. 'I am certain all will be well.'

'When you...' Philippa paused for a moment and changed the subject. 'Anthony says William Goodwin is completely smitten, can talk of nothing but you.'

'But why?' Bess burst out. She needed to be married but could think of no sensible reason why a man would want her.

'A million reasons,' Philippa answered quietly. 'He likes the way you look, you talk, you act. He likes that you are not frivolous, that you do not seek men's attention. He just likes you.' She asked, wonder in her voice, 'Have you never been in love?'

'Never.'

'Not even...'

'No,' Bess said firmly. 'I thought I was in love with him but he...,' she forced out the words she had never spoken aloud, 'he loved someone else. I did not know until after we were married. He was courteous, treated me with respect but every moment he was with me he was wishing I was that other girl.' There were tears in her words. 'I thought I had done something wrong, I tried to win him but my efforts made him angry.'

'Oh Bess.'

'It shames me even now. They wanted him to marry me so, obediently, he did his duty. He even recited the false words his father had given him when he was courting me. And I believed him. He did not need to. Had he been honest, I still would have married him—I always did what my father told me to.' She sat up in the bed. 'This is what makes me so angry with Edmund Wyard. He must be ten years older than Myles was and still he is following his mother's orders, although he knows how unsuited he and Lucy are.' She flung herself back onto the mattress. 'The stupid callous man!'

Kate groaned, 'Will you two stop muttering. Some of us need to sleep.'

'Yes,' Avisa called from the other bed, 'if you will not talk loud enough for the rest of us to hear, be quiet and go to sleep.'

Philippa put her mouth to Bess's ear and murmured, 'Lucy should show some spirit too. And you, you make the most of William's feeling for you. This is your best chance. Whether you love him or not, you will make him an excellent wife. Better him than a vile old man.'

'Much, much better,' Bess agreed.

~

The marriage of Philippa Beckingham and Anthony Compton took place in the parlour of Sir Hugh and Lady Allingbourne's London residence. The room was festooned with greenery. Philippa wore a gown of silk brocade, the bodice and the sleeves embroidered with small beads, and an open ruff decorated with delicate cutwork. She was led to Anthony by her father and attended by her sister and the young unmarried women of Lady Allingbourne's household.

Bess blinked away tears as she heard the promises made, promises that spoke of love, a love that was so rarely present, or died soon after marriage. But there was love between Philippa and

Anthony and, if the Lord was good, it would grow. They were both free hearts and came willingly to a marriage that pleased both family and friends.

The lavish banquet that followed in the hall ended with a dramatic masque performed by professional players accompanied by the blast of trumpets, and thunder and lightning conjured by drums and flashing torches.

~

Edmund Wyard was seated beside Lucy Torrington. His mother had made it exceedingly clear that, in her view, he should marry Lucy. As the players extolled the virtues of women, and wives in particular, he felt irritation rise at the young woman. He had tried to talk to her during the feast, but her answers had been brief and invited no further exchange. Were not young women trained in the art of conversation? A fine marriage this would be, held together by duty alone. He studied Anthony Compton and his new wife sitting at the high table. Theirs was a marriage arranged by family yet it seemed to hold far more than duty for them both.

He glanced at Lucy—her face was plump, her hair and lashes an unremarkable brown, her eyes a washed-out blue, and her lips surprisingly narrow. She appeared to be lost in her own world. He could not imagine coming home to her. In fact, he could not imagine her as wife to anyone. Although she was a sturdy young woman, there was something unworldly about her, as if she were seeing things others could not.

He wanted a wife of flesh and blood. Someone like Alyne, kind and warm and loving, someone who did not judge him and find him lacking. Alyne could make him forget, for a time, the brutality he had been part of in Ireland. He heard again her bubbling laugh and, overwhelmed with loss, he drained his cup. Turning to the servant waiting patiently to one side with the wine jug, he held his cup out again.

Why had his mother even suggested this woman? It would be better if he did not marry, better to appoint a decent house steward. But a steward could not sit beside a man at a banquet, could not dance with him and make him laugh.

What had the Stoughton woman said? *If I were a man, I would do exactly as I pleased.* Perhaps he should try.

The players had begun to dance, Anthony and his wife with them, inviting others to join. He handed his cup back to the servant and turned to the young woman beside him. 'Mistress Torrington, would you care to dance?'

She blinked as if seeing him for the first time and nodded.

He led her out, grim-faced, as they joined the couples arranged down the centre of the hall.

~

Today Bess was Philippa's guest, free to enjoy herself. She had taken every offer to dance. William Goodwin was not present but his father was. As Bess moved around the room in a lively galliard, she had been aware of Master Goodwin's scrutiny. William must have mentioned her to him. When the dance finished, she expected him to approach her, to invite her to dance. Dancing was an easy way to gain a sense of your companion through light conversation. Goodwin turned away and spoke to the man standing beside him.

Lady Allingbourne caught her eye and indicated that Bess should join her.

'Bess, I am sorry to ask you this but would you mind taking Lucy in hand?'

'Oh dear, what has she done?' Bess groaned. 'Or, I suppose as this is Lucy, not done?'

'She is seated with Edmund Wyard, but I doubt she has said six words to him all afternoon. He did dance with her but they both looked as if they were being subjected to a form of torture.' There was exasperation in her kindly face. 'Would you mind joining them for a short while? Once you get them talking, you may slip away.'

'Very well, my lady,' Bess said, knowing that for certain, as soon as she left them, the conversation would quickly halt.

By the time Bess found the pair, Avisa had planted herself between Wyard and Lucy. Smirking, Thomas Rawson watched them from the other side of the room.

'Did you know, Edmund, that Lucy writes poetry?' Avisa said.

He scowled and did not reply.

'Ay,' she continued, a sly smile on her lips, 'poetry to an unattainable love.'

'Avisa,' Bess said sharply, 'I am sure that Master Wyard has no wish to hear of our poor attempts at verse.' She looked directly at Wyard. 'They are nothing more than exercises to keep our minds nimble.'

He remained silent.

'Avisa, Clemence wishes to speak with you,' Bess said. It was a ruse agreed between them to draw Avisa away from trouble. Bess did not want her returning to Thomas to sit laughing at Wyard from the other side of the room.

'But I want to dance,' she pouted.

'She needs you to help her attend Lady Allingbourne.' Bess was stern.

Avisa rolled her eyes and flounced off.

Lucy was humming with the music, her mind elsewhere. Bess, thinking she must check whether Lucy's *friend* was somewhere in the crowd, sat herself between them.

'I am surprised you are still here, Master Wyard. I heard you were to join the Earl of Leicester's army.'

The scowl she thought one of his essential features faded. 'Yes, I am to serve Sir William Pelham who I was with for a time in Ireland. He is waiting to be given permission to leave.'

'So, it could be soon?'

'The sooner the better.'

'It must be difficult to wait when you would rather be elsewhere.'

'Especially knowing I will be of more use there than here. I am not much good at the idle life. Dice and drinking for any length of time are not the way to ready yourself for battle.'

'I would rather not think too much on that,' Bess said quickly. 'I believe you have an estate in Buckinghamshire.'

'Ay, a very pretty place. There is an excellent steward, my father saw to that.'

Bess suspected there was a story behind his last statement but it was not her business. 'I suppose stewards are necessary if you do not have a wife to manage it for you. What manner of farm is it?'

'You are interested in farming, Mistress?' he said, surprised.

'I grew up on my father's manor in Suffolk. It always interests me to hear how others manage their estates.'

'Bucklings is mixed—oats, barley, some wheat, sheep. There are several orchards. The black cherries are the best I have ever tasted.' He gave her a crooked smile, 'If I am back next summer, I will bring you some.'

'Thank you, sir,' Bess smiled. She felt a surge of warmth for this man. Perhaps all he needed was someone to take a little interest and not make sneering comments. She turned to draw Lucy into their conversation, only to find her seat empty.

'La! Where has that girl gone?'

'I did not see her slip away,' Wyard shrugged, unconcerned. 'Well Mistress, that is your duty done.'

'My duty?'

'To play the go-between.'

'I was that obvious?'

'Nay, but I have long experience of my mother's machinations.'

'Lady Allingbourne asked me to get you two talking. Your mother would never ask *me* to do anything.'

'You know my mother well?'

'I have met her a number of times.' Bess fought a smile. 'The last was most unfortunate—I nearly bowled her over. She has no high opinion of me.'

He gave that crooked grin again. 'Filial duty prevents me from commenting, but I would say I have formed a vastly different opinion.'

Bess blinked, surprised to realise that she actually liked Edmund Wyard. 'Thank you, sir.'

'I know I am not greatly skilled at talk but I can dance.' He stood and bowed, holding his hand out to her.

'It would be a delight, Master Wyard,' Bess smiled and thought him much misjudged.

~

With the newly married couple bedded in style in Lady Allingbourne's main bedchamber, the guests made their way back to the hall—some to continue with their carousing, others to bid goodnight before retiring to bed.

Bess thought she was the first to enter the chamber she shared with the other women. As Mall helped her undress, she noticed movement in the shadows at the far end of the window. Motioning Mall to stop, she crossed to the window. Lucy stood in the dark, her head bowed, her eyes closed.

'Lucy,' she said sharply.

Lucy took a deep breath, her hands clenched at her sides.

'What are you doing?'

'Nothing,' Lucy stuttered, 'nothing.' She turned to face Bess.

Kate and Avisa came through the door together, chatting excitedly and began to take off their finery with the help of Mall and another maid.

'Where did you go this afternoon?' Bess hissed, her voice low. 'You left without taking leave of Master Wyard.'

'I am sure he was happier talking to you than me.'

'Whether he was happier or not, it is no excuse for your discourtesy. Where did you go?' Bess struggled to keep her voice low. 'I did not see you for the rest of the day.'

Lucy looked away from Bess. 'You did not look hard enough, I was present all afternoon.'

'If I find you have been meeting that man again...' she breathed heavily through her nose and did not continue.

'What man?' Lucy asked, wary.

'Do not pretend ignorance—the man from six months ago, the one we have already spoken of.'

'You do not understand,' Lucy said quietly.

On the other side of the room, Kate had begun a long tale of a broken heart as Mall combed out Avisa's hair. Avisa seemed not to be listening but rather straining to hear Bess and Lucy's murmured conversation.

'There is little to understand,' Bess whispered. 'You are besotted with the man. We both know he is here in London. You saw him in the crowd near the Royal Exchange last week. Lady Wyard will not want you as a good-daughter if she finds you have been dallying with other men?'

Lucy glowered, showing the stubbornness of a child. 'You may think what you like of me, the whole world can,' she said sullenly. 'All that matters is what I know is in my heart. I value true virginity above all else—purity of the heart and purity of the body.'

'You protest too much. Purity of the heart is one thing, virginity does not outlast the wedding night.'

'No!' Lucy was emphatic. 'I will never marry.'

The others stared over at them. Lucy lowered her voice. 'I will live a virgin, like our Queen.' It had the sound of an afterthought.

'And how will this happen if you keep associating with your dissipated friend.'

Lucy's face flushed. 'He is not dissipated.'

'Unless I have your firm promise not to see him again, I am going straight to Lady Allingbourne.' Bess jerked her head angrily. 'I should have taken this to her six months ago.'

Lucy reached out and touched Bess's arm. 'I have made no arrangement to meet him again. After tomorrow he will be gone.' She choked back a sob, 'I doubt I will ever see him again this side of death.'

'I suppose that will have to do,' Bess scowled. 'But, remember, I will be watching you like a hawk.' She saw the tears welling in Lucy's eyes. 'I scold because I worry,' she added gently. 'This could ruin your whole life. It is not only my lady but your parents who would be disturbed if they knew of this.'

'I know well that many things about me disturb my parents.'

Bess put her arms around Lucy who laid her head against Bess's shoulder.

Avisa, dressed in her bed smock, strolled over. 'What are you two whispering about? He could always marry one of you and have the other as a mistress. That's about his style.'

'What are you talking about?' Bess snapped.

'Edmund Wyard. I presume that's who you are fighting over.'

Both pairs of eyes widened.

'It is not always about men, Avisa,' Lucy said, exasperated, and walked towards the bed.

Bess fought the urge to slap Avisa. 'You spend too much time in the company of Thomas Rawson.'

'He is amusing.'

'You have a care.' Bess sat on the bed and eased off her shoes. 'Lady Allingbourne will not tolerate light behaviour in her women. Now get into bed.'

When Bess finally laid her head on her pillow, she thought on Philippa's advice. William Goodwin was her best chance. It was good she was not in love with him. Her mind was not addled by emotion so she could dispassionately weigh the benefits of such a match. William would bring her everything she wished for and she, in turn, would make him the best of wives. She was tired of constantly watching the behaviour of other young women who had a wealth of advantages but no sense at all.

15

The second day's festivities were lavish with as many guests, some who had been present yesterday, some new.

William Goodwin, not his father, was a guest today. 'I hardly dared hope,' he beamed as he was seated next to Bess.

Bess returned his smile but did not tell him that it had been Lady Allingbourne's decision to alter the strict seating order to encourage his interest.

As he settled himself into his seat, two serving men approached, one with a ewer of water and a towel, the other a bowl. William busied himself washing his hands. He placed his napkin on his left arm and turned to Bess, running a finger against the fabric of her embroidered sleeve. 'Very pretty cloth.'

'Do you not recognise it?' Her eyes sparkled. 'I bought it from you not much more than a month ago, when we first visited your father's shop.'

'Cloth does not interest me the way it does my father and my brothers.' His eyes rested on her face. 'For me, the wearer always makes a difference.'

Bess flushed and glanced away to the high table. Philippa and Anthony sat side by side, unaware of those around them. Philippa was radiant. If she had been in love with Anthony yesterday, today she adored him. He was solicitous towards her, eating from the same plate, offering her the best pieces first.

'Bess,' William called her attention back. 'Are your duties finished for today?' He offered her his goblet.

'If my lady wishes it, I will have to wait on her but for now I am free.' She placed her hand over his as she sipped from his cup.

A servant approached with a platter of beef braised in a rich gravy. William lifted the choicest slices and placed them on Bess's plate. It was as much a statement that he was courting her as if he had employed the Town Crier. She accepted his attention, her eyes lowered.

A troupe of musicians played—viols, lutes and tambour—a pleasant accompaniment to the hum of conversation along the tables. On the other side of the room, sat Lucy day-dreaming as Wyard, who had turned away from her, spoke to a portly red-faced man who was laughing raucously at everything Wyard said.

William followed Bess's gaze. 'You know Edmund Wyard?'

'I have met him two or three times. Yesterday, Lady Allingbourne asked me to play Cupid for Lucy and Master Wyard.' She continued watching. ''Tis strange but I have never seen him so animated. I wonder what he is talking about.'

'Some war tale no doubt,' William said, unsmiling. 'The man is obsessed with Ireland. I doubt he has much to say that would interest a woman.'

'I am not so sure.' Bess's face softened. 'I had an interesting talk with him yesterday about his estate in Buckinghamshire.'

'That sounds enthralling,' he said dismissively. 'He is a grown man. Can he not do his own wooing?'

'Their parents want them to marry,' Bess said. 'But, unfortunately, Lucy has no wish to marry at all. I doubt he cares much whom he marries.'

'A fine recipe for a marriage made in Hell.'

'Perhaps they will warm to each other once they are man and wife.'

'No—there must be some common ground in the first place, some respect, for flame to kindle. Marriage is too close a bond to be undertaken without the slightest hint of warmth.' He frowned, 'I doubt a grown woman who let herself be talked into marriage to a man she despised would have the wit or spirit to understand her husband's business.'

Bess's eyes widened. 'You consider a wife has a place within her husband's business?'

'A wife is meant to be a helpmeet. Even if she takes no active part, she must understand enough to give her husband the support he needs.'

Bess felt a rush of warmth for William. 'That I have so often argued,' she said forcefully. 'Some men pay stewards to run their estates in their absence. Why would someone whose allegiance is based on payment care more for your estate than a wife who with every fibre of her being wants what is very best for you?'

'Why indeed?' William agreed. 'Many a merchant's widow has taken over her husband's business and continued it to prosper and to grow.'

The dishes continued to come—artichokes, buttered crabs, oysters; tarts and pies and custards. Bess and William talked throughout, Bess learning much of William's life, his travels and his family—brothers, younger sister, beloved mother, and his father, respected, forceful and still with the final say in the lives of his adult children. After the suckets, marchpane and comfits were served, the dancing began in the chamber adjoining the hall.

As William and Bess made their way through the crowd, Clemence tapped Bess on the arm. 'Bess, my lady wishes to speak with you.'

Bess smiled at William, rueful. 'I will return as soon as I can.'

William shrugged, clearly irked, but said nothing. He leant against the wall in the other chamber, arms folded, watching the dancers, refusing offers from women keen to dance.

Lady Allingbourne was still sitting at the high table. 'I have not had the chance to speak with you, Bess. How was it yesterday with Lucy and Edmund?'

'Not well, my lady,' Bess answered. 'Master Wyard can be drawn to talk. If Lucy used her wits, they could find common ground.'

'They seem no better today. Oh, he looks about to leave her.' Lady Allingbourne nodded to where Edmund Wyard had risen from his seat.

'Master Wyard is not hard to talk to, Lucy is the problem—she is not interested. Even were Master Wyard as persistent as Thomas Rawson, nothing would be gained. Lucy is not ready to marry.'

Lady Allingbourne sighed, 'Margaret will have to look elsewhere, unless both she and Sir Peter wish to drag the girl to the altar.'

Bess thought of Wyard—he did not have the eyes of a man who would be happy with an unwilling bride. 'I do not know Master Wyard well but I doubt he is set on marriage at any price.'

'You are right.' Lady Allingbourne touched Bess gently on the arm. 'Go dear and enjoy yourself, William is waiting so patiently by the door.'

Bess wound through the milling guests but, before she could reach William, Thomas caught her by the hand.

'Now Bess, you owe me a dance.'

'But William...' She tried to pull away.

'Let William wait a few minutes more.' He nodded to where Philippa and Anthony led the bransle. 'It looks like marriage has its pleasures.'

Bess ignored his insinuation. 'They do look happy.'

'I could do as much for you.'

'Thomas!' Bess groaned, rolling her eyes.

The music changed and they took their place with the other dancers for the pavane. 'But you love me, do you not?' He bent and kissed her hand.

'What are you doing?' Bess pulled her hand away and glanced towards William, glowering in the doorway. 'Trying to make William jealous?'

'That would not take much,' he laughed.

As they stepped forward together, he said, 'It does not hurt to have a man know he's not the only one. Fear of losing you will make him get to the point quicker.' He smirked, 'Whatever that point may be.'

The dance brought them face to face. 'I do not play such games.'

'You should learn. It is as much sport as riding or hawking.'

'For you perhaps.'

As they turned about Bess noticed not only William but Wyard was watching her.

She turned away from Thomas when the dance ended to find Wyard in front of her. When he bowed and asked her to dance, she could not refuse.

As they skipped beside each other in the galliard, Bess asked, 'Should you not be courting Lucy?'

'The girl is not interested.' They faced each other. 'As the saying goes, there is a good store of fish in the sea.'

As Wyard began a series of leaping steps, Bess realised that he was a fine dancer, light of foot and energetic. She supposed he was skilled at most physical activities. Many of a soldier's skills depended on poise and balance—sword play and manoeuvring a horse needed more than sheer physical strength.

He stopped and Bess now danced in front of him.

Lady Wyard stood in the doorway talking to Lady Allingbourne, her eyes narrowed as she caught sight of Bess.

'Your mother does not seem happy.'

'I am not following her instructions faithfully,' he said with a crooked smile as they stepped forward together, hands held. 'She said I would win Mistress Torrington's heart by spending the day giving her my undivided adoration.'

'You did not think to try it?' Bess said playfully. They let go their hands and stepped away.

'It is cruel to try to win a heart by lies,' he answered. All ill thought Bess had ever entertained towards him melted away. Wyard stepped forward to meet Bess again. 'Besides, I wanted some pleasure from this evening.'

Bess raised an eyebrow.

They danced down the room, side by side, holding hands once more. 'I wanted at least one dance with you.'

Surprised at the unexpected gallantry, Bess smiled unguarded as she turned towards him. 'If you are not careful, Master Wyard, you will soon have the way with words of Master Rawson.'

His smile broadened with genuine amusement. 'Heaven forfend!'

As they exchanged places she saw, again, Lady Wyard's frosty stare. 'Oh dear, your mother does seem displeased.'

'I am sure she is.' He gazed over her head towards the edge of the room. 'And that fellow by the door looks as displeased as my mother.'

Bess glanced towards the door. 'Poor William. Every time he has approached me, I have been whisked away. When this dance ends I must go to him.'

'You two are betrothed?' They stepped side by side.

'No.' All Bess had were hopes.

'He has the look of a man who knows what he wants.' The dance finished and Wyard bowed to Bess. 'I wish you well

Mistress Stoughton.'

Although he smiled, Bess glimpsed sadness in his eyes.

'Thank you, Master Wyard.' Bess curtsied to him.

'Call me Edmund, I am sure we will meet again.'

'I do hope so,' Bess answered.

William pushed through the other dancers to her. 'Now, for certain, it is my turn. Even if the Queen herself demands you attend her, I will not let you go.' It was not said playfully.

'I cannot be uncivil to my lady's guests.'

He scowled as they stepped forward together, side by side. 'What is Rawson's game?'

'It is all a game with Thomas,' Bess said evenly. 'It means little.'

The music changed and they progressed through an energetic canario, William still unsmiling. Then they danced La Volta and, with the exuberance of the dance, his ill humour vanished.

All through the dance Bess was aware of Wyard watching them and was struck with the strange thought that it would be pleasant to be able to be in two places at once.

~

Bess and William walked along a path recently swept clean after a light fall of snow. The naked branches of the tree at the centre of the garden were stark against the overcast afternoon sky. William drew Bess close, linked her arm through his and led her to a seat recessed in a hedge against the garden wall. The seat was dry, wiped down minutes before by a servant.

They sat close together in silence. The music from the house drifted on the chill air. One or two other couples, noticeable by bright splashes of colour among the clipped bushes, lingered in the unexpected privacy of the empty garden.

'Bess,' William took her hand in his. 'You must know how I feel for you.'

Bess began to speak but he placed a finger against her lips. 'Let me finish or I will never get it out. We have not known each other long but I have the measure of your worth.' He laid his hand against her cheek. 'Marry me.'

Bess hardly dared to breathe. 'But your father?'

'I'm certain my father will agree,' he answered quickly.

Suddenly she wanted to weep. 'But I have nothing to bring to a marriage.'

'Ah, my dearest love,' he sighed. 'You bring yourself. I deem that worth more than influence or wealth.'

'William,' Bess sighed, 'you are so kind.'

He attempted to protest but she hushed him, her fingers against his lips. He held her hand there, breathing warmly on her fingers as she tried to concentrate on what she had to say. She needed to marry, but more, she wanted an honest marriage. 'Your feelings for me are clear as clear. I like you well but I fear my feelings do not have the depth of yours.'

He drew her hand away from his lips. 'A woman cannot afford to be free with her heart until marriage is assured. Once we are betrothed, I am certain you will find a love equal to mine. If you do not, at first, my love is enough to enkindle like in you.'

The poetry of his words touched Bess and she welcomed his warm lips on hers, but felt no answering flame. Still, this was a better beginning than her last marriage where she had thrown her passion at a man who feigned it and, in the end, told her that he did not love her, nor ever had.

William drew back, his fingers trailing down the side of her face and around her neck. 'I am not asking for a yea or nay today. All I want is that you consider it, that you give me the hope that it is possible.'

This was what she wanted, the answer to all her hopes and prayers. 'It is possible. I wish to marry you but we must seek permission from both your father and Lady Allingbourne.'

'Could we not marry first and tell them later? We are both of an age.'

Bess's heart was sinking. 'You tempt me but it would be a hard way to start a marriage—it would set your family against me.' Doubts crept up on Bess—did William want to follow this course because he knew his father would not approve? How long would his feelings last in face of his whole family's hostility?

'You forget I have a lawyer's way with words.' William pulled Bess close. 'I can convince them of anything.'

She laid her head against his chest and listened to the regular beat of his heart beneath the fine linen and brocade.

He held out his hand as the snow began to lightly fall.

Bess and William watched as the gentle flakes melted the moment they touched his skin.

16

L ady Wyard rapped sharply on the door of the bedchamber and entered without waiting for a reply.

Edmund glanced at her as he tied on his cloak. Hayes, beside him, held his hat and gloves.

She had to concede that Edmund presented an imposing figure. He was of average height, well-muscled, with the posture of one used to command. The dark velvet jerkin with embroidered gards worn over a damask doublet added to the effect but, she supposed, the elegance of his dress said more of the effort taken by his tailor. She doubted her son was one to give much thought to fashion. He was worth every penny she would demand from Sir Peter Torrington as a marriage settlement.

Dame Margaret gave Hayes an icy glare. 'Edmund, I wish to speak with you.'

Hayes made no move to leave until Edmund nodded to him.

Dame Margaret carefully arranged her skirts as she seated herself in a chair beneath the window. She forced a smile and said, 'I wondered what you intend to do about Lucy Torrington.'

Edmund adjusted the poniard hanging at his back. 'Nothing.'

'She seems a pleasant little thing.'

'I would not know,' he shrugged. 'In all she has barely spoken a dozen words to me.'

'I found her quite talkative,' Dame Margaret said. In truth, Margaret Wyard had been the talkative one last night in her effort to draw the girl out, to elicit more than three-word answers. 'Perhaps when you get to know her better.'

'I have no intention of getting to know her better.' He stood there, the image of his father, immoveable, his mind made up.

'She will bring a large dowry.' It was the girl's greatest asset.

'I do not care. She has none of the qualities I want in a wife.'

'And what would they be?' Dame Margaret could not help

herself. 'I suppose you would prefer someone like that..., that widow?' She had seen him fawning over her, smiling, bowing. If he had used even half the effort on the Torrington girl there would be no need for this discussion.

'Widow?' he frowned, not understanding.

'The Stoughton piece.' Ill-mannered, disrespectful and penniless. 'Apart from you, she danced with most of the men there last night.'

'It was a wedding feast, Mother.' He pulled on his gloves. 'I suspect most of the women there, young and old, danced with a number of men.'

'Edmund!' Her voice was sharp. 'This is the very best of matches.' Why did he not see it? Marriage had nothing to do with personal wishes—it was for strengthening the family, making alliances, increasing wealth and power. She understood too well why young women were reluctant. She had been forced to her duty at sixteen. Had she been able to follow her own inclinations, she would never have married but what good would that have done anyone? Dame Margaret continued to stare at her son. She had no patience with his peculiar reluctance. Marriage was never as difficult for a man as it was for a woman.

'If Lucy Torrington is not to your taste, you can always follow your father's example. Take a mistress—Elizabeth Stoughton,' she almost spat the name, 'if that is your fancy.'

He strode to the door but turned, his hand resting on the latch. 'I do remember, Mother.' His face was white with contained anger. 'I will never accept such an arrangement. If you will excuse me, I have business to attend.'

Dame Margaret sat staring as the door closed behind him, her eyes narrowed with calculation.

~

The light from the parlour window fell onto the cloth panel spread across Bess's lap. New bed hangings had been sewn by professional embroiderers but the centre panel of the bed-cover was to be done by Lady Allingbourne and her ladies. Bess was embroidering cornflowers around the edge.

Avisa, her back to the fire, watched Bess as she sewed. 'You did well last night, Bess, with half the men present chasing you.'

Bess stared at her, dumbstruck.

'I know Thomas chases after any woman, eligible or otherwise, but as well as your lawyer, Edmund Wyard was eyeing you like a starving fox that has sighted a plump goose.' Avisa held her hand out, admiring the glitter of the stone in her new ring in the firelight. 'His mother will have a thing or two to say about that.' She put her head on the side and said, 'Property considerations aside, most men would prefer you to Lucy. You clearly would be far more...'

'Do not dare finish that sentence,' Bess snapped. 'It does you no credit to be mouthing coarse fancies. You would do well to show Master Wyard respect. He has spent years fighting for this country while Thomas Rawson, where you no doubt heard these statements, was wasting his life in idle pursuits and dalliance.'

'I am sure Thomas would be delighted to hear you say that,' Avisa pouted. 'He seems to have a great liking for you.'

'You have a care with him. He is betrothed to a well-dowered woman. His only interest in me is that I am one heart he has failed to deceive. As for William Goodwin, he is no mere lawyer. He is highly regarded by many at court and I suspect his family is as wealthy as yours.'

'That I doubt,' Avisa said sullenly. 'And they have no lineage.'

'A lot of good lineage does if you have no money,' Bess scowled. 'Now come here and help me with this embroidery.'

Avisa flounced over and took her time arranging her skirts before she seated herself opposite Bess. She lifted the other side of the bed-cover. 'What are these supposed to be?'

Bess glanced up. 'Cornflowers.'

'This one looks like a twenty-legged spider.'

'Unpick it,' Bess frowned. 'Where is Lucy? She was supposed to be helping with this.'

'She was here but said she was going to the privy and might be a while.'

'She said that?' Bess's frown deepened.

'Ay, not that I wanted to know.' She picked up a small pair of shears and a needle from the basket on the floor beside Bess.

Struck by a sudden thought, Bess sprang up, her sewing falling to the floor, and sped towards the door.

'Perhaps she is off meeting her lover,' Avisa smirked as she carefully lifted a thread from the flower with the needle and snipped it.

Bess pulled the door open. 'Her lover?' She turned back, a sick feeling in the pit of her stomach.

'Edmund Wyard,' Avisa laughed nastily. 'I know he fancies you but with Lucy...'

'Avisa!' Bess said through gritted teeth, slamming the door behind her.

~

Bess paused at the hall window wondering why Mall was heading across the courtyard to the street. She would be needed in an hour or so to help the younger women dress for the masque they were performing for Philippa and Anthony's guests. A gust of wind whipped past the girl, flicking at the hood of her cloak to reveal not Mall's raven hair but a light brown. Lucy glanced quickly towards the house, adjusted the hood, and slipped through the archway into the street. Alone.

Panic caught at Bess. The man, whoever he was, had not left yet and Lucy was going to bid him farewell. She was a fool to have trusted Lucy. Girls in love, illicit love, were the most duplicitous creatures on earth.

Bess ran up the stairs to the bedchamber and grabbed her cloak and hat. By the time she reached the street, Lucy was gone. Making a swift calculation, Bess headed south along Bishopsgate Street. Despite the icy weather, the streets were busy. Keeping away from the horses and carts and wagons lumbering along the street, she ducked and wove through the crowd. Everywhere she stepped someone was in her way. A pedlar trundled his handcart into her path nearly tripping her. A knot of women blocked her way; gloved hands pulling their cloaks tight, they stood talking heedless of those around them. She accidentally knocked an old man's elbow and turned to apologise only to be faced with a stream of spittle and abuse.

Bess could have wept with frustration but hurried on. As the tower of St Peter Cornhill came into view, she glimpsed what she took to be Lucy's cloak. If truth be told, it was like so many others, but the woman moved with Lucy's purposeful gait. Bess slowed, keeping her distance, not to be seen should Lucy look back. Bess *would* catch them and give the man a piece of her mind too. It would be useful to know exactly who he was when she took her complaint to Lady Allingbourne.

Lucy turned off Gracechurch Street, the cries of country women selling winter vegetables fading behind her. Bess entered streets she had never trod before as she hurried to catch up. Snow began to lightly fall.

Bess kept Lucy in sight, scurrying through narrow streets where the upper stories of the houses overhung so far that the light and the snow barely reached the cobbles. Lucy crossed a wider street, the aroma of baking pies lingering on the air, and entered a maze of lane-ways meaner than the last. Refuse was piled in mounds against the walls and clogged the kennels running along the middle of the street. It was winter but the stink was enough to make Bess cover her nose and mouth with her hand.

Something squelched underfoot, cold through her thin soles. Bess looked down and cursed herself. Her new slippers, made for dancing or treading on floors strewn with sweet herbs, were stained and smeared with muck. In her haste she had not thought to change them or put on pattens. Her cloak was of good cloth, beneath it the deep green of her gown flashed like a beacon with each step. Lucy had been prepared, a drab dress beneath an unremarkable cloak—she could have passed for a servant.

Lucy turned another corner and Bess followed her into an alleyway. Here the houses leant as if sinking into the mud underfoot. A couple of shabby urchins squatted in a shadowy doorway and whined, their grimy hands outstretched for alms. Away from the constant clatter of the carts and the calls of apprentices and pedlars, the noise was intermittent—shouts and moans, thumps and whispers, the high-pitched wail of a baby.

A lank haired woman leant against the doorjamb of a narrow house, a thin cloak pulled around her. She watched Bess pass, as intent as a cat sizing up its prey.

Bess pulled her own cloak tighter. Head down, teeth chattering, stones and broken refuse stabbing her feet through the tattered soles of her slippers, she hurried to catch up with Lucy. She lost her footing. Sliding in the mud, she grappled for the wall to keep from landing in the slime. The hems of her skirt and cloak were heavy with the foul mud.

Lucy plodded on. She turned to stare into a doorway, to answer a comment thrown at her. Bess caught sight of her profile and whimpered. It was not Lucy but a woman twice her age, her face hardened to the life lived in these parts.

Bess pushed past the woman into another lane, trying to appear as if she knew where she was going. But this was an unknown London and she no longer knew which was south, which north. She feared she was walking round and round the same streets, the same malicious eyes following her through the gloom. If she could see a landmark, a church spire, a street she recognised, but with the buildings practically toppling towards each other across the narrow lanes, it was hard to even see the sky. Tears welled in Bess's eyes but she would not give in to them. Footsteps thudded behind her, slowing when she slowed, increasing when she rushed. Was it her imagination? Or her heart pounding?

~

In an upper room, not two streets from Lady Allingbourne's house, Lucy knelt, her head bowed, one amongst a dozen in the candlelight. She raised her head and, resting her eyes on the back of the man at the front of the room, joined her voice with those around her as they murmured responses to his prayers in the age-old tongue she had learnt at her grandmother's knee. Her mind drifted, serene, until that ecstatic point when the Eucharist was raised aloft—a shaft of light that pierced the gloom of mundane life. When her turn came and the transfigured bread touched her tongue, time and place no longer existed, only Christ himself and his representative who stood before her with smiling blue eyes and faded hair—a man who inspired in Lucy a martyr's recklessness.

~

Robert Hayes lounged against the low wall surrounding St Saviour's churchyard, alert despite his careless demeanour, his hand resting on his sword hilt. He gazed up at the gulls circling overhead, scraps of white against the grey sky.

Edmund Wyard stood in the churchyard, head bent, staring at the simple gravestone. The names of Alyne Perry and her son

John were engraved there and the date 1583. The grave was well tended, as were a number of others, even if their places were marked only by a wooden cross. Other gravestones were tumbled and fallen or overrun with weeds. Hayes had convinced Wyard that the grave would be better cared for if he paid Hayes' cousin, someone Hayes could hold to account, rather than the fat-faced verger.

Hayes glanced at his master's face. The misery that had marked it for months after hearing of Alyne's death was gone. Two years was long enough. She had been a goodhearted lass, despite her earlier calling. He supposed she had taken to it out of need rather than inclination. She had given it away willingly once Wyard had taken up with her. Sensible too, she knew she could never be the wife he needed.

Wyard did need a wife, Hayes thought, but not someone like that pale girl his mother was trying to force onto him. That was a marriage that could easily be as big a disaster as his parents'.

Hayes stood up as Wyard came down the path towards the gate. Wyard said nothing but Hayes fell in step with him as they headed toward the Stairs and the wherry that would take them back across the river.

17

Bess caught a glimpse of sullen sky as the street widened. It was less noisome, with patches of ground, here and there, clear of refuse. A group of men huddled in the doorway of a mean tavern; Bess kept close to the wall opposite as she passed.

'Hey darlin', what's the hurry?' one called.

His mates joined in. 'Special customer?'

'His lordship waitin' fer y'?'

There was malevolence in their braying laughter.

'We'll give y' a better time than any softsword gentleman.' The last word carried a world of contempt.

The tallest, hollow cheeked with a jagged scar down the side of his face, detached himself from the group. He stalked alongside Bess and caught her by the elbow. 'Not so fast, my lovely.'

Bess shook him off and ran, shoving her way past an elderly man hobbling on a crutch, almost bowling a child over. At the next corner the street opened out onto a landing dock, busy warehouses at one side. The snow was no more than a damp film. Gulls cried overhead, people milled about, some going to the wherry, some carrying loads on their shoulders.

Bess glanced back, the man was still following, weaving with confidence through the crowd. She slipped into the next lane-way but it led nowhere. She turned to leave but he blocked her way. Bess's heart thudded, her mouth was dry.

She tried to push past him.

He grabbed her by the shoulders, his fingers digging in, and forced her against the wall. He pawed at her hair, held her face between his rough fingers, squeezing until she winced with pain.

'Now my lovely, what do y' 'ave fer me?' His leering grin showed a row of broken yellowed teeth.

Bess twisted away to avoid the reek of his ale-sodden breath.

He pulled her face around. 'Y' want t' end up as pretty as me?'

A blade pricked at her throat.

Bess swallowed and said, her voice shaking, 'I have left my purse at home.'

His eyes glittered. 'There's more than one way t' pay.' He sliced the front of her gown, the razor-sharp blade ripped through the lacings of her bodice and the smock beneath, pricking her skin. His free hand tugged her skirt upwards.

Bess tried to summon what was left of her courage. She gasped as he was wrenched away from her. She heard his head smack against the wall opposite, the crunch of breaking bone as a fist slammed into his face. Two men set upon him with a vengeance using fists and boots.

Bess pulled her cloak around herself and fled, the sound of her own name echoing in her head. She ran blindly out across the landing, turning at the next corner into a wider street. The sky spread out above her, apprentices and pedlars called their wares, housewives and craftsmen went about their orderly business in clean linen and neat clothing. Bess saw their sidelong glances—her hat was gone and her hair had come loose. Holding her cloak tight to hide her damaged gown, she pulled the hood over her head and slowed her pace.

Footsteps still thudded behind her.

'Bess!' She halted, wild-eyed, fearful, no longer with the strength to run. 'Bess.'

She burst into tears at the sight of a familiar face.

Edmund Wyard put his arms around her and held her close. Her hood fell back and he brushed his hand over her tumbled hair. 'You are safe now.'

Bess leant against him, trembling. Passersby stared but she did not care.

As her sobs subsided, he tilted her face up, concern in his hazel eyes. 'There is an inn not far from here, quite respectable.' He pushed a stray lock of hair behind her ear. 'We can sit there. It will give you a chance to compose yourself.'

Bess nodded. As long as she was in his arms, she knew no harm could touch her.

~

Hayes caught up not two minutes later, keeping behind them, alert to their surroundings, as Edmund, a protective arm still at Bess's waist, hurried her through the crowd towards the Old Swan Inn. Hayes took a seat next to the door of the taproom and ordered himself a mug of ale. The innkeeper, a cheerful man in a clean apron, guided Edmund and Bess to a chamber at the rear of the inn. It was clean and furnished with a long table with benches at either side. Edmund seated Bess in the tall chair at the head of the table then turned to the innkeeper and ordered wine and food.

Bess watched Edmund's every move as they waited for the innkeeper's return, her eyes still dilated with fear. She hunched in the chair, her knuckles white as she grasped her cloak tight.

Edmund wished he could keep her wrapped in his arms until she felt safe again. He wondered if he was prompted more by his own desires than Bess's need. He took off his cloak, went to the hearth and stoked the fire.

'Is he dead?' her voice creaked.

'Does it matter?' Edmund asked gently. He unbuckled his sword belt and laid his rapier on top of his cloak on the bench.

Bess shuddered, 'I do not know.' Her teeth chattered; she clenched her jaw hard.

'He would have had no mercy on you, Bess,' he said as he took his seat. If he had not arrived when he did... It did not bear imagining.

'I know, but...' She stopped as the innkeeper entered bearing a tray with bread, cheese and a bowl of steaming pottage. He was followed by a boy carrying goblets and a jug of wine, and a maid with a towel and a bowl of warm water. They set it all on the table and left.

Bess stared at the pottage. 'I am sorry, but if I eat anything, I will be sick.' She covered her mouth with her hand.

'You need to drink something at least, to help dispel your fright.' Edmund poured wine into both goblets. 'Aqua vitae would perhaps be best but I do not want to explain to Lady Allingbourne why I have had to carry you home.' He handed the cup to Bess.

As she reached out to take it, her cloak fell open displaying not only the slashed gown and bodice but her breasts beneath the linen of her ripped smock. She tugged her cloak tight around her, huddling in the chair.

Edmund forced himself to look away. 'You can wear my jerkin.'

'But you will be cold.'

Still not looking at her, he said, 'It is warm enough in here, and I have a doublet and a cloak.' He undid his sleeveless jerkin, laid it on the table in front of Bess, and went to the window. He stared out into the deserted yard at the now steadily falling snow.

Bess gave a tiny cough.

Edmund turned back. The jerkin hung loose over her clothing. Her hair was neater, twisted into a plait, her hands and face washed clean. She had folded her cloak and laid it neatly on the other bench. The fear had faded from her eyes.

He washed too and sat down, cut a slice of bread and cheese and held it out to her. 'Try to eat something.'

Bess took the bread and nibbled but seemed to have trouble swallowing. She put it down and took a sip of wine, then a mouthful.

Edmund took a long draught from his own goblet. The wine was smooth and rich, probably stronger than was good for Bess. Warmth flowed out towards his limbs; he hoped it was having the same effect on her. Helping himself to the rich spicy pottage, he watched her as she drank her wine. She had pushed the bread and cheese away.

'What were you doing, Bess?'

Bess concentrated on a painted cloth hanging on the wall showing Robin Hood and his merry men.

'You must know there are parts of this city where it is not safe for a woman of your standing to venture, especially alone.' He knew he sounded like a censorious father. 'It is not fitting either.'

Bess swallowed another mouthful of wine. Her teeth had stopped chattering.

'I do know that.' She took a ragged breath, struggling against tears. 'I did not think.' Bess shook her head as if to clear it of unpleasant thoughts, shifted in her chair and held out a foot. 'My slippers are ruined. They were new, made especially for the wedding.'

Edmund stared at the slipper with its torn sole and soiled embroidery, the stained hem of her skirt. He would not be distracted. 'You left home unprepared. Why?'

'Because,' her shoulders slumped as she gave up the secret, 'one of the ladies slipped out, unattended, to a tryst. She had sworn to me there was no man. I followed her without thinking. I hoped to catch them both and put an end to it.'

'What sort of man would arrange to meet a woman where I found you?' He could barely credit it. 'It is the haunt of whores and pickpockets. Only a lowborn serving man, or worse, a scullion, would make an assignation in such a place. And this is one of Lady Allingbourne's women?'

Bess looked down at the swirling wine as she played with her cup. 'I doubt they were meeting where you found me,' she sighed. 'I discovered far too late that I was following a stranger. I got lost trying to find my way back.' Tears welled again. 'I am certain I was walking in circles.'

Fear returned to her eyes but he made no move to comfort her. 'Which lady are we speaking of?'

Bess stared ahead, her mouth shut tight.

It was not fair to interrogate her like this. 'I suppose I need only look at your companions and decide who appears so love-struck that she would follow her swain into the back alleys of London.'

'I do not know where she went. There may be a sensible explanation. I do not want to besmirch her name if I have been mistaken.'

Edmund scoffed, 'You are too trusting.' He set his cup down and winced as he stretched his hand.

Bess reached out and traced her fingers gently along his grazed knuckles. 'Your hand, is it very bad?'

His skin tingled at her touch and he fought the urge to take her fingers and draw them to his lips. 'Nay, a few scratches. I am more used to swordplay,' he said. 'Brawling is a young man's sport.'

She had colour in her cheeks now. He spooned pottage into a bowl. 'Eat up or you will be getting lightheaded and I will still have to carry you home.'

'I feel much better now.' Bess tasted the pottage and started to eat as if she was ravenous. 'You had better eat some more otherwise I will eat it all.'

'There is nothing wrong with a hearty appetite.' There was something about her reminded him of Alyne. 'So much about you is surprising, Bess. You are not what you seemed at first.'

'And what did I seem to be at first, Master Wyard?'

'At first I thought...' his voice trailed off. What he thought had come from her denial of all knowledge of the young messenger, and what he had assumed to be her relationship with Lady Allingbourne's steward. The first time he had seen her, she was standing on the steps of Allingbourne Hall holding her arms out for that child. That image was one of comfort.

His eyes rested on her face. There was more beauty there than in prettier women. 'I suppose I thought you no different from other women.'

She pulled a face at him. 'You thought me a flirt of light morality?'

'That is not what I thought at all,' he gasped.

Bess leant against the back of her chair. 'First impressions are often misguided. I thought you stern, aloof and humourless.'

'And now?' He held his breath.

She took another mouthful of wine and sighed with what sounded like contentment. 'I know you to be kind and honourable. You keep a stout fence between yourself and the world but one day I will break it down and make you laugh until you can barely breathe.'

Alyne could always make him laugh. He gazed at Bess and said nothing.

Bess drained her cup and poured herself more wine. 'Forgive me,' she glanced up at Edmund, 'I have spoken out of turn.'

'Nay, not at all. I would that...' It was better left unsaid. He needed to be sure. She deserved to be wanted for herself, not because she reminded him of someone else. He reached for the wine jug and poured what was left into his own cup. 'I should finish this.'

He gazed at her, thoughtful. 'Will you tell me something? That boy at Allingbourne Hall, young Geoffrey, who was he?'

Bess sipped her wine in silence.

'There was a clear family resemblance.'

'If I tell you, all the kind thoughts you have had of me will disappear.' She straightened her shoulders and said, 'That was me. I am Geoffrey.'

'You?' He was incredulous. 'Why?'

'I know it is scandalous.' She kept her eyes on his face, a plea in them. 'You think this is worse than a girl slipping out to secretly meet a man?'

'It depends on the reason.'

'I was running away from home.' She sounded glib.

'Be serious! Surely I deserve the truth.'

'Why did he matter so much to you?'

'He was so young and unprepared, a danger to himself. I wanted to give him the advice he sorely needed.' His mouth twisted. 'I feel a fool.'

'Never, never feel that, Edmund.' Bess reached out and placed her hand on top of his. 'You were trying to do a kindness. The only person this reflects badly on is me.'

'So why?'

She groaned, 'Because I am willful.' She sat up, her back straight, her jaw tight. 'My father had called me home for the christening of his youngest child but it was a pretence. He had arranged for me to marry a neighbour, Dick Litchfield, an aged man I despise,' she shuddered. 'The thought of him makes my flesh crawl. When I refused, my father locked me in my room. I escaped with the help of my sister. I would rather be dead than married to that man.'

'Do you not think your father has your best interests at heart?'

'My best interests!' she scoffed. 'His only interest is in a parcel of land Litchfield would give him control of on our marriage.' She stared at Edmund, 'Do you believe parents always do what is best for their children?'

He did not reply, he knew what parents did.

'Marriage should be between people who at least have some liking, some hope of living comfortably together.' She frowned, intense. 'Do you truly not care whom you marry?'

'Of course, I care,' he said, guarded.

'But had Lucy been willing, you would have married her.'

'Not necessarily.'

'You are a man—free to go where you like. You can choose

whomever you like. Why do you let your mother do the picking for you?'

'No one is ever truly free,' he answered evenly. 'The final decision is mine, not my mother's.'

'Yet she selects the stable from which you choose. Would you let your mother select your horses for you?'

His mouth twitched at a smile. 'For all you know, my mother may be a fine judge of horse flesh?'

'Is she?' Bess arched an eyebrow, smiling.

'Nay,' he smiled back. 'But one thing I do know, you have had far too much to drink.' He took her cup from her. 'I will escort you home.'

Edmund stood and took up her cloak, drawing it around her.

As he buckled on his sword belt, he said, 'Promise me something.'

Bess's eyes were clear, free of anxiety. 'Whatever you ask.'

'Tonight, dance with me.' He moved closer. 'I want more than a single dance.'

He gazed at her pink lips, parted by a shallow breath. He could kiss the tilted end of her nose, move with gentle kisses to the corner of her mouth. His own breathing was shallow but he held himself in check.

Perhaps she read his mind. She lowered her eyes. 'You have saved me twice. It would be churlish of me not to, though I must be careful from now on.'

'Why?'

'If you were to save me again that would make three times. Then I would be bound to you for life.' Although Bess had started out playfully, her tone became serious. 'I would not want you burdened.'

'Would that be so bad?' It would be easy to take her in his arms, to forget the discontents of his life. But was he merely seeing in her a reflection of his own desires? He was a fool, imagining what was not. He stepped away from her. 'Is this a polite way of saying that you would prefer not to dance with me except as a means of getting me to pay attention to Lucy Torrington?'

'No, Edmund. Never.' She touched his arm. 'My mind is

addled at present. Nothing would give me greater pleasure.'
  He wanted more than anything to believe her.

18

'B ess! Bess!' Avisa shook Bess furiously. 'You must get up.'
Bess struggled up, still not fully awake.

'Clemence has been looking for you everywhere. You were supposed to help us dress for the masque.'

Bess fell back on the bed, her eyes shut. 'My head aches, please go away.'

'Bess,' Avisa whined. 'I need you to help with my hair, Mall is making such a mess of it.' She leant over Bess and shook her again. 'Pwah! Your breath is vile.' She gaped as understanding dawned. 'You have been drinking.'

Ignoring the pain of her thudding head, Bess sat up and swung her legs over the side of the bed. She was wearing a clean smock, and her feet had been washed. She had had the presence of mind to tidy away her soiled clothing, but she had the vaguest memory of it. 'I have not, it is your imagination,' she muttered.

Reality crashed down on her—not only the memory of her terror and Edmund's kindness, but the shame of her familiarity with him. She flushed at the thought of his arms, strong and protective, and his lips so near. How she had longed for him to kiss her and, for a few breathless moments, she had thought he felt the same. Bess closed her eyes and moaned. She must have been much more than a little drunk.

Avisa sprang back. 'You're not going to be sick?'

Bess hunched forward on the side of the bed. 'Nay, she groaned, 'I think I have an ague.'

Avisa pressed her hand to Bess's forehead. 'Your head is cool. I will get a posset brought up for you.'

'No Avisa, I doubt it will be of use.' Bess slid off the bed. 'I'll dress and help you with your hair.'

She pulled out the gown she had planned to wear from the press and dressed quickly with Mall's help, finally wriggling her feet into her older slippers. They would suffice but it was a pity she had ruined her new shoes.

Bess stood behind Avisa, combing her hair.

'What is the matter, Bess? You look so sad.'

'It is my headache.' She peered around the room. 'Where is Lucy?'

'She's with Lady Allingbourne. Old Lady Wyard has been here since the masque and demanded Lucy's company. Do you think Lucy will marry Edmund Wyard?'

'I doubt anything will come of it.'

'I could not marry him,' Avisa said. 'He is far too ugly.'

Bess scowled as she arranged Avisa's hair around a beaded tire. 'You would do far better to judge a man by the way he behaves than by a few marks on his face.'

'It is more than a few marks.' Avisa shuddered. 'I am glad I am not Lucy because Lady Wyard seems set on it.'

Bess pushed the final pin into place. 'All finished.'

Avisa took the small mirror that lay among the scattered combs and pins and cosmetic pots on the table beside her and peered at herself. Satisfied, she put the mirror down, stood and twirled in front of Bess.

'You look lovely,' Bess said.

'Then why does no one want to marry me?' Avisa wailed. 'I thought Thomas did but....' Her voice trailed off.

'Thomas is betrothed—that is the end of it. You must have a care of men like him, their only interest is in dalliance.'

Avisa's face brightened. 'But dalliance can lead to marriage.' It was more a question than a statement.

Bess concentrated on Avisa—her flawless unlined skin, her eyes untroubled by experience despite her pretence of worldliness. Avisa was much younger than she tried to appear and had a girl's belief in happy endings.

'That rarely happens, more often the poor girl is left with a reputation for lightness or worse.' Bess closed her eyes and rubbed her fingers between her brows. When she opened them Avisa was staring at her, her mouth set in a sullen line, awaiting an answer more to her liking. 'Sensible young men seek their father's approval before paying court. I am certain your father will find the best possible match for you when the time is right.' Bess knew that was not always true but could think of nothing else to say. 'Be patient, there is plenty of time for you.' She saw the disbelief in Avisa's vivid blue eyes. 'You are only seventeen.'

'The Queen's grandmother married at twelve and I am much older than that.'

Bess pressed her lips together. 'That was years ago, it is different now.'

Clemence bustled in carrying a small parcel. 'Where have you been, Bess?' she said sharply. 'My lady wants us all in the hall as soon as possible.'

'I will not be long.'

'This package has come for you, by a serving man no less, no mere apprentice.' She placed the parcel on the end of the bed. 'Something familiar about him,' she muttered.

Bess unwrapped it quickly. Inside was a new pair of embroidered slippers similar to her ruined pair but of far better quality.

Clemence looked from the slippers to Bess's gown, they were of a similar shade. 'You were intending to wear them today?'

Bess nodded. What else could she say?

'These craftsmen,' Clemence tutted, 'they leave everything until the last moment. Another hour and it would have been too late.'

As Bess slipped her hand into one, her fingers touched a folded paper. 'You two go down, there is no point in all of us being late.'

Once the others had left and Mall was tidying the table, Bess withdrew the paper from the slipper. A single line was written there:

To help you fulfill your promise. E.W.

E.W.? Edmund Wyard? What promise? Bess could remember no promise. The slippers were a godsend but it was not proper— not proper of Edmund to send them nor of Bess to accept them. It was unseemly for a woman to accept the gift of apparel from a man not her husband or her betrothed. She placed the shoes on the floor and slipped them on; they were a perfect fit. Both Clemence and Avisa had seen them, they would ask why she was not wearing them and there was no way she could explain. She had no choice.

'Mall,' she asked, 'did you lend Lucy your cloak this morning?'

'Yes, Mistress Torrington wanted it for the masque. She returned it about an hour later. Said it was not suitable after all.'

'You may help me with my sleeves now. And my hair—dress it simply tonight.' Bess had no wish to draw attention to herself.

~

It was a less formal evening with fewer guests, a supper followed by singing and dancing. Bess was certain William Goodwin had been invited, but he was not present. She tried to push away the thought that it had something to do with his father's attitude to a marriage between them. She studiously avoided looking to where Edmund sat glumly beside an equally glum Lucy. Forcing herself to forget the morning, Bess gave her attention to the elderly cousin of Lady Allingbourne's seated beside her.

When the dancing began, Edmund rose and moved away from Lucy without asking her to dance. To Bess's relief her companion expressed the wish to dance, but he had vigour enough for a single stately pavane. As they withdrew from the other dancers, Edmund approached them, bowing to Bess's companion.

'Would you mind, sir, if I borrowed your dancing partner for a while?'

'Not at all young man,' he beamed. 'Who am I to stand in the way of Love's progress.'

Edmund bowed again and took Bess by the hand. He gave her a lopsided grin, 'Have you forgotten your promise, Bess?'

Two lines formed between her brows. 'My promise?'

They moved away from the dancers and stood near to the wall. 'That you would dance with me tonight.'

'Of course, but you must forgive me, Master Wyard, my memory of this morning is rather vague.' A flush spread up her cheeks. 'I would have locked myself away this evening with the shame of it, but I would have had to offer my lady an explanation.'

'Bess,' his eyes caressed her face, 'there is no shame. All your actions this morning, your unclear memory, are nature's way of dealing with a fearful event. Try to forget it all now.'

Bess could not meet his gaze. 'And now I owe you more. Your

kind gift has saved me yet again.'

He bent his knees slightly so he could look into her face. 'Does that count as the third time?'

'The third time?'

He straightened up. 'You suggested if I saved you a third time, I would hold your soul in my hand.'

'I said that? It sounds too poetic for me.'

'Perhaps not those exact words. Rather, if I were to save you one more time, you would be bound to me for life.'

'Forgive me, I do not know why I said such a thing. And even if you were happy with such a proposition,' she smiled weakly, 'I doubt a pair of shoes is enough.'

'Perhaps not, but I am glad you accepted them. I hope you can view them as a gift between friends. I had no use for them and no one else need know.'

'How did you come by them?'

Pain flickered in his eyes. 'They were intended as a gift I never had the chance to give.'

Bess knew he was thinking of the whore. She should be insulted but Edmund Wyard was different from other men. His behaviour was not always the most courtly, but his actions seemed to be inspired by the best of intentions. To his mind he would be giving something intended for a woman he had loved to another whom he cared for. Bess was certain he did care for her, as a friend perhaps, or a sister.

She watched the dancers. 'It is time I honoured my promise.'

'And that promise was for more than a single dance.'

'Was it?' Her eyes sparkled. 'We shall see.'

He was an excellent dancing partner and they progressed through bransles, corantos and galliards to La Volta and back again. Bess lost the will to do her duty and see that Lucy and Avisa were behaving well, that other guests had someone to dance with or to talk to. Between dances they sat to one side and talked and Bess thought of nothing but the moment, forgetting all her worries and even her hopes of marriage to William Goodwin. She would happily have spent the whole night in Edmund's company but, as the night wore on, they both became aware of Lady Wyard's basilisk stare.

'I should save Mistress Torrington from spending the entire evening with my mother.'

Lucy was seated beside Lady Wyard at the other end of the room, lost in her own thoughts.

'Are you aware that Lucy fears she will be forced to marry you.'

'I would never marry an unwilling woman.'

Bess gazed at him, sorry for her harsh judgement at other times. She wished to tell him that she thought the woman he did marry should count herself blessed. Instead she asked, 'When do you sail?'

He shrugged. 'Sir William still awaits Her Majesty's pleasure, so tomorrow I am returning to Bucklings Hall to play the farmer until it is time to leave.'

'Edmund, if I do not see you before you sail, I pray God keep you safe.' She reached up and kissed him on the cheek.

He took her hand in his, squeezing it gently. 'Thank you, Bess.' His eyes were filled with a longing she did not understand.

As Edmund walked off towards his mother and Lucy, Bess still felt the touch of his fingers on hers. She sighed and seeing Philippa sitting by herself, went over to her.

'I have had no chance these last few days to do more than smile at you across the room.' She kissed Philippa. 'You look so happy.'

'I am, Bess. I wish we could stay here longer—we are going to Hertfordshire tomorrow. I am to stay there with Anthony's aunt when he returns here. Sir Hugh says he needs him back within the month. It will be ages until we can go to his estate.' She grinned at Bess. 'So, you and Edmund Wyard.'

'What of me and Edmund Wyard?'

'You two stand together like an old married couple, comfortable in each other's company.'

'He is one of the kindest men I have ever met.'

Philippa's eyes widened. 'You have certainly changed your tune.'

'I have had the chance to know him better.' She looked around at the guests. 'I thought William would be here tonight.'

'I did too,' Philippa said without thinking, smiling at Anthony as he walked into the room with Thomas.

A week ago, Philippa would have been the first Bess told of William's proposal, but Philippa was so wrapped up in her own good fortune that the lives of others were of no more than passing interest. And that was how Bess thought it should be for a newly married woman.

Anthony was drawn into a dance with Lady Allingbourne but Thomas strolled towards them looking smug.

'Whose heart have you broken now?' Philippa called to him.

'Only your new husband's. I have won a fair sum from him at dice.'

He bowed to Bess. 'Now Wyard has decided to dance with his intended...'

'His intended?' Philippa and Bess said together.

'Young Lucy.' He held out his hand to Bess. 'I will take the opportunity to dance with you.'

'What about me?' Philippa said with a toss of her head.

'I am sure your husband would not be happy to find that, after taking his money, I was trying to take his wife as well.'

'You may dream,' Philippa smiled.

As Bess and Thomas stepped forward, hands held, into the line of dancers, Thomas said, 'What have you done to poor Goodwin?'

'What do you mean?'

They turned to face each other. 'I met him this afternoon at the Bell Savage Inn. He was well in his cups bemoaning the faithlessness of women and you in particular.'

Bess broke away from Thomas and pushed through the other dancers. He followed her into the adjoining chamber, where a group of guests were singing accompanied by the virginal and lute.

'Bess,' he caught her hand and led her to a seat well away from the singers. 'Tell me what has happened.'

Bess hunched forward, her hands clasped in her lap. 'William asked me to marry him. I expected him to be here tonight to tell me if he had his father's approval.'

'I am sorry, but this afternoon he was talking as if you had done him a great injury.'

'I have done nothing.' A large tear rolled down her cheek. She brushed it angrily aside. Why was she crying? She cared for William but did not love him. But without him her future plunged into darkness again.

'I told him he was mad but he was too far gone to understand.'

'Are you sure of what he was saying?'

'He was reviling you as faithless.'

'Faithless?'

She thought of Edmund. In the aftermath of fear, she had for a few moments misread his kindness. It was ridiculous, she might as well set her sights on the Earl of Essex as on Edmund Wyard. But William did not know of that, no one did. And whatever she had imagined, she had not acted on it. She had not been faithless. No, most likely William's father had forbidden him to marry her and, for some perverse reason, William was blaming her for it. Anger surged through her.

'What is the matter with you men? You have the world at your feet and yet you venture nothing. You always do as you are told no matter what your age. Your fathers say *No* and to preserve your high opinion of yourselves, you find a way to twist it so the woman is to blame. I am a mere woman yet I refused when my father arranged for a loathsome old man to marry me.'

Thomas blinked in surprise.

'In my position I suppose you or William would have married a horrible old woman.'

'I suspect marriage is harder for a woman.'

'Indeed, it is,' Bess glared at him.

He reached over and grasped her hands. 'Do not blame me for what has happened between you and Goodwin.'

'I have no idea what has happened.' She looked at him for understanding. 'You have known him longer than I have, is he given to sudden passions?'

'Nay,' Thomas shook his head, 'he is a steadfast boring fellow.'

Bess blinked back tears.

'Oh Bess, do not take it to heart.'

'How can I not, if he calls me faithless?' She shook off his hands and, catching sight of Lucy moving toward the door, sprang up and followed her.

By the time Bess reached the door, Lucy was across the adjoining chamber.

'Lucy, wait,' Bess called to her.

Bess caught up with Lucy, saying, 'Quick, come in here.' She opened the door to the unlit parlour.

Lucy went in ahead of Bess and waited in the gloom, frowning as Bess fumbled to light a candle on the cabinet to one side of the door.

She seated herself on a chair within the light-fall of the candle, her hands clasped demurely in her lap.

Bess remained standing. 'Where did you go this morning?' she snapped.

'I was here all morning with Lady Allingbourne.' Lucy's face betrayed nothing.

'Do not lie to me, I saw you leave.' Bess grabbed at Lucy's wrist and tried to pull her from the seat. 'We will go to my lady and leave her to decide what's to be done.'

Lucy wrenched her arm back. 'And what would my lady say about you sneaking in, reeking of drink, then spending the afternoon snoring your head off like a drunken sot?'

'Do you know what happened to me?' Bess's eyes blazed. 'I saw you slip out this morning in disguise. I followed you. I hoped to catch you and prevent you from shaming yourself but clearly you are beyond shame. You disappeared into the meaner parts of this city. I tell you, no man who had a care for you would arrange to meet in such a place.'

Lucy rolled her eyes. 'You are making much out of nothing. I went no further than Eastcheap. I needed some pins and everyone else was so busy, I thought it the easiest way to get them quickly.'

'What a ridiculous story!' Bess took a deep breath. 'Listen to me, I gave no thought for my own safety. Trying to follow you I got lost.'

Lucy gnawed on a fingernail, not looking at Bess.

'I was accosted by a vicious man who held a knife to my throat. As I had no purse to give him, he thought he would take his pleasure in other ways. He ripped open the front of my gown.' Her voice wavered but she fought to stay calm. 'The worst would have happened had not Edmund Wyard arrived.'

'Edmund Wyard,' Lucy sneered the name, 'what was he doing in such parts?'

Bess's fingers itched to slap her. She held her hands tightly together at her waist. 'You listen to me. I could have been killed or worse and yet all you do is mock my rescuer. I am tired of your lies. We are going, now, to see Lady Allingbourne.'

'No Bess! Please!'

'Even if you do not care for your name and your honour, I do—because your behaviour casts a poor light on Lady Allingbourne and the rest of us.'

'I beg you, do not go to her.' Lucy's face had drained of colour. 'I will tell you the truth, but you have to promise to tell no one else.'

'I will promise nothing of the sort. You are coming with me to Lady Allingbourne.'

'Please Bess,' she spoke barely above a whisper, 'I went to Mass.'

'You what?' Bess gaped.

'I know you heard,' Lucy said quietly. 'The man you thought was my lover is a priest, a holy man.' Her eyes brimmed with tears. 'He is leaving England tonight.'

'You are a Papist?' Bess breathed.

'I have been a Catholic since I was a girl and went to live with my grandmother.'

'But Papists are traitors.' Bess felt ill. She thought of the impaled heads above London Bridge. 'They plot to kill our queen. Think of Dr. Parry on trial when we were in London last year.'

'Not all Catholics plot against the Queen.'

'Priests plot with Spain. Have you heard nothing of the last time Spain had a toehold here. The land reeked with the stench of burning flesh. Have you not read the Book of Martyrs?'

'It is all lies.'

'Do not be such a fool. Ask anyone over forty, they all remember.'

'The martyrs in this land are Catholic. Each year the number increases. What of Father Mayne, Father Kirby and Father Campion, my grandmother's friend, at whose hand I first received the Body of Christ? All saintly men, all dead for no other reason than their faith.'

'And who aids these men?' Bess spat back. 'England's enemies—Spain and France. They are traitors, all of them.'

'No! Their blood will bring salvation to this land.'

Bess spoke through gritted teeth, 'What would you do if the Pope were to send an army with the purpose of establishing papistry in this land again?'

Lucy screwed up her nose and said irritably, 'That stupid question! Its sole aim is to trick and condemn Catholics no matter how they answer.'

'And you have not answered it.' Bess sat heavily on a chest just beyond the pool of light. 'I should go to Lady Allingbourne and tell her of your madness.'

'And make a martyr of me too!' Lucy said, defiant. 'Go to Lady Allingbourne. I no longer care. I am ready to die for the one true faith.'

'You are the greatest fool I have ever met. You have a chance of marriage with the kindest, most honourable of men and you choose instead this treasonous stupidity.'

'Edmund Wyard,' Lucy scoffed.

'Yes, Edmund Wyard. You do not deserve him.'

'You think so highly of him, marry him yourself.'

'I would if he asked me,' Bess blurted out.

'I will never marry. I intend to consecrate myself to God's service.'

Bess sprang from her seat and hurried towards the door.

'You'll not tell Lady Allingbourne?' Lucy called after her.

'No, you stupid, stupid girl. I need time to think.' Bess slammed the door behind her.

She stopped halfway across the darkened chamber, her hands pressed against her face. What should she do? Lucy was playing with treason but Bess did not want to be responsible for Lucy's imprisonment or death. Nor did she want to place such a burden on Lady Allingbourne. Although Lucy was nearing twenty-one, she was unworldly. Perhaps all this was nothing more than a girlish fantasy and, with the man gone, Lucy would return to her senses. Bess prayed she was right.

19

It was as if the snow had held itself in check for Philippa's wedding, but once the newlyweds had departed, it more than made up for its restraint, snowing heavily for a week.

Bess watched the snowflakes settling on the window panes, slowly piling on the window sills and blanketing the garden. Her hopes chilled with each day that dragged by with no word from William. She was sure Thomas had misunderstood. She had done nothing that could be described as faithless. If only he would visit. If she could speak to him, all would be right.

~

The goldsmith in Cheapside sent a message to Lady Allingbourne that the necklace she had ordered before Philippa's wedding was ready. Tired of being cooped inside, Lady Allingbourne decided to risk the weather rather than wait for him to deliver it. Snow still lay heavy on the ground and the wind was icy, but bright patches of sky showed through the clouds. She went accompanied by Bess and two footmen.

When they stepped out of the goldsmith's shop, Bess caught sight of William on the other side of the street heading towards his father's shop. She glanced at Lady Allingbourne who nodded.

Bess called to William and hurried across the street, her pattens clattering on the cobbles. Although William could not help but see her, he strode on. Bess tried to increase her speed, her pattens sliding on the icy slush and mud in the middle of the street. She would have landed in the muck but for the steadying arm of an elderly gentleman. He sent his man after William who had now reached his father's door.

William glared at Bess but waited all the same.

Bess smiled in thanks to the gentleman, who bowed to her and went on his way.

William stood silent, his eyes colder than the air around them.

Her heart sat like a leaden weight. 'William, what is wrong?'

'You dare ask me that?'

'What have I done?'

'Do not try to trick me by feigning ignorance,' he scowled.

'I do not play tricks,' Bess said angrily. 'I have no idea what has set you against me. Tell me so I can honestly deny it.'

'Deny that you were with Wyard two days after Compton's wedding? I saw you,' he sneered. 'I was on my way to meet my father at our warehouse in Billingsgate and there you were, in his arms, oblivious to the spectacle you were making. I followed you, saw you go into the Old Swan Inn together. That is not the behaviour of an honest woman.'

'There is an explanation,' Bess said quietly, 'an explanation that is decent and understandable and in which I am innocent of anything you imagine.'

He took two steps towards her. 'Explain it to me.'

'I was attacked by a ruffian and Edmund saved me.'

'Saved you? What were you doing abroad, unattended?'

Judgement and disbelief were plain in his face. How could she make him understand? He would need to know the whole story and Lucy's part in it. Bess knew the zeal with which William hated Catholics—he would denounce Lucy for certain. To protect Lucy, she would have to lie to him. That would mean starting marriage with a lie, if he took her at her word.

'Why did you not come up to us? Why did you not ask me to explain?' She fought to keep back the tears. 'Instead you skulked after us, judging me unheard.' She saw a flicker of pain and longing in his eyes. 'Your protestations of love were as shallow as anything mouthed by Thomas Rawson.'

'My father said you spent the first day of the wedding entirely in Wyard's company.' His voice lacked its earlier conviction.

Bess walked away from him, towards Lady Allingbourne waiting outside the goldsmith's shop. She did not know if she wanted William to follow her. She did know that, even if he accepted her explanation, he no longer had faith in her innate honesty. A good marriage did not need romantic love but it did need trust. When she reached Lady Allingbourne, she looked back at the Goodwin's shop but William had gone.

~

Bess and Lady Allingbourne made their way home in silence. Once inside the house Lady Allingbourne asked quietly, 'What is the matter, Bess? What has happened between you and young Goodwin?'

'Nothing, my lady. That was something that had no future. I did not meet his exacting standards.'

'You felt for William?' she caught Bess's hand in hers.

'I liked him well enough but I had not lost my heart.'

'You are very pale.' She touched the palm of her hand to Bess's cheek.

'I feel unwell. If you will permit me, I will lie down for a little while.'

'Of course, my dearest Bess.'

Bess went up to the bedchamber and lay on the bed, the curtains drawn. She sobbed, weeping for her misplaced hopes. All that beckoned was a future lived under the shadow of Dick Litchfield, a future drained of light and laughter.

Part 3

20

April 1586

Edmund Wyard jolted awake, his heart racing, his mouth dry with fear, screams echoing in his head. He lay still, his breathing slowing as he became aware of his surroundings. With a loud groan he climbed out of bed and grabbed a fur-lined coverlet from the pile of bed-covers that had fallen to the floor. He wrapped it round himself and walked to the window. The courtyard was bathed in grey light, the usual babble of waking birds strangely muted. A still landscape devoid of life, it had the nightmare quality of his worst dreams, his worst memories—Carrigafoyle Castle. He shivered, closed his eyes and tugged the coverlet closer.

He thought he had left his nightmares behind in Ireland. But now the screams rang in his ears, the stench of slaughter lingered in his nostrils, and the image of a woman cowering beneath a blood smeared sword burned in his memory. The slaughter of women and children was not the act of honourable men. But what if, as Sir William Pelham had argued, the babe in arms was tomorrow's enemy, his mother the seedbed of future traitors, and the killing of the innocent a necessary example to the guilty. Edmund had been grateful the order to join Sir William had reached him too late. He had arrived to face the aftermath of the attack, grim as it was. Edmund opened his eyes and stared out to the pale light breaking along the horizon. But this time his dream was not memory, the woman had Bess Stoughton's face.

The nightmares had started three months ago, after that cutthroat by the Thames. For the first time in his life he had felt real fear, and not for himself. He would have killed the bastard but Hayes beat him to it. His overriding urge had been to see Bess safe. These months of waiting were allowing fear to prey upon his mind. It was time to act—he would not wait for Pelham but would get leave from Sir Francis Walsingham, the Queen's

Principal Secretary, to join Lord Leicester as soon as possible.

Warmer now, Edmund stretched out in his large empty bed, beneath the coverlet. It did not help that he was living like a monk, but he was not a green youth filled with mindless desire. He needed a woman he cared for, a wife. And a child, children to fill up the empty corners of this house. When he had first held his new nephew in his arms, his namesake Edmund, he had been astonished by the tenderness he felt for the child. How much more if he had been his own son? It would give a purpose to all his struggles.

Bess Stoughton drifted through his thoughts again. Wherever he had gone since his return, a succession of women had tried to catch his attention—pretty young women thrust in his way by calculating parents, and widows sure of their attractions eager for a more auspicious second marriage. He saw the disgust in their eyes as they lingered on the discoloured pits marking his skin but, for most, his wealth more than made up for his unsightly face. Few saw past it to the man beneath and none, save Bess, had seen him as anything other than a prospective suitor. There had been no intent behind Bess's words other than, at first, to get him to talk to Lucy Torrington. And surprisingly, Bess seemed to enjoy his company.

Edmund thought of the moment in the Old Swan when he had looked into her unguarded face and was certain she had wanted him to kiss her. And if he had? He threw himself to the other side of the bed. She was confused, her judgement impaired by drink and fear. It was wrong to consider it. She had reminded him of Alyne. Poor Alyne, she always had more sense than he had. He had wanted to marry her, but she had refused; she had a keener sense of the way the world worked. He hoped he had brought her comfort and safety for those last few years.

And Bess? When he thought of her, Alyne no longer came to mind. Bess had the upbringing and the manner to stand by his side. Her family was of gentle birth even if not highly placed. All she lacked was wealth and he had enough for both of them. For certain, she was by now betrothed to Goodwin.

Edmund threw off the bedclothes and climbed out of bed. He gazed out the window as he pulled on his breeches. The sky was pale with the dawn. By the time he was dressed and in the stables, it would be fully light and the birds would be in full throat. He would ride out and see how he felt on his return.

~

The music of a consort of viols, lute, cittern and recorder drifted through the door of the banqueting chamber where the invited guests of Lady Hopeton feasted on sugared delicacies, Lady Allingbourne among them. The attendants waited in the outer chamber, Bess sitting next to Margery Williams, a waiting woman she had known since her first visit to London ten years earlier. For no reason she could define, Bess was happy. The shadow that had hung over her these last few months had faded as the household had returned to its usual London patterns and Lucy had given up her secret meetings. Bess was now certain marriage to William Goodwin would not have worked. Despite his pretty way with words, his feeling for her had been shallow—he had so readily, willingly almost, believed the worst of her. Those who said romantic love was no basis for marriage were right.

Through the open door, she could see Lady Wyard's rigid back. With Edmund gone from London, Lucy was more at ease, believing Lady Wyard had discarded her plans for a marriage between them. Bess was not so sure. Each time Lady Wyard visited, she singled Lucy out, drawing her into stilted conversation.

'Bess,' Margery raised her voice, 'you are daydreaming.' She gave a sly smile. 'Who is it?'

'No one,' Bess sighed. 'Spring makes me lighthearted.'

If she thought seriously about it, she had no reason to feel lighthearted at all. In five months her father would demand a reckoning and she would have nothing to give him. It was time she reminded Lady Allingbourne of her offer to help. Why could life not go on just as it was? And if, eventually, the opportunity for marriage arose naturally, she would take it. Bess suspected that, provided it was not brought to Lady Allingbourne's attention, she could stay as long as she wished. Of course, if her father took it into his head to insist to Lady Allingbourne that she come home, she would be lost. But it was April, spring was truly here, the weather was warmer, green shoots were pushing through the damp earth and Bess felt like singing. She had for days.

Margery elbowed Bess. 'You are still not listening. It must be a man.'

'Nay,' she smiled.

'Have you heard from Philippa?'

'Philippa was never much of a letter writer. Her aunt wrote to Lady Allingbourne that she had accompanied Philippa to Anthony's estate in Berkshire. She is finally getting the chance to use the skills learnt from Lady Allingbourne.'

'Any talk of a baby yet?'

'The letter came nearly a month ago. It would be far too early to tell anyone even if she suspected.'

Margery gazed at the subtleties decorating the banqueting table, one in the shape of a cornucopia with moulded fruits and flowers spilling from it, the other a fanciful castle, both now in some disrepair. 'Do you think we will get any of what's left?'

'Not with the cost of sugar,' Bess laughed.

'I'd love one of those marchpane fruits in that great horn,' Margery continued to stare at the subtleties. 'And has Lucy lost that dreamy look?'

Bess's heart lurched. Sharp-eyed Avisa had said nothing so Bess had assumed no one else had noticed.

'What dreamy look?' Bess said slowly.

'We were taking wagers on who she was in love with.'

'In love?' Bess's voice creaked.

'That love-struck look stands out a mile.'

Bess tried to appear puzzled and said, 'I have no idea.'

Margery launched into a long, long tale of one of her lady's love-struck women. It was all too complicated and Bess allowed her attention to wander. Among the male attendants seated together in the corner closest to the door, was a man she could not place. He was in his thirties with a ruddy outdoor face and a wiry strength beneath his well-cut livery. He had the look more of a soldier than a courtier's man. Occasionally Bess caught him watching her. He was familiar but, although she racked her brain, his name eluded her.

Chairs scraped in the banqueting chamber and the guests drifted out into the garden with its maze and its pleached arbours leading to the river. The attendants moved in to see if their ladies and gentlemen required them. Lady Fellowes beckoned Margery to help her from her chair. The old lady leant heavily into her as she shuffled slowly down the steps into the garden. Lady Allingbourne looked across at Bess and shook her head while she continued talking to Lady Hopeton. Bess waited for the crowd to leave the room before she followed, captivated by the play of the afternoon light on the window panes, her spring contentment still possessing her.

'Bess.'

Her heart thumped beneath her tightly-laced bodice. She smiled so broadly that a dimple appeared in her left cheek. 'Edmund.'

They both stared at each other, wordless.

Happiness shone in Edmund's face.

Bess thought it strange that a man whose face was a mask when playing cards, could at other times be read as easily as a book. Life must have been dire for him these last months to show such pleasure at seeing her.

She broke the silence. 'How are your cherry trees?'

'My cherry trees?' He smiled as understanding dawned. 'In ravishing blossom. I will arrange with my steward to send you the pick of the crop.'

Bess's eyes twinkled, 'I will only accept them if they are brought by your hand alone.'

'Then I must see this campaign is brought to a speedy end so I can be back in time for the harvest.'

'And how have you been enjoying the life of a farmer?' Bess realised they were flirting—something rare for her and, she suspected, unknown for Edmund. It was a game, a harmless pleasant game.

'Well enough, though my estate runs efficiently whether I am there or not.'

He gave a crooked smile that made Bess pause for breath.

'We have discussed this before.'

'Indeed. You will be pleased to hear I have come to your way of thinking—a wife would be a better manager.' He held out his arm to her.

Bess shook her head. 'I am not a guest today. I am attending

Lady Allingbourne.'

'I will be a manservant then and walk with you.'

They walked slowly across the room, trailing the last of the attendants.

A voice boomed from behind them, 'Ho! Wyard! What are you doing here?'

A great burly man of about Edmund's age with a bushy untrimmed beard strode towards them. 'Never took you as one for indoor sports.'

He did not wait for an answer but stepped between them and threw his arms across their shoulders. 'And who is this?' He beamed at Bess, 'Your lady?'

'Alas, no. This is Mistress Stoughton, one of Lady Allingbourne's women.'

He lifted his arm off Edmund, staring hard at Bess. 'Bess? Little Bessie Askew!' he said with a gap-toothed grin as he looked her up and down. 'My, you have grown up.'

He grabbed her and gave her such a smacking kiss that Bess was sure it echoed out into the garden. 'You married that milksop Stoughton.'

'Myles died three years ago,' Bess answered evenly.

'So, you're a widow and sly Ned here sees his chance.' He jerked his head in Edmund's direction. 'Well, I am between wives at present and if he's not quick he may have some competition.' He grabbed a fistful of fruit from the plundered cornucopia and crunched on one. He turned to Edmund 'So why are you here dallying with the ladies and not in the Low Countries?'

'I planned to go with Sir William but he has not been given leave yet.'

'Pelham?' he spluttered, scattering sugar everywhere. 'Ah, Ned,' his face was suddenly dreamy, 'remember him on that march through Dingle. You could not fault him. Expected nothing of the meanest foot soldier he did not expect of himself.'

Edmund did not answer.

He slapped Edmund on the back. 'I had better go and make my apologies to Lady Hopeton as I was meant to be here earlier.' He strolled out the door still munching on the marchpane fruits.

'You know George Raynsford,' they laughed together.

'I served with him in Ireland. A man of immense passion and few doubts.'

'He is Lady Allingbourne's nephew,' Bess smiled. 'I have not seen him for years. Even when he was younger, we thought him the very image of a pirate.' Her light laughter echoed in the empty room. 'We had better join the others.'

They walked out into the garden and towards the water, a space between them, the last of the attendants not far ahead.

'Are you staying long in London?' Bess asked.

'I hope not. I have decided not to wait for Sir William and I am arranging a pass to join the Earl of Leicester.' He smiled at Bess, 'I feared my mother had a likely maid lined up when she browbeat me into coming here today.'

'And did she?' Bess found she had to force a smile.

'Fortunately not, though I am glad she made me join her.'

Bess watched the swans gliding on the river.

'Where is Master Goodwin today? I heard you were to be betrothed.'

'Where did you hear that?'

'Thomas Rawson intimated as much.'

'He tattles like an old woman and stretches truth to see the effect it has.'

'Are you betrothed?'

Bess recognised the unpolished face Edmund usually presented to the world. A subtler man would have guessed the answer.

'I was but a passing fancy.'

'Well, that is his loss,' he said cheerily.

Bess quickly asked, 'When do you sail?'

'A few weeks yet. I need permission to join the Earl of Leicester and have business to attend. And I need to hone my skills. I have been permitted use of the tiltyard at Whitehall, and Rocco Bonetti, the Master of Arms who runs a school in Blackfriars, has agreed to practice swordplay with me.'

'I would have thought you had little to learn.'

'Warfare in Ireland is played by different rules.' Seeing Bess's puzzlement, he added, 'It is always good to have a new opponent—there is little Hayes and I can do to surprise each other.'

As they turned away from the river Bess caught sight of Lady Wyard watching them from the rise ahead. Head held high, she stalked over to Lady Allingbourne. Lady Allingbourne glanced at Bess.

Edmund followed Bess's gaze. 'You have been with Lady Allingbourne a long time?'

'Since I was seventeen. I was with her until I married, just as Philippa was. After my husband's death, she welcomed me back as one of her waiting women. She has been most kind.'

A footboy ran up to Edmund. 'Excuse me, sir, Lady Wyard bids you come to her.'

'Thank you,' Edmund nodded but did not move away from Bess.

The lad waited, bouncing on the balls of his feet.

'I will go to her anon.'

'She told me to wait for you.'

Edmund's shoulders slumped, as if the effort of resisting his mother's wishes was almost too much.

Bess touched his arm. 'Go to her, it will be easier in the long run.'

'Anything to keep the peace,' he sighed. 'I will see you again.'

Bess's eyes lingered on him as he walked off towards his mother. She wondered whether his parting comment had been a statement or a question.

~

Robert Hayes strolled among the other attendants in as cheerful a mood as any there. He was glad to be on the move again, and not back to Ireland. He had been talking with one of Lady Hopeton's women, a woman of about his own age who seemed to enjoy his company. There was the lightest undercurrent of flirtation.

He watched Wyard tramp towards his mother, a footboy at his heels like a diligent sheepdog. He could see Wyard was taken with Mistress Stoughton. He relaxed in a way that Hayes had rarely seen, and never with a lady. The situation was not to the old Lady's liking—Hayes had noted the narrow-eyed glare.

Wyard stood dutiful and polite in front of his mother. Lady Wyard was smiling at him, making an effort to be pleasant, something rare for that old woman. She was more used to giving orders as Hayes knew only too well. He wondered what game she was playing. She seemed well pleased with herself. It had to be for more than drawing her son away from Mistress Stoughton.

Hayes continued watching the pair. If Wyard wanted to follow his own path, he needed to be as alert with his mother as ever he was in enemy territory. But who viewed their mother as the enemy?

Maud Wilson poked Hayes playfully in the ribs, 'Robin, you haven't heard a word I said.'

'Forgive me,' he said. 'I was pondering the lives of our betters up ahead. Despite all their advantages, they seem to make no better a hand of life and love than we do.'

Maud rolled her eyes and laughed, 'Is that not the truth? Still I would rather be rich and make a sow's ear of my life than poor.'

Hayes laughed with her and thought it a pity he had no better life to offer Maud.

~

Lady Allingbourne said little as she and Bess travelled home by barge. Bess sat quietly, lulled by the rhythmic slap of the oars and the glitter of the late afternoon light on the water. It had been a pleasant afternoon. Her most vivid memory was of George Raynsford asking if she was Edmund's lady, and Edmund's reply, *Alas, no.* Was it courtliness? But he was not usually a courtly man. She did not dare try to understand it.

21

Lady Allingbourne sat with her eyes closed, her hands resting in her lap on the velvet night gown she wore over her fine linen bed smock, as Bess combed out her thick greying hair.

'Bess,' she said carefully. 'I noticed you with Edmund today.'

'My lady?' She would offer nothing.

'He seems to be drawn to you. You are aware Lady Wyard still has hopes of Lucy?'

'If you will excuse me,' Bess could not help herself, 'I think her hopes misguided. Edmund has said he has no wish to marry Lucy, nor she him.'

'You are right,' Lady Allingbourne nodded, 'but Margaret can be like a terrier with a bone once she has her mind set on something. She has firm beliefs on the way the world should work and can be cruel to those who step in her way.' She turned her head to look up at Bess, the shadow of concern in her eyes. 'Is there anything between you and Edmund?'

'No, my lady,' Bess answered with a defiant tilt of her chin. 'I do not know why he seeks me out,' her voice softened against her will, 'but I find him pleasant company.'

Lady Allingbourne gave a gentle laugh. 'You are one of the few. That may be why Margaret has it in her head that you are scheming to marry Edmund.'

'In truth, I am not.' No matter how much she enjoyed his company, she knew the way the world worked—Edmund Wyard was beyond her reach.

Bess began to plait Lady Allingbourne's hair and forced herself to say what was expected. 'Would you have me tell him not to speak with me?'

'Certainly not. Whether you are in my house or outside attending me, you will act as you always have, with kindness and courtesy.' She reached up and caught Bess's hand. 'You are one of the best girls I have ever had with me. I wish life had been kinder to you.' She sighed, 'If I had been blessed with a daughter and she had been like you, I would have counted myself the happiest of mothers. And now, we must give active thought to finding you a husband.'

'Thank you. My father allowed me until Michaelmas, at the latest, to find someone. September will be here in no time.'

'Give me two weeks or so and I'll see what I can do.' Lady Allingbourne tapped a finger against her lips, thoughtful. 'Will you get the pink gown from the press for me.'

Bess shook the folded skirt and bodice out and carried them to Lady Allingbourne.

'I have not worn this in over two years. You may take it and alter it. Most of your gowns are dark. It is time you dressed to draw more attention to yourself.'

'Thank you, my lady.'

Bess was delighted. Most of Lady Allingbourne's discarded gowns were given to Clemence who passed on the duller colours that did not take her fancy. This gown was of a rich peach colour in damask and Bess had sleeves that would complement it. It would not take too much work for Bess to adjust it to fit herself. As she left the room, the gown over her arm, she realised she had not lost her lighthearted mood. All in all, it had been a pleasant day in which Lady Wyard was but a minor irritation.

~

Dame Margaret sat upright in her chair; years of discipline had made her erect posture second nature. Edmund, sprawling at ease in the chair opposite, his legs extended towards the brisk fire, appeared not to have heard her. He had been lost in a daydream and was blinking as if he could not grasp what she had said.

She repeated herself.

He gripped the arms of the chair. 'You have done what?'

'Do I need to repeat myself a third time?' She tried to keep the irritation from her voice.

He flung himself out of the chair and paced the room. 'Without reference to me?'

'I have a copy of the marriage contract, you can look over it. I am certain, if it is not to your liking, it can be altered.'

159

'Not to my liking!' He appeared stunned. 'The whole notion is not to my liking.'

'But Edmund,' she said, 'I am your mother. I do know what is best for you.'

'I am a man of thirty-one, not a child.'

'No matter what the age, a mother always has her child's best interests at heart.' She wondered if he would be more tractable had she given in to his demands for cloying hugs and kisses as a child. But was that not what his nurse was for? Besides, it was not the way to make a man who stood strong in the world. And, of course, he had so strongly reminded her of his father.

She forced a weak smile. 'Your brother was like you when I arranged his marriage to Eloise.' She could see his disbelief.

'Eloise has bloomed since their marriage. She was as plump and awkward as young Lucy.' Plump for certain, awkward with her good-mother to be, and unwilling until she met John. When they were introduced, she had looked him up and down as a farmer would a new draught horse or a bull, and then she had smiled at him, radiant. And he, fool man, had fallen under her spell.

Margaret Wyard had to admit it was hard to imagine Lucy Torrington displaying ungoverned emotion as Eloise did, but that was no bad thing. Eloise was undisciplined, too familiar with her women, lax and overly fond of her children, and with John she behaved, at times, more like a mistress than a wife. She would have to take Eloise in hand when she returned to Northamptonshire. No, Lucy Torrington was perfect—docile and demure and, Sir Peter had assured her, obedient.

'It is pointless to even consider the matter,' Edmund said. 'I am preparing to leave for the Low Countries.'

'You said yesterday Sir William was still in Lincoln.' Dame Margaret was certain she had caught him out. 'That he had not been given permission.'

'I have decided to go alone. I am seeing Sir Francis Walsingham next week. He will give me the necessary pass and letters.'

'Sir Francis and I were neighbours as children.' She sounded like an old woman in her dotage with nothing but reminiscences to warm her, but she did not care. She had to get him away from that scheming woman. Florence Allingbourne's assurances meant nothing—she was not a good judge of character, always ready to believe the best of her favourites.

Edmund stood with his back to the fire. 'They are crying out for men. Half those who promised to go have remained at home. No matter that you were friends as children, I doubt Sir Francis would deny me leave just to fit in with your marriage schemes.'

'You do not see the benefits now but in ten years you will thank me.'

He shrugged, unconvinced.

'Sir Peter is very generous—the settlement is everything we could wish for.' She thought again of the Stoughton woman. 'Edmund, I will not see you throw your life away on that wh...' She forced herself to stop. He would not be won this way.

Edmund's eyes glittered as he watched her.

Dame Margaret feared he had read her heart as she saw, for a brief moment, a calculating ruthlessness best reserved for the enemy in battle. He spun back to face the fire, his hand resting on the mantle as he stared into the flames.

'I will look at the contract but I promise nothing more.' Scowling, he turned to his mother. 'There are to be no announcements. Nothing will happen until I return from the Low Countries.'

'But the betrothal can take place immediately.'

'No.' His mouth was set in a grim line. 'I will not rush.'

'That is acceptable.' Dame Margaret did not understand what had changed his mind but she would not question it. In time he would see the wisdom of this marriage. 'I will let Sir Peter know and see whom he wants to talk to Lucy.'

'I will. No one else is to raise the matter with her.'

'I am certain you can win her over.' She had seen the charm he had wasted on Stoughton.

'I hope so.' He bowed to his mother. 'Now if you will excuse me, Mother, I am going out to get drunk.'

Dame Margaret remained seated in front of the fire and heard him, on the stairs, yelling for his man and the thud of the door as he strode out to the street. She was doing what was best for him. It was clear even he realised it now, though with the same ill grace his father had often displayed.

~

Overnight Bess's lighthearted mood evaporated. She woke aware of the cool reality that a burst of sunshine, pleasant company, a new gown and Lady Allingbourne's interest did not ensure her future.

The day was spent quietly at home. The women sat sewing with Lady Allingbourne in the garden, making the most of the mild afternoon sunshine. At the sound of footsteps on the gravel path, they all looked up.

Edmund strode towards Lady Allingbourne, the footman almost running to keep pace with him.

'Edmund, welcome,' she smiled as he bowed to her. 'It is a pleasure to see you again.'

He stood, stiff and awkward. 'May I speak with you alone, my lady?' He was again the gruff and seemingly charmless man Bess had first met.

'Of course.' Lady Allingbourne rose from her seat and passed the placket she was embroidering to Bess. 'Ladies, we will continue our sewing in the parlour.'

Bess looked up at Edmund as she placed her own sewing in the basket with Lady Allingbourne's. Although his dress was immaculate, his face was haggard, his eyes bloodshot. He turned away from her.

Biting her lip, Bess went into the parlour and stood where she could see through the window into the garden.

Avisa and Clemence came and stood alongside her. Only Lucy sat and took out her sewing.

Although Edmund scowled as if he were imparting unpleasant news, a slow smile spread across Lady Allingbourne's face. She squeezed his hand and walked into the house.

Edmund waited on the garden seat, staring away from the house, his fingers drumming on his knee.

Lady Allingbourne came into the parlour smiling. 'Lucy, go out to Edmund, he wishes to speak with you.'

Lucy glowered but did as she was told.

'He has finally seen sense,' Lady Allingbourne said to no one in particular. She settled into her chair. 'Ladies, time to get on with our sewing. And Bess, close the window. We cannot have them thinking we are straining to hear what they are saying.'

Bess glanced into the garden as she pulled the casement shut.

Edmund, hunched forward, was speaking with a serious intensity. Lucy sat beside him, her hands clasped tightly in her lap, her mouth set in a sullen line. When he finished, Lucy was open-mouthed. She beamed at him and gave a most unmaidenly whoop of laughter.

Bess went back to her seat and took up her sewing.

~

Edmund did not stay long. He refused Lady Allingbourne's offer of supper and left without acknowledging Bess's presence once.

Bess was silent through the evening meal and excused herself as soon as it was finished, pleading a headache.

As she lay on the bed, the curtains drawn, it hit her like a pounding wave, bowled her over, knocked the breath out of her. Of all the men in the world, she wanted Edmund Wyard, no one else. Her much vaunted common sense had deserted her—she was as foolish as a green girl. He was kind and polite but he had never said anything to give her hope of more. Yet somehow, against all reason, she had allowed the dream to form. She knew why he was drawn to her—she was no threat, she was like a sister. Once he came to know Lucy better and learnt to be at ease in her company, he would show her the same good-humoured side Bess had seen yesterday. And Lucy would learn to love him too. Sick with jealousy, large scalding tears ran down Bess's cheeks. *To those who hath shall it be given, and to those who hath not even what they have shall be taken away.* Was that not the story of her life?

She must have drifted off to sleep. She had a vague memory of Avisa and Lucy talking in whispers as they prepared for bed. It was only when Lucy climbed in beside her that she woke.

'So. You and Edmund Wyard.' She had meant to whisper but it came out as a hiss.

'Yes.' Bess heard the smile in Lucy's voice. 'He said…'

'I do not want to hear your secrets,' Bess cut her off and turned her back to Lucy as a great pang gripped her throat. Edmund was a man—he had far more freedom than Bess could ever dream of—yet, despite his posturing, he was happy to throw it away and follow his mother's orders.

22

Edmund was not the most ardent of suitors. Three days passed before he called on Lucy again. It gave Bess time to come to terms with her foolishness. Edmund had not said or done anything to encourage her. Her own desires had convinced her that his pleasantries were different from the overblown compliments of other men. She must ignore her misguided yearnings and be sensible. Still, she did not understand why Lucy had agreed. Perhaps it was a sign that Lucy had outgrown her Papist dreams. Or else, if she had not, Edmund had promised her freedom to practice her treasonous faith. How would he have known unless he were a Papist too? She could not ask Lucy, afraid that even in asking she would betray her greensick fantasies. The most important matter for Bess was to ensure she not be tied to a man she abhorred. She must hold Lady Allingbourne to her word that she would help her find a husband. To do that, Bess needed to show herself to good advantage. So she sat quietly and, with swift deft stitches, altered the peach-coloured gown and tried not to listen while Avisa and Clemence asked Lucy teasing questions which Lucy parried with surprising humour.

~

Bess stood at the window of the parlour reading, her book tilted towards the light.

'Good Even, Bess.'

She looked up to see Edmund in the doorway.

'We did not finish the story today and I need to know how it ends,' she said sheepishly.

He closed the door quietly behind him. 'What are you reading?'

Bess's heart thumped. Why had he shut the door? 'The story of Icilius and Virginia.'

'And does it end well?'

'No, Virginia dies.'

He was not listening, his face alight as if he were pleased to see her. 'That is a very pretty gown. It suits you well.'

She gasped, a flush spreading up her cheeks. 'The author says here *link where you love; that you may be married to a man rather than money.*' Her eyes glistened as she snapped the book shut. 'A pity more do not think like that.'

Bess forced herself to look at Edmund. 'Are you dining with us tonight?'

'I am.' He moved closer to her. 'Bess, I need…'

She stepped around him. 'I must go, Lady Allingbourne will be wondering where I am.'

She hurried out, her mouth a tight angry line. Edmund was as bad as Thomas Rawson. It was clear he was about to be betrothed, yet he thought he could toy with her.

~

The whole household was present for the evening meal in the hall, Sir Hugh and his attendants as well as Lady Allingbourne and her women, and the guests, Edmund Wyard and George Raynsford. It was not a formal meal and the members of the household mixed freely with the guests, sitting where they liked. Avisa placed herself between Thomas Rawson and George Raynsford and was encouraging one to outdo the other in the generosity of their compliments.

Bess tried not to watch Lucy and Edmund, their heads bent towards each other whispering. Lucy was radiant; she had blossomed since Edmund's proposal. Edmund, looking much happier than four days ago, glanced at Bess and gave her a crooked smile.

Bess turned her head away.

Despite their whispering, there were no caresses, no hand-holding, no stolen kisses. It gave Bess no comfort. She saw the care Edmund took with Lucy as he selected morsels for her plate and offered her his goblet. Never once did their fingers brush but… Bess beckoned a servant for a cup of wine and forced her mind away from unwelcome imaginings.

When the meal finished and the servants cleared away the dishes, the musicians who had played restfully during the meal broke into livelier tunes. Sir Hugh and Lady Allingbourne led the group in a pavane and then retired for the night. Before Clemence followed Lady Allingbourne from the room, she whispered to Bess, 'Keep an eye on Avisa. I am not sure we can trust George to treat her as a sister.'

'If you prefer, I will attend Lady Allingbourne tonight.'

'Nay, you stay and enjoy yourself.' She started towards the door but turned back. 'And Bess,' she whispered, 'I should not say this but that gown suits you better than it did Lady Allingbourne. Now go and draw George's attention away from Avisa.'

It was what Bess had intended to do but not for Clemence's reason. George was diverting company. He made her feel as if she were seventeen again with not a care in the world.

The formal dancing gave way to country jigs—dances they had learnt as children, energetic and good natured. George grasped Bess's hand and pulled her into a roundel.

Later, as the music started for Sellenger's Round, George dragged Bess away from the dancers. 'Come and sit down, Bessie, I need a drink.'

Bess sat herself at the table while George grabbed a jug of wine from the sideboard and two goblets and brought them over. He poured himself a large measure but gave Bess a third of what he had for himself. He raised an eyebrow saying, 'We cannot have you befuddled while you're around me.'

Blushing, Bess lowered her eyes.

He reached over and pinched her cheek. 'I could always make you blush.' He threw his head back, drained his cup, and gave a contented sigh. 'I'm getting too old for this.'

'You're not so old, George.'

'Half-way through my life if I am granted the customary three score and ten.'

Bess shivered. 'Let's not think of that.'

George watched the dancers. 'So that is Ned's fancy. I wonder what the attraction is.'

'His mother is much taken with the size of her dowry.' Bess could not keep the bitterness from her voice.

'Ah! The old lady is still getting him to dance to her pipe. Edmund Wyard is a damned good soldier and one of the most honourable men I've ever met. 'Tis a pity he does not stand up to his mother.' He continued to stare at the dancers. 'His father was the same. Never laid down the law to Maggie but went off quietly and did exactly as he wanted. Set his mistress on that estate at Bucklings Ned has now. Only went home when he had to, mainly to see his children. It made her more bitter than she already was. From what I've heard, even as a girl, Maggie could freeze a man with a single glance. A man needs a wife who can keep him warm.' He stroked his bushy beard, thoughtful. 'No doubt young Lucy is virtuous and wealthy, but I doubt she would keep a man warm in bed.'

Bess stared straight ahead, her jaw tight.

'Oh Bessie,' George put his hand under her chin and turned her face to his. 'You've lost your heart to him.'

Bess jerked her head away. 'I have not,' she said, her eyes glistening.

George pulled her to him. 'Consider me your big brother and tell me your troubles. I would marry you myself but I suspect you are one of those women with strange ideas of fidelity.'

Bess tried not to smile. 'George, you always were incorrigible.'

'And I've got worse with age,' he grinned. 'Now, Ned is glaring at me,' he laughed lightly. 'I wonder why that is?'

George got up and pulled Bess to her feet. 'Let us go for a stroll in the garden. That will put the cat among the pigeons.'

'I am here to make sure Lucy and Avisa behave themselves, not to go sneaking into dark corners myself.'

'So 'tis your duty alone that prevents you?'

'Are you ever serious?'

'Never if I can avoid it.'

'It's time we danced again,' Bess smiled at him. He made her feel happier than she had for days.

~

As the night wore on, they tired of dancing. A couple of Sir Hugh's men joined the two musicians at one end of the table and played dice while the rest sat together at the other end. George lounged next to Bess, his arm stretched along the settle behind her; Lucy and Edmund were side by side, a distance between them; Avisa sat close to Thomas.

Bess wondered how best to separate them. She could ask Avisa to fetch something for her but Avisa would refuse if she were enjoying herself.

Clemence, who had come back in, had no qualms at all. 'I believe there is room enough for me on that bench,' she said as she wriggled her diminutive form between them.

'Clemency,' George barked with laughter, 'the gallants have no hope with you to guard the maids' virtue.'

'Someone has to take care. A girl's head is easily turned by sugared words.'

'I have no need for sugared words, one look and 'tis pure love for my person.'

'Neither pure nor love are words I would use concerning you, George.'

He grinned at her. 'Perhaps not but, for certain, when my daughter is old enough, I'll entrust her to you.'

'It is a pity you all do not keep in mind that young women are someone else's daughters and sisters.' Clemence gazed at the men in the group. 'They deserve as much protection and respect as your own.'

'Ah, but we cannot help ourselves, women are sirens, calling us to our doom.'

'Your doom?'

'Marriage,' George laughed.

'From what I see, men are as keen to marry as women and, in my short experience of that state, men get the far better deal.'

'You married the wrong man. You should have married someone like me.'

'You!' she spluttered.

'There is much to recommend me—I am lusty, and amusing, and you would want for nothing.'

'But you'd not be faithful.'

'You cannot have everything. I would be very *kind* to you.'

Bess bit back a smile—she had never before heard the word given such a meaning.

'A kind man would be faithful,' Clemence said primly. 'It is the foremost quality I would seek in a husband.'

Thomas was watching George, his dislike clear. He drained his cup and poured himself another drink. 'We know what Bess wants in a husband,' he said. There was an undertone of malice in his voice. 'She does not care as long as he is rich.'

Stung, Bess snapped, 'I have said nothing of the sort. Marrying for money alone is as ridiculous as marrying for love. However, gold will keep a woman warmer than a man, and,' she added forcefully, 'gold is far more reliable.'

'You have a point there.' George placed his hand on Bess's shoulder and rubbed it companionably.

Edmund watched them from the other side of the table. Although his face was expressionless, his good humour had faded.

'How can gold keep you warm?' Avisa looked at Bess as if she were mad.

'It can buy you clothing and food and shelter and does not lose its lustre.'

'But would not a man who adored you be better?'

'Love,' Bess scoffed, 'is a much overrated emotion, most often used by men to lead silly girls astray.'

'Avisa, Lucy,' Clemence said, 'you listen to Bess, she speaks much sense.'

'And we know what Avisa wants,' George winked at her. 'Rich for certain, handsome too, and totally captivated by her.'

Avisa twisted her mouth, 'That would do to begin with.'

'That puts you out of consideration, Tom.'

Thomas bridled, 'Why?'

George bared his teeth, grinning. 'You may be rich and pretty from a maid's view, but you're not besotted with Avisa or you would not have been enticed so easily into a betrothal to someone else.'

'Some of us put duty before our own pleasure.'

It had not occurred to Bess that Thomas might be marrying for duty alone, having no particular liking for the woman he was to marry and that he, like Edmund, was doing as he was told.

'George,' Bess said quietly. 'Does Thomas not want this marriage?'

'At first he did,' George lowered his voice, 'but the poor lad has discovered that his betrothed is impervious to his charms. She is a strong-minded young woman of unassailable virtue who, no doubt, will have the running of that marriage—her father has ensured the contract is to her advantage.' He grinned broadly, 'And, to make matters worse, Tom was caught *in flagrante* but not quite *delicto* with another young maiden of gentle birth.'

Bess's eyes widened in surprise.

'Ay, her virtue can still be considered intact. Her father took the matter to Sir Hugh who has had stern words with our Tom, most particularly about discretion.'

'No love talk in front of the company,' Thomas called to them.

Bess wondered if, beyond his love problems, Thomas saw George as a rival. For certain George's exuberant personality drew more attention than Thomas's good looks.

Clemence beamed at Lucy, sitting quietly beside Edmund. 'I need not ask, Lucy, who the man of your dreams is.'

Lucy said slowly, 'The attributes a man should have are kindness as you said, honour, and steadfastness in his beliefs.'

As Lucy spoke, Bess knew for certain Lucy was still firm in her Catholic faith. She was chilled by the thought that Edmund might be a traitor too. The realization that he was a Papist must have overcome Lucy's previously avowed wish never to marry. But Edmund was about to go to fight in the Low Countries to help free them of the yoke of Catholic Spain. It made no sense unless he was misleading them all and intended to fight with England's enemies. Bess could not believe she had so misread him.

'No girl,' George boomed, 'describe the man—tall, short, dark, fair, shapely legs.' He slapped his heavily muscled thighs. 'Winning smile,' he grinned wolfishly.

'It is what is in a man's heart that counts, not appearance,' Lucy said.

Avisa gave a little shudder. 'I could not marry an ugly man no matter how rich.'

'So that puts you out of consideration, George,' Thomas smirked.

'I'll admit it's not my looks the ladies remember most.'

'Looks hardly matter,' Clemence shrugged. 'Most men end up as ugly as sin.'

'The question is,' George said with mock seriousness, 'are looks important? He winked at Bess as he poured himself another drink. 'I'm quite taken by a comely face and a buxom body, and if that can be coupled with a fair dowry and a pleasing manner, I have no complaints.' He turned his attention to Thomas. 'Tom, what's your opinion of a fair face over a large dowry?'

'I prefer the dowry. Her looks do not matter much. If she is not to your fancy, you do not have to be in her company often. Wyard here would agree with me.'

Edmund said nothing. He was staring at Bess and, by the stern set of his face, he had passed a harsh judgement on her.

Bess shifted, uncomfortable.

'You have said little, Bess, what sort of man do you want?' Edmund asked.

Bess glared at him. 'One with strength of character, one who would place me first.'

'And if the parents of such a man were set against you?'

'I would expect him to make his own decision.' She lifted her chin as she spoke.

'But what of the injunction: *honour thy father and thy mother?*'

'If you wish to quote scripture at me, what of the verse that says a man shall *leave his father and his mother, and shall cleave unto his wife: and they twain shall be one flesh?*'

'That is the case once a person is married,' he said, 'but before marriage a child's first duty, after God, is to father and mother.'

Bess was aware of no one else in the room but Edmund, taunting her. 'Yes, such a duty that he would readily accept someone forced on him by his parents, someone he cared little for, perhaps even despised?' She drew a ragged breath. 'It makes a mockery of the notion that marriage involves the union of two souls.'

'Bess.' George put his goblet down and placed his hand on hers. 'Bess, it does not matter,' he said quietly.

'Parents do try to choose wisely for their children,' Edmund said without conviction.

Bess shook George's hand away. 'Do you believe that?' Her voice dripped with scorn. 'A wise parent would be guided by their child's wishes. From what I see about me, most parents care for nothing more than dowry and connections. And their spiritless children follow without objection.'

She sat back, trembling, shocked at her own outburst.

'Well, ladies,' Clemence said brightly, breaking the silence in the room. 'It is near time for us to retire but, perhaps, we should sing a few rounds of something cheerful first.' She beckoned to the musicians at the other end of the table.

Bess took the opportunity to slip away to the privy.

~

The sound of a madrigal drifted through the darkened chamber adjoining the hall. Bess walked over to a window and stared into the moonlit garden. She had no wish to return to the hall and force a cheerfulness that had faded now she was out of George's company. She touched her forehead against the cool glass of the small panes and blinked back tears.

'Bess.'

She started at the sound of her name and turned to see Edmund move out of the shadows at the other end of the window.

He stepped closer and said, his voice rough, 'What is between you and George Raynsford?'

'What business is it of yours?'

He brushed his fingers against her cheek and, before she thought to draw back from him, his arms were about her crushing her to him. His kiss was fierce, ungentle. Life had not prepared Bess for the flame that swept through her. She wrapped her arms around Edmund, answering him with equal hunger.

The door to the hall opened and skirts swished as a woman came out.

Bess had no will to move away from Edmund. She would be caught but she did not care. Edmund drew her deeper into the shadow, blocking view of her with his body. The woman, whoever she was, passed by without noticing them.

With the sound of a male chorus answering the alto, reality took hold. 'What are you doing?' Anger surged through her. 'You are about to be betrothed to Lucy.' She tried to push him away but he held her fast.

'I am not. This is a ruse to gain time so I can marry the woman I love.'

'And who would that be?' She would not believe unless he said it.

'You, Bess. You,' he breathed.

They stood in the dark, staring into each other's eyes, breathing the same breath.

The door opened again—two women this time, their skirts rustling as one followed the other through the chamber. The second one paused for a moment halfway across the room, then hurried on. By then Edmund's lips were on Bess's, gentle now but insistent, and nothing else mattered. It was as if she had not existed until this moment and from now there was no life that was not with Edmund Wyard.

His lips were against her forehead. She could feel his heart beating against hers. 'Bess,' his voice was low and breathless. 'I love you.'

There was one answer, the words she had not dared to form. 'I love you, Edmund.' She began to weep slow, quiet tears.

He held her face between his hands and kissed the tears away. 'I am going to marry you. Nothing will stop me.'

The door opened again. Would they not leave them in peace?

'I must go,' Bess tore herself away.

Edmund watched as she disappeared into the dark at the far end of the room, the sound of her slippered feet fading.

George gripped Edmund's shoulder. 'You take care of her, Edmund, or you will have me to answer to.'

23

Bess lay staring into the darkness while Lucy snored gently. She could feel Edmund's lips on hers, the brush of his beard against her cheek, the scent of his skin. Yet even as joy thrilled through her, uneasy thoughts gnawed. Why was Edmund pretending to court Lucy? Why was there need for *a ruse to gain time*?

Lucy muttered and rolled onto her side.

Bess eased herself onto her elbow and watched Lucy as she slept. If Edmund was using Lucy without her knowledge, he was not the man Bess thought him to be; she should have nothing more to do with him. But when she thought of him, her will drained away.

As the sky began to lighten, Bess drifted towards sleep.

~

Blear-eyed with lack of sleep, Bess forced herself out of bed and groaned as her feet touched the floor.

Lucy, already dressed, looked back across the room as she pulled the door open. Her chin trembling as if she were about to weep, she glared at Bess and slammed the door behind her. Bess's heart sank—Lucy loved Edmund too and had caught sight of them last night.

Avisa's blue eyes twinkled with mischief, as she wriggled her feet into her slippers. 'I saw Lucy and Edmund kissing last night.'

'Where?' Bess padded to the bowl and water jug that stood on a small cabinet behind the door. It was her worst fear. He was misleading them both.

'Just outside the hall. They thought they could not be seen in the dark.'

'And you have been teasing her?' She bent over the bowl and splashed water on her face.

'Of course.' Avisa sat down for Mall to dress her hair. 'And she

175

denies it. They are about to be betrothed so I do not understand why she is pretending nothing happened.'

'Lucy is easily upset.' Bess turned, towel in hand, water glistening on her cheeks. 'It is best if you leave her alone, no matter what you think you see.'

'But it is fun teasing Lucy.'

'Avisa,' Bess shut her eyes as she dried her face. 'Please be kind.'

'If I must,' Avisa screwed up her nose. 'But if I catch you, I'll give you no mercy.'

Bess drew a quick breath. 'And who would I be kissing?'

'George Raynsford.'

Bess laughed, 'If you catch me kissing George, you may tease me as much as you wish.'

~

Bess played the virginal while Avisa and Clemence sang.

Tomorrow the fox will come to town,

Keep, keep, keep, keep, keep!

Lady Allingbourne was bent at her embroidery, her spectacles perched on her nose, still working on the heavily decorated placket. It was covered with flowers, in blue and red and yellow, entwined with green leaves.

The door banged open and George strode in. He bowed to his aunt, winked at Bess, grabbed Clemence around the waist and danced her across the room singing with her.

And cry as loud as you can call,

O—keep you all well there!

Bess smiled at the sight of George, a great bear of a man, dancing with tiny Clemence, the top of whose head came up to his chest. George filled any room he entered and brought with him a palpable atmosphere of good humour. When Bess started playing a gavotte, George swept Clemence off her feet.

The dance finished, George flung himself onto the stool next to his aunt and grinned at Clemence who was forcing herself to frown at him.

'Go on,' he said, 'you enjoyed it.'

Lady Allingbourne shook her head. 'George, you are little different from that very naughty boy who came to stay with us twenty-five years ago.'

'I do my best Auntie.' He turned his full attention on her, almost kneeling the stool was so low. 'Have you given thought to my proposition?'

'I have, but with you leading the party I have the greatest fears.'

'Name one girl,' he said with the cheekiness of a boy, 'one girl under your care that I have led astray.'

'Well,' Lady Allingbourne said slowly.

'They all hope I will. Even Clemency.'

'Indeed!' Clemence hid her face behind a book she had picked up. George leant over, winked at her, and turned the book the right way around.

Lady Allingbourne gazed over her spectacles. 'I suppose there will be no harm in it.' She did not sound convinced. 'It is not as though you are proposing to stay out all night as many do. Who else, other than my ladies, will you be taking with you?'

'I would prefer to have them to myself but, I suppose, Ned can come and a few of Sir Hugh's men.'

'Ah!' Lady Allingbourne smiled, 'I understand.'

'You know you can trust him.'

'I know I can trust Lucy. I expect you want me to bring a breakfast for your May gatherers.'

'Better than leaving it to me. We would end up with too much drink and not enough food.'

'Then I *would* have to worry about my ladies.'

George eased himself off his knees. 'Ladies,' he said, 'tomorrow is May Day and my gracious aunt, against her better judgement, has agreed to let me take you maying. I may even crown the woman of my dreams with May blossom.

Avisa whispered in Bess's ear, 'It might be you. He clearly has a liking for you.'

'George loves all women.' Bess gazed over at him. 'He is more like a brother, a good-natured but mischievous brother.'

'My brothers are nothing like that,' Avisa said, disbelieving.

Lady Allingbourne pulled another silk from the basket on the floor beside her and threaded her needle. 'Will one of you go and find Lucy?' She spoke to no one in particular. 'I am sure she will be pleased.'

Bess stood up quickly. 'I'll go.' It was her best chance to speak with Lucy alone.

~

Bess found Lucy sitting on a low stool facing their bedchamber window, so lost in thought that she did not hear Bess enter. When Bess got closer she realised Lucy was kneeling, her eyes closed.

'Lucy,' Bess said gently.

Shocked out of her reverie, Lucy jumped, dropping something that fell to the floor with a soft patter. She reached down quickly, scooped it up and held it in her tightly closed fist as she stood.

'What do you have there?'

'Nothing.'

'A nothing you want no one to see.' Bess held out her hand. 'Show me.'

Lucy held her fist tight but Bess caught her by the wrist and prised her fingers away. A string of dark, polished beads with a small cross attached, lay curled in the palm of Lucy's hand. Rosary beads.

'Oh Lucy,' Bess gasped, 'you fool. Do you want to get us killed? It is treason to own these gewgaws.'

'I do not care. I am ready to die for my faith, if I do not die of shame first.' She trembled, her voice sharp with anger. 'The single reason I agreed to take part in this game of Edmund's is that it will give me the chance to set my life on the path I wish, but Bess,' her nostrils flared as she spoke, 'I will not allow you to use me to cloak wantonness.'

'Wantonness?' Bess's voice rose. 'I have never been wanton.'

'What of your behaviour last night?'

'What do you mean?'

'You allowed George to paw you publicly then flung yourself into Edmund's arms.'

'George was not pawing me,' Bess spoke over her. 'That is just his way. I imagine had you been seated beside him, he would have done the same.'

'I would have made him stop. I would never allow a man to touch me with familiarity.'

'And so create a sour mood for all present.'

'And you did not do that with your nasty squabble with

Edmund?'

'I did not mean to argue with him. I thought...' Bess closed her eyes.

'I do not understand why Avisa thinks it was me,' Lucy glared at Bess. 'You two bickered with the venom of a married couple. Then you disappeared within minutes of each other. Anyone with eyes could see what was going on.'

'People see what they suppose to be the truth. They do not use their eyes.' And Bess was glad they did not. 'Forgive me, Lucy,' she pleaded. 'I love him.'

'I know that, and he does love you.' Lucy was calmer now. 'But I do not want my name stained as someone who wallows in the flesh.'

'It was hardly wallowing in the flesh.'

'No matter how you describe it, it was something I would never have done.' Her mouth was set in a thin judgmental line. 'You must restrain yourself until a week from Monday.'

Bess blinked, puzzled.

'When he marries you,' Lucy said, now looking puzzled herself. 'Did he not tell you?'

In their brief time together last night, other things had seemed more important than talking. 'He did not tell me the date.'

'As we will be returning to Allingbourne Hall at the end of the month, I will ask Lady Allingbourne for permission to stay for a couple of weeks with my aunt who lives out beyond St. Giles. I am certain she will allow you to attend me. I will witness your marriage to Edmund and, instead of coming to St Giles, you two can spend the time together.'

'I did not know you had an aunt in London.'

'My grandmother's sister. My father has no love for my mother's family so we rarely see them.' Lucy frowned, 'I hate that I must be party to your lies.'

'Yet they help you with your own plans, Lucy.' Bess forced herself to ask, 'What are they?'

'I am arranging to go to France to join the Ladies of Syon at Rouen.'

'The Ladies of Syon?'

'It is a convent—I am going to become a nun.'

'Have you told Edmund this?'

Lucy shrugged, 'No. The fewer people who know my plans, the better.'

'That is wise,' Bess said quickly. 'Edmund would see it as nothing more than the basest treason.'

'Treason,' Lucy scoffed. 'This has nothing to do with states and kings. It is something I have wanted to do for as long as I can remember. Edmund's charade is Heaven sent.'

'Please, Lucy.' Bess lowered her head, rubbing her fingers between her eyebrows. 'This is madness.'

'If it is madness,' Lucy's eyes shone as she spoke, 'it is a madness blessed of God.'

24

The women rose before daybreak and rode out with George, Edmund and several of Sir Hugh's men to collect May blossom. Sir Hugh and Lady Allingbourne were to follow later, bringing the breakfast feast.

Well beyond the city walls, the still, foggy air carried wood smoke from the bonfires where others had spent the night wrapped in their cloaks, some in languid pairs, waiting for the first light to collect the dew-laden blossom of the hawthorn.

They dismounted near a large copse and the handful of servants who had come with them took charge of the horses and set about building a fire. It was hard to tell the women apart. George had insisted, to add to the atmosphere of revelry, that the women wear the identical cloaks and vizards he had provided. Only Clemence, because of her diminutive size, could be easily recognised.

George helped Bess down from her palfrey. As she waited while Edmund assisted Lucy and Avisa, George drew Bess's arm through his and patted her gloved hand. 'Bessie, as you can see all of you look the same in the fog, so who is to know who is with whom?'

Bess turned to him, wary. If George knew, surely it would not remain secret for long.

He bared his white teeth. 'Even through that mask I can tell a worried face.' He bent his head closer to Bess. 'It is too long a story for now but I owe Ned my life, and I will give him whatever help he wants without question. When you two are together anyone can see you are two halves of the one coin. Even his mother sees it. Why do you think she hates you so much?'

Bess swallowed, 'Hates me?'

'I saw the glint in her eyes as she watched you and Ned together last week.'

'Why would she hate me?'

'Ned needs a woman to love him, to stand beside him, not a slip of a girl Maggie imagines she can bend.' He stared into her eyes through the slits in her vizard. 'And as for him lacking strength of character…'

'I did not mean that.'

'Now Ned has made up his mind, I tell you, he will forsake all for you and old Maggie will lose what hold she has on him. If she knew, she would use any means to thwart your plans.'

'You are frightening me. All I want is to love Edmund and to be happy.'

'And you will, but keep it quiet until he gets back, otherwise you'll get no peace from her.'

Clemence hurried over and said to Bess as she handed her a set of clippers, 'Lucy, you should find Edmund.' She glanced around at the cloaked figures. 'Now, where is Bess? I want her to keep you in order, George, and I will watch Avisa. Thank the Lord Thomas Rawson has come down with that cold.'

'Ay,' George said dryly, 'an accommodating married cold named Hilary.'

'These disguises are a ridiculous idea.' With an angry toss of her head, Clemence moved off towards Avisa who was now hanging off the arm of one of Sir Hugh's men.

Bess and George strolled towards the thicket.

'Look at that, the poor love is all aflutter. She cannot work out which girl is which, who to watch and who to let go. She has been told to allow Lucy some freedom today; my lady trusts Ned not to do the wrong thing.'

Edmund appeared from nowhere. 'Lucy, have you seen Bess anywhere?'

When Bess smiled, his face lit up and he took her hand. 'George, you are a master schemer.'

'Years of practice.' He rubbed his hands together. 'Now off with you. I am certain I saw a great bough of blossom through those trees.'

~

Edmund and Bess made their way, side by side, through the trees, the sounds of their companions softening as they walked on.

Edmund stopped beneath a gnarled oak and threw his cloak over a fallen log to cover the damp moss. Bess sat, and as Edmund lowered himself onto the log, she undid her cloak and pulled it around them both.

He lifted off her vizard and drew her close. His kisses were gentle. Bess clung to him, kissing him back, slowly and completely, drifting in his arms towards a place where all that existed was the two of them.

'I am leaving in three weeks,' he whispered, his breathing uneven. He pressed his lips into Bess's hair.

She closed her eyes and gave a muffled groan.

His lips brushed against her eyelids. 'We can be married tomorrow week by licence.'

She lay her head on his shoulder. 'Why does there have to be this secrecy?' The reasons George had given seemed so far-fetched.

Bess leant against him as he moved his arm to her waist.

'I fear my mother's wrath, not for myself, but for you when I am gone.'

'Surely there is little she can do if we are firm in our love.'

'Oh Bess, you do not know her. She has a ruthless anger. She paid ruffians to beat my father's mistress. They tried to cut a W for whore into her forehead. Edith struggled so much that all they managed was a single slash. Mother was shamed by Father's infidelity. He did not flaunt Edith and I doubt many knew of it until the attack. Father bought Bucklings then and lived there with her. She was unwilling to be seen.'

'What was she like?'

'I met her a single time. She seemed a kind and modest woman who loved my father deeply. They were in their middle years when they met. She gave him the love and warmth Mother never would.' He sighed as if torn between love and understanding for his father and duty to his mother. 'Edith was no strumpet.'

'But why can we not marry quietly without this pretence?'

'My mother has already begun negotiating the marriage settlement with Sir Peter. If she knew about us, she would do everything in her power to prevent us marrying. I hoped by agreeing to court Lucy, I could defer the negotiations until I returned from the Low Countries. Once she knows of our marriage, I must be with you until she accepts it. When I explained it to Lucy, she was delighted. She has great affection for you and has even found a way for us to be together for my last weeks here.'

Bess raised her eyebrows, wondering if affection would have been reason enough for Lucy to agree had she not had plans of her own.

'She wants to stay with her mother's aunt. Her father is marrying again and she is afraid he will forbid his children from having anything to do with their mother's family.'

Bess saw no point in saying that Lucy's mother was alive. She doubted Lucy had told so outrageous a lie. Bess had noticed recently that Lucy had the knack of leading people to draw the wrong conclusions through ambiguous statements and sentences left unfinished.

'We will be married Monday next with George and Lucy as our witnesses. And, while Lucy stays with her aunt, we will be together in my brother's house in Coleman Street. Mother is returning home on Friday. Lucy will ask Lady Allingbourne for leave to visit her aunt, and request that you go with her. She is certain Lady Allingbourne will not deny her and, no doubt, I will be permitted to see you both safely there.'

'You have it well planned.'

He grinned, 'I have had the help of that seasoned campaigner George Raynsford.'

'Did it occur to you I might have changed my mind since we last spoke?'

'Never. I saw your face when George first asked if you were my lady and knew then, with certainty, it was what you wanted.'

'And how long have you wanted me?'

'Always. Even before I knew you. I have been searching for you all my life.'

Bess laughed, 'I wish I could say such pretty things. All I can say is that I love you.'

'That is more than enough.'

In the distance she heard Avisa squealing, Clemence's high pitched giggle and a man's booming laugh. Bess traced her fingers along Edmund's lips. He caught her hand and kissed the fingertips one by one. Still holding her hand, he rested his head against hers. They sat together, not speaking.

Bess closed her eyes and listened to his breathing, in time with her own. This was different from anything she had ever felt. There was no need to pretend, to strive to be other than she was. She was not in love with Edmund; she loved him, wholly and entirely. There could be no talk of infatuation or intemperance, for their promises to each other, spoken and implied, were enduring, more binding than a formal handfasting.

The fog had cleared and the sun shone in shafts through the trees.

'We had better collect some May blossom,' Edmund said, resigned already to the mundane world. He stood and offered his hand to Bess.

As Bess rose, she reached up and brushed her lips against his. He grabbed her to him and kissed her hard.

'I had better find Lucy now,' he said.

Bess waited as he disappeared between the trees.

~

Bess cut small branches of white hawthorn as she walked back towards the others. By the time she came out of the copse, she had a large armful of May blossom.

Sir Hugh and Lady Allingbourne had arrived, rugs had been laid on the ground, cushions strewn about and hampers opened.

As Bess, her vizard swinging from her wrist, added her May blossom to the mound on the small cart that had arrived with Lady Allingbourne, Avisa ran up, her eyes large, and whispered loudly, 'I saw Edmund and Lucy in the woods. They were...,' she smirked.

'For Heaven's sake, Avisa, you are imagining things.'

'But they were lying on the ground together, fumbling under Lucy's cloak.'

'You did not see their faces, did you?' Bess's eyes blazed. 'You have no idea who it was.'

'But the cloak was just like this,' Avisa pouted.

Bess shook her cloak. 'These cloaks are common stuff, hundreds of women wear them. It could have been any of two dozen couples in these woods at present.'

Avisa's mouth twisted, 'I am certain.'

'You saw what you wanted to see. And you will not say a word of your fantasy to Lucy.'

'But...'

'No! Avisa!' Bess grasped Avisa's wrist, her fingers digging into the skin. 'This is a malicious slander and, if I hear another word of it, I will take the matter straight to Lady Allingbourne.'

Avisa scowled, her lips turned down, a picture of petulance.

'Go and have breakfast and forget about it all.'

Avisa flounced away and sat as far as she could from Bess, ostentatiously nursing her wrist.

Breakfast was laid out for them: mulled wine and bread and cheese, chicken and pie—far heavier fare than they usually ate, but today they had hearty appetites.

Bess joined the rest and lowered herself onto a rug.

George flung himself down beside her, offering her his chicken leg. 'Go on Bessie, have a nibble.' He leant close and whispered into her ear, 'Give the impression you are completely smitten by me.'

Bess held the chicken leg and took a small bite. 'I do not know Lady Allingbourne would be happy with that.'

'Not at all,' he grinned. 'She has asked me what I feel for you—she sees me as your perfect suitor.'

'Oh George, what did you say?'

'That I would be delighted if you were willing to accept my imperfections. She has given me leave to court you.'

Her eyes swam. 'If my heart were not taken, I could think of nothing better.' George was so much larger than life, warm and generous, that a woman could love him and, perhaps, learn to close her mind to what he may or may not do while he was away from her.

'Now we must get into the spirit of this,' he reached over to draw Bess into a kiss.

Grinning at him, Bess brushed his hand away.

Over George's shoulder, she noticed Lady Allingbourne watching, a gentle smile on her lips. Bess turned as Lady Allingbourne's smile broadened.

Edmund, his arms filled with blossom, came into the clearing with Lucy. Edmund helped Lucy to sit and brought her food, offered her his cup to drink from. He did not look once at Bess, and Bess forced herself to look away.

'You are thinking to marry again?'

'It is about time,' George said, 'My daughter needs a mother. And I would not mind providing her with a few brothers and sisters.'

'Do you have anyone in mind?'

'Apart from you?'

Bess rolled her eyes at him. 'Ay, apart from me.'

'Now Clemency—I would enjoy uncovering the fire beneath that prim exterior. And she would be a fine mother to my girl. But, unfortunately, as I want more children, she is too old.'

'What about Avisa?'

George gave a gap-toothed grin. 'There's one who likes to lead men a merry dance.' He winked at Avisa, who rolled her eyes and poked out her tongue. 'I've been chasing her through the thicket since you left.' He raised his eyebrows at Bess. 'And caught her.'

'And …?'

'I gave her a chaste kiss on the cheek. She's a little young for me.'

'Avisa is eager to marry.'

'Is she?'

Avisa was now flirting with another of Sir Hugh's men.

'Some girls are ready at her age, but not that one. She needs a year or two to learn that the best men are not always those with the prettiest faces and the finest way with words.'

'Some women never learn that,' Bess said. 'And Lucy, what was she doing while you were chasing Avisa?'

'She went on determinedly picking blossom. She is a sensible girl.'

Lucy sat, her eyes shut, basking in the sun, a picture of contentment.

Sensible, Bess thought, when she was not playing traitor's games. She shivered.

George put his arm around her. 'Come here, I'll keep you warm.'

'Not too warm,' Bess warned him.

~

'Ned, it's time you gave up.' George slapped Edmund on the shoulder as he got up from the table in the hall. He strolled over and stood with his back to the small fire in the hearth. Everyone else had retired early, but he, Edmund and Thomas, remarkably recovered from his cold, stayed playing dice.

'Let him be,' Thomas said, tossing the dice in his cupped hands.

Edmund stretched his arms above his head. 'George is right,' he stifled a yawn. 'I should go home.'

'One more roll, Raynsford?' Thomas called to George who had wandered to the window and was staring into the darkening garden.

George turned back to the room. 'One more. Then I will seek my chaste cot too.'

'Chaste cot! You!' Thomas scoffed.

'In my aunt's house, it most certainly is.'

Edmund stood and rolled his shoulders.

'You two are showing your age tonight,' Thomas laughed.

'Age be damned!' George snorted as he slid into the seat opposite Thomas. 'We rose before dawn, laboured in the woods hewing branches of blossom. We have been to church, danced around the maypole and otherwise entertained virtuous ladies all day. But you, I dare say, tumbled out of a certain someone's bed at midday and have not done service even to God today.'

'I did service in other ways,' Thomas smirked.

George raised an eyebrow, unamused.

Thomas sighed loudly, 'I will listen to two sermons Sunday next.'

'Indeed you will. I will hold you to that.'

'Ned,' George called to Edmund as he crossed towards the door, 'I suggest you take a stroll in the garden to gather your wits before you venture out into the dark and dangerous streets.'

'I suppose it would not hurt.'

'I'll rouse Hayes for you when I go for my own man. I expect they're keeping that pretty Welsh maid from her bed.' He nodded to Thomas, 'You keep your eyes off that one—we need to leave something for those who serve us.' He grabbed the dice, rattling them in his hand. 'Two more tosses and I will go to bed.'

Thomas grinned, sure of his luck today.

~

Edmund's footsteps crunched on the gravel path as he walked towards the flowering plum at the centre of the garden. It had been a difficult day, except for the dream-like interlude in the woods. He had spent the day in Lucy Torrington's company. She was a kind-hearted girl but she said little and, for most of the time, was lost in her own dreams. And George, the best man to have beside you in a fray, making the most of it all, pretending he was besotted with Bess. The worst had been that he had to feign indifference to Bess.

In the waning light, the shadows were dark beneath the tree, almost as if there was a figure there.

His heart leapt. 'Bess,' he whispered.

She answered with his name.

As he came closer, he saw the joy in her face. 'What are you doing out here?' He glanced towards the window of the hall.

'Escaping the bustle of the maiden's chamber. I needed quiet to savour my memories of today.'

He moved close and said quietly, 'Are we alone?'

She nodded and wound her arms around his neck, pulling his head down. The weight of the whole frustrating day drained away as she kissed him. If every day could end this way.

'Today was the worst torture I have ever been through,' she whispered, 'worse than toothache.'

'Worse even than a broken arm.'

Their kisses lengthened, time falling away as they clung together, aware only of each other. Edmund, reluctant, broke the spell as his lips brushed Bess's jaw line. 'A week and nothing else will matter,' he murmured, breathless.

'A week,' she sighed.

'Are you sure you do not want to wait until I return?'

'Why wait longer than we must?' She tightened her hold on him and buried her face against his chest. 'Why must you go?'

'I am needed there and I have given my word.'

'I need you here.' Her voice was muffled by the cloth of his doublet. 'If anything should happen to you, I could not bear to live.'

'Bess,' he raised her chin and stared deep into her eyes, 'I give you my word, I will come back.'

'Do you always keep your word?'

'I do. No matter what happens, I will come back to you.' He had life before him now, and he would allow nothing to keep him from it.

25

The black palfrey stood patiently beside the mounting block as the groom made one last check of the girth strap and stirrups. Dame Margaret twitched her riding switch against her skirts, her lips a tight line. 'I had hoped...'

'Mother,' Edmund interrupted, 'I made it quite clear that nothing would be done until I returned.'

She gave an angry shake of her head. 'There is time enough for you two to be married before you go. Florence says the girl is besotted with you.'

'Lady Allingbourne exaggerates. I see no point in marrying Lucy to leave her.' It sounded so plausible, so considerate. Yet he was marrying Bess to do exactly that. He could not live without the thought that she was his. If he were to die, which he had no intention of doing, he would have lived enough. Two weeks with Bess Stoughton as his wife was worth more than an eternity with any other woman.

'Edmund!' Lady Wyard snapped. 'You give the impression of a smitten man yourself.'

'I have much on my mind.'

'I thought your father left his affairs in good order.'

'He did,' he frowned. 'I have a number of other matters to see to: arms, another horse, provisions.'

Lady Wyard rolled her eyes as if he were talking of trifles. 'I had best be on my way. I wonder what disorder Eloise has managed to create in my absence.'

Edmund said nothing. He bowed to his mother and waited as she mounted her horse and rode out into the street followed by her small army of attendants. He turned back to the house feeling lighter than he had for weeks. He would spend the morning with the sword master then dine at Lady Allingbourne's where he would watch Bess as she sat beside Lucy, and anyone observing would assume his eyes were on Lucy. And Bess would sit thinking, she said, of nothing but him, appearing to gaze at George. If Lady Allingbourne had taken Bess on yet another errand, he would find a way of passing the time with Lucy, or if she had gone too, with George. Chess was good, and Lucy was a surprisingly adept player. All George needed was an audience. Somehow, Edmund would contrive a few moments alone with Bess. He ached to hold her in his arms, told himself it was enough, but knew the moment he saw her it was not. It was a constant battle to maintain his restraint, harder still because he sensed Bess felt the same. It would be so easy, kiss by kiss, breath by breath, to be swept on, but Bess deserved nothing less than the honour of marriage.

~

With less than a month until their return to Essex, Lady Allingbourne made lists of tasks to be done before they left. She required Bess's attendance as she arranged a pair of tapestries for the Hall, and visited the grocer in Bucklesbury to order spices too expensive to be trusted to their usual supplier—saffron, ginger, and sandalwood for colouring. Even Lucy demanded Bess's company on a single lengthy trip. Bess supposed Lucy assumed, rightly, that Bess would require no explanations. First, they visited a draper on Cornhill Street where Lucy organised two modest gowns of a sober elegance that suited her. They trudged across the city to visit a man of law just beyond Ludgate. Bess waited outside the lawyer's chamber not daring to imagine what Lucy was arranging inside. Then on to a cordwainer, a glover and finally to a goldsmith in Cheapside where Lucy bought two heavy gold chains. Bess knew Lucy was preparing for her journey, taking what she could of value with her, but Bess pushed it from her mind. For Bess, these days were shot through with unease that a day would pass without seeing Edmund.

Yet when Bess stayed at home, the mornings were endless as she waited for Edmund. Once he arrived, whole afternoons and evenings flew. The moments they found themselves alone—beside a staircase, in the corner of a window, in the garden—were an eternity in themselves. A timeless place where the touch of his fingers on her skin, his lips on hers, stirred such an intensity of longing that she had no will to resist. Yet he always drew back.

Although he said nothing of it, Bess knew Edmund's thoughts. There must be nothing sordid in their loving, nothing rushed or fumbled in darkened corners. He would come to her as her husband in a union that was blessed by God and man.

The week dragged on, felt longer than a year but, when Monday morning arrived, it seemed to have passed in the blinking of an eye.

~

Lucy, George and even Edmund had disappeared within moments of their arrival at the Wyards' house, leaving Bess alone in the parlour. It was smaller than Lady Allingbourne's yet more elegantly furnished with a polished table, a turkey rug draped over a large chest and an inlaid cabinet holding burnished plate. A virginal stood in a corner, and an imposing portrait of Lady Wyard in a gilded frame dominated one wall.

Bess turned her back on Lady Wyard and went to the window, staring out into the walled garden. A sparrow flew down and perched precariously in a young pear tree. Bess watched the slender branch bobbing under the weight of the bird and wondered at her own reputation for good sense. She had stated often the common wisdom that love was no basis for marriage, yet here she was about to enter into a secret marriage for love alone. All that mattered to her was that she would be with Edmund. She knew it was right when she was with him, more right than anything she had ever done.

~

The parlour door opened silently and Lucy called to her, 'Come Bess, time to get ready.'

Bess followed Lucy up the stairs to a light-filled bedchamber. The scent of roses drifted through the open casement from the garden below. Bess's best gown and sleeves were spread on the large curtained bed, the slippers Edmund had given her beside them.

Lucy closed the door. 'Goodness, you look as if you are going to your execution.'

'Am I doing the right thing?'

Lucy's eyes were full of sympathy. 'Do you love him?'

Bess nodded. 'But everyone knows that romantic love is no

basis for marriage.' She spoke as if she were trying to convince herself.

'You are wrong there,' Lucy said quietly. 'From what I have observed, marriage is a barren place without it. This I do know, we are only given one chance to follow our hearts. If you walk away now, you will regret it for the rest of your days.'

Bess knew Lucy was speaking as much about herself but that did not make her statement less true.

'We do not want to keep them waiting too long.' Lucy unlaced Bess's sleeves.

With a long shuddering sigh, Bess gave up her doubts.

~

When Lucy opened the door to the parlour and ushered Bess in, the room seemed to be filled with men—not only George, and Edmund's man Hayes, but others Bess had never met. Edmund was speaking to a man who was clearly the clergyman while another, in the sober garb of a lawyer, listened intently to them both.

George beamed across the room. 'Bessie, you are ravishing.'

Edmund smiled at her and introduced the clergyman and the lawyer by their names.

'Now Ned, let's get you married.' George picked up a garland of roses, rosemary and hawthorn blossoms that had been sitting next to a small pile of documents on a table against the wall.

Lucy took it from him. 'What a romantic thought, Edmund.'

'I'm the one you should be smiling at,' George said with mock affront. 'Ned here has not a romantic bone in his body.'

They took their places, Bess and Edmund in front of the clergyman, Lucy and George at either side, while the lawyer watched on. Hayes remained by the door.

Bess thought of the tales of secret marriages, but they were stories of witnesses dragged in off the street and priests who could not be found afterwards. This was not a secret marriage but a private one, in front of friends. What man intent on deceit calls in his lawyer to witness it?

Bess stood beside Edmund in the sunlit room, the carolling of birds drifted in from the garden. She breathed in the scent of roses. This was right, the path she was ordained to follow. She said the words she had said once before, but now she said them as a solemn conscious vow.

The clergyman asked for the ring and Edmund groaned, 'I forgot to buy a ring.'

George gave a roar of laughter and slapped him on the back. 'Give her your own ring.'

Edmund twisted off the ring he wore on his little finger, a single diamond set in an antique band.

As he slid it on Bess's finger, she was glad he had forgotten. She would rather wear a ring warm from Edmund's finger containing something of his essence than a circle of cold metal without meaning or history.

Bess closed her eyes as Edmund kissed her, a brush of his lips against hers. When she opened them, the sunlight shone through the windows touching each person in the room. It seemed as if the world had been made anew.

Lucy hugged Bess. 'I wish you all the joy life can bring.'

'We are not quite finished.' Edmund led Bess to the table where the lawyer had spread several large documents. 'Bess, I am granting you, a small manor I have bought in Surrey. You will also have the usual third of the income from Bucklings, but if I should die without issue, it is not entailed so it will pass to you. No matter what happens, you will be cared for.'

Bess's eyes swam with tears. 'Nothing will happen to you.' She said it as a charm against the future.

'I will come back. I have promised you.'

Edmund and Bess signed the documents in the presence of the lawyer and the celebration began. Hayes slipped from the room and within minutes footmen entered carrying flasks of wine and platters with quail and partridge, baked meats, wafers and marchpanes, gingerbreads and jellies.

All toasted the bride and groom. The clergyman and the lawyer did not stay much beyond the end of the meal but Lucy and George lingered. George especially, with his booming voice and his good humour and his teasing, made it a real wedding feast.

~

Bess and Edmund stood side by side in the courtyard, a space between them, as they bade Lucy and George goodbye. Edmund went back into the house, Bess following him in silence as he climbed the stairs. Words no longer were enough.

He held the door to the bedchamber open.

Bess walked to the window and gazed again into that small, perfect garden.

Edmund crossed the floor to her. She did not turn but waited. He placed his hands on her shoulders and she leant against him, feeling the warmth, the strength of his body. He turned her to him and brushed his lips against hers. She opened her lips, pouring her soul into her kisses, every fibre melting as he pulled her tight against him. Bess clung to Edmund, she knew he would never let her go. Her past fears, her painful memories were nothing now. Nothing existed but the two of them and the love that flamed between them.

~

The sun was pouring into the room when Edmund woke from a deep sleep, untroubled by nightmares for the first time in months. He lay stretched out, his back warm against Bess. She ran her hand along his side, pressed a kiss between his shoulder blades. Edmund rolled over to face her. Smiling, she closed her eyes and pressed her nose against his chest, drinking in the scent of his skin.

His fingers played in her unbound hair. 'What shall we do today?

Bess reached up and kissed him lightly.

'And after that?' His eyes shone.

'I want to spend the day with you,' Bess sighed contentedly. 'Nothing matters other than I am with you.'

He raised an eyebrow. 'The *whole* day in bed?'

'Why not? We are storing firewood against the winter.'

'Perhaps we could go to the playhouse.'

'Then there will be no secrecy.'

'If I could, I would pay the Town Crier to call from every corner that I have married you.' He held Bess tight against him. 'But I do not want you to face my mother alone. Her anger is something to behold.'

'That I do know—she tried to make Lady Allingbourne dismiss me.'

His eyes widened with surprise. 'Why?'

'I near knocked her heels over head,' Bess grinned.

'Tell me the story,' he chuckled. 'Leave nothing out. It sounds as if you tackled her like a lout playing football.'

'Your mother playing football, there's a thought.'

Bess sat up, her hair falling loose around her. Edmund gazed at her, enraptured by the beauty he saw in her—the flawless skin, the perfection of her body, the lovely face alive as he had never seen it before.

She told her tale of Lady Wyard, imperious, expecting all to stand aside for her; a small child, surfeited on marchpane and wafers, green-faced and whining that he was going to be sick; and a disrespectful waiting woman more concerned with keeping the floor clean than treating her elders and her betters with dignity. Bess acted out the parts, changing her voice and her expression like a player on the stage.

'And had we stood aside and waited, your mother would have skidded in the vomit and landed on her elegant bottom.'

Edmund lay in the bed helpless with laughter. When he regained his breath, he said, 'You said one day you would make me laugh until I could barely breathe.'

'You have a lovely laugh.' Her eyes twinkling with mischief, Bess tickled him.

Edmund wriggled away but fought back, laughing. The tickling quickly turned to teasing caresses and once more they were lost in their new-found delight.

~

The pattern of their days was simple—sleeping late, loving and laughing, reading aloud, singing in the parlour and playing the instruments where each had the better skill, dancing unaccompanied. They needed no one else within their world and, although they disciplined themselves to live for the day, for each moment, time did not stand still.

~

They sat together in the morning sunshine drinking in the sight of each other, speaking of anything other than their imminent parting and the empty months ahead. The close future dropped away as they imagined the steps they would take on Edmund's return, how he would come to Bess and, among friends, they would announce their marriage to Lady Allingbourne. They considered whether to go next to John Wyard in Northamptonshire or to Bucklings Hall, deciding on the latter to allow themselves some time together before facing Lady Wyard's fury.

Neither heard the footsteps on the gravel path. They started as George, suddenly beside them, said, 'God help us, Bessie, what have you done to the man? Ned looks happy.'

Lucy had followed George. 'You both look happy.'

'We were until you two arrived,' Edmund grumbled as he rose from the seat.

Bess's heart twisted as she recognised a pain that mirrored hers.

~

As they rode back to the Allingbournes' house in Bishopsgate Street, Bess said, 'You had better tell me, Lucy, what you have been doing, seeing we have spent the fortnight together.'

'Living the life of an elderly lady: resting, reading, sewing, chatting, taking short walks.'

'And that is all?'

'What more could there be?'

Bess dared not think. 'Your aunt, describe her, I should know that much.'

'Old, slight stoop, white hair, a northern accent that has never left her. Utterly devout.'

Bess knew exactly why Lucy had sought this aunt out. There would have been more than devotion here—plotting and planning for what was called treason. But how could Bess stand between Lucy and her dream?

~

Lady Allingbourne looked knowingly from Edmund to Lucy and sighed, 'Such a pity.'

As neither said anything in reply, she said, 'When do you two leave?'

'This afternoon,' George answered. 'We hope to make Harwich by nightfall tomorrow.'

'You too?' Bess groaned.

'Ned talked me in to it.' George pulled Bess to him and gave her a quick hug. 'No fuss please, Bessie.'

Bess shook him off and hurried from the parlour, fighting tears. She stood in the entrance hall, in the shadow of the stairs, and waited, a great knot of anguish in her chest.

George and Edmund strode towards the door to the yard, the jingle of their sword-belts echoing in the hall. Edmund turned as Bess whispered his name. His arms were around her, his lips on hers. When he drew back, she gazed deep into his eyes. 'Come home to me, my love. Come home safe.'

'I promise you, Bess, nothing will keep me from you.'

George stood near, his bulk hiding view of them from the yard. 'Ned, there's someone coming.'

Edmund kissed Bess fiercely then tore himself away. He did not look back.

George caught hold of Bess's hand. 'Bessie,' he whispered, 'I will keep him safe for you.'

Bess touched his arm. 'Keep yourself safe, George.'

Lady Allingbourne stopped at the foot of the stairs and saw the tears glistening on Bess's lashes. With the care of a mother, she put her arm around Bess. 'We will pray for them both.'

They climbed the stairs together.

'I had hoped for a betrothal before we returned home,' Lady Allingbourne said. 'Did Edmund visit Lucy often while you were at her aunt's?'

'No, my lady.'

'Oh dear! Has Lucy done anything to discourage him?'

'No, but there is friendship there,' Bess said carefully.

'Friendship is a good basis for marriage, many marry with far less. Perhaps once Edmund returns.' She smiled at Bess. 'And what of you and George?'

'We are friends.'

Lady Allingbourne nodded, seeming to understand more than was offered. 'Perhaps we will have more than one betrothal when they return. That should make your father happy. And I barely had to lift a finger.'

26

The following afternoon Lady Allingbourne and her ladies sat in the garden sewing, no elaborate embroidery today but household mending—linen smocks and shirts. Bess's mind drifted as she sewed, memories of recent days washing through her. A thrush alighted on a branch of the plum tree and broke into open-throated song. Bess smiled, remembering another sunlit garden.

~

An apple tree was espaliered against the garden wall with new leaves unfurling a tender green. Bess and Edmund sat beneath it feeding each other sweet orange segments, telling tales of childhood.

'When I was about nine or ten, playing football with the stable lads, Father joined us. He must have been nearing forty but he had the energy and exuberance of a man half his age. A few others left off their work and joined in too. He had the knack, whenever he was home, of suddenly turning an ordinary day into a holiday.' Edmund's eyes were bright with memory. 'A rough game it was, with few rules, and ended more as a wrestling match, Father was no better than the rest. Mother discovered us and berated Father for behaviour unbecoming of his station. In truth, her public admonishment was the unbecoming thing.' The happiness drained from his face as he spoke. 'Father took it as he always did, with good humour, winking at us as he left. He caught Mother around the waist and jested that she was jealous she could not play the game. The look she gave him would have frozen the tropics. I am certain he cared for her and, had she answered him with even an ounce of warmth, he never would have strayed. A year or two later he met Edith.' Edmund frowned, still torn by love and duty towards both his parents. 'He never said a word against Mother ever, never used her to justify his infidelity. Edith loved him for himself, gave up everything, even her good name, to be with him.'

Edmund gazed past Bess, his frown deepening at the sight of a footman hurrying towards him with a letter. He wiped his hands on a napkin, took the letter and roughly broke the seal.

Bess waited until the footman disappeared into the house. 'Will the servants tell your mother of me?'

Edmund scowled as he read but said, distracted, 'Nay.'

'Is something wrong?'

'Not at all. More orders from my mother.' He crumpled the letter and batted it across the garden. 'The servants are my brother's and before that my father's. They owe no allegiance to my mother.'

'Who do they think I am?' Bess busied herself wiping the juice from her fingers. 'Your mistress?'

'They know you are my wife, although they have been warned to say nothing of it to my mother.'

Bess gazed into Edmund's eyes. He gave the crooked smile that had warmed her to him from the start.

'But you are my mistress—mistress of my heart, mistress of my dreams.'

She set the tray with its orange peels and crumpled napkins on the ground next to their seat and moved closer to him. 'I wish I could say such pretty things.'

'All you need say is that you love me, that is worth far more than a hundred sonnets, a thousand pretty similes.'

Bess brushed her fingertips across the pitted scars on his cheek. Edmund caught her fingers and held them, a flash of pain in his eyes.

'You are perfection to me, Edmund.' She had pressed her lips to his cheek. 'Every part of you I love exactly as it is.'

And he had kissed her worshipping fingers.

Bess closed her eyes, feeling again the heat of his lips on her skin. It was as if he were with her.

'Look at Bess,' Avisa's voice rang out. 'She's in love.'

'Do be quiet, Avisa!' Lucy sprang to Bess's defence. 'It is possible to be happy because the day is beautiful and the birds are singing. It does not always have to be about a man.'

'It usually is though,' Avisa pronounced smugly. 'But look at Bess smiling at nothing.' She was keen for the others to notice.

'She is daydreaming.'

Bess blinked at Avisa, shocked that she had betrayed herself.

'So, did he offer you marriage?'

'Who?' Bess was blinking hard, at a loss to understand how Avisa knew so much.

'George, of course.' Avisa screwed up her nose, 'I know he is not the prettiest and he is old and decrepit, but he really seemed taken with you.'

Bess laughed, relieved. In her eyes George was the perfect image of virility.

'And Bess,' Avisa added earnestly, 'he is rich. You should consider him. You are not so young yourself, you cannot afford to be too particular.'

'Avisa,' Bess gasped, open-mouthed, more amused than offended.

Lady Allingbourne's face mirrored Bess's. 'Avisa...'

She stopped at the sound of a commotion in the entry hall, the shouts of an angry man, the softer remonstrations of a footman. The noise had barely died away when the footman hurried through the garden towards the group of women.

He bowed, 'Excuse me, my lady.' Flustered, he did not wait to be asked to continue. 'Sir Peter Torrington is here. I have put him in your private closet.'

'Thank you, Walters.' Lady Allingbourne took off her spectacles and, unhurried, folded her sewing and placed it in the basket beneath the book they sometimes read while sewing. She walked sedately towards the house, followed by Walters. The women watched in silence. Clemence took up the book, cast a forbidding glance at the other women, and began to read.

Avisa raised her eyebrows at Lucy, questioning, but Lucy dropped her head and concentrated on the placement of stitches in so mundane a task she could almost have done it blindfolded. Bess did the same. Aware of Clemence's glare over the top of the book, Avisa was forced to get on with her sewing in silence.

The sound of shouting could be heard above Clemence's reading, but she read on as if nothing else were happening.

After five minutes or so, Walters came for Lucy. She too took her time folding her sewing away. Avisa watched her, large-eyed, keen for an explanation. But Lucy did not look directly at anyone.

As soon as Lucy had stepped into the house, Avisa asked, 'What do you think is going on?'

'It is none of our business,' Clemence said curtly and continued reading.

Bess's heart lurched when Walters came for her.

Avisa, sewing still in hand, jumped up and seated herself beside Clemence. 'Will we be called too?' she asked eagerly.

Clemence did not take her eyes off the book. 'I have no idea,' she answered as if the words were written on the page.

~

Sir Peter Torrington stood at the window of the small chamber where Lady Allingbourne did her household accounts, staring down into the garden. He turned as Bess crossed the room. He was a greying, heavy-set man with nothing of good humour in his face. Bess saw no resemblance to Lucy.

Bess curtsied to him and to Lady Allingbourne.

Before she could take the seat indicated by Lady Allingbourne, Sir Peter began. 'Mistress Stoughton, you were with my daughter for most of Edmund Wyard's courtship of her. Did it appear to you he was toying with her affections?'

Bess's instinct was to say Edmund had never courted Lucy. Instead she met Sir Peter's fierce scrutiny and, hoping she appeared honest, said, 'It appeared to me that what was between them was more friendship than romantic love.'

'Friendship? The idea was he convince her to marry him, not that he become her friend,' he said incredulous, as if there was something unnatural in the proposition that a man and a woman could be friends.

'As I said, Sir Peter,' Lady Allingbourne put in, 'in the beginning Lucy would barely speak to him but with perseverance and Bess's good graces, I would say they did become friends. I even thought Lucy felt more for him, though she denies it, and I doubt she would admit to any kind feeling for him now.'

'Margaret Wyard assured me he had convinced Lucy to marry him.' He was struggling to understand what had happened.

Lady Allingbourne pursed her lips, puzzled. 'There were times, especially in this last month, when I would have sworn he was in love with Lucy. The way he used to look across the room...' She turned to Bess.

'I can only judge by what they said. Lucy made it clear she had no wish to marry Edmund and he respected her wishes and did not press her.'

Sir Peter glowered at Lady Allingbourne. 'If what you say is true, perhaps the man was daydreaming about this other woman and you have been misled. He is as big an addle-pate as my daughter. Bah!' he snorted, 'I do not understand it! The man has a fierce reputation as a soldier, yet when it comes to women... How can he be such a fool?' He paced the room. 'Whoever this woman is, her dowry will not compare to my daughter's. What he is after can be bought for a few pence on any street corner.'

Lady Allingbourne looked away from Sir Peter, her contempt barely veiled. She moved in her chair and faced Bess. 'Sir Peter met Edmund on the road to Harwich late yesterday...'

'And I asked him when he intended to marry my daughter,' Sir Peter interrupted. 'The brazen-faced rogue said he did not, that he was already married.'

'He was here yesterday and made no mention of it,' Lady Allingbourne said.

'Some underhand affair no doubt. I would not want to be Wyard's piece when his mother hears of this.' He gave a nasty grin. 'You should have seen old Christopher's trull after she had her face sliced.'

Lady Allingbourne ignored him and said to Bess, 'I wonder if Edmund married the woman while you and Lucy were visiting her aunt.'

'Her aunt?' Sir Peter bellowed.

'A Mistress Parkinson.' Lady Allingbourne paused. 'Her grandmother's sister, I believe.'

'And a damned Papist reputed to harbour priests.' He stared hard at Bess.

Bess gripped her hands together in her lap. It would be safest with this odious man to volunteer nothing.

Lady Allingbourne swallowed loudly. 'Bess?'

'I saw nothing to make me think...,' her voice trailed away.

'Could you tell a Papist if you saw one?' Sir Peter sneered. His small dark eyes narrowed. 'You're not one yourself?'

Colour crept up Bess's cheeks. 'I am not!'

Lady Allingbourne placed a hand on Bess's wrist.

'The girl's not to be trusted.' Sir Peter slammed his fist into his hand.

Bess jumped, fearing he was speaking of her.

'She knew she was not to go there.'

'You made no mention of it to me, Sir Peter,' Lady Allingbourne said.

'No mention of this is to be made to anyone,' he snarled. He loomed over Lady Allingbourne, pushing his face towards hers. 'If this gets out, your whole household will be suspect.'

Lady Allingbourne strained away from him. 'Surely not!'

He straightened up. 'I am taking Lucy home so she has no chance to act on any ideas that stupid old crone has given her. I've had enough of this indulgent fancy of letting children have a say in whom they marry, of getting to know each other first. I will take her home once I have settled my business in this godless town. She is not to leave this house.'

Lady Allingbourne nodded to Bess to rise and said to Sir Peter, 'Do you want Lucy to keep to her room?'

'Yes,' he scowled, then shook his head. 'No. But she is not to set foot outside the house.' He glared at Bess. 'You can trust your household?'

'I most certainly can,' Lady Allingbourne replied.

Sir Peter called to Bess as she opened the door, 'Tell my daughter to be ready to leave on Sunday.'

Bess curtsied to him and closed the door quietly.

~

Bess burst into the bedchamber. 'Lucy, your father says he is taking you home on Sunday.'

Lucy shuddered, surprised, as if coming back from a dream and scrabbled something from her lap into a closed fist. Fear washed through Bess—the rosary beads.

Lucy rose calmly from her seat on the chest by the window. 'Does he? Then I must bring my plans forward a few days.' She walked to her coffer against the far wall and slid the beads into it. 'I need your help, Bess.'

Bess had no wish to know anything of her plans but how could she refuse?

'I expect he'll not allow me to leave the house.'

Bess shook her head.

'In that case, will you run an errand for me tomorrow? I will write a note for the merchant, it will not take long.'

'That is all?'

'Yes. I will not involve you further. I would not want you to suffer after I am gone.'

'You are leaving?'

'As soon as it can be arranged. Definitely before Sunday.'

Bess hugged Lucy. 'I pray God keep you safe.'

'He will.'

'But what if you are caught? You will be facing more than an angry father.'

'I know that, but I also know that this is God's will. If I am taken, it is because He has chosen me for a martyr's crown.'

Bess groaned, 'Lucy, I am afraid for you.'

'Do not be. Prayer will keep me strong.' Her face glowed, radiant and unworldly.

~

Both Lucy and Clemence were already in bed and asleep when Avisa and Bess quietly entered the bedchamber.

Avisa sat on the edge of the bed she shared with Clemence and kicked off her slippers. 'Oh, I almost forgot,' she said airily, 'two letters came for you this afternoon when you were with Lady Allingbourne and Sir Peter.' She tiptoed to the cabinet behind the door and collected the letters. 'One is from Philippa but I have no idea about the other. The seal has been disfigured and the boy who brought it could tell me nothing.' She looked at Bess, eager for an explanation, as she handed them over.

Bess glanced at the writing but opened Philippa's letter first. She smiled as she read. 'Philippa is expecting a child.'

'Ooh, when?' Avisa beamed. 'Can we go to her lying-in?'

'December, she thinks. You will have to ask Lady Allingbourne.' She handed the letter to Avisa.

As Avisa read, Bess turned away and, under cover of spreading her bed smock out, slipped the other letter beneath her pillow.

She would read it by moonlight once Avisa was asleep.

~

Bess lay awake. She could hear, between Clemence's gentle snores, the softer sound of Avisa breathing with the regular rhythm of sleep.

She slipped from her bed to the window and stood, holding the letter between her palms, her eyes closed, trying to recapture her strongest memory of Edmund. It did not work. She broke the seal and tilted the paper towards the window. Although the moon gave off a bright light, she strained to read. There was no greeting nor was it signed but it was addressed to her in his hand. It was not a letter, no detail of where he was or what he was doing, instead Edmund had sent Bess a sonnet.

I know this pain, this anguished lonely night.
My life was so before you gave your heart
To me and God did bind us man and wife.
Two souls now one, no man can drive apart.
Your Love's alchemy has so altered me,
My ice bound heart thawed by your loving glance,
That every breath and thought I have is thee,
Though parted we may be by time and chance.
The darkened earth deprived of sun so waits
The jealous moon to pass, and likewise I,
Deprived of sight and touch of thee, do ache.
I know our souls are one, yet still I sigh.
When this eclipse is done, beloved wife,
United we will be for all of life.

As Bess read she heard Edmund's voice as clearly as if he had been standing with her.

27

Bess asked Lady Allingbourne for permission to make a few small purchases for Lucy, and Lady Allingbourne, trusting Bess, agreed without hesitation.

After buying pins, ribbons and stockings, Bess followed Lucy's precise instructions and arrived at a small shop in Birchin Lane as the bells sounded the hour. She handed Lucy's sealed note to the shopkeeper. The stooped old man, when he saw the seal, excused himself and left Bess standing in the shop with the footman who had accompanied her. Bess was uneasy, she knew this was no usual purchase. She told herself she was merely helping a friend to escape her father's rigid plans, but what if there was more to it? Lucy could be embroiled in a Papist plot. There were whispers everywhere of plots and schemes. Two priests had been captured and taken to the Tower only last month.

She stared around the shop with its jumble of second-hand furniture, clothing piled high in panniers, exotic carvings and painted vizards spread along a table against the wall, and wondered how Lucy came to know of such a place. She did not doubt this shop was run by Catholics. It shocked her that there was no easy way to tell who was a Papist and who not, that so near to where they lived, nearer even, Papists could be plotting to destroy them.

There was no one Bess could turn to for advice. She told herself over and over that she was simply helping a friend. Edmund, were he here, would not see it this way. She had heard him talking to George—Catholics were the enemy, agents of Spain who would do anything they could to tear down all that was good in their blessed land. At the thought of Edmund, a now familiar ache gripped Bess's throat. Her longing for him was a physical pain, as if a part of her had been torn away.

The rattle of a cart in the street and the cry of a pedlar brought

Bess back to the present. She glanced at the footman who stood staring out the door.

The shopkeeper shuffled in and handed Bess a small package. 'Tell your Mistress it is set in train,' he whispered.

'My mistress?'

'Use no names,' he hissed between gritted teeth.

Bess dared say no more.

She shivered as she stepped into the street. Had Lucy described her as her maid in the note to protect her? What had Lucy entangled her in that she needed protection?

~

In little more than a week, they would be leaving for Allingbourne Hall. Bess hoped that her misery would be more bearable away from London. Lady Allingbourne thought Bess was missing George so she did not have to hide her unhappiness. Perhaps this separation was easier for Edmund to bear. He had so much to do and he could at least say he was married. She could imagine him telling Sir Peter. But for Edmund's mother, they would have announced their marriage to all who knew them.

Bess woke on Saturday with a headache, more miserable than ever. She joined the other women in the parlour embroidering the centre panel of Lady Allingbourne's bed-cover. She could not see well enough to thread her needle, the colours of the threads ran into each other. Beside her Lucy hummed happily as she sewed.

'You are surprisingly cheerful for someone about to be banished,' Avisa said.

'It is no banishment,' Lucy said brightly. 'I am going where I will be happy.'

'But your father's estate is in the middle of nowhere, and I doubt there are any interesting men there.'

Lucy shrugged, 'I like a life that is simple.'

Avisa coughed, smothering a giggle.

Bess struggled to pull herself out of her lethargy. She turned to speak to Lucy and whimpered as pain burnt across her head.

'Bess, what is wrong?' Lady Allingbourne's voice was sharp with concern.

Bess shut her eyes. 'A headache.'

'Go and rest,' Lady Allingbourne said gently.

~

Heavy raindrops slid down the outside of the window of the bedchamber. As Bess pressed her head against the cool glass, the memory of another time she had done the same and what had followed caught at her. Everything she did reminded her of Edmund. She fought down a sob. Who would have thought loving someone could bring such pain? Bess went to the bed and lay down. She spread her hand on her bodice where, beneath the layers of clothing, she wore the small pouch she had made to hide Edmund's ring. It contained his sonnet too. What had he written?

...and likewise I,
Deprived of sight and touch of thee, do ache.

Their longing was the same. She closed her eyes and fell into a deep sleep.

~

Bess woke with a start.

Lucy's face loomed close, pallid in the dimness of the room. 'I did not want to leave without saying goodbye.'

'Lucy, do take care.'

'I will.' Her eyes shone. 'The angels of God watch over me.'

Bess struggled up. 'Look at you, you are plumper than a pigeon.'

'I cannot carry much so I have worn everything I can. I have a dozen layers on and can just get my uppermost bodice done up. I need a placket like a woman with child.' She raised her arm, a cloak draped over it. 'You will not mind if I take your cloak?'

'Why?' Bess frowned.

'A disguise,' Lucy grinned, obviously enjoying the intrigue. 'If I wear my own, I might be stopped as soon as I stepped outside the door. Say I stole it.'

She bent and kissed Bess on the cheek.

Bess caught Lucy's hand. 'I wish you well, Lucy.'

'And I wish you and Edmund all the happiness in this world.' Lucy tied the cloak and collected up a small bundle.

'God keep you,' Bess whispered as Lucy closed the door.

Bess lay staring at the tester. Her head still pained her, her whole body ached. She was not sure whether she was suffering from an illness or from misery. With Lucy gone, there was no one left who knew of her love for Edmund. Fleetingly she had possessed something beautiful and with each day that passed it seemed more and more a dream.

She closed her eyes and slept.

~

Bess was lost in a grey world, her only comfort was Edmund's presence at her side. She saw her mother ahead, as pale as she had been on her deathbed. As Bess ran towards her, she faded into the darkness. Bess turned back to Edmund, but he was no longer there. She sensed him, not far away, and ran through the gloom, glimpsing now and again the shape of him ahead. She ran through narrow winding streets, unseen threat at every turn. He was beyond her reach, no matter how hard she ran or where she searched, she could not find him. And the grey light of her dream world drained away to darkness.

~

'Wake up! Bess! Wake up!'

Bess woke with a jolt, blinking into the flickering candlelight. She moaned, overwhelmed by fear that she would never see Edmund again, and lay still, weak with imagined loss.

'Bess! Bess!' Clemence bent over her, Lady Allingbourne beside her holding the candle. 'Do you know where Lucy is?' Clemence's voice rose, edged with panic. 'We cannot find her anywhere.'

'No,' Bess mumbled. Her head no longer ached but the despondency of her dream settled on her.

Deep shadows marked the worry in Clemence's face. 'Has she been given a sleeping potion of some sort?' she said to Lady Allingbourne.

'Nay, Clemence,' Bess said slowly. Even speaking was an effort. 'I am unwell, that is all.' She struggled up and swung her legs over the side of the bed and sat there.

Lady Allingbourne stepped back. 'Bess, Sir Peter Torrington is here. He urgently needs to speak with you. Lucy has disappeared.'

Clemence helped Bess from the bed and Bess submitted, resigned, to her fussing as she was made presentable.

~

Lady Allingbourne shepherded Bess into the parlour to a seat by the empty hearth and sat beside her.

Bess tried to concentrate on what Sir Peter was saying as he paced round and round the room with an air of restrained menace.

'Did you know she was planning this?' he barked.

'No.' Bess closed her eyes, tired to the bone.

Sir Peter stood in front of her, his hands on his hips. 'You were as close as any to my daughter.'

She forced her eyes open. 'Yes.'

'Has she taken Wyard's perfidy to heart?'

'Lucy never wanted to marry him.'

He scowled, 'Is it possible she had a passion for someone else?'

'No.'

'She was happy to be returning home,' Lady Allingbourne said.

'If she said that, it was a barefaced lie,' Sir Peter snorted. 'She has always hated Stamthorpe, took every opportunity to be away. Why do you think she spent so much time with her grandmother? Vile Papist crone. If I had known...' He glared from Lady Allingbourne to Bess. 'And she never left the house?'

'No,' Bess and Lady Allingbourne said together.

Sir Peter crossed his arms and scowled so deeply that his dark bushy eyebrows made a single line. 'If I knew what she had planned, I would know what to do.' He walked to the fireplace and stared into the empty hearth.

Bess sensed he was not talking about Lucy but how to protect himself.

'We will delay our departure until we have word of her,' Lady Allingbourne said.

He swung back to face the women. 'When are you planning to leave?'

'A week from Monday.'

'If she has not appeared by then, we'll not find her.' He stroked his beard, fear in his eyes. 'If anyone comes asking, do not mention the aunt.'

'But...' Lady Allingbourne frowned, not understanding.

Sir Peter turned on her. 'You stupid woman, you have aided and abetted a Papist. If I know anything, the fool girl is on her way to France to become a nun.' His voice dripped venom. 'No one doubts my loyalty, but you, lady, have harboured a Catholic viper in your bosom.' He strode across the room and wrenched the door open. 'She will have been consorting with other Papists while she was here and you have done nothing to stop her. That makes you a traitor too and we both know the penalty for treason!' He slammed the door behind him.

All colour had drained from Lady Allingbourne's face. 'I did not know,' she sobbed.

Bess went to her and laid her head on Lady Allingbourne's shoulder. Lady Allingbourne caressed Bess's cheek. 'Dearest Bess, you look worn-out. Go to bed and do not worry. I hope he is wrong and Lucy has slipped away to another aunt or cousin. Who could blame her with such a father?'

Bess returned to her bed in deeper misery. By keeping quiet, by helping Lucy, and even by marrying Edmund, she had deceived Lady Allingbourne. Lady Allingbourne trusted her, had done as much for her as a mother, yet Bess had betrayed her. Bess hoped there would be no accounting.

Part 4

28

July 1586

Bess lay in the long twilight staring at the pattern on the tester above her bed. Fears, suppositions and near certainties jostled in her mind, pushing sleep out of reach. Clemence muttered in her sleep and turned over.

Bess sighed and closed her eyes. She had barely begun to doze when she jerked awake. Shuddering bangs echoed through the darkened house. Rough voices shouted, doors slammed, feet thudded on the floor below. Clemence lay beside Bess, wide-eyed, rigid with fear.

Avisa had jumped out of her bed and was pulling on her velvet night gown. 'It's the Spanish come,' she cried, her voice quavering. 'We'll be ravished in our beds.'

'Do not be ridiculous,' Bess snapped. 'We would have had some warning.' She was trying as much to calm her own fear. She slid out of bed and put on her woollen night gown, sliding her feet into her slippers lying on the floor beside the bed.

The door slammed open and a heavy-set man peered in, his features malevolent in the flickering light of the lamp he held, his eyes lingering on the women in their night clothing.

'You lot,' he barked. 'Downstairs. Now.'

Avisa tilted her chin up, held herself erect. 'May we not dress first?'

'Move!' he bellowed. The lamplight shone off the barrel of the dag in his other hand.

Clemence whimpered as they were herded through the door and down the stairs. Ahead, Bess saw a group of maidservants huddled together as they were forced, also at pistol point, into the small parlour next to the hall. Their guards stood at either side of the door.

Lady Allingbourne, ashen-faced, sat in a hard-backed chair in the middle of the parlour. She too was dressed in her night attire.

Alan Fossett stood behind her, a swelling above one eye. Avisa ran straight to Lady Allingbourne and knelt, cowering against her side. Lady Allingbourne put a protective arm around her.

The room was in chaos: hangings pulled from the walls, chairs and stools overturned, coffers and cabinets opened, their contents spilled on the floor as a couple of men rifled through them.

Bess went to Lady Allingbourne. 'Are they robbers?'

Their faces were uncovered; they wore no masks or muffling scarves.

'Quiet! No talking,' roared one of the guards at the door, a wiry man holding two dags.

Lady Allingbourne gave the slightest shake of her head.

'Pursuivants,' Alan hissed. 'The Queen's priest hunters.'

A tall dark man, dressed in the Queen's livery, strode into the room. His heavy-lidded eyes surveyed the room slowly. 'None of you will leave this room until were have scoured out every damned priest hole in this house.'

Lady Allingbourne rose from her seat. 'I can assure you, you will find nothing. I can vouch for each member of my household.'

'Present? And past?'

Lady Allingbourne's hands were gripped tightly together at her waist. 'If I knew that a member of my household was a secret Catholic, I would dismiss that person.'

Bess closed her eyes. Lucy was the reason for the search and Bess, by keeping silent, by helping her, had brought this on Lady Allingbourne.

The clatter and thump of the search continued. At times it sounded as if they were trying to demolish the walls of the house itself. Bess picked up a chair from the floor and placed it beside Lady Allingbourne's. Clemence did the same, warily, the pistols following their slightest movement.

The tall man came again to the door and gave the briefest of bows to Lady Allingbourne. 'I will question each and every member of your household until I have the truth.'

Lady Allingbourne remained in her seat, composed. 'And my husband, have you questioned him as well?'

'Sir Hugh is well known as an honourable man of unwavering loyalty. But women left to their own devices are not so trustworthy.'

'My loyalty is no less unwavering than my husband's.'

'If that is so, Lady Allingbourne,' he gestured at the disorder, 'you will consider this a small price to pay in our search for hidden traitors.'

'You could have done this by daylight,' Lady Allingbourne groaned, 'and come into my house as guests rather than breaking in like brigands.'

'The traitors in your household would have had time to hide the evidence of their perfidy.' There was the hint of a smile beneath his beaked nose. 'In haste something is always left behind.' He bowed to Lady Allingbourne. 'Now, my lady, if you will come with me, there are questions to be answered.'

As Lady Allingbourne followed him, one of the guards stepped forward to take her arm but she stared at him along the length of her nose and he thought better of it. She walked out, her head held high. Those left in the room remained in their places. The guards withdrew, locking the door behind them.

No one had the will to speak. Avisa hunched in Lady Allingbourne's chair, rocking, her eyes tight shut. Alan stood behind her, staring into nothing. Clemence, her head bent, worried at the corner of a thumbnail. Bess wrapped her arms around herself and prayed in silence.

~

One by one they were led away for questioning. Bess's turn came as dawn was touching the horizon. Their inquisitor, Master Rogers, had set himself up in Lady Allingbourne's privy chamber. It was a beautiful room with windows offering a commanding view of the river, fields and orchards of the estate. The walls were hung with tapestry, and embroidered hangings, some the work of Lady Allingbourne and her women. But now the floor was strewn with papers and the contents of upended coffers. A number of the hangings were ripped from their backing cloth.

Rogers seated himself in Lady Allingbourne's padded chair, his dark face almost demonic in the grey dawn light. 'Mistress Stoughton,' he said.

Bess drew her night gown tight, aware of her near nakedness before a complete stranger. She had no sense of private desire in

Roger's intense gaze. Anything he did was with cold calculation, and she feared that more.

'Sit.' He pointed to the stool in front of him.

'So Mistress, what of these?' A string of rosary beads dangled from his fingers. 'Do you know it is treason to possess such baubles?'

Bess nodded.

'And if I were to tell you they were found in your coffer.'

Bess swallowed. 'I would say you were lying.'

'Yet you know what they are.'

Her head swam with panic—he was accusing her of being a Papist. She knew she had done wrong by law in helping Lucy, but she was a friend and she owed her a debt. Had Lucy put them in her coffer? Would that be enough to get her hanged?

'How do you know what they are?' Rogers persisted. He snapped the questions off, barely giving Bess time to answer.

'Where have you seen such items?' 'How long have you been a traitor?' 'How often have you attended the Papist Mass?' 'Give me the name of the Papists, the traitors you know.'

Bess's face contorted, her eyes filled with tears as she tried to answer, afraid she was answering the wrong question, that no matter what she said she would be found guilty.

'I am not a Papist.' 'I am not a traitor.' 'I have never been to a Mass.' 'Lady Allingbourne's is an orderly household. We go every Sunday to the parish church. There are prayers morning and night. In London we go to hear the preachers at St Paul's.'

'I am not a Papist,' she said earnestly. 'I would die to protect the Queen.'

Rogers stopped his browbeating, staring at Bess as if he could see into her soul. When he opened his mouth again, the bluster was gone.

'And Lucy Torrington,' he said quietly. 'where is she now?'

'I do not know.' Bess's voice creaked as she spoke, 'She ran away.'

'And why did she do that?'

'In truth, I do not know.'

'Come, Mistress Stoughton, do not take me for a fool.' He stood and advanced on Bess, pushed his face so close that she could see the pores of his skin, the red threads in the whites of his eyes. 'Why did she disappear?'

Bess tried to keep her breathing even. 'Lucy was afraid her father would force her to marry.'

Rogers frowned. 'A woman with no desire to marry is unnatural.'

'It is not unnatural to wish to have some say in whom we marry.'

'You were her closest friend. You knew what she was planning.'

Bess leant forward. 'My closest, dearest friend is Philippa Compton who has been married six months. We shared our true thoughts, I never did that with Lucy.'

He moved back to his chair. 'Even now the flower of our men is fighting Spain's Catholic forces in the Low Countries.'

'I do know that,' Bess nodded. 'Some men I know well are there, George Raynsford and Edmund Wyard.' It was a balm to say his name aloud.

'Anyone who has the slightest suspicion of Papist plotting and holds her tongue for friendship's sake is siding with their enemy.' He glared at her, contemptuous. 'If Masters Raynsford or Wyard were to die, any person who had given aid to a Papist would have as good as driven the sword into their bodies.'

Bile rose in Bess's throat. She covered her mouth with her hand.

'An honest person would come at them with a sword so they could see her for what she was. Think Mistress Stoughton, think of George Raynsford, think of Edmund Wyard, their sightless eyes staring from their pallid faces, their matted and torn doublets soaked with their life's blood, their brains spattered on the ground from the shattering wound of a Spanish sword. Think Mistress Stoughton that anyone who aids the Papists aids their killers.'

Bess closed her eyes and choked down a sob. Her voice quaked, 'But Lucy would never harm... She only wanted...' Bess stopped, sweat filmed her forehead. Her mouth twitched with a familiar weakness.

'What did she want?' Rogers growled.

Bess sprang from the chair and ran towards the door. It was

blocked by a guard. Rogers was at her side, gripping her arm.

'No!' Bess wailed and bent over, vomiting onto the floor inches from Rogers' fine leather boots. He jumped back from her. Bess remained bent double, heaving, retching long after her stomach was empty. She had not eaten since the night before so all that pooled on the floor was acrid bile. Bess slowly straightened up, her hand clamped over her mouth, tears running freely down her cheeks.

'Sit.' Rogers pointed to the stool, his nostrils narrowed, his lips pursed with distaste. 'Get a maid to clean that up,' he barked at the guard at the door.

He returned to his chair. 'An interesting reaction.'

'I am unwell, sir,' Bess said weakly. She did not want the first person she told to be a priest hunter tormenting her. She wiped her fingers across her lips. She needed to rinse the bitter bile from her mouth but she would not ask, would not give Rogers the pleasure of refusing.

'Now tell me what Lucy Torrington wanted.'

'Who knows what she really wanted?' Bess shrugged. 'I only know what she did not want—to be forced to marry. You might ask her father where she is.'

'I know where she is—in France. She found her way to the Ladies of Syon at Rouen.' His eyes narrowed. 'Did you know she was a Papist, that she was plotting to become a nun?'

Bess knew Rogers would never believe her if she denied all knowledge of Lucy's hopes and dreams. 'I did not know Lucy was a Papist until a few months before she disappeared. It is not a crime unless that person fails to attend Church or plots treason, is it not?' she asked, her brow furrowed with worry.

'Times have changed,' Rogers scowled. 'None are to be trusted now. You had no inkling of her plans to go to France?'

'She did say, once or twice, that she wished never to marry.'

He glowered. 'And you said nothing of this to anyone?'

'What could I say? I did not understand it myself. I assumed she was afraid of the type of man her father would choose for her,' Bess shrugged. 'I never thought...' The light film of sweat glistened on her forehead. In truth, Bess had first thought that Lucy was indulging in girlish fantasies. It was not until those last few weeks that she had realised how seriously Lucy held her dreams.

'To get to France she needed help and I can assure you it did not come from her father.' His nostrils twitched again. 'He has been most helpful in suggesting where we might look for her abettors. Anyone who helped her is nothing but a Papist herself. Do you know what their ends are?'

Bess, her hands clasped tight in her lap, nodded.

'The Papists wish to overthrow this country, to murder our queen, to force us to Romish ways. Do you want the Spanish to rule this country through a puppet like the Queen of Scots? This is no fantasy, Mistress. Have you heard nothing of Ridolfi, of Throckmorton, of Parry, all men who schemed to kill our queen?'

Behind Bess, water slopped on the floor as the guard muttered at a maid to get on with it and clean the mess.

Rogers scowled at them and asked quietly, 'And Anthony Babington, tell me what you know of him?'

Bess stared at him. 'I cannot. I do not know the name.'

Rogers continued, 'You are aware of what has been happening in the Low Countries? Did you hear of the sack of Antwerp last year? You must have heard some years ago of Haarlem, of Zutphen, of Mechelen. Capitulation will not save anyone. In Naarden, when the town surrendered, the ordinary townsfolk were massacred, old men, women, children and, I have even heard, unborn babes ripped from their mothers' wombs.' His dark eyes smouldered with fierce outrage. 'That is the future of our country if these Papists have their way. Anyone who so much as lifted a finger to aid Lucy Torrington in her flight is on the side of these murdering dogs.'

Behind them the door slammed.

Bess was Lucy's friend but she agreed fervently with all he said. She had argued as much with Lucy, though not near as eloquently. She knew that, in her own way, Lucy was a fanatic. If it had been the price of her freedom, would Lucy have willingly joined with such plotters?

'I would never have taken Lucy to be a traitor,' Bess said miserably, hugging her arms tight against her stomach.

'Anyone who supports the Catholic cause is a traitor.' Rogers sat erect in the chair. 'But what of you Elizabeth Stoughton? What of your part in her escape? You even accompanied her on her sally to a man of law.'

'I went to a lawyer with her, out beyond Ludgate, but she left me to sit outside the room. I know nothing of what she arranged there.'

'She went there to raise a loan against the land her grandmother had bequeathed to her. Her father said it was to form part of her dowry,' Rogers almost smiled.

Bess wondered if he disliked Sir Peter.

'He was most upset to find that if he wants it, he must pay out her loan. He regards it as theft from himself although his daughter had turned twenty-one a month before she left and so owned the land.'

'I did not know.' She looked up at him and hoped he saw that she was truthful. 'I love England. I would never knowingly do anything that would help those who would destroy the lives of men like George Raynsford and Edmund Wyard.'

Rogers was not put off. 'But what have you done unknowingly?'

Bess clung to the truth that she was no traitor and that Lucy's quest had been personal. As Rogers continued to interrogate her, she limited her answers to what was asked, offered nothing more, and hoped that, in the end, Rogers merely took her to be a fool.

~

By midday the pursuivants had gone leaving chaos behind them. Not only were hangings ripped and furniture broken but throughout the house, here and there, the walls had been ripped open in the search for secret hiding places, priest holes.

Lady Allingbourne surveyed her damaged rooms and said with anger directed as much at herself as anyone, 'None of this would have happened if we had come home once Philippa's wedding was over.' She turned to Bess. 'We lingered in London far too long. Next year we will be home by Easter.'

Bess thought of Easter next, wondering if, by then, Edmund would have come home to her.

~

It took days to get the house in order, to clean up the mess, arrange carpenters and craftsmen to fix the walls and the furniture. The torn hangings were set aside for the ladies to mend.

One afternoon as Lady Allingbourne and Bess were sitting quietly in the parlour stitching, Lady Allingbourne said, 'I heard you were unwell while our *visitors* were here.'

Bess kept her eyes on her task. 'I was frightened, my lady.'

'We all were, Bess.' She took Bess's hand in hers. 'If there is anything you wish me to help you with, I would be most happy.'

It was clear Lady Allingbourne suspected something, but she would imagine it involved George. Bess doubted she would be happy to take her part against Lady Wyard. It was time Bess let Edmund know.

'If I were to write to George, could you arrange for my letter to be sent to him?'

Lady Allingbourne glanced at her, understanding more than was said.

'He asked me to write sometimes.'

'Of course I will, my dearest, but it may take some time to reach him. I'll send him a few lines too.'

So Bess sat down that night and wrote to Edmund, enclosing her letter in a sealed note to George.

~

Bess wondered how it was ever possible to have secrets. She thought she had successfully hidden her condition, yet Lady Allingbourne suspected, and Alan Fossett too.

Bess was a little apart from Lady Allingbourne, Clemence and Avisa as they collected lavender from the garden. Alan came over to her and held her basket as she continued to snip the lavender stalks. 'If you need me, Bess, I will do anything to help.'

Bess glanced at him, wary. The bruise above his eye was now a yellowy-green. He gave the impression of being so frivolous at times, but beneath it all was a kind and thoughtful man.

He lowered his voice, 'Does the father know?'

Bess glanced quickly over his shoulder; the others were too far away to hear. 'What makes you think?' she whispered.

'I have sharp eyes. If he will not marry you, I am happy to. I know you deserve better than the position of a steward's wife, but it would avoid scandal.'

Bess stretched up and kissed him on the cheek. 'Alan, you are a true friend.' She put her garden shears in the basket and linked her arm through his. 'I will tell you the truth.'

They walked to the far end of the knot garden, the gravel crunching beneath their feet.

'You must promise you will say nothing of this to anyone.'

He twisted his mouth. 'Whatever you ask.'

'I married Edmund Wyard in May.'

Alan opened his mouth, disbelieving. 'That pompous…'

'He is nothing like that once you know him.' Bess's eyes softened with memory. 'He is so much more wonderful than you could ever imagine.'

'He must be to have captured your heart,' Alan said grudgingly as he put down the basket and took both her hands. 'But what are we to do with you? His mother is a ferocious old beast, no wonder you are saying nothing. Do you know when Wyard will return?'

Bess's lashes glistened in the sunlight. 'No, but I have written to him to tell him of the child.'

'Once he knows, I am sure he will come.'

Bess knew it was not so easy. Edmund was a man of duty and would not come home until he was satisfied that duty had been fulfilled. She supposed she would have to face Lady Wyard alone. But she would wait until she heard from Edmund and be guided by him. If he were here, she would be the happiest woman in the world.

29

22 September 1586

There was no hint of dawn. The air was chilled and the fog so thick that Edmund could barely see five yards ahead. He sat on his horse among Sir John Norris's handpicked cavalry near the Warnsfeld church about a mile from Zutphen.

Edmund was well armed for battle in casque and cuirass, vambraces strapped to his forearms, greaves and cuisses on shin and thigh. Others favoured less armour having abandoned their cuisses at least. Edmund was taking no chances in their skirmishes this time. For the first time in his life he looked beyond the end of the battle; he wanted to live, he had someone to live for—even more so now.

When George had brought him the letter yesterday he had not opened it immediately but had made his way to the edge of the camp on the rise outside the village of Warnsfeld. After reading the letter, he had stared away from the trenches. The countryside surrounding Zutphen stretched across a plain. Long rows of poplars grew at the roadsides, windmills were dotted here and there, as well as farmhouses with orchards and gardens. With the depredations of battle and occupation smoothed away by distance, it appeared to be good farming land. He thought of Bucklings. Bess should be there now, not worrying at Allingbourne Hall, fearful of what his mother would do. His child should be born at Bucklings. His child. He was to be a father. Edmund beamed, his happiness dispelling the unease he had about the planned ambush tomorrow. He would do his duty here then go home, be with Bess, raise his children, live his allotted span.

Edmund had turned back towards the camp and scowled. The sooner they had done what they had come for the better, but he feared this was a campaign that would drag on. There seemed no order. There were not enough men and they were poorly provisioned. Lord Leicester was not decisive enough, more concerned with display and honours. The nobility among them were divided and quarrelsome, feuding over perceived insults. Their Dutch allies were often slighted and not shown adequate respect. Despite the discord, the petty defeats and retreats, there were individual acts of courage, behaviour to make a man proud to be English. Perhaps, Edmund thought, he had had his fill of soldiering. As he reached the centre of the camp, George had stridden up and thrown his arm across his shoulder.

'That scowl hides nothing, Ned. I see beneath it a happy man.'

Edmund had broken into a lopsided grin, 'I'm to be a father.'

'Congratulations.' George had slapped him on the back. 'I will have to double my watch on you. If anything happens, Bessie will deal with me more harshly than any Spaniard.'

~

Beyond the soft snorting and blowing of their own horses, they could hear the faint creaking of wagon wheels and the tramp of soldiers' feet. The supply train was approaching with its load of wheat and barley, butter, cheese, and beef sent by the Spanish commander, the Duke of Alva, to relieve the English siege of Zutphen. The English hoped to repeat their earlier success at Antwerp, so that by capturing the supply convoy they would ultimately gain Zutphen. Once they had Zutphen, with Deventer and Kampen in the hands of their allies, the United Provinces, they would control the Ijssel River. It gave them a large foothold and hope of real victory against the Spanish.

Apart from the two hundred cavalrymen waiting with Sir John Norris, three hundred pikemen followed with Sir William Stanley. A much larger group of infantry was held in reserve. Norris and Stanley, foremost among those on the English side who had been at each other's throats, had put aside their differences and even sworn friendship, vowing to die side by side in her Majesty's cause.

No scouts had been sent out so the only warning the English had was the increasing rumble of the approaching supply train. The English commanders had crossed the river from their camp and made their way through the mist to join the rest: Lords Essex, Willoughby and Audley; Sir Philip Sidney, Sir William Russell and Sir William Pelham, who had arrived a month after Edmund, now carrying wounds from Doesberg where he had stepped between Lord Leicester and an assassin. Even Lord North, wounded with a musket shot to the leg, was riding with one boot off.

As dawn broke, the fog lifted suddenly to show the long train of wagons moving slowly towards Zutphen, protected by more than four thousand Spanish troops—cavalry and mounted arquebus men, pikemen and musketeers. They had even had time to throw up their own entrenchments.

The Earl of Essex roared, 'Follow me, good fellows, for the honour of England and of England's Queen!' as he raced towards the enemy's cavalry, splintering his lance on the lead Spanish horseman, toppling both horse and man.

The waiting over, exhilarated, Edmund spurred his horse forward with the rest, charging through the Spanish cavalry, turning aside, bowling over those in his way until his lance too shattered against a Spaniard's chest, propelling the man from his horse. His foot caught in his stirrup, the cavalryman was dragged beneath the hooves of his rearing horse and trampled by those struggling around him.

They pushed the Spaniards back over their own line of pikemen, only wheeling back in the face of a volley of Spanish musket fire. But the English reformed and charged again. At times the English force seemed to be swallowed by the enemy. They fought with a fury of splintered lances and clashing swords; smashed bone and spurting, seeping blood; reeking acrid smoke and blasting muskets; screaming, rearing, thundering horses and shouting, roaring men.

The Spanish horsemen faltered and broke before the English and fell back to their musketeers. In the rain of musket fire George Raynsford's horse was shot from under him. He laid about him with his curtal-axe slashing, wounding any enemy within his reach, and by sheer brute strength forced his way across the field. When Edmund caught sight of him, he had found himself another horse and was plunging towards the Spanish lines. A pikeman came at him but George, despite his bulk, nimbly swerved out of his way. He hacked down, blood spurting from the pikeman's neck as he crumpled to the ground. As George straightened up, a musketeer fired upward from near the trenches and caught him full in the face, his casque blown off with the force in a welter of blood and flesh. Time slowed as he turned aside and Edmund caught sight of the ravaged face as George slumped backwards and fell from his horse. Blind fury raged through Edmund. He charged forward, slashing indiscriminately, bearing down on the musketeer as he attempted to reload. The man raised his musket but before he could fire, Edmund chopped him down, hacking into him, almost decapitating him.

A third time they charged, thundering toward the enemy ranks. Edmund was reckless of danger, grimly satisfied each time a Spaniard collapsed as he hacked his sword through flesh, grinding it against splintering bone. Pain seared up Edmund's back as he wheeled his horse. He held himself rigid and forced his horse on but the edges of his world darkened. As he slowly toppled from his horse, he wondered why it was said that in his last moments a man saw his whole life pass before his eyes. All he saw was the face of his wife, Bess—but then, she was his life.

~

The battle lasted ninety minutes. The teamsters controlling the wagons had fled with the first assault and the soldiers, both English and Spanish, had struggled to take control of the horses. The wagons, under protection of Spanish troops sent out from Zutphen, had forced their way slowly nearer the town while the battle raged. In the end the English were forced to fall back when the Spanish infantry came up and opened fire upon them. That day little except enduring honour was gained by the English.

~

Robert Hayes, grim faced, blood spattered, marched through the English camp. The relief was palpable. Tales of valour were already being exchanged and embellished as wine-skins were passed from man to man. Hayes had no heart to join them. Twelve cavalry dead, they said, twenty-two foot soldiers, and he had seen each one, even the unmistakable body of George Raynsford, his ruined face modestly covered. Hayes knew what must be done. He would watch and wait. When he was sure the field was clear, he would go out and search. Edmund Wyard would not lie unrecognised in a foreign grave.

30

October 1586

Bess stared up at the few high clouds scudding across the washed blue sky. After a week of overcast days, today was a pleasant surprise. A mild breeze rustled through the trees surrounding the formal garden of Allingbourne Hall, their foliage bright with autumn colours. She watched a leaf tremble in the air and slowly drift to earth as she wondered where Edmund was, whether he had received her letter, how soon she would hear from him. The ache of her longing for him was now a constant part of her existence.

Behind her she heard Lady Allingbourne's patient attempts to get Avisa to unpick the black work she was embroidering on a linen shirt. Lady Allingbourne was sitting on a stone bench beside Avisa, basking in the sunshine. An unseen skylark broke into burbling song as it rose into the air. Bess closed her eyes, her lips parted in a sigh of wonder at the butterfly-like fluttering within her. She placed her hand at her waist, smiling to herself. The child had quickened.

Bess bent over an open rose to breathe in the scent but half the petals fluttered down as she touched the plant. She pinched off the spent bloom, dropping it to the ground, and walked back along the gravel path, aware that Lady Allingbourne was watching her.

Avisa looked up. 'Help me Bess,' she wailed, 'I'll never learn to do this properly.'

Bess took the shirt from Avisa. 'You need to sew slowly, and watch very carefully, so that your needle enters exactly the place it came out.' She sewed a few careful stitches and handed it back to Avisa.

'I hated it when my mother tried to teach me and I am no better now,' Avisa pouted. 'When I am married, I will pay someone to do the black work for me.'

Bess avoided Lady Allingbourne's eye and bit her lip, fighting a laugh.

'We'll leave for Berkshire in a fortnight for Philippa's lying in,' Lady Allingbourne said over Avisa's bowed head, 'that will give us time to travel at a leisurely pace.'

Avisa stopped her sewing. 'I wish I could come too.'

'You know why you cannot come,' Lady Allingbourne was stern. 'You are a young maid and could have no proper role there.'

Avisa's lip quivered as she stabbed her needle into the cloth.

Thinking it would have to be unpicked again, Bess said, 'Put that away for now. We will try again tomorrow.'

Avisa gratefully bundled the shirt into her basket and almost skipped towards the house with it.

As Lady Allingbourne watched her go, she said, 'I had a letter from Margaret Wyard yesterday. She has been in London for the last two months. I gather she had a falling-out with her good-daughter and to Margaret's surprise John sided with his wife.' Lady Allingbourne gave an uncharacteristically malicious laugh. 'Margaret seems to forget that even docile girls who marry young grow up and gather strength and ideas of their own.'

'Lady Wyard is at their London house?' Bess hated to think of Lady Wyard staying where she and Edmund had been together, walking where they had walked, sitting where they had sat.

'Ay, she has no liking for her dower estate. I suppose she could have gone to Bucklings Hall,' she shrugged, 'but she has an understandable aversion to the place. She is still doing her best to find Edmund a wife.'

Bess scowled, 'But he is already married.'

'It seems Sir Peter was the only one Edmund told. I have not heard of it from anyone else and Margaret clearly knows nothing of it.'

'We will know the truth when Edmund returns.' Bess struggled to keep the longing from her voice.

'She will be more than annoyed if he is married. She already has another girl in mind, the daughter of a London goldsmith.' Lady Allingbourne stopped at the sight of a dust-covered messenger striding along the path towards them.

He bowed and said, breathless, 'Lady, I bring dire news from your brother.'

Lady Allingbourne sat motionless, not daring to breathe.

'Your nephew, Master George Raynsford, was killed in battle in the Low Countries near three weeks ago.'

She strangled a sob.

Bess grasped Lady Allingbourne's hand, battling her own tears. 'What happened?'

'It was at a place called Zutphen. Our men fought most valiantly, a force of not much more than five hundred men against over four thousand Spanish,' the messenger said proudly. 'The casualties on the English side were few but thirteen of our cavalry and twenty-two foot soldiers were killed. The enemy lost more than two hundred men.'

'George,' Bess sighed. He was a man so full of life and good humour, she could not imagine a world that did not contain him somewhere.

'Sir Philip Sidney, Lord Leicester's nephew, has taken a wound in the leg,' the messenger continued. 'He is recovering at Arnhem.' He frowned. 'Master Wyard was killed too.'

Bess gasped, the breath knocked out of her.

'Master Raynsford was the first to die and it is said Master Wyard more than avenged his death before being struck down himself.'

Bess walked towards the house, away from Lady Allingbourne and the messenger, her cheeks wet. If Edmund was dead, she did not want to live. But she held Edmund's final gift within her—a newly quickened life.

~

Bess stared out at the rain lashing the garden of the Wyards' London house. She doubted the sun could ever shine there now that Edmund would not return. A month had passed since his death and, for most of that time, she had not sensed that he was gone. Every bright memory of that month haunted her.

Behind her, the portrait of Lady Wyard glared out from the parlour wall. Bess had learnt to ignore it on her last stay but now, with the lady herself present in the house, it was not possible.

'Bess, come sit by the fire,' Lady Allingbourne called to her.

Bess went to the hearth and stretched her icy fingers towards the warmth.

Lady Allingbourne rose and placed her hands on Bess's shoulders. 'Sit down,' she said. 'It is time for us to talk.'

Bess remained standing. 'I need to lie down. My head pains me.'

'Bess,' Lady Allingbourne's brow was furrowed, 'we must…'

Bess's desolate grey eyes gazed directly into Lady Allingbourne's. 'Not now,' she said quietly, 'but once we have returned from Philippa's lying in.'

Lady Allingbourne turned back to the fire and frowned into the dancing flames.

~

As Bess climbed the stairs to their bedchamber, the bedchamber she had shared with Edmund, she made a decision that could no longer be delayed. She had seen the way Lady Wyard's eyes had strayed to her waist when they had arrived. Despite the tight lacing she was becoming stout. Another month and she would need to wear a placket if her clothes were to fit decently. Lady Allingbourne more than suspected but thought George was the father. If he had been, she would have made sure Bess and the child were cared for. But this was Edmund's child and deserved all that was due to it. Lady Wyard might despise Bess but, surely, she would welcome her dead son's child.

Lady Wyard never acknowledged Bess's presence unless forced to do so. Bess supposed it could be the deadening weight of grief. She too struggled to do what was required of her. But Bess had not seen Lady Wyard shed a single tear, not even when they had arrived, diverting from their planned journey to Philippa's. Lady Allingbourne had thrown her arms around Lady Wyard and wept. Lady Wyard had stood rigid, looking not as if she were controlling her sorrow, rather that she felt none. But who can judge what another feels?

~

Later, when Bess came to think of it, it seemed Lady Wyard made it easy for her. They had been sitting in the parlour, the irrepressibly friendly Cicely Ramage, one of Lady Wyard's women, playing the virginal while the others sewed. Bess was embroidering delicate flowers around the hem of a small gown she was making for Philippa's baby.

Lady Wyard folded away her embroidery and rose from her seat. 'Alas, Florence, I must leave you as I have household matters to attend in my closet which will not wait despite the pleasure of guests.'

Hester Shawe, her waiting woman, as humourless as her mistress, started to rise but Lady Wyard shook her head.

Not wanting to appear to be chasing Lady Wyard, Bess finished a row of split stitch.

'If you will excuse me, my lady.' She put her sewing down and stood.

Lady Allingbourne nodded and continued with her own sewing.

~

Bess waited in the chamber she shared with Lady Allingbourne, summoning the courage she needed to face Edmund's mother. She straightened her shoulders and, with trembling fingers, drew out from her bodice the pouch where she kept his ring. She slipped the ring on her finger, savouring the weight of it and the thought that it had encircled his finger too. He had worn it for so many years, something of him must remain in it.

Outside the door of Lady Wyard's closet which adjoined the main bedchamber, Bess swallowed a large breath and knocked. There was silence. Perhaps Lady Wyard was not there and she would have to steel herself again some other time.

As she stepped away from the door, an imperious voice called, 'You may enter.'

Lady Wyard was sitting at a table beneath the window, her clasped hands resting on the polished wood. In the dull afternoon light her skin was unlined, her flesh so spare that, at a distance, she was as flawless as a young woman. Closer, her white hair and the wrinkles on her face and neck gave her age away, but it was clear she had been a beauty in her youth. Her dress, rich and elegant, was always immaculate, not a hair, not a thread out of place.

Bess's instinct was to run from the room but she owed it to her child to stay.

Lady Wyard turned slowly in her chair and stared down her nose at Bess.

Bess curtsied to her.

Lady Wyard continued to stare in silence.

'Lady Wyard, I would speak with you, if I may,' Bess said, a slight tremor in her voice.

'It would appear that is exactly what you are doing.'

There were several chairs and stools arranged around the room but Bess did not sit; she doubted Lady Wyard would invite her to. She stepped closer and blurted out, 'My lady, before your son Edmund left for the Low Countries, he and I were wed.'

'Were you indeed? I suppose you will now tell me you are with child.'

'I am.'

Lady Wyard gave a nasty smile. 'How convenient for you my son is dead and cannot deny your claims.'

'We were wed last May,' Bess's voice caught, 'by licence. There was a clergyman and witnesses.'

'But, alas, you cannot remember the names of these witnesses.'

'Of course I remember their names.' Bess struggled to keep her voice even. 'George Raynsford and Lucy Torrington. Edmund's man, Hayes, was also there.'

'How convenient! George Raynsford is dead, most likely Hayes as well, and Lucy Torrington has disappeared. And do you know the clergyman's name?'

Bess blinked. Edmund had introduced him but she had made no effort to remember. 'No, I do not but Edmund's man of law would know. He was present too. We signed contracts which he took away with him.'

Lady Wyard sat up straighter.

'I cannot recall his name but I am certain he is Edmund's usual man of law.' Bess realised, in that moment, how weak her story sounded.

Lady Wyard's cold, hard eyes did not leave Bess's face. 'This is a cruel fiction designed to take advantage of my son's death.'

'I would never do that.' Tears welled in Bess's eyes. 'I loved Edmund. The wedding took place in this house. You need only ask the servants—Edmund told them I was his wife.'

Bess stood, uncomfortable, under Lady Wyard's unblinking stare. When she did speak, there was such contempt in her voice that Bess wished she had never come to her.

'You have invented this fanciful tale to cover your shame at the expense of my son's good name. I am not tricked so easily. I suggest you take yourself to the country and hide there.'

Bess drew a ragged breath, 'Do you not care what becomes of your grandchild?'

'My grandchild?' She shrugged, 'I suppose it may be a by-blow of Edmund's—he always did have a taste for low women.' She paused, a malicious twist to her mouth. 'Ay, there were whispers on my return here that Edmund had kept a whore in this house before he left for the Low Countries.'

Anger surged through Bess. 'I am neither a whore nor am I low born. My mother could trace her family's lineage to a knight who came to England with the Conqueror.'

'Lineage can easily be forged.'

'That is true.' The contempt in Bess's face equalled Lady Wyard's. 'We all know of mere shopkeepers come into wealth who have paid for an invented pedigree and within a generation or two their sons *and daughters* conduct themselves as if they stand higher than the true nobility.'

Lady Wyard's nostrils narrowed. 'You will not repeat your slanders against my son or you will feel the weight of my wrath.'

'What will you do? Have my forehead carved with a W?'

Lady Wyard hissed between her teeth.

'I am your son's wife.' Bess spoke each word with the force of truth.

'You have no proof.'

'Not in my hand. A few judicious questions and I will find his lawyer. When I have the contracts he holds, I will take them to Edmund's brother John, the head of your family. I will show him that I wear his brother's ring.'

Lady Wyard's eyes went to Bess's fingers. 'Show me.'

Bess held out her hand.

'Come nearer that I may see it properly.'

Bess stepped closer to Lady Wyard.

Lady Wyard gripped her hand, staring intently at the stone and the pattern of the band. Her mouth set in a vicious line, her grip tightened and she twisted the ring from Bess's finger. Had it been tighter she would have pulled the finger out of joint.

Bess held her breath as Lady Wyard held it up, turning it in her fingers. 'It is my son's ring.' Her face softened.

Bess exhaled slowly.

Lady Wyard slipped the ring onto her own finger. 'Now hear me, Elizabeth Stoughton, my son said this ring was stolen from him. I have no doubt you took it from him when you were whoring with him.'

If that were true, everything that has passed between them was a lie. Bess felt as if the ground had fallen away beneath her. 'When did he tell you it was stolen?' Her voice was little more than a whisper.

Triumph blazed in Lady Wyard's face. 'I had a letter from him, written the day before he died. He was bereft at the loss of the ring. He valued it highly—it was given to him by his father. He would never have given it away.'

'Unless,' Bess answered, willing herself to believe her own words, 'he was giving it to someone he loved more deeply than he had ever loved before.'

'Utter nonsense, girl,' Lady Wyard spluttered. 'You have listened to too many romantic tales.'

'May I see the letter?' Bess asked. She needed to see the words in Edmund's own hand before she would accept the truth of Lady Wyard's claim.

'No, you may not. I have to prove nothing to you.' She leant back against her chair and stared at Bess, calculation in her eyes. 'I have pity for you though. I will say nothing to Lady Allingbourne, even though as a friend I should. I am satisfied to have my son's ring. I will leave you to cover your shame as best you can, provided you cease plotting against the memory of my son. Now go.'

Bess did not curtsey but turned her back on Lady Wyard and walked from the room. She stopped outside the door feeling the baby's trembling movements. Bess laid her hand against her waist and whispered, 'Oh child, what are we to do?'

In her bedchamber, Bess climbed onto the bed and crawled under the coverlet. She pulled her feet up, curling into herself and wept into the pillow. Later, when she was warmer and was certain she could bear company again, Bess washed her face and went down to join Lady Allingbourne, her smile forced, her eyes glittering as she pretended a brittle cheerfulness.

31

November 1586

Bess woke from a dreamless sleep. For the first time since she had heard of Edmund's death, her mind was clear. Tomorrow she would go as planned with Lady Allingbourne to Philippa's lying-in. She would confide in Philippa and Anthony; Anthony would know who Edmund's man of law was. Then she would write to the lawyer and ask him to contact Edmund's brother. She was certain John Wyard would honour Edmund's wishes.

As Bess forced herself out of bed, she wondered why she had not thought to do this sooner. The answer was in the desolate longing that consumed her and made even the simplest action an act of will. The only light in this dark world was their child.

Bess had been spared facing Lady Wyard the previous evening. She had left the house attended by a single footman soon after Bess's interview and had not returned in time for supper. Bess was sure she would not be so blessed today.

~

Margaret Wyard sat with her guests in the parlour. Florence Allingbourne had, at last, stopped her talk of her nephew and Edmund. How could their souls rest with this constant calling up of their memories?

Bess Stoughton was sitting on the other side of the room, her head bent, pretending to concentrate on her sewing. Dame Margaret wondered what scheme the deceitful creature was hatching now that her plot to use Edmund's death to hide her shame had failed.

Dame Margaret sewed a few more careful stitches and stopped, the needle still in her hand. Was it possible Edmund had used the ruse Stoughton claimed, the fanciful secret marriage? It was unlike what Dame Margaret knew of him. She studied Bess through narrowed eyes. Would he have given her the ring? What had she said? He might give it to *someone he loved more deeply than he had ever loved before.* That *was* like Edmund. She tightened her lips. Edmund was fool enough to have married the impudent piece. She needed to visit Edmund's man of law and see if Stoughton was telling the truth. If Edmund had foolishly married her, she would have dower rights over Bucklings. There was poetry in that—a strumpet living off property bought for another strumpet. He might even have left all his property to her. No. Dame Margaret would not permit her family's property to be thrown away on a scheming whore and her spawn. Her grandchild indeed!

'Margaret!' Lady Allingbourne raised her voice.

Dame Margaret jerked, startled out of her reverie. 'Forgive me, Florence, I was thinking of Edmund.'

Tears welled in Lady Allingbourne's eyes. 'It is hard at times.' She grasped Dame Margaret's hand. 'He and George were such friends. In those last few weeks...' she choked back a sob. 'We miss them both.'

Dame Margaret glanced at Bess who was sitting with her head bowed, her sewing crumpled in her hands. Cicely Ramage leant across and squeezed Bess's hand. Dame Margaret glared at Ramage and determined to deal with her later.

'They are gone and we must bear it,' Dame Margaret spoke as if displays of grief were a weakness.

'Oh Margaret,' Lady Allingbourne moaned. 'We cannot forget them. They...'

'I think I mentioned to you that I visited Alice Cathcart, the lace-maker, yesterday,' Dame Margaret spoke over her. 'She is making me two cartwheel ruffs. I took off my carcanet for her to measure me and left it behind. I am surprised she has not sent it back.' She paused and said slowly, 'Florence, would you permit your woman, Stoughton, to collect it for me. Cathcart lives two streets from here. I would send a footboy but it is very valuable.'

'Of course.' Lady Allingbourne nodded to Bess.

~

As Bess and the Wyards' footman stepped out into the street, he was called back in to receive further instruction from Lady Wyard. Not wanting to face the lady again, Bess slowly paced in front of the house, wondering if this errand was a test of some sort. If Lady Wyard expected she would steal the carcanet, she would be sorely disappointed.

Bess turned to find two hard-faced men close behind her.

'Elizabeth Stoughton?' the taller of the two barked.

'Yes,' Bess answered, instantly wary. She resisted the urge to run back into the house.

He moved even closer, his dark soulless eyes staring into hers. 'You will come with us. We have a warrant for your arrest.'

Bess backed away from him. 'For my arrest?' She almost laughed with the improbability of it. 'Show me this warrant,' she said with an authority she did not feel.

The other man, broken nosed and pugnacious, fumbled in his pouch and pulled out a piece of parchment. He unfolded it and shook it towards Bess.

She searched it quickly—her name was there and it was signed and sealed. 'There must be a mistake.'

'No mistake,' the shorter one said as he grabbed her arm. Before Bess could react, the taller man had her other arm and the pair had bundled her around the corner into the back of a covered wagon. She was thrown onto the floor and one held her as the other tried to tie her up.

'Cease your threshing girl,' the short man snarled.

Bess started screaming. There were people everywhere in the street, someone would help.

The shorter man slapped her hard across the face and shoved a gag into her mouth as the other bound her.

The taller man jumped from the wagon, calling to the driver. The wagon rumbled off.

Shuddering with muffled sobs, Bess struggled upright and slumped against the wagon side. As her eyes adjusted to the gloom, she noticed her remaining captor had settled himself into a corner of the wagon on a pile of sacks and, once he was satisfied she was resigned to her fate, had closed his eyes.

The wagon rattled over cobblestones. Outside Bess could still hear the sounds of the city—the cries of apprentices and pedlars, the scream of gulls, the general hubbub. Her mind raced with possibilities. If what they had shown her was a true warrant, there would be an official of some sort at the end—a gentleman, no mere ruffian, someone who would see this was a mistake. She had not read the warrant other than to see her name, and they had not told her the charges against her. Her stomach churned at the thought that Lucy had been involved with the dreadful plots on behalf of the Queen of Scots. Surely, they would have come for her sooner. If not Lucy, then Lady Wyard? But if she wanted to be rid of Bess, a knife between the ribs in a crowded street would be easier and more permanent. Bess's heart lurched at the thought that it might still come to that.

Her guard appeared to be asleep. Bess wondered if she could wriggle to the end of the wagon and fling herself out. But would anyone in the street help her? Her captors would be on her before she could get away. And the baby could be hurt. Bess shivered and drew her knees up.

~

The wagon shuddered to a halt.

The taller guard appeared at the end of the wagon and together with the man who had travelled with her, they manhandled Bess out into the open. Her legs gave way but she was hauled upright and braced herself unsteadily against the wagon as her feet were untied.

The sky was so overcast it seemed night was setting in early. The bulk of Westminster Abbey towered over them as Bess, gagged and hands still bound, was led across the yard of a smaller church to a private house. A light drizzle settled on everything.

She was propelled through a low doorway and down steps into a small cellar. Thick wooden doors with metal grilles were set into two of the walls. The room was bare except for a table and two chairs, one either side of the table.

The taller guard removed her gag. 'Do not bother screaming, my darling.' He ran a broken-nailed finger across Bess's cheek. 'No one will care, even if they hear you.'

The other laughed unpleasantly and untied her wrists. 'And no hitting out either or we will be forced to bring you to your senses,' he said with hopeful menace.

They pushed Bess through the door at the end of the room. She slipped on the shallow steps and fell hard on the slimy floor.

The heavy door banged shut, the humourless laughter of the guards fading as they sauntered away.

Bess rubbed her knee through the cloth of her gown. She slowly pulled herself up and peered through the dark. Where the other room had been almost austere, this one was no better than a sink-hole. Grey light trickled through a small grate near the tall ceiling where the wind whistled in and rain seeped down the slimy wall. The floor was damp and slippery, a mound of sodden straw piled behind the door. In a deluge, Bess had no doubt, the room would flood. The grille in the door would give a good view of a pair of manacles that hung loose from high on the wall. Bess's breath caught. Anyone locked into them would hang several feet off the floor.

Pulling her cloak tight for warmth, Bess edged carefully around the room to the driest corner, opposite the manacles, and eased herself onto the floor.

She placed her hand protectively on her belly in answer to her child's fluttering movements. Perhaps he felt her fear. 'Oh, little one,' Bess whispered, 'what has happened to us?' A tear rolled down her cheek as she remembered the time when this child had come into being—the sun had shone, Edmund was alive and the world had been filled with hope. She dashed the tear away with the back of her hand.

If she had committed a crime, Bess knew she should be brought before a justice and charged. She could not be kept here forever to die locked away. Lady Allingbourne would worry when she did not return and would search for her. People like Bess did not disappear.

~

Exhausted, Bess managed to doze fitfully through the endless night. By the time the gloom of the cellar lightened, Bess was stiff and cold. Her teeth chattered and she was hungry and thirsty. She eased herself up and stretched her aching muscles. The baby pushed gently at her.

'Good morning, little one,' Bess said aloud, needing to hear her own voice.

The sound of horses and shouted greetings carried from the courtyard. A door slammed at a distance. The aroma of baking bread drifted on the air.

Bess's mouth watered and her stomach grumbled; she had

eaten and drunk nothing since dinner yesterday. Was she to be left to starve? But were not women with child kept alive until, at least, the baby was born? She crossed her arms and hugged herself tight. She must find a way to contact Edmund's brother. Even if she could not be saved, she must ensure that Edmund's child was cared for after she was gone.

Bess twitched with fright as the door was flung open and the taller man from yesterday peered in. Unwilling to soil his boots, he stood on the uppermost step and jerked his head, 'You! Out here!'

The light from a lantern at one end of the table shone off the snowy ruffs and glittered on the doublet buttons of a gentleman seated at the table.

Relief washed through Bess at the sight of him. He was clearly a man of some standing. He would see her arrest was a mistake. Bess drew herself up and walked towards him.

'Sit,' he ordered.

Bess pulled her cloak tight and sat in the chair opposite him.

A jug and a platter with cheese and newly baked bread were set on the table, a knife and mug beside them. He poured himself a large measure from the jug. His Adam's apple bobbed as he swallowed. He put his mug down and wiped the back of his hand across his mouth. His clothes were of a better cut than his manners.

He sat forward, resting his elbows on the table, his hands linked together as if in prayer. 'Mistress Stoughton.'

There was a quality to his smooth voice that made Bess's flesh creep.

'I am Mistress Wyard.'

He gave a nasty broken-toothed smile, 'So you claim.'

Bess stared at him. If he knew that, Lady Wyard was behind it all. 'I do not have the honour of your name, sir.'

'Master Richard Topcliffe.' He rose and sketched a courtly bow, then sat again and said conversationally, 'Do you know why you have been brought here?'

'Because Lady Wyard wants to be rid of me.'

'Lady Wyard is the least of your worries,' he smirked, his pale eyes unnerving. 'There is nothing in your life you would wish to remain in the shadows? Nothing you have done that would bring upon you the severest punishment?'

'Nothing,' Bess swallowed, her mouth dry.

He broke off a piece of bread and chewed slowly. 'I know you for a liar then.' He continued to chew as he spoke. 'Every word you say will be judged in that light.'

He speared a lump of cheese with his knife and chewed slowly, savouring it. Bess was spellbound by the thought of food and the unedifying spectacle of Topcliffe's open-mouthed mastication.

'Do you deny you are a Papist?'

Bess laughed with relief. It was so far from the truth, so easily disproved. She had nothing to fear.

'You find your situation amusing?'

'Not at all, sir, but it is laughable that anyone would suggest such a thing.'

He watched her closely. 'You were a bosom friend of that Romish slut, Lucy Torrington.'

'Lucy was no slut,' Bess said, colour rising in her cheeks. 'I have never known a more modest girl.' There was something in Topcliffe's staring eyes that reminded her of the brigand by the Thames. 'I..., I...,' she stammered, 'I met her for the first time two years ago when she came to live at Allingbourne Hall.'

'Yet in that time you became so close that you were willing to help her to escape to the Papist stew at Rouen. No one but someone of the same vile creed would help a *modest* girl do that.'

'I am not a Papist,' Bess enunciated each word separately.

'So you say. Yet you stayed at her Aunt's house at St Giles—a house riddled with priest holes. You accompanied her to her man of law, helped her as good as sell her father's property. Did you also help her sew the gold coins into her garments?'

Bess frowned. 'I did not know she did that.'

'Indeed,' he snorted, 'she was a brazen creature.'

'When I first met her, I thought her a mouse, easily imposed upon.'

'Easily led astray.' He glared at Bess. 'It will go better with you if you give us the names of all those you have had dealings with.'

'I know no names. I am not a Papist.'

Topcliffe got up, moved around the table and perched on its edge. He leant forward and lifted Bess's face to examine it better.

'It would be a waste to have you locked away in a convent, though no doubt the priests would welcome the addition to their leaping house.'

'I am not a Papist,' Bess said through gritted teeth. 'I never have been and never, ever will be. The idea of entering a convent is abhorrent to me.'

Topcliffe folded his arms across his chest and continued to stare at her. He stood abruptly, as if he had come to a decision and moved back to the other side of the table. 'You will willingly give me the name of every Papist you have ever met by the time I have finished with you,' he said, expressionless.

He snapped his fingers and one of his lackeys appeared from the shadows, grabbed the lantern and followed his master from the room. As soon as the key rasped in the lock, Bess sprang up to the table. She scrabbled at the bread and cheese left on the platter, crushing as much as she could into her mouth, fearful they would return and take it away. It was more delightful than any banquet dish she had ever tasted. As the minutes passed, she slowed her chewing and took a long slow draught of the small beer.

As she ate, Bess noticed, through the gloom, a narrow pallet in the corner of the cellar. When she had finished her meal, she went and kicked at it gingerly. No creature she could see scuttled out. She would not think of the insects that might be living there. There were no blankets but she had her cloak. With the door to the damp cell closed, the room was not unbearably cold. Bess curled up on the pallet, her cloak pulled tight, and immediately fell into a deep sleep.

~

When Bess woke, she had no idea of the time of day. Intermittent noise carried from the yard outside so she assumed it was still daytime. The platter and jug had been cleared away while she slept and a jug of small beer and a dish of pottage left in their place. She hungrily ate the tepid tasteless mess, relieved that they did not mean to starve her. The baby stirred and that gave Bess comfort. She loosened the lacings on her gown—she would not hide her condition any longer.

~

Bess was left alone for the rest of the day. As she paced the room, trying to keep from panic, she noticed the other door and tried the latch. It would not budge. She stood on tiptoes to see through the grille—the room was dark but she could make out what seemed to be a large frame set in the middle of the room. Bess shuddered, the hair on the back of her neck rising. Suddenly afraid, she stepped back quickly, no longer wanting to see inside.

Panic bubbled up again. She clamped her hands over her mouth against the scream that was building in her. They had said no one could hear. And who would even care if they thought she was a Papist. She tried to slow her ragged breathing, her hands now spread across her belly as the baby fluttered frantically.

'Do not be afraid, little one,' Bess said aloud. 'I will find a way out for you at least. And while we are waiting, I will tell you a story.' She choked back a sob. 'One day, just on dusk, as I was riding to Allingbourne Hall, I met a man…'

32

The following morning Topcliffe barged into the cellar, her two abductors clattering down the steps moments after him. They positioned themselves, smirking, one each side of the locked door Bess had peered into yesterday.

Topcliffe stalked over to Bess, grabbed her by the arm and dragged her towards the cell she had first been locked in. He flung the door open, wrinkling his nose at the stink. As Bess had been given no pail to relieve herself into, she had used the squalid cell as a privy. There was no doubt many had before her.

He sneered as he looked her up and down, 'A little confinement and women turn into sluts.'

Bess held herself erect. 'I am dressed modestly but, as you are aware, at present I do not have the means to keep myself as I would wish.'

He wrenched her arm and pointed to the manacles hanging from the wall. 'Tell me what you know or I will hang you in the air and have no pity on you.'

'I have told you, I know nothing of Papists,' her voice trembled.

He pulled her away from the door and forced her against the wall.

'I will have the truth from you. By the time I am finished with you, you will welcome death like a lover, you will cry out for him but he will be tantalisingly beyond your reach. I can stretch out the moment of death exquisitely.' Tugging at her doublet, he pulled it open and sent several buttons bouncing across the floor. He forced his hand down her bodice and grasped her breast. 'I know men and women intimately. I know where to touch, where to leave off touching.' He pinched her viciously and withdrew his hand, leering as Bess whimpered.

Topcliffe moved away and roared for his men.

Bess's knees gave way as the men charged towards her. She slid down the wall, trembling, too terrified even to cry out. She tried to curl into herself, her arms protecting her belly. They grabbed her arms, hauling her up, and propelled her across the cellar and up the steps. Sobbing with fear, Bess stumbled into the daylight, almost blinded after the darkness of the cellar, and was marched into the house itself and up the stairs.

Topcliffe stopped at a door. 'A word of advice, Mistress, because I have a liking for you.' His tongue slipped along his lip. 'Keep a civil tongue in your head with Sir Francis Walsingham. He has no liking for unruly women.'

Despite her distress, Bess's heart skipped a hopeful beat. Sir Francis was a man of high standing, he would understand this was a mistake.

The room Bess entered was like those she had lived her life in—carved tables and chairs, hangings on the walls, clear light shining through glass windows.

Sir Francis sat beside the table, a dark serious man with heavy-lidded eyes. Bess stood in front of him. Topcliffe placed himself behind her, near the door.

Sir Francis stared at Bess, his thoughts unreadable. 'What is your name and station?'

'I am Elizabeth Wyard, a married woman,' she rasped, still trembling, her breathing uneven. 'I am a waiting woman to Lady Allingbourne.'

'Wyard?' He glanced at a pile of papers on the table. 'The *marriage*,' he said with distaste. 'We will deal with that later. You are otherwise known as Stoughton.'

She took a deep breath, steadying herself. 'Yes,' she said, 'and my maiden name was Askew.'

'How long have you been a Papist?'

'I am not a Papist. I never have been. I never will be,' Bess answered firmly.

'Do you deny you aided the Papist, Lucy Torrington, to escape the country?'

'I did not knowingly aid her.' The only thing she had done was collect a small package for Lucy—and hold her tongue.

'You would have me believe that, although she was your

friend, you did not know she was a Papist?'

'Not with certainty until a few weeks before she disappeared.'

'You must have had suspicions.'

'No, Sir Francis. Lucy went to church with us.' Bess thought better of mentioning Lucy's frequent Sunday agues. 'She did not speak openly of her beliefs.' Bess was surprised by her ability to speak half-truths. She was not being completely honest, but neither was she telling outright lies. 'In many ways Lucy had the simplicity of a girl rather than a woman.'

'Yet this *simple girl* managed to get herself to Rouen.' He frowned, 'Are you saying you knew nothing of her plans?'

'She mentioned a dream of being a nun.' Bess gazed into the light from the window. 'I took it to be a childish fantasy she would outgrow.' Even had she taken her concerns to Lady Allingbourne, Bess doubted the outcome would have been different. Lucy would have been sent home to her father but would still have found a way to follow her dream.

'You have been quite reckless in your judgements,' Sir Francis glowered, 'perhaps willingly so. You happily spent time with Torrington's aunt, a notorious Papist and concealer of priests.'

'I never stayed with her aunt.'

Sir Francis picked up the papers and shook them at her. 'You claimed to Master Rogers...'

'I was lying.'

'And the truth is?'

'Lucy did go in May to stay with her aunt, but I remained with my husband at his brother's house in Coleman Street.'

'Your husband Myles Stoughton has been dead over three years.'

'Edmund Wyard and I were married in May.'

Sir Francis' face reddened. 'Ah, the so-called marriage.'

Bess drew herself to her full height and said with a calm dignity, 'It was a true marriage before a minister of the church and witnesses.'

'All of whom are conveniently dead or gone.' He drew a heavy breath through his nose and looked at that moment as if he carried the sorrows of the world. 'While this marriage is not my immediate concern, it hurts me that someone would so besmirch the name of one of our heroes of Zutphen for her own ends.'

Bess closed her eyes as tears spilled down her cheeks. 'Edmund married me.'

'I do not believe you,' Sir Francis glared. 'He would have done it openly. He was never anything but honest. But you, you are a different sort. You even stole the ring his father had given him. Enough of this!' He slammed his hand on the table. 'Tell me of the Catholics you know in your own home and in the other places you visit, the names of priests, the places where you have heard the Popish Mass. It will go easier for you if you do.'

Bess's knees buckled again and she stumbled forward, gripping the table for support. 'I know nothing of these things, I am not a Catholic.'

Sir Francis appeared unmoved by her obvious distress. He held out a string of rosary beads. 'Lady Wyard said she saw you praying with Papist trinkets such as these.'

'She is lying,' Bess gasped. 'I have never used such beads.' Sweat filmed on her brow. 'Please, Sir Francis,' she whimpered. 'I feel unwell. May I sit?'

Sir Francis eyes narrowed. 'Topcliffe, a stool for this woman,' he snapped.

Bess sank heavily onto the stool Topcliffe brought over. She wrapped her arms tight around herself to still the trembling that wracked her whole body.

'Yet, Stoughton,' Sir Francis continued, 'you know what these beads are.'

'I saw Lucy with something like them once, maybe twice.' Bess's voice quavered as she spoke.

'You are the most dishonest woman I have ever met. Most Papists are willing to give voice to their faith, are proud of their allegiance to Rome. Yet you seek to hide it in the hope you will escape and continue in your treasons. Most would rather remain silent than lie.'

'I am not lying,' Bess cried. 'It is the truth. I am not a Papist, I am a true Englishwoman.'

'What would you do if the Pope were to send an army and declare that his only object was to bring the kingdom back to Catholic allegiance?'

Bess held his gaze, 'I would take the part any good English man or woman would.'

'A deceitful response,' Sir Francis sneered. 'You do not answer the question directly.'

'I would defend the Queen of England.' Bess paused, wondering if that was enough. 'I would defend our gracious sovereign, Queen Elizabeth.'

'How do I know you speak the truth or what you know we want to hear? You have already admitted to being a liar.' He glanced at Topcliffe. 'Master Topcliffe, take this woman away and see if you can get the truth from her.' He glared at Bess. 'If you will not be honest, we will have to force the answers from you.'

As Topcliffe grabbed her arm, dragging her up from the stool, Bess held her gown taut against herself. 'I am with child, Sir Francis. I expect the baby to be born next February.'

'No one told me of this,' he frowned at Topcliffe.

Topcliffe shrugged, 'I did not know, Sir Francis.'

'Lady Wyard knew,' Bess said quietly, 'I am surprised she did not mention it to you. It was the only reason I went to her.'

Sir Francis scowled and said, exasperated, 'Topcliffe see this woman is kept in close confinement.'

His eyes blazed as he snarled at Bess, 'You have delayed the final reckoning but, once this child is born, we will use every means at our hand to wring the truth from you.'

~

Bess knew no one would help her. No one. Not her father nor Lady Allingbourne nor even Philippa if they suspected she were a Papist plotter.

She sat on the straw in a cell in the Gatehouse Prison and laid her hands protectively over her belly. The baby's movements were still strong. 'What will life be for you, little one? If I die now, you will too. Perhaps it would be better for us both.'

Bess stared into the dark. She was terrified by the thought of facing a prolonged pain-wracked death like that endured last September by those Papist traitors who had plotted to set the Queen of Scots on the English throne. The deaths of Anthony Babington and his fellow conspirators were so barbarous they had even disturbed the hardened London crowds.

Edmund had promised that he would come back to her no matter what happened. What had he meant? That even if he were dead, he would come? It was time for him to honour his promise—and Bess would welcome him with open arms.

33

Margaret Wyard watched as Hester Shawe took Cicely Ramage to task. 'You were told when you joined us that the highest standards are expected of Lady Wyard's women.'

'But I did nothing wrong,' Ramage said, a note of defiance in her voice. 'Sir Philip spoke first, he asked me a direct question and I answered him.'

Shawe peered along her bony nose. 'More than that, you were flirting with him.'

'I was not!'

'You were laughing.'

'Yes, he made a jest and I laughed. To have ignored him would have been discourteous.'

Morris, Dame Margaret's third woman, kept her head down stitching doggedly, as if fearful that Shawe's anger would spill over on to her.

'It is clear Sir Philip saw in you a woman easily seduced. This is a respectable household. If I so much as catch you glancing towards a man again, you will lose your position here. Now get on with your sewing.' Shawe looked towards Dame Margaret who gave a slight, approving nod.

Ramage, her mouth set in a sullen line, took her place beside Morris and began to sew. Dame Margaret realized now that taking on Ramage had been a mistake. She was a cousin of some sort of Eloise's. Plump, talkative and forward, she showed the same frivolous behaviour as that ungrateful girl. Shawe was right to question the woman's morality. She had been flirting with Sir Philip. To say Sir Philip had initiated the conversation was irrelevant. Men had an unerring sense of who was easy to seduce. Cicely Ramage was not going to use her position here to gain favours from Dame Margaret's guests. Ramage was a widow, old enough to know better, her two children in service elsewhere. She should be past interest in men but some women were whores at heart.

Dame Margaret took up her own sewing and withdrew the needle. Three women were more than enough. She did not understand Florence Allingbourne and her desire to surround herself with young women. They were nothing but trouble. Perhaps Florence did it because she had not been blessed with children. Yet even one's own children were not always a blessing. Dame Margaret stabbed the needle back into the cloth.

The clatter of horses in the yard carried through the house to the silent room. Dame Margaret moved in her chair, straightening her posture. She was not expecting guests. Perhaps it was John come to beg forgiveness for banishing her. He should have taken a rod to Eloise for her insolence, not sided with her. Men were so weak—John, his father, Edmund. Not all men though, not her own father. Her father had demanded respect, and received it from his wife, his children and his servants. His word had been law and, as in the wider world, if you broke the law you were punished. If her husband, Christopher, had been more like her father, he would have been a man she could respect. And Christopher's sons would have known the obedience due to their mother.

Her visit to Edmund's man of law had convinced her Edmund had married that scheming woman. The lawyer had been so wary, unwilling to give her Edmund's will or his Deeds and had asked where *Mistress Wyard* was. The fool had wanted to apply for Probate right away. She had managed to convince him to wait, telling him there was a later will in possession of her elder son. Soon though, the lawyer would contact John and the marriage would come to light. She was at a loss what to do next.

Dame Margaret adjusted Edmund's ring which she wore on her right hand. She had acted in haste going to Sir Francis. It had been easy to convince him the Stoughton woman was a Papist traitor, especially as she had been close to Lucy Torrington. Dame Margaret had not considered, when she made the claim, that a traitor's property was forfeit. If she had contained her anger and got Stoughton to bring her the lawyer's papers proving the marriage, Dame Margaret could have destroyed them. And then arranged for Stoughton to meet with an accident. But there was a world of difference between allowing the law to take its course and arranging a person's death. Perhaps the Good Lord would intervene and Bess Stoughton would die in prison—so many did.

The door opened silently and Margaret Wyard paled.

Edmund stood before her, thinner, paler, dark smudges beneath his eyes. The dead knew everything. He had come to accuse her, to harry her to her own death. She saw her own fear mirrored in the faces of her women. They could see him too.

'Mother,' he gave a lopsided grin as he limped towards her. 'You look as if you have seen a ghost.'

'I thought you were dead,' she croaked.

'I am not so easy to kill, especially with Hayes behind me.'

Ramage, the stupid creature, burst into tears. Shawe hissed through her teeth at her to keep quiet.

'You did not think to let us know,' she snapped, weak with relief. 'We have been grieving for you.'

'Forgive me, Mother.' That irritating grin was still plastered to his face. 'I was injured and not quite myself for several weeks. It is only since I arrived in England that I realised I was supposed to be dead.' He gave a half-hearted shrug.

'It is such a relief, Edmund.' And she meant it.

He seemed so lighthearted; she had never seen him like this. Dame Margaret closed her eyes. She must say nothing about the Stoughton woman until she had thought things through.

'Shawe, have Edmund's room made ready.'

Shawe rose from her seat but paused, watching her mistress and her son.

'I will stay tonight. I am going to Allingbourne Hall tomorrow.'

'Florence Allingbourne has gone to Berkshire, to Philippa Compton's lying-in.'

'Was Bess with her?'

'Bess?'

Ramage opened her mouth to speak but was stopped by Shawe's narrow-eyed glare.

'Bess Stoughton, one of her women. So high,' he raised his hand level with his eyes, 'brown hair, grey eyes, a dimple.' He touched a finger to his left cheek and grinned, 'I am sure you know her.'

Dame Margaret pressed her lips tight together.

'Who was attending Lady Allingbourne?'

Dame Margaret felt the old irritation rise. 'I have no idea. I took no notice of her women.'

He looked at the women but the younger two had their heads down now, concentrating on their sewing. Hester Shawe's stared blankly ahead.

'She would have gone with Lady Allingbourne,' Edmund said. 'Philippa and Bess were close friends. I'll go to Berkshire.' He smiled, happy, thinking of Stoughton, no doubt. 'If you will excuse me, I will go and clean away the dust of the journey.'

Edmund bowed to his mother and, as he straightened up, caught sight of her hand resting on top of her sewing. 'That is my ring. How did you come by it?'

Dame Margaret was silent, unable to think of a plausible answer.

'She came to you.' There was fear in his face now. 'Of course, she would, she thought I was dead.'

'Did you think I would believe you had married such a low born slut?' she said, scorn dripping from every word.

'A low born what?' he snarled.

'A slut—a woman who uses her flesh to lead men from their duty.'

'Madam, have you never heard of love?'

'You talk like a greensick girl. Marriage is a business concerned with property and connections, it is not to be entered for private pleasure. *She* has no property and no lineage of any account despite her claims.'

'Who are you to talk of lineage? Three generations ago your family were nothing but shopkeepers.'

Dame Margaret reeled as if struck. 'How dare you speak to me in this way? I am your mother.'

'My wife came to you because she was with child.'

Her eyes widened, how did he know that?

'And you turned her away. Not only that, you stole the ring I had given her.' He held out his hand. 'I will have it back.'

Dame Margaret, white faced, twisted it off and tossed it into his open palm.

'Where has Bess gone?'

'I have no idea.' She did not meet his eyes. 'I suppose she is with Florence Allingbourne.'

Ramage jumped up and blurted out, 'No, she is not, sir.'

Dame Margaret tried to glare her down. She would turn the brazen baggage out into the street.

'Mistress Stoughton went missing four days ago. We could not find her anywhere.'

He glowered at his mother. 'Madam! What have you done?'

'How was I to know she told the truth?' Dame Margaret shrugged, as if talking of a matter of little weight. 'You did not tell me you had married.'

The room was quiet now except for the hiss of settling logs in the fireplace. The women sat silent, almost afraid to breathe, as Edmund fought to hold back both rage and fear.

'Bess told you and showed you my ring,' he said hoarsely, his voice little more than a whisper.'

'She could have stolen it.'

'She was in dire need and you took it from her.'

'Why did you not tell me?' This mess, it was his own fault. 'All this could have been avoided.'

'I feared what you would do to Bess when I was not here to protect her.'

Margaret Wyard fought down a shudder. It was not natural for a man to look at his mother with such hatred in his eyes.

'You have a reputation.'

'That slut deserved it,' she spat.

'My father never flaunted Edith. He loved her.'

'Love,' she scoffed, 'is the pretty name men use to disguise their lust.'

'If you truly believe that, I pity you.' He turned his back on her and walked toward the door, his limp more pronounced.

As soon as the door had closed behind him, both Dame Margaret and Shawe rounded on Ramage. 'How dare you!'

Shawe slapped her hard across the face. 'You will learn to speak only when spoken to, you ungrateful wench.'

'No, she will not have time. Ramage, you will leave this house immediately.'

'He said Bess was his wife,' Ramage sobbed. 'Why should he not know?'

'You stupid woman,' Shawe and Dame Margaret said together.

The women's voices dropped away, aware of Edmund standing in the doorway.

'It appears Lady Wyard no longer needs your services,' he said to Ramage, 'but my wife will need a waiting woman. You may stay here until I return with her.'

'She will not,' Dame Margaret's voice was icy. 'I will not have her under the same roof…'

'Madam,' Edmund spoke over her. 'This is my brother's house not yours. You have your dower property. I suggest you take yourself there. When John hears of this, he will support me.'

'You are my son, I demand…'

'You have lost all right to demand anything of me,' he shouted. 'Bess and I were married in the sight of God. The clergyman said, *These whom God hath joined together, let no man put asunder.* It seems to me this was your intention. It is unforgivable.

'I am leaving for Suffolk tomorrow, by way of Allingbourne Hall, and want you gone from here by the time I return.'

Dame Margaret stopped herself from saying, *Well, you'll not find her there.* She watched as her son walked away from her. He always was the most difficult of children, he deserved no help.

34

Edmund cursed himself and cursed his injuries. He lay in bed at Allingbourne Hall, every muscle aching. He should have been able to make the whole journey easily in under two days but they would not reach Woolham Manor until the day after tomorrow. His fear for Bess had deepened once he had spoken to Clemence and Avisa and learnt of Lucy's disappearance and their visit by the pursuivants. If Bess was not alive, his whole life was without purpose.

Hayes moved quietly around the candlelit room, making sure all was ready for an early departure tomorrow. Edmund owed him his life, not that he remembered it. When Hayes had not found him among the dead and injured, he had scoured the battlefield. He had discovered him, finally, near the Spanish trenches, hidden beside the corpse of a horse, stripped of anything of value, his leg broken, his ribs bruised. Hayes had proved to be a domineering nurse and, once he was convinced Edmund was recovering, had begun to nag with the persistence of an established wife.

'You have done your share, sir,' he had said. 'With a baby coming and no one knowing you are married, I would say the Mistress needs you.'

Edmund had laughed at him, although he yearned to go to Bess. 'Are you sure it's not that you want to get back to some lass who has taken your fancy? That cheerful woman of Lady Hopeton's?'

'Alas, no,' Hayes answered, a glimmer in his eyes at the mention of Maud Wilson. 'Nothing you do here will make a difference. It will be months, years, before this mess is set right.'

And he was right—this war would not be won quickly and certainly not this campaign.

Hayes had persisted, 'You were lucky to be spared this time. Who's to say you will be so fortunate the next. Mistress Wyard needs you.'

In the end it required little effort. Sir William Pelham had asked that Edmund attend him on the journey to bring Sir Philip Sidney's body home. Sir Philip's leg wound had not healed and within a month of Zutphen he was dead.

It was almost as if Hayes had the second sight. Bess needed Edmund more than he could ever have imagined. He had hoped by this to be resting his head in her lap, his cares laid aside. It was an image that had kept Edmund going through the months away. He would never forgive his mother if Bess...

He refused to imagine it.

~

Edmund cast an assessing eye over Woolham Manor as they rode towards the house. It was a sizable estate and well-ordered, but perhaps not large enough to provide dowries for six daughters.

The groom of the stable came out as soon as they rode in. Edmund dismounted carefully. Still moving like an old man, he limped towards the house and left his horse to Hayes and the groom.

He was ushered into the hall by a bustling motherly woman of a similar age to the groom. She left him, saying she would find the Master. Edmund gazed around the hall with its aged beams, its hangings, its armorial banner above the high table. This was a manor house in the old style.

His heart lifted at the sound of light footsteps behind him. He turned, his face already alight, only to see a girl of about ten. She was fair where Bess was dark, but there was something of Bess in her face.

'Who are you?' she asked. She was a serious-faced child, the dignity of an aged matron in her manner, although her question had been unpolished.

Edmund bowed to her. 'I am Edmund Wyard. I have come to see your father, but if your sister is here I would rather see her.'

Her brow wrinkled. 'I have seven sisters.'

'Your sister, Bess.'

'Bess is not here but you may sit while you wait for Father.' She indicated a settle against the wall. 'Goody Perris has gone to find him.'

'Whom do I have the honour of addressing?'

The child curtsied. 'I am Joyce Askew.'

Edmund sat carefully and stretched his left leg out in front of him.

She put her head on one side. 'You have hurt yourself.'

'It was a while ago but I am almost mended,' he gave a sad lopsided grin. 'Miss Askew, do you know where Bess is?'

'You may call me Joyce,' she smiled at him. 'We've not heard from Bess for months and Father is very angry with her.' She sat next to Edmund and continued, 'He wanted her to marry Master Litchfield but she ran away and has not come back. Master Litchfield is 110 and has bad breath. She was supposed to come home weeks ago. Father has written to Lady Allingbourne telling her to send Bess home.'

'Lady Allingbourne is in Berkshire at present,' Edmund said. 'And Bess cannot marry anyone.'

'Why not?'

'She is married to me.'

'Oh!' Joyce looked him up and down.

Edmund fought the urge to laugh. The child was weighing him as a farmer would a prize cow. She did not seem pleased.

'Bess did not tell me.'

'We thought it best to wait until I returned before telling anyone.'

'But I like weddings.' Joyce's bottom lip quivered. 'Where were you?'

'I have been in the Low Countries.'

She opened her eyes wide. 'Were you at Zutphen?'

'I was.'

'Are you a knight?'

'I am.' Edmund gave an awkward grin. 'The Earl of Leicester knighted me following the battle.'

'Can I come and live with you?' Joyce asked, awed.

Edmund blinked.

'Bess said I could. When I told her Master Litchfield had asked to marry me first, she said I could come and live with her once she had a good husband.'

'For certain, you are too young to think of marriage.'

'That's what Bess said too. My cousin, Jane, is marrying him and that has made Father very, very cross. Aunt Elinor will live with them. I heard Mother say Master Litchfield is going to get more than he bargained for.' She stopped, her brow furrowed, and said, 'I do not know what that means but I am certain she will make sure he says his prayers and goes to church.' Joyce jumped from her seat at the sound of a door banging behind the screen. 'Here is Father.'

Edmund gripped the arm of the settle and rose.

Joyce beamed at her father. 'This is Bess's husband.'

Askew's wary interest changed instantly. He glowered at Edmund.

Edmund stepped forward and bowed. 'Edmund Wyard, sir.'

Askew grasped his hand, vice-like; Edmund resisted the temptation to increase his own grip in answer to the man's challenge.

'Father,' Joyce said, 'Sir Edmund was at Zutphen.'

Askew's eyes narrowed, still distrustful. 'Sir Edmund, eh? At Zutphen?'

'Indeed, sir.'

'Sir Edmund was injured there,' Joyce put in.

'Come to the parlour.' He led Edmund towards the steps to the dais. 'My daughter is not with you?'

'No, sir, that is why I am here.'

Joyce was dismissed, unwilling, to get Mary Perris to bring them refreshment. The men sat in the parlour as Edmund explained the circumstances of their marriage and Bess's disappearance.

'Do you know where else she might go?' Edmund asked.

'I suppose she could have gone to her sister, but that is a long journey. What of her friends?'

'She was on her way to Berkshire with Lady Allingbourne for her friend Philippa Compton's lying-in. I stopped at Allingbourne Hall on my way here but she was not there. It is possible she has gone to my brother in Northamptonshire,' Edmund shrugged, 'but I doubt it. I do not want to spend precious time racing over the countryside when I should be searching in London.'

'Does Bess know you have returned?'

Edmund's brow creased with worry. 'She thinks I am dead.'

'Poor Bess,' Askew exhaled. He seemed to have aged in the time they had been talking. Perhaps he too saw the fearful image of a woman's body floating in the Thames that had been haunting Edmund.

~

Edmund spent the night at Woolham Manor. It was a well-run household. There was a simplicity to the life here, with all the spaces in the house filled with the squeals and laughter of young children. The evening meal was subdued, each person present caught in their own thoughts of Bess. They put Edmund to sleep in the bed that had once been Bess's. He dreamt of her as she was in May and it made waking harder.

Edmund forced himself into the saddle and rode towards London. He was certain the answer lay there. As soon as he arrived, he went straight to his lawyer, catching him as he was leaving for the day. He said Bess had not been to see him but Lady Wyard had. Edmund was convinced she knew far more of Bess's fate than she had revealed. But she was no longer in London and, even had she been, how does a man interrogate his mother?

It was too late to do anything else so Edmund rode back to the Wyards' London house and fell heavily asleep as soon as his head touched the pillow. He woke in the middle of the night from a dream he could not remember, weighed down with a sense of doom. It was as if Bess had disappeared off the face of the earth and all that was left of her was the memory of a handful of May days, days of a love and passion that had burnt deep into his soul and altered him for good. Life without Bess was unimaginable, but that was what he faced.

He threw himself onto his side and swore as his leg twinged again. As he eased himself onto his back a thought struck him. Sir Francis Walsingham. Heedless of his aches, he sat upright. Sir Francis seemed to know everything that happened in England. So small a matter might not have come to his attention, but there was a chance, a slender chance, that he knew something. It was the best hope Edmund had.

35

Edmund arrived discourteously early at Sir Francis Walsingham's imposing house in Seething Lane, a short walk away from the brooding presence of the Tower of London. He was sure the footman took satisfaction in informing him Sir Francis was at present residing at his manor at Barn Elms.

Edmund limped off to find a boat to take him to Barn Elms. After waiting impatiently for a wherry, Edmund chafed at what seemed to be slow progress as the boatmen rowed up river. He could take no pleasure in the sight of the riverbank mansions and their gardens or the lush countryside, wondering instead whether it might have been swifter to ride. At least, if he were riding, he would be doing something, not sitting useless depending on the efforts of others.

When they arrived at Barn Elms, Edmund scrambled from the boat, ordering the boatmen to wait, and raced towards the house as fast as his limp allowed. He was ushered, after a short wait, into a wood-panelled chamber. The light from a tall mullioned window fell onto a large paper-strewn table where Sir Francis Walsingham was at work, reading from a closely written document and dictating to the secretary seated opposite him.

Sir Francis relaxed, smiling, as Edmund was announced. He came around the table and grasped Edmund by the hand before he had time to bow. 'It is good of you to visit me Edmund. Come sit by the fire.'

Edmund followed Sir Francis to the fireside, his limp pronounced.

The secretary did not move from his place, but continued scribbling and reading, seemingly unaware of what was happening elsewhere in the room.

Sir Francis glanced at Edmund's leg, 'I presume your injury comes from Zutphen.'

'Ay,' Edmund answered.

Sir Francis's face was grey and drawn, with the marks of lingering illness and of grief.

'You have my deepest sympathy, Sir Francis. Sir Philip Sidney was the bravest of men, a fine commander with care for all who served with him. England mourns his loss.'

Edmund sat in the chair indicated by Sir Francis and asked, 'How fares Lady Sidney?'

'My daughter is as well as can be expected. She has suffered great loss, not only her husband but her baby was stillborn.'

The breath caught in Edmund's throat, 'It is a cruel thing.'

'And we thought you gone from us too.'

'My man Hayes and the Lord himself seem to have had other ideas.' In the presence of others' grief, he felt as if he should apologise for being here almost hale. 'I received a shot to my back but my cuirass protected me. The blow knocked me from my horse but by some miracle I was not trampled. My man Hayes, that most unlikely angel of mercy, scoured the field later and found me near the Spanish trenches, insensible.' He paused for a moment, caught by memory. 'I wish I could have done as much for George.'

'George Raynsford,' Sir Francis shook his head slowly, 'another fine man lost to England.' He closed his eyes for a long moment. When he opened them, sorrow had been put aside. 'Much as it is a delight to see you, Edmund, I am sure you have come for a reason other than to pass time with an old man.'

'Am I so transparent?' Edmund said, sheepish.

'Not at all, but tell me what I can do for you.'

'I am trying to find someone who has vanished into thin air. I hoped you might have heard a whisper...'

'A woman?' Sir Francis winced as he moved in his chair.

'My wife.'

Sir Francis leant back, frowning.

Edmund gazed steadily at Sir Francis. 'We were married privately in May. We did not make our marriage public because I was leaving and I thought my mother would make life difficult for Bess if she knew.'

'I presume we are speaking of Elizabeth Stoughton.'

Hope flared in Edmund. 'You know of her?'

Sir Francis' face was unreadable. 'She has come to my attention.' He tapped his fingers on the arm of his chair. 'I was told there was no marriage, that she was a dishonest woman seeking to exploit your death for her own ends.'

'Who told you this?'

When Sir Francis did not answer, Edmund said angrily, 'My mother.' Taking a deep breath, he swallowed his fury, and asked, 'Do you know where Bess is now?'

'She is being held at the Gatehouse Prison until she can be properly questioned.'

Edmund sprang from his seat and limped about the room. 'Why? What is she supposed to have done? What lies has my mother told?' He turned to Sir Francis. 'My mother is not an honest woman.'

'These are harsh words for a son to utter.'

Edmund clenched his jaw. 'They are the truth.'

Sir Francis held up his hand. 'Now wait, I was already aware of Elizabeth Stoughton. She was involved in a conspiracy to aid Lucy Torrington to defraud her father and to flee the country. Lucy Torrington is a hardened Papist.'

'I did not know that,' Edmund slumped into the chair. 'But I will not believe Bess's part in any conspiracy until I hear the confession from her own lips.'

'Apart from that, your mother claims she saw her with rosary beads and uttering Papist oaths.'

His mother had denounced Bess! She could have told Edmund how to find her but had held her tongue, letting him waste a week searching while Bess was locked away in the squalor of a prison. He would never forgive her.

'My mother is lying,' he said bitterly. 'I spent two entire weeks in Bess's company. In that time, we were never apart. She had no Papist beads, we went to church together, she has a copy of the Prayer Book. She is as faithful an Englishwoman as any I have known, and more honest too.'

'But last May she spent time in the household of Mary Parkinson, a Papist and protector of priests, of Jesuit traitors.'

'Last May?' Edmund was confused. 'Who is this Mary

Parkinson?'

'The sister of Lucy Torrington's late grandmother.'

Edmund nodded, understanding. 'Bess told Lady Allingbourne she had stayed with Lucy at her aunt's house to hide the fact that she was with me.' He laid his palms open to Sir Francis. 'Is it any wonder we wanted to keep this marriage secret? You see what happened once my mother knew of it and I was not here to protect Bess. She has done everything in her power to destroy her.'

Sir Francis rubbed the flat of his hand along his thigh, thoughtful. 'Elizabeth Stoughton tells much the same tale as you.'

'Because it is the truth!' Edmund raked his fingers through his hair. 'What are the conditions of her imprisonment?'

'She is kept as many others are. As she is with child, although she has been closely questioned, she has not been brought to the ultimate test.'

'The ultimate test!' Edmund flung himself from the chair and paced the room again. 'You would rack her?'

'Sometimes it is the only way we can find the truth,' Sir Francis exhaled as if he were exhausted. 'These are terrible times and without recourse to such means we will never prevail. We cannot permit England to be overrun as the Low Countries have been. Imagine the Sack of London.'

Edmund groaned, 'I have seen what the Spanish can do.' He eased himself into the chair again, his leg stretched out before him. 'I will swear on my life that Bess is an innocent caught in a web of lies and deceit spun by others.'

'Tell me this Edmund, did Mistress Stoughton...'

'Sir Francis please, give her her due, call her Mistress Wyard— she is my wife, she carries my child.'

Sir Francis nodded. 'Did Mistress...?' He paused and smiled tiredly. 'If you are insisting that I address her correctly, I should call her Lady Wyard, Sir Edmund. Now, did Lady Wyard ever say anything to you of the Romish faith, or speak kindly of its followers?'

'No, we never spoke of such things.'

'What did you speak of?'

Edmund frowned, uncomfortable. 'What do you imagine, Sir

Francis? We were newly married.'

'It would help if you were a little more exact.'

Edmund gazed into the past. 'We spoke of love, of the future, the family we would grow.' He stopped and asked quietly, 'May I see her?'

'That can be arranged.'

'What must I do to have her released?'

Sir Francis considered Edmund, assessment in his eyes. 'Mistress Stought... Lady Wyard,' he corrected himself, 'has been insistent from the beginning that she is not a Papist. She answered most questions as a good Englishwoman should. We took it she had not learnt yet to dissemble, preferring instead the outright lie. In the Gatehouse she has distanced herself from the other Papists.'

'It seems Bess's guilt has been assumed from the start.'

'Your mother's evidence was damning. We could not dismiss accusations made by someone of her standing.'

'I understand in these times you must follow every suspicion offered in your attempt to root out the traitors in our midst, but I tell you Bess is no Papist. She is not a traitor. I will stand whatever surety you demand if you will release her to me.'

'I am unsure...'

Edmund spoke over him, 'You doubt my fidelity? I have fought Catholics and traitors most of my life.'

'I know you for an honest man, Edmund. I will take you at your word and release your wife into your custody. The charges still stand but I will have them re-examined in light of the half-truths that have been told.'

The anxiety drained from Edmund's face. 'Thank you, Sir Francis.'

Sir Francis twisted in his chair and called to his secretary, 'John, write to the Keeper of the Gatehouse ordering him to release Lady Wyard, formerly Stoughton, into the custody of her husband and bring it here for signing.'

Edmund watched the secretary as his pen scratched swiftly across the page, afraid to speak in case Sir Francis changed his mind.

Once the letter was signed and sealed, Sir Francis handed it to

Edmund. 'Take this to Master Pickering, Keeper of the Gatehouse. He will release your wife to you.'

Edmund resisted the urge to kiss him. 'Thank you, Sir Francis, you will not regret this.'

'Your wife must be careful not to associate with Papists of any sort. If she does it will cast suspicion on you both.'

'I will take her home and we will both live quiet uneventful lives.'

'I would we could all do that. I will speak to your mother—I will not be used as an instrument in petty feuds but, Edmund,' he paused and leant forward, 'when the worst of your memories of this have passed, you must find it in your heart to forgive your mother. Despite everything, you have a duty to her after that which you owe to your wife.'

'Sir,' Edmund said, wondering if it would ever be possible.

~

Bess lay on the straw in her small dank cell. Vermin of all sorts scuttled about each time she moved. The air was foul with the stink of the uncovered slop pail. She had not been mistreated—there had been no beatings, no manacles, but that did not mean she had been treated kindly. She was given a meagre amount of food. A blanket had been pushed through the door to her. She did not know by whom. Perhaps another prisoner with greater means who was not as closely confined? It would not have been one of the gaolers; they did little without payment and Bess had no money. She feared it was a Papist who had taken pity on her and that she would be judged harshly for accepting their charity.

The child, whose movements grew stronger with each day, gave her comfort. When he lay still she was bereft, fearful he would never move again. He gave her hope. She longed for Edmund to come for her but the child was life itself pushing towards the light. How cruel it was that something so wonderful could be born simply to suffer and die.

Bess looked up as the door groaned open. Her heart leapt—Edmund had come! He was pale against the gloom in his light coloured doublet and snowy ruffs. He was not as Bess remembered him. He was thinner and tired and there was suffering in his face. His death must have been painful. Perhaps he suffered too because they had been so long apart. She knew in that moment how much he loved her. His was no resurrected body—he had forsaken Heaven to be with her.

He stood in the doorway. 'Bess,' his voice rasped.

Bess pressed her hand against the damp wall as she slowly struggled upright. Behind Edmund, lamplight flickered. Heaven or Hell, it did not matter, she would be with him. The baby would have to come too, poor mite. It was right, the three of them would be together.

Bess reached out to Edmund and grasped his hand. It was warm and solid. She glanced back at the straw, expecting to see her bodily form lying there but there was nothing. She stopped where she was, disbelieving. 'Are we dead, Edmund?'

'No, Bess, we are both very much alive.'

'But they told me...,' her voice trailed off.

'I was missing for a while and injured, but I am here now, and whole.' He put his arm around her waist. 'Come quickly, you are free.'

She tried to pull away. 'I am vile, I stink, there are vermin in my clothing.' She was near to tears. 'Please, do not touch me.'

He drew her closer. 'I do not care.'

~

Edmund lay beside Bess, watching her as she slept. Emotions raged in him: relief that he had found her; fear that she had, in some way, been damaged beyond mending; smouldering anger at his mother.

When he had brought Bess home yesterday, Cicely Ramage had prepared a bath for her. He would have left Cicely to help Bess wash but Bess had wanted him to stay. Edmund sat beside the tub as Bess settled into the steaming bath. She had been in that place for a little less than two weeks. Her skin was raw and scratched and she had lost flesh on the scant diet. The largest part of her was her rounded belly. Edmund's eyes shone with unshed tears, overwhelmed by his love for her.

Cicely poured water down Bess's back, across her shoulders, through her hair, lathering the hair with scented soap. Bess said little but lay in the bath, a gentle smile on her lips whenever she looked at Edmund. It was as if she did not quite believe what she saw.

Edmund had gone to her coffer and opened it, looking for a bed smock. There on the top lay the slippers he had given her. He had picked them up and traced his fingers over the embroidery recalling the spirited woman Bess had been.

He had held her through the night, held her safe, ignoring the ache of his own desire. It had to be put aside until Bess was herself again. He remembered dimly the belief that it was not right for a man to lie with his pregnant wife.

Edmund traced his fingers along the side of her face. To his eyes, Bess was the most beautiful woman in the world. Slowly Bess opened her eyes and smiled at him, a waking smile from those blissful days in May.

Memory clouded her happiness. 'They say the baby in the womb takes on the sights his mother sees.' Fear was vivid in her eyes. 'Will our son be misshapen? Or, being so long in the dark, will he be blind?'

Edmund's stomach churned with dread; he knew the common wisdom. 'Bess, he will not be blind. Two weeks in the dark out of nine months will make little difference.'

Edmund held her tighter, pressed his lips against her forehead. 'You are safe. You and the baby.'

'I should be so happy,' she murmured, touching her fingers against his lips, 'but I am fearful still that this is a dream and I will wake back in that place.'

'I promise you, you are here with me.' He caught her fingers and rubbed them against his beard. 'Does a dream feel like this?'

Bess smiled, but her eyes still held disbelief.

'Think of it as a bad dream you have woken from. In time, even the memory of it will fade,' he said with a confidence he did not feel.

36

December 1586

If Bess had her way, she would never walk the London streets again. They were not safe—you could turn a corner and have your whole world crumble. And she would have Edmund always at her side, but she knew a man could not live his life within the enclosed walls of a house.

Edmund went out every day, often to Bonetti's fencing school in Blackfriars. He looked well, had put on weight and lost his limp. Sometimes, when he gazed into Bess's eyes she saw fear there, fear for her. She forced herself to church each Sunday, walking warily along Coleman Street between Edmund and Cicely to St Stephen's—only because Edmund had said that if she did not go it would look like recusancy, a Catholic's refusal to attend the established church. He wanted her to come out with him to the playhouse, to St Paul's, to stroll through the colonnades at the Royal Exchange, but she would not go. He suggested they invite guests to dine but there was no one Bess wanted to see—she had all she wanted in that house.

Even Cicely had tried, whether at Edmund's bidding or not, Bess did not know.

'The weather is a little better today, Mistress. Perhaps we could go to Cheapside. Remember, the Master said you should arrange to have some new gowns made.' She had smiled so brightly, as if she were the one contemplating a new gown. 'A pretty new gown always lightens the spirits.'

For the first time in her life Bess could have as many pretty new gowns as she wished, but now she knew they were of such slight importance.

'Not today.' Aware of Cicely's disappointment, she said, 'Perhaps you would arrange for a mercer to bring us cloth and get a tailor to come too.' But Bess knew that was not what they wanted. She forced herself to say, 'If Edmund came with us I might…' There was no point in finishing.

'Mistress, I am certain he would if he were here, but he has other business to attend to.' She said it gently, 'He cannot always be with us.'

Cicely was right. Bess saw the patience Edmund took with her, knew he chafed at the circumscribed life they lived, but she could not throw off the fear.

Bess spent her days by the fire in the parlour, sewing with Cicely. She had, at last, begun preparations for her child—binders and swaddling bands, tiny smocks and bonnets, as well as plackets so she could still decently wear her clothes. Thought of the baby for the most part brought her joy. He moved strongly, for certain he would be an active happy child. Bess made herself believe Edmund's assurances that two weeks in the dark would have done him no harm.

She knew she should be happy—she had everything she had ever dreamt of, but she was afraid. She knew how easily it could be snatched away. Even Edmund's news, three days following her release, that Sir Francis had found the accusations against Bess baseless, brought no relief.

~

Icy wind rattled the window as Bess and Cicely sewed together in the small parlour beneath a tapestry bought by Edmund to hang in place of his mother's portrait.

'It is getting too dark,' Cicely said, packing away her sewing. 'I'll light the candles. You should finish too, Mistress.' As she bustled about, she said, 'I remember Lady Allingbourne saying you are gifted at the virginal.'

'I would not go so far.' Bess smiled at Cicely, 'You play well yourself.'

Cicely dimpled at the compliment. 'Why not play something now?'

Bess had played nearly every day since she had first learnt as a young woman in Lady Allingbourne's care. Now, she no longer had the heart.

Cicely went to the instrument, propped open the lid and sat down. She played skillfully for a few bars then began striking the wrong notes with such frequency that it was clearly deliberate.

'Are you trying to force me to show you how to play that?' Bess laughed lightly.

'Perhaps,' Cicely grinned. 'Play a few notes and see how you feel.'

Bess took Cicely's place at the virginal. She placed her fingers on the keys. There was no need to think, the music flowed back. It was a balm, clean and comforting, and she began to hum.

Somewhere in the house a door banged in the wind. A few minutes later Edmund poked his head around the door. Bess saw the hope in his face that at last their trials were over and thought her heart would break.

She knew she must somehow regain what she had been. What she was now was not enough for him or, in truth, for Bess herself.

'Look who I met this afternoon,' Edmund said as he opened the door wider. Anthony Compton strolled across to Bess and kissed her.

'Well, are not you two the secret ones?' he beamed. 'And look at you, Bess. Stand up and let me see.'

Bess rose as he took her hands and, eyes smiling, said, 'And when is little Edmund to arrive, Lady Wyard?'

Fear shuddered through Bess as she glanced frantically about the room.

Anthony watched her, puzzled. 'Has he not told you?'

'Told me what?' Her voice creaked, near to tears.

Anthony let go of her hands and rolled his eyes. 'Sir Edmund here was knighted following Zutphen. It took Lord Leicester to recognise his worth.'

'There was some difficulty kneeling, with my leg strapped to a board.'

'You should have told me.'

The others in the room no longer existed.

'I had better things to say to you.'

'Edmund,' she whispered, her breath taken away by the look on his face.

'Lord help us,' Anthony said, 'married six months and still love-struck. So Bess, when is the baby due?'

'In February.'

Anthony walked to the fire and held his hands towards the

warmth. 'I am surprised you are not with Philippa.'

'I was on my way there but...' She stopped herself and said brightly, 'When Edmund came home, I decided to stay here.'

'Philippa said Lady Allingbourne seemed unable to explain why you had not come.'

Anger flashed in Edmund's eyes but Anthony was not looking.

They spent a pleasant evening talking and playing cards, singing and telling stories. It reminded Bess of evenings at Allingbourne Hall. It was the way life should be lived.

As Anthony was leaving, he said, 'I am off to Berkshire on Monday. Philippa expects the baby will be born within a couple of weeks. Come with me, Bess. We can organise a coach. I doubt it will slow us very much.'

'I would like to but...' As she cast about for an excuse she realised she did want to be with Philippa. She caught Edmund's hand and held it tight. 'Would you mind?'

'Of course not.' And, as if to counter a change of mind, he added, 'I will travel with you.'

~

They lay curled together in bed that night, Edmund warm against Bess's back, his hand spread at her waist feeling the movements of their child.

Bess spoke into the darkness. 'I am not so sure I should go.' It was easy to agree but the reality of travelling in the open terrified her.

'Bess, you need women around you, people who know what to do when your time comes.'

'I will be a burden on Philippa if I stay until our baby is born.' There was panic in her voice.

'You would have been with her had this not happened. Think of those weeks as a dark path through the woods, but you are now back on the open road in the sunshine.'

She heard the care he took when he spoke.

'And once you got to Compton's, it would not have been long before those sharp-eyed women worked out that you too were with child. I suspect you would have had him there anyway.'

'Do you not want your first child born at Bucklings Hall?'

'I do, but what I want more is for you to be safe.'

Bess pressed her face into the pillow. 'It would free you to do those things you must,' she said, desolate.

'Oh Bess!' He buried his face in her hair. 'I want you happy.'

'I want to be myself again.'

'Bess, I love you.' His voice was muffled.

'I love you, Edmund, more than anything in Heaven or on earth.' She spoke with more force than she had used since he had rescued her. 'I am afraid, but I will go.'

37

The coach halted in the courtyard of a substantial two-storied manor house. The spire of a grey stone church could be seen at a distance behind its gabled roofs.

As Edmund helped Bess step down from the coach, the main door flew open and Philippa took a few steps into the yard. She held out her arms calling, 'Bess.'

Bess almost ran to Philippa and threw herself into her arms. She sobbed, tears flooding out as a great well of sorrow overflowed. Philippa held her tight until her trembling stopped. She stepped back and ran her eye over Bess's figure. 'Bess, I did not know. Lady Allingbourne said nothing.'

'No one knew,' Bess sniffed, smiling through her tears.

Philippa's women clustered around them. 'Mistress, please come inside.' 'You should be in your chamber.' 'It is far too cold out here.'

Philippa and Bess, still holding tight to each other, walked into the house together.

Anthony laid his hand on Edmund's shoulder. 'At times like these, women are best left together.'

Grooms and stable-boys had rushed up and were leading the horses away, other servants unloaded Bess's baggage.

'Come inside and have something to eat and drink. It has been a long slow journey.'

Edmund exhaled as if a weight had been lifted from him. 'Longer and slower than you can imagine.'

~

Anthony refilled Edmund's goblet and returned to his seat beside the parlour fire.

'It is hard to credit that anyone would act as your mother did. I heard tales of what had happened to your father's mistress,' he shrugged, uneasy. 'Some thought your mother justified as she was so publicly shamed. But this is different—Bess is your wife.' He stared into his cup. 'How is Bess truly? She seems so much quieter than she was.'

'In her body she is well, and she says the baby is lively. But it is as if she has lost her spirit.'

'It would shake a strong man to go through what Bess has.'

'It was not only the imprisonment. Once she knew she was with child she worried for me and for the future of the child. Then for near a month she thought I was dead. And, when she sought help from my mother...' He did not finish.

'Bess can stay with us for as long as she wishes. She can have the baby here. The place is overflowing with women.'

'Better here than at Bucklings. We have not had time to set up our household there.'

They both turned at the sound of a light rapping. Lady Allingbourne pushed the door open. 'If you will excuse me, Edmund, may I have a word?'

Edmund remained seated, his face hard as she crossed the room.

Anthony stood, offering his seat to Lady Allingbourne, and moved away towards the door.

'Stay, Anthony,' Edmund called to him. 'There is nothing Lady Allingbourne has to say that cannot be said in front of you.'

Anthony said, as he opened the door, 'Nay, I want to see Philippa before I go to bed.'

Lady Allingbourne perched uneasily on the edge of her seat waiting for Edmund to speak, but he was staring steadily into the fire. As the door closed behind Anthony, she burst out, 'Forgive me, Edmund.'

'Forgive you what?' He continued to watch the glowing logs.

'Everything. Bess has told me what happened.'

He glared at her, his eyes dark and hard. 'She disappeared into thin air and you did not stir a finger to find her.'

'I was afraid she might have followed Lucy. With all that has been happening—Babington and the Queen of Scots—I wanted to draw no more attention to my household.'

'Has Bess ever done anything to make you suspect she was a Papist?'

Lady Allingbourne shook her head, her eyes on the floor. 'Nay, but I never suspected Lucy either.'

'It seems you have little knowledge of what goes on under your own roof.'

Lady Allingbourne rubbed her fingers hard across her forehead. 'And then your mother...'

'My honoured mother,' he said bitterly.

'Your mother sent Bess out on an errand, to collect a valuable carcanet. Bess left without the footman who was to accompany her. When she did not return, it looked as if Bess had stolen it.'

Edmund snorted, 'I doubt the carcanet even existed. It was an excuse to get Bess out into the arms of those sent to arrest her. My dearest *mother*,' he said the word as if it were a curse, 'wanted Bess to disappear.'

Lady Allingbourne stared at her hands clenched in her lap. 'I confided my other fear that Bess was with child and that I thought poor George the father.' She glanced quickly at Edmund's stony profile and hurried on. 'I did think that, but whenever I tried to raise the matter Bess would change the subject. Your mother said she doubted that it had anything to do with George. She claimed to have heard, some months ago, that Bess had become involved with a serving man in Lady Hopeton's household and they had probably run off with her carcanet.'

'You believed that of Bess?'

Lady Allingbourne twisted her fingers hard. 'It was not what I expected of her but I did not know.'

'You have known Bess since she was a girl. How could you not know?' He drew a deep breath. 'No matter who the father was, were you not concerned by her disappearance?'

'I hoped she had gone to a place of safety to have her baby.'

'And left her belongings behind?'

'That's what Lucy did.'

'Did she? I heard she took as much gold as she could sew into her clothing.' Edmund got up and poured himself another drink from the jug on the sideboard.

'Your mother said I need not wait, she would make enquiries.'

'And you happily left without a backward look.' He sat down again and took a long draught from his cup.

'Had I raised a hue and cry, what good would it have done? Even had I known she was locked away as a Papist, there was nothing I could do.'

'You could have seen she was kept in some comfort.' His steady gaze was unforgiving. 'Ah, but I forget, that might have drawn attention to your household.'

Lady Allingbourne bowed her head, a single tear dripped off her nose. She wiped it away and held her hand against her mouth as she stifled a sob.

Edmund put his goblet on the floor next to his chair and stood. 'There is one person to blame for this and she will never be punished. She sought the death of a good-daughter, but instead, all she has gained is the death of a son's love.'

'Surely not,' Lady Allingbourne gasped.

'Why does no one see it?' He paced the room. 'It would have been more honest to have taken a dagger and stabbed Bess through the heart.' He stopped and stared steadily at Lady Allingbourne. 'You remember the scripture—the Lord said of marriage that a man and a woman are *no more twain, but one flesh*. No one can harm Bess without harming me.' His eyes glistened in the firelight. 'She asked nothing of me other than I love her and made me happier than I have ever been. But my mother, in her malice, has tried to destroy Bess for no other reason than she loved me.'

He grabbed his cup, drained it and slammed it onto the sideboard.

After he had gone, Lady Allingbourne sat trembling in the firelight, tears running freely down her cheeks.

~

Edmund strode across the empty courtyard to where Hayes stood with the horses. He turned back at the sound of Bess's voice.

'You are leaving without saying goodbye?' She stood in the doorway, a large kerchief wrapped around her shoulders over her woollen night gown.

'I thought you would all be still abed.' He gave a half-hearted grin. 'I am not brave enough to venture into the women's chamber.'

'We would not have eaten you.' Her smile was as weak as his. 'I woke early and came looking for you.' She glanced up at him and recognised the pain in his eyes. She longed for his lopsided grin, longed for him to feel nothing but awkwardness. But there was not much to smile about these days. 'When will you be back?'

'Christmas at the latest. I am going to see my brother, John, then to Bucklings.' He frowned and changed the subject. 'How is it with Philippa?'

'The midwife says soon, perhaps today.' She stepped closer to him. 'You were right to make me come. The past already has the feeling of a dream.'

'More a nightmare.'

'Yes, but I have woken up.' She paused, her eyes on his face, as if she were memorising every feature. 'There was a time,' she said slowly, 'when I measured life's pains by whether they were better than life with Dick Litchfield. And Edmund, two weeks spent in the Gatehouse Prison was far better than a life spent with him. I would endure a month there, a year even, if that was the price of spending the rest of my life with you.'

'Bess,' he breathed her name as he folded her in his arms, brushing his lips against hers.

Bess knew Edmund had come home hoping to lay down his burdens; instead had taken up more. She wanted to weep for him.

He moved away from her and mounted his horse. 'What will I bring you as a New Year's gift?'

Bess gazed up at Edmund, her eyes brimming with the love she felt for this man, more beautiful with his marked skin and gruff manner than the handsome gallants with their shallow eloquence. 'All I want is you. Come home to me and I will be the happiest of women.' She knew the truth of her words as she spoke them.

'Keep yourself safe, my dearest love,' he said as he saluted her and rode off, Hayes behind him.

~

Two weeks it had taken at a punishing pace. He had ridden first to Northamptonshire to his brother. It was a relief to find his mother absent. Edmund had set the whole sorry story before John, and he, while understanding, had taken the same position as Sir Francis, saying that, in time, Edmund must find it in his heart to forgive his mother. Eloise, weeping for joy at the sight of him, had said, 'John is far more forgiving than many of us.' She was bracing herself to welcome Dame Margaret for Christmas but had ordered him to tell Bess to expect her for the lying-in. Edmund had then travelled to Bucklings Hall. It seemed emptier than when he had left it last, a place of dreams deferred. He took stock with his steward but had no desire to plan for anything. From now on, any decision would be made with Bess at his side. Finally, he had ridden back to Berkshire.

~

Edmund and Hayes rode steadily through the dusk. Although Edmund had hoped to make Compton's by nightfall, it would be fully dark by the time they arrived but, on this of all nights, the household would be up late.

It was on dusk he had first met Bess—a determined woman who had defied her father and ridden near forty miles disguised as a boy. He had intended to write to her but written words meant so little. He needed to see her, to judge how she was, to tell her what was in his heart.

He urged his horse faster.

~

A stable-boy rushed out to take their horses as they rode into the courtyard. The sound of carols carried from the hall. The log would, no doubt, have been dragged in and the cup passed around. Tonight, Edmund left his horse to the ministrations of the stable-boy and strode towards the house.

He followed the singing into the hall and stood at the back. Most of the household were present. He searched the crowd but could not see her.

Philippa was there, the swaddled baby in her arms, Anthony beside her beaming proudly.

The crowd in the hall sang,

Sit you merry, Gentlemen
Let nothing you dismay

Edmund joined in full voice. He was not singing loudly or off key but several heads turned. None was Bess. His eyes raked the crowd again. She was not here. She was everything to him; for certain, he would have sensed it if harm had come to her. And there should be signs of mourning but the hall was decorated as for any Christmas with holly, ivy and beech boughs.

O fear not said the Angel

Behind him a woman sang,

Let nothing you affright

His waist was encircled by her arm and they sang together,

this day is born a saviour

of virtue, power and might

Edmund looked into the smiling eyes of the woman he loved more than his own life. Her cheeks had filled out, her skin glowed, her hair was glossy. She took his hand and placed it at her waist as their child aimed a hefty kick at him.

Bess smiled at Edmund, her eyes clear and untroubled, and he answered her with a crooked grin.

Epilogue

February 1587

Although the February winds lashed them, Edmund still paused at the final rise to survey Bucklings. The fields were dark and the trees bare but the beauty and order of the farmland with the house at its centre lifted his spirits. Even as they lifted, they plummeted again with fear. Today, tomorrow perhaps, Bess would give birth and that was a trial as great as any she had suffered so far. Sometimes women, even strong healthy women, did not rise from childbed. He prayed that God would spare her.

Death surrounded them, often taking the brightest and the best. Two days ago, Sir Philip Sidney had been buried at St Paul's after lying in state at the Minories in Aldgate since November. Edmund had marched in the funeral procession mourning not only Sir Philip but, privately, George Raynsford too. The citizens of London had turned out, their heads bowed, their voices hushed as the long procession passed towards St Paul's. Poor men and soldiers marched, gentlemen and yeoman servants, chaplains, noblemen, aldermen, the Lord Mayor of London and three hundred London citizens in arms. A splendidly adorned war horse was ridden by a young page trailing a broken lance. The coffin, draped in a black pall embroidered with Sidney's arms, was carried by fourteen men and followed by great Lords including the Earls of Leicester and Essex, Lords Willoughby and North, all who had served with Sir Philip on that fateful day. Pennants had fluttered above the solemn tread of the mourners.

Edmund had not stayed for the gatherings afterwards where soldiers met and told the black and humorous tales they alone fully understood. He had taken his leave of Lord Leicester and Sir William Pelham, for he needed to be away, back in present life, looking towards the future. He needed to be with his wife.

~

The house was ominously silent as Edmund dismounted in the

courtyard. Had he done ill by giving in to Bess's insistence that she come to Bucklings Hall once Twelfth Night had passed? He had thought the women at Compton's had taken leave of their senses, but he was powerless before their massed arguments. Lady Allingbourne had sworn she would take better care of Bess than she would a daughter. And Bess had not found the slow careful journey demanding. Her delight at Bucklings, both the house and the estate, had been worth the worry and the tedious journey made almost at walking pace over muddy roads. Three weeks ago, as he had ridden towards London cursing the timing of his betters, he had left behind a quiet household already settled into an orderly domestic life.

The stable-boy waited at the gate as Edmund led the horse to him.

A whooping shriek shattered the silence.

Edmund dropped the bridle and raced towards the house.

'Sir Edmuuuund!' The high-pitched scream echoed off the walls of the courtyard.

He collided with a small flurry of skirts and streaming hair. 'Joyce?' he gasped.

She bounced in front of him. 'It's a boy! It's a boy!'

He thought he was a strong man but his eyes brimmed. 'A boy.'

'I have been watching from the window for you all morning.'

He was not listening. 'And Bess?'

'I do not know.' Joyce's brow furrowed. 'They will not let me see her.'

Fear gripped him by the throat. He grasped Joyce's hand and raced towards the house, slamming through the door, pulling her behind him. At the staircase, he swung Joyce up and carried her as he took the stairs two at a time. He set her down at the door to the bedchamber and stood, breathless.

The door opened and Lady Allingbourne stepped back to let them enter. The room was crowded with women. Edmund walked slowly forward, hardly daring to breathe. Philippa was here, not long churched; and Cicely, of course; Eloise as she promised; even Emma, Bess's stepmother; and a woman so like Bess she could be none other than her sister, Ann. Somehow, they had been summoned without Edmund being aware of it.

The women moved aside to let him through.

And there was Bess, in the centre of what had been his lonely bed, tired and radiant. With one arm, she cradled a swaddled bundle, the other she held out to him.

Edmund bent and kissed her, his eyes swimming, unable to speak. He sat on the bed beside her, gazing down at the red-faced, sleeping infant.

'Is he not beautiful?' Bess smiled, her own eyes wet with joy.

'He is,' Edmund sighed.

'Might we call him George?'

'I can think of nothing better.'

Bess handed the baby to him, slid her arm around his waist and rested her head against his shoulder.

The child cradled in his arms, Edmund bent his head and brushed his lips against the infant's forehead.

The past was done with, all that mattered lay ahead.

Historical Note

Forsaking All Other is set between July 1585 and February 1587. The historical timeline is accurate and where actual events are described, they are as close to the historical record as I could make them. The story itself and the major characters are all fictional. For the most part, historical personages are mentioned rather than given an active role except for Richard Topcliffe and Sir Francis Walsingham. I have tried to present these two people in a way that is in keeping with what is known of them. My view of Richard Topcliffe echoes the contemporary view. He was a man who revelled in his role as interrogator and torturer of Catholics and, by the 1590s, had his own 'strong room' for interrogating prisoners in his house in the grounds of St Margaret's churchyard, Westminster. In 1592 he raped Anne Bellamy, a young Catholic woman imprisoned in the Gatehouse Prison, as a means to getting her to reveal the whereabouts of the Jesuit priest, Robert Southwell. I have drawn on the depiction of Topcliffe by Jesuit priest John Gerard in his autobiography (*The Autobiography of a Hunted Priest* translated from Latin to English by Philip Caraman, 1952). Gerard was captured in 1594 but managed to escape in 1597 despite injuries resulting from torture. Although this source has its biases, Topcliffe was seen as an unsavoury character at the time—his nephew Edmund even renounced the family name, in part because of his uncle's notoriety.

In the case of Sir Francis Walsingham, I do not subscribe to the highly coloured and, at times, ahistorical view of him presented in popular culture. He was a complex man living in dangerous times. He had not only heard of the atrocities inflicted on Protestants during the Spanish occupation of the Netherlands but, a Protestant himself, was eye-witness to the St Bartholomew's Day massacre in Paris. As Robert Hutchinson says in *Elizabeth's Spymaster* (2006 p.261), to dismiss him as the Elizabethan equivalent to an SS Reichsführer or a NKVD head 'conveniently discounts the callous reality of the times in which Walsingham lived and the challenges he confronted almost daily.' In keeping with the multi-faceted man found in modern biographies such as Hutchinson's and Derek Wilson's *Sir Francis Walsingham. A Courtier in an Age of Terror* (2007), the advice I have him give to Edmund to forgive his mother is plausible and echoes his conciliation between Lord Beauchamp and his father, the Earl of Hertford, after the former's clandestine marriage in 1582.

The attitude of the English to the Irish that I present is accurate for this period. While I have taken artistic licence in having Sir William Pelham say that 'the babe in arms was tomorrow's enemy, his mother the seedbed of future traitors', he did believe that 'the example of terror must light upon some' and so it was acceptable to slaughter innocent non-combatants as a necessary example to the guilty ('Tudor Ireland: Anglicisation, mass killing and security' by David Edwards in *The Routledge History of Genocide* Eds. Cathie Carmichael and Richard C. Maguire, 2015). In this he was no different from many others. Sir Henry Sidney, a previous Lord Deputy of Ireland, even joked about the countless number of Irish common people, 'varlets' in Sidney's parlance, that he had killed (*Age of Atrocity: Violence and Political Conflict in Early Modern Ireland* by David Edwards, Padraig Lenihan, Clodagh Tait, 2010, p.74). Unfortunately, the massacre at Carrigafoyle Castle, where not even women and children were spared, was not unique in 16th century Ireland, nor over the eight hundred years of occupation.

I have tried to ensure that my fictional characters' attitudes and actions are in keeping with the time. Many of the sources I have consulted in writing this novel can be found on my website, catherinemeyrick.com.

While I have tried to depict the times accurately, I must admit to an obvious anachronism in the dating of the chapters. The Julian calendar was use in England up to 1752 although its use across most of Europe ceased in 1582. With this calendar, the year ran from 25 March (Lady Day) to 24 March. This means that Sir Philip Sidney died on 17 October 1586 and was buried on 16 February 1586 as 1587 did not commence until the following month. For ease of understanding, I have used the Gregorian calendar which we currently use, where the year starts on 1 January. Interestingly, despite using the Julian calendar, the

Elizabethans referred to the gifts exchanged around 1 January as New Year's gifts.

The title of this book, *Forsaking All Other*, is a reference to the declarations which would have been made by Bess and Edmund individually at their marriage in 1586 which are those of the 1559 *Book of Common Prayer*. The declaration *And forsakyng al other, kepe the onely to her, so long as you both shall live* and the vows themselves are central to the traditional understanding of Christian marriage and encompass not only sexual fidelity but also the reordering of loyalties and obligations from parents to spouse, allowing no other person to come between the couple. This is explicitly stated in the marriage ceremony with a quotation from St Paul: *For this cause shall a man leave father and mother, and shalbe joined unto his wife, and thei two shalbe one flesh* (Ephesians 5:31). This sentiment can also be found, almost word for word, in the Book of Genesis (2:24) and the Gospels of Sts Matthew (19:5) and Mark (10:7).

The lyrics quoted in this novel are from Tomorrow the Fox, a 'freemen's song' collected by Thomas Ravenscroft (1588-1635) and an early version of the popular carol, God Rest Ye Merry, Gentlemen. Although these date from slightly later than the 1580s, I have worked on the premise that many songs were in use long before they were written down. The quotation from the story of Icilius and Virginia found in chapter 22 is from George Pettie's *A petite pallace of Pettie his pleasure contaynyng many pretie hystories by him set foorth in comely colours, and most delightfully discoursed* (1578), a book written with young women in mind. Edmund's sonnet to Bess is my own work.

Language is always an issue in historical fiction—whether to try to come close to the language used in surviving records and contemporary literature or to take a modern approach. The historical novelist, Josephine Tey considered that if characters 'did not sound quaint to each other, then they have no right to sound quaint to us' (*The Privateer* 1977, c.1952. p. 254). Although it is impossible to write a story set in the 16th century that sounds fluent to the modern ear without drawing on the words that have enriched our language in the intervening centuries, I have attempted to avoid the use of thoroughly modern terms and have limited myself to using those contractions that can be found in

Shakespeare's writings. During this period Yes and No as well as Ay and Nay were equally used, with Yes and No used for more emphatic expressions; I have used both in this way. Occasionally, I have also used 16th century terms rarely heard now because I do want to give the sense that this story took place in the foreign country that is the past. I hope I have achieved something that is both readable and historical in flavour.

Acknowledgements

I would like to thank a number of people who have helped me on the long road to publication. Several members of the Historical Novel Society have read and made extremely helpful comments on the novel in its various stages of development, especially historical novelists Juliette Godot, Linda Hardy and L.S. Young. Most especially, I would like to thank Jeanne Greene, also of the HNS, who critiqued the novel in detail and helped in so many ways to bring it to its mature form. I would also thank Lyndsey for her meticulous proofreading and her advice on numberless aspects of both writing and history. Thanks also go to Denise McKay for her advice on all things equine, any mistakes in this area are solely due to my misunderstanding. My sister Gabrielle has been an unfailing support, reading early drafts and never wavering in her belief that Bess and Edmund's story needed to make its way out into the world. Last but not least, I am indebted to my husband and children for their support and forbearance over many years when my attention was inclined to wander away from immediate concerns to the 16th century.

About the Author

Catherine Meyrick is a librarian with a love of history in all its forms. She has a Master of Arts in history and is also a family history obsessive. Although she grew up in regional Victoria, Catherine has lived her adult life in Melbourne, Australia.

You can find out more about her at her website
catherinemeyrick.com